Cassandra, Lost

Also by Joanna Catherine Scott

The Lucky Gourd Shop

Charlie and the Children

Indochina's Refugees: Oral Histories from
Laos, Cambodia and Vietnam

Breakfast at the Shangri-La

Cassandra, Lost

Joanna Catherine Scott

St. Martin's Press New York

CASSANDRA, LOST. Copyright © 2004 by Joanna Catherine Scott. All rights reserved.
Printed in the United States of America. No part of this book may be used or reproduced
in any manner whatsoever without written permission except in the case of brief
quotations embodied in critical articles or reviews. For information, address
St. Martin's Press, 175 Fifth Avenue, New York, N.Y. 10010.

www.stmartins.com

Library of Congress Cataloging-in-Publication Data

Scott, Joanna C., 1943–
    Cassandra, lost / Joanna Catherine Scott.—1st ed.
        p.   cm.
    ISBN 0-312-31942-8
    1. Van Pradelles, Cassandra, d. 1815—Fiction.   2. France—History—Revolution,
1789–1799—Fiction.   3. Americans—France—Fiction.   4. New Orleans (La.)—
Fiction.   5. Women—France—Fiction.   6. Lafitte, Jean—Fiction.   7. Maryland—
Fiction.   8. Pirates—Fiction.   I. Title.

PS3569.C638C37   2004
813'.54—dc22
                                                                2003058180

First Edition: March 2004

10 9 8 7 6 5 4 3 2 1

In memory of

Cassandra Deye Cockey Owings van Pradelles

and with gratitude to her descendants

for allowing me to use their family history for this novel.

Special thanks to

Joshua F. Cockey of B and Cecil Offutt

of Cockeysville, Maryland,

and

Charles Kilgore of League City, Texas,

for their enthusiasm and support.

I hope you like the story.

Author's Note

*W*HEN I FIRST WENT TO LIVE IN COCKEYS-
ville, a small town north of Baltimore, I found an old graveyard in
which a simple obelisk rose above the other stones. It read: "Cassandra D. van Pradelles. Lost at Sea, 1815. Aged 40 years."

And then came a voice behind me—an old man in a greatcoat and
a flat tweed hat inquiring who I was and what I wanted in his family
burial ground. I asked about Cassandra. She was, he said, an ancestor
of his, and sweeping off his hat, he introduced himself—"Joshua F.
Cockey of B"—pronouncing the name with an archaic flourish.

We became friends and Mr. Cockey gave me access to his
extensive family papers, from which I learned the bare bones of
Cassandra's dramatically romantic story. The question I was left
with was: *Why? What caused all this to happen?*

Since the peculiar province of the novel is the exploration of
causes and effects, of actions and their consequences, it is this
question I have set out to answer in *Cassandra, Lost*, a story about
the joys and perils of following the heart.

Acknowledgments

My GRATITUDE GOES TO MARY GOLDING Hogya, for her patient reading and rereading of the manuscript; my agent, Miriam Altshuler, for her help in molding it into its final form; and, of course, my editor, Dori Weintraub, who bought it for St. Martin's Press.

Thanks to Ruth Mascari, Marj Ashcroft, and Joan Grabowski, for their classes on Baltimore history and on piracy and privateering; the Reverend David Rivers of the Gloria Dei Church in Philadelphia; Sally Lightburn, museum docent, of Paris; and the staffs of the Maryland Historical Society, the Johns Hopkins Library, and the Archdiocese of New Orleans.

Thanks also to the staff of the North Carolina Collection, UNC-Chapel Hill, for their support; and to the Weymouth Center for the Arts and Humanities in Southern Pines, North Carolina, for granting me a residency.

Cassandra, Lost

1

IT RAINED THE DAY CASSANDRA RAN OFF
with the Frenchman. The storm swept from the northeast, howling
from its high perch in the Endless Mountains down across the
Pennsylvania border into northern Maryland. Across lush farmland
it came, beating at wheat and corn that rose rank after rank, field
after field, flattening the crop which sprang back up behind,
resilient, bred to sudden weather. Swept barking and hooting down
the middle road from York, ripping at the roofs of farmhouses and
taverns, shaking windows in their frames and lifting chickens
off their feet. Mill wheels rattled savagely; dogs cringed and whined
and wedged themselves beneath the safety of their masters' chairs;
a lace-bottomed petticoat, escaped from someone's clothesline,
danced and billowed in the air above the ancient Shawnee hunting
grounds. At the sharp ridge of the John and Thomas Forest, the
storm appeared to hesitate, as though gathering force to leap down
and thrash the plantations of the Cockey Valley before funneling
down it like a torrent down a pipe to drown Baltimore Towne.

Cassandra Deye Cockey Owings stood on the front verandah of Owings Hall, her family's plantation home, and watched it come. She both loved and feared these sudden evening storms, the way the sky above the ridge turned purple as a bruise and churned, the way the birds fled out of it, each one a screaming line drawn in the sky, the dangerous fresh smell. But today she stood there tense, hoping it would turn away, or if not turn, come suddenly, be over suddenly, and gone, because up there, on the ridge above the pond, her Frenchman had promised he would wait for her—and now look what hung above his head.

Where was Papa? Where could he have got to? If he did not come at once this storm would prevent him and then who knew how long it would be before she could get a final answer from him? Impatiently, she whisked her riding crop against her long full skirt. The light nankeen flew up and wrapped around the crop and she bent to disentangle it with deft movements of her fingertips. "Good," she said, "not even a small tear," and smoothed the fabric into place with the self-conscious gesture of a girl who has dressed for an occasion.

A little dog, a Pekingese named Baby, sniffed busily around the bottom step, the long hair of her back lifting in the rising wind. "Here, Baby, come here, girl," Cassandra called, but the little dog shoved her nose into the angle between step and ground, whining and scratching at the dirt.

A turkey vulture rose above the woods below the house, and then another and another. One by one they vanished in a wide loop to the right behind the house, then reappeared on the left to glide low above the broad sweep of front lawn, where they performed an intricate arcing dance, swooping and hovering, hanging inches off the ground, now angling a wing and climbing to float, then sink and float again, their wingtip feathers spread like the fingers of a hand.

Gazing up toward the ridge, Cassandra saw the boiling clouds bulge out and swell, like a bully who has summoned up the courage to attack. She saw the great oaks plunge like startled horses, saw the sudden forward movement of the clouds. The turkey vultures rose together on strong wings and fell into the woods. Slow raindrops burst against the fine crushed limestone of the drive. Rain slashed across the boards of the verandah as she backed off toward the open door.

"Here, Baby, come inside."

The little dog scuttled past and stood inside the doorway, legs braced, growling at the rain. Cassandra felt the door swing against her arm and stepped aside. It closed sharply, sucked into place by a vacuum in the atmosphere. Then, with Baby scrambling behind, she climbed the stairs.

At the landing she stopped, peering through the window at the rushing sky, watching it burst in a flood over the house, obliterating the ridge. The noise was wonderful. The elm tree by the window leaped and thrashed. The rain came down in slanting, roaring sheets, smashing against the stone wall of the house as though in an attempt to batter it down. Then it drew off and smashed again.

The window clouded with her breath and she set her riding crop down on the sill, rubbing her hand across the pane to clear it. "Oh, God," she whispered, "please let it be quick. Please let it pass. Please, please don't let it ruin everything."

She cupped her hands against the glass and set her forehead on them. Someone was out there in the rain. No, she was not imagining. Out there, at the edge of the woods below the house, half-hidden by the overhanging trees, she could see her Frenchman like a ghost inside the rain, set astride his big black stallion, looking up toward the house.

A noise behind her and she started, but it was only Eudie at the linen press above her in the passageway, her arms full of heavy crimson fabric. "Such a storm, Miss Cass," the old Negro woman called above the din. "I barely got Miss Colegate's gown inside from airing afore it got completely ruinated. Get off there, you bad thing, you," she said, nudging aside with her toe the little dog, who was dancing around her, scrabbling at her skirt. "Go on now. You be tearing up my onliest good work dress." She set the crimson gown inside the press and pushed the door shut, giving it a shove with both hands to get it completely fastened, then came and leaned over the stair rail, looking down into Cassandra's face. "You be all right, Miss Cass?"

"Yes, Eudie. Just a little nervous of this storm."

Eudie clucked her tongue. "There, there, child, don't let some silly storm be causing a depression of your spirits. We have enough of that with your mama. You go on and lie down on your bed and rest yourself. This storm be nothin'. It'll pass." And with Baby at her heels, she shuffled off toward the servants' stair at the hallway's farther end.

"Come here, Baby," Cassandra called. "Oh, don't then. Silly little dog." She swung back to the window, but Benedict was gone.

The rain had eased and came down now only in a drizzle. Behind it, the sun swam in the sky. Cassandra went back down to the verandah. Surely Papa would come soon. And surely when he came he would have softened. All her life he had given in to anything she asked. Sometimes, at first, he would refuse, but then she would shake her curls and, tugging at his whiskers, cover his face with kisses, and before long he would relent. He would relent today. Yes, she was confident of that. The moment she had his answer she would have her horse brought round and go to Benedict with the good news.

She looked up at the ridge again. But would she be too late? Had Benedict already gone, washed off by the storm? No, he had sworn to wait till dark. And had she not seen him sitting out there in the rain? Had it not been a message to her that he would shelter in the woods until the storm was past? He would wait impatiently, he had said, praying that her father's decision on their union would be reversed. She looked up at the sun. It looked back damply down at her. There was still time.

Above Cassandra's head, her mother Colegate lay on her white embroidered counterpane, a new French novel facedown on her breast, listening to her daughter pace the boards of the verandah. She knew what ailed the child. She wanted to go down and comfort her. Last night, when John had sat in bed and argued with himself, she had wanted to take her daughter's side but could not find the words. Oh, she was a helpless thing, always on the verge of saying something, never saying it. So often she had wanted to stand up to him, to argue forcefully, to back him down and make him go her way, but she could never do it. And this subject of a husband for Cassandra was not one in which he would brook interference. The child had always been his favorite. From when she was a tiny thing, his face would melt and his choleric nature turn to cream-churned butter when she came trotting on her baby legs, holding up her arms to him. Many times Colegate had taken the little girl on her knee only to have her slip away to climb onto her father's knee or cling against his leg. She loved Cassandra too, she did, but sometimes she thought John loved his daughter more than he loved her. She had confessed her jealousy to God so many times she feared He had grown tired of her.

And now she had another sin to add to her confession. Knowing full well that John would not approve, she had encouraged Cassandra's romance with the Frenchman. She had left them on their own without a chaperone when Lieutenant van Pradelles had come to call. She had even let them go into the woods alone and stay for hours one day when John was not at home. In her deepest heart she half agreed with John that this man was not the match Cassandra ought to make, but she could not help herself. He was so handsome. All the ladies were in love with him. And—yes, she admitted it—she fancied him herself. She almost felt that by falling in love with her daughter he had fallen in love with her. Lieutenant Benedict François van Pradelles—it was like a name out of a novel.

And his voice!—it made her loins melt. When he spoke to her in French it was as though a hero of romance had stepped clean off the page. Her own French, which was adequate for reading, seemed so gauche, so straight out of the schoolroom. Cassandra, though, thanks to her tutor's diligence, was facile in the language, she and Benedict conversing as though it were her native tongue. Colegate thrilled to hear them.

So when John came, would it be yes? She wanted it to be so. She sighed. Why could she not be more sensible? She stared up at the ceiling, at the repeated curves and angles embossed into its metal, each one going nowhere, returning on itself.

Below, on the verandah, Cassandra stopped her pacing and

stood gazing down the drive as though the intensity of her desire would make Papa appear. Surely this storm had not made the roads so bad he could not pass? How long would she have to wait before he came? A day? Two days? A week?

No, here he came. At last he came. Yes, it was his horse slipping and sliding on the soggy road, his large proud figure riding, it seemed from this distance, cheerfully. Now he was stepping his horse along the limestone drive between the double row of sycamores. They soughed and sighed above him. Now coming round the bright green circle of the lawn, his horse caked to the fetlocks in red mud. At the bottom of the steps, the pair came to a halt, the horse twitching first one foot and then another, releasing little sprays of mud. Papa's broad-brimmed hat dripped water and his shirt clung wetly to his solid arms and back. Still, he smiled across his broad red face and Cassandra felt her heart smile back at him.

"Papa?"

A high yipping started at the corner of the house and Baby came careening with her tail in a commotion. John clicked his tongue and laughed down at the little dog bouncing on her back legs up and down below him, her forelegs paddling at the air. The horse twitched patiently.

"Stop it, Baby," Cassandra called, and when Baby didn't, she came down the steps and swept her up. "Stop it, I said stop." She looked at John above the wriggling dog. "Papa?"

"I have good news." He produced from his vest pocket a heavy silver watch and clicked it open. "But I'm soaked and starving from this ride. Go up and dress yourself for supper."

"But, Papa . . ."

He was gone in a skitter of wet gravel.

Cassandra hurried back inside and upstairs to her bedchamber. She tore off her riding clothes and snatched up the gown laid out on the bed, calling impatiently to Susannah to button her. The mulatto girl, who had been dozing on a low stool in the corner of the room, jumped up. The grandfather clock in the front hall began to sing its song, and by the time it bonged two bongs, the gown was on and buttoned; by the third, a white kerchief was arranged neatly in its bosom; by the fourth, Cassandra was hurrying back toward the stairs; and by the sixth, she was on the bottom step.

As the sixth deep tone rang out and faded, the house came alive with bustling and voices. Her sister Charlotte and brothers John and Thomas came clattering, with their tutor Mr. Meekum limping on behind, Penelope clinging to his left hand, Mary to his right, and excitable Charcilla skipping at his side. Baby Fanny came frilled and bonneted in the arms of her wet nurse, staring with big eyes silently about her.

Their mother appeared above them on the staircase, looking wan and lovely in her crimson gown. She was supported at the elbow by old Eudie, who looked more in need of support than her mistress, and came down step by step as though she were made of porcelain and would break in pieces at the slightest jolt. The assembly in the hall below fell silent, looking up at her.

"Such a to-do," she sighed. "Think of my poor head." She reached the bottom of the stairs. "Come," she said, and they all followed her into the parlor, the children teasing each other and laughing.

In the corner by the window, a shriveled-up old woman waited in a high-backed wheeled armchair. This was Great-aunt Deye, who had come alone from England many years before and spent her life here as the lover of a married man, dead now for almost twenty years. The children filed before her, setting their lips against her papery cheek. As each one came she smiled a tremulous smile. "Is that you, Tommy? Have you come again?"

"No, Great-aunt, it is Charlotte."

"It is Mary."

"It is Penelope."

"No, Miss, it is little Fanny," and the baby was held up to her cheek.

Great-aunt Deye ignored all these denials. As each child set its lips against her cheek, she said, "Tommy, you have come then."

Cassandra, being the eldest, came last. Looking down at Papa's aunt, she felt pity surge in her. She had been a beauty in her day. Her portrait, hanging above her on the wall, might have been a portrait of Cassandra—the same black curls, the same dark flashing eyes, the same pale skin with the soft pink sheen of roses at the cheek. Now she sat each day in her wheeled chair by the parlor window, calling out to everyone who passed, "Is that you, Tommy? Have you come again?"

The kissing of Great-aunt Deye concluded, John and Thomas rolled her chair across the parlor rug and through the wide connecting doorway to the dining room, where they settled her at the table. Colegate, upright in her stays and crimson gown, arranged herself at its far end, Cassandra at the near end, on the side, the children in between, Mr. Meekum too. Fanny's wet nurse sat apart, on the leather ottoman from Egypt, where she unbuttoned her blouse and set the baby to her breast. Colegate turned her eyes away. It was so indelicate, but John insisted that the family eat supper all together no matter how young they might be.

She looked at Mr. Meekum, who was leaning down, whispering to Charcilla. She had never quite approved of having a man to teach her daughters, but John had been impressed with his credentials, so she had consoled herself with the thought that the fellow was no beauty, with his legs deformed by rickets and a head that seemed too heavy for his neck, perhaps from a surfeit of brains.

The passage doorway opened with a rattling of its knob, and here came Papa, with smiling face and brilliantly white shirt, stock impeccably tied above a frilled jabot. He bent to greet his wife, who turned her face aside. "Be careful. My blue devils have been on me the entire day. My poor head aches fiercely."

He bent to kiss Great-aunt Deye, who raised her hand to his whiskers, whispering. "Yes, dear, it's Tommy come again," he said kindly, and she leaned her head against his chest and sighed.

"Come now," he said, lifting aside his coattails as he settled his haunches down into the armchair at the table's head, and when he had given thanks, he rubbed his hands together like a playwright who has just hatched a successful plot, smiling slyly at Cassandra. "We have more than food to give thanks for tonight, my dear. But let us eat."

Cassandra felt her insides tremble. "But Papa, can you not tell me now? I've waited the entire day."

"Indeed you have, my dear. And I have labored on your behalf. It's clear you've reached the age when a woman becomes restless. A good husband is what you need to settle you."

A breath of relief came out of her. "Oh, thank you, dear Papa."

"And so," he went on, "I've ridden half the day, through rain and storm"—he laughed an easy laugh—"and have had a conference settling the matter for you."

"A conference, Papa?" What, had he gone somehow to meet with Benedict? Had they conferred? Where? Up on the ridge? This was very strange.

"Yes, indeed, a conference. But first things first." And he lifted his spoon and made a loud noise sucking at his soup.

Cassandra knew there was no point in pressing him and so she waited, toying with her food while he ate heartily. At last he wiped his whiskers with his napkin and, setting it down on the table, leaned confidingly toward her. "Here, give me your hand. I've had a conference with Samuel Worthington. His son Mordecai is much taken with you, as you know, and so we have come to an agreement on a settlement of properties and investments that will benefit both families. You are to marry in the fall."

Cassandra felt a pounding in her head and a sensation in her belly as though she had been hollowed out. She snatched her hand away. "Marry Mordecai? That dullard with his pockmarked face?"

A shadow of displeasure came across John's eyes.

"Indeed, child, it's a good match. You will have a husband of position and property, someone serious, who will be attentive to your needs. Someone who will establish you in fine style close to your own family. As for dullard, that may be what you think now, but a more mature eye will see reliability. And as for pockmarked, I thought I'd raised a daughter of sensibility and perception. What matters pockmarked? Mordecai is well set up and strong. You have fallen in love with a smooth skin and a seductive eye, but *look* at this Frenchman, this Lieutenant van Pradelles. He's so thin and willowy the slightest breeze might carry him away, his step is soft and feminine, and his delicate white hands good only for flicking here and there, for kissing with his own mouth so he can blow nonsense at impressionable girls—yes, I've paid note to his foppish Frenchman's ways. I like the fellow well enough, but he lacks the haunch and thrust to dominate even the weak emotions of a woman. Only a silly woman judges a man's potential as a husband by the nature of his skin, or by the fancy flicking of his hands."

Cassandra felt hot blood rushing in her cheeks. She felt again the way Benedict's hands had flickered like butterflies against her loins and inner thighs the afternoon they spent together in the woods. Once more she smelled the apple pomade on his smooth black glossy hair, saw her ivory locket on its crimson riband at his heart, felt the tiny pop of buttons on her gown and the release, heard the slipping of her bodice strings . . .

"Cassie?" Her father's eyes were on her face. They seemed to hold a knowing look, as though he understood what had already made her the happiest of women and would replace those delicate inquiring fingers with the rough hands of a clod.

"Feminine?" she whispered. "Foppish?"

From behind her came a smothered giggle. Her father, who had drawn his breath in for another speech, let it all out in a rush and looked along the table. His younger children froze in their places, staring at him wide-eyed. In the silence, Fanny's wet nurse coughed. Glancing toward her, Cassandra saw her catch Mr. Meekum's eye. She saw her father see it too. She saw embarrassment suffuse him.

"Out!" he said, and springing from his chair, strode to the door and flung it open. "Out of here, the lot of you! Yes, you too, Charlotte, and you, John. No, Thomas, you may *not* stay. This is none of your concern." And he marshaled them pack and parcel out into the hall and closed the door. "To speak of such things before nursemaids and children!" he said, turning back into the room.

A listening expression came across his face. He swung back to the door and flung it open. Feet skittered up the hall. Someone giggled on the stairs. Cassandra saw the cords rise on her father's thick red neck. He stuck his head around the jamb and bellowed like one of his own bulls. The sound echoed and re-echoed, bouncing off the wooden walls and metal ceilings, returning on itself distorted and alarmed. When it died away, the stairs had fallen silent. Then the furtive sound of creeping. A door closed overhead.

John stood with the doorknob in his hand, his head cocked to one side. "There," he said at last, and closed the door.

He came back to his chair and lowered himself into it. "Furthermore," he went on, as if nothing had disturbed the conversation, "you are too young, this Frenchman is too old. He is your senior by twenty years."

"Only seventeen, Papa."

"By almost twenty years."

"But John." Colegate's voice was just above a whisper. "You are older than I am by *more* than twenty years. When my father complained of it to you, you said a woman needs a man with some experience to guide her."

John shrugged impatiently, turning to look at her. "What would you have me say, woman? Yes to a gesturing Frenchman in my daughter's bed?"

Into her silent reprimand, he said, half-sulkily, "We know nothing of his family, his background."

"We know his parents are aristocrats, that they are at court, that they attend King Louis and Queen Marie Antoinette."

"We have his say-so for it. We've never met these people."

"We'll meet them shortly. He expects them any day from France."

"Refugees!"

"Émigrés, rather. There's no shame in that. And certainly no shame to have a son who fought with General Rochambeau at Yorktown. A hero of that battle, so they say."

"Yes, yes, a hero in a battle. Very nice. But what good are medals if he has no money? And since we're on the subject of what people say, they also say that after Yorktown, your hero took to piracy. A pirate, Colegate! You would marry off our daughter to a *pirate?*"

"You yourself had shares once in a privateering vessel."

John's face flushed up to the hairline. His voice took on a harsher note. "So you would stand up for him? How so? No, don't sit there staring, woman, with your mouth agape. If you would speak for him, speak up."

"He . . . he's very handsome . . ."

"Pah! You read too many romances."

"He's good company." Colegate faltered and ran on. "He tells a story well."

"So, company enough. But what of that? Does that qualify him for marriage with my daughter? Face it, wife, the man has no stability. He tells a million stories of his travels, each one in a different place. First he is in Saint Domingue, then in the Carolinas, then Virginia, Kentucky, and now here he is in Maryland. Can the man not stay still in one place for a minute? It seems to me he's wasted all the best years of his life in wandering about. As a result, he has no more money than he can jingle in his pockets."

Cassandra, who had been listening to this interchange with her head turning from one speaker to the other, sprang up in agitation. "Papa, that's quite unfair. Benedict has applied himself with diligence since he arrived in Baltimore, to provide for his family, who may arrive here in a difficult circumstance."

"As paupers, you mean, ready to throw themselves upon our charity."

"I do not doubt the lieutenant will provide for them," said Colegate, and then, with a quick glance at Cassandra, as though she would gather courage from her daughter's fieriness, "He *does* work hard. Why, every lady in society has had him show up at her door offering his merchandise. He has a fine eye for a lovely weave and such a hand for sketching up designs—"

John cut her off. "Yes, yes, a merchant flipping his hand beneath a length of fabric, offering trinkets to the ladies, who then persuade their husbands they will die without them. I myself have been persuaded more than once, I grant you that. But tell me this. How does this gift for selling me a length of silk or a piece of Belgian lace give the man the right to steal my daughter?"

"I think she is not stolen. Here she stands."

"The man is an adventurer, with his eye set on the lands and fortune Cassandra will inherit. I think this Frenchman is not stupid. He has cast his net out for an heiress and in it he has caught our daughter. Listen to me, Cassie, this Frenchman has no fortune here, no property. And his country is in tumult. They are murdering each other in their beds, hanging each other from lanterns in the streets.

Yes, you know it to be true. You read the newspapers. You have met émigrés and heard their tales. Some horror is fermenting over there in France. Who knows if this fellow's family will make it out of there at all? As for their lands, who knows what their mad compatriots will think of doing next? Confiscate them? Carve them up and hand them out for fools to ruin? Worse, if all goes well in France and his family retains its lands, he could well carry you away to be a stranger amongst people who care nothing for you."

He looked up, almost pleadingly, into Cassandra's face, but she stood before him with her eyes accusing, the breath heaving in her breast. An unbearable emotion seemed to rise up in him. His face swelled and tears came into his eyes. "Cassie, dearest daughter, pay attention to the father who brought you into the world, and your seven brothers and sisters also. Surely, with eight healthy children to commend me, you must admit my claim to understanding the needs of a woman. A solid, sturdy man is what will bring you satisfaction, a man who can father on you solid, sturdy children. This sighing after the smooth skin of a coxcomb will bring you to no good, no good at all."

Cassandra turned to Colegate. "Mama? Will you not persuade him?"

But Colegate seemed not to hear the question. At her husband's mention of the needs of a woman, she had half started from her chair and now sat on its edge with an extraordinary expression on her face.

"Cassie," John said, and seized her by the wrists. "Cassie, my own darling girl."

From her wheeled chair halfway down the table, Great-aunt Deye called out in her quavering old voice, "Is that you, Tommy? Have you come at last?"

Cassandra turned to look at her, and saw herself in years to come, sitting lonely in some nephew's corner, calling out for Benedict. She spun away and fled out of the room.

When she appeared, breathless, in the kitchen, half a dozen faces looked up at her in surprise. Susannah, who had been sitting on a stool spooning corn bread into her mouth, clattered her spoon into the metal pan. "Miss Cass? What is it?"

"Fetch my horse, Susannah."

"But Miss Cass, you have no hat, no cape. Let me run upstairs and fetch them."

Cassandra seized her by the arm. "No, do not go up. Is that not your cape hanging on the wall? Lend it to me. Don't stand there with your jaw hung open, girl. Fetch me the cape."

And as Susannah danced about her, making little questioning noises through her teeth while she adjusted the cape across her mistress' shoulders, the others in the kitchen sat gaping at this phenomenon—Miss Cass borrowing a slave's cape, what was this?

Cassandra looked around at their astonished faces. "None of you has seen me here this evening. Come now, Susannah, quickly, fetch my horse."

Within moments she was in the saddle. "If anybody asks for me, say that I grew restless, and desiring exercise, went riding in the south meadow."

"Miss Cassie, it grows late for riding out."

"Do as I say."

"Yes, Miss. Oh, Miss Cass, be careful of the little dog!"

But Baby had already come dancing out in front of her and, before Cassandra could pull her horse aside, was tangled in his hooves. She hauled on the reins and swung around, the horse rearing like a dancer on his two hind legs. The little dog ran off into a bush, limping with her tail turned down and Susannah running after.

Cassandra hesitated, glanced up at the sky—the sun was falling fast—then dug her heels into the horse's flanks and she was headlong, flying for the ridge.

_2_

IN THE WOODS BELOW THE RIDGE THE TREES
dripped constantly. Cassandra drew Susannah's cloak about her, but
still felt drops running down her neck and back. It was a hot evening, though, and she barely felt that she was wet. The sun gleamed
low behind the trees, slanting red and silver shafts through lacy dog-
wood branches, touching the top leaves of the ferns with brilliance.

Within minutes she had passed the pond, barely glancing at the
spot where she and Benedict had lain that afternoon they spent
together in the grass. Now she was at the creek bank. The creek
was swollen from the rain, rushing down across its bed of tumbled
stones so violently that her horse jibbed, turning his head aside
and rolling back his eyes. She spoke softly to him, coaxing, patting
her hand encouragingly against his neck, until he set one cautious
foot into the shallow water at the edge. Gradually, he picked his
way across and scrambled through the wet ferns on the farther
bank with a triumphant little snort. She swung him round and set
him on the trail winding to the top.

Though willing now, the horse made his way hesitantly, slipping from time to time on mud or slick wet undergrowth, while the tree trunks slowly blackened against brilliant orange sky. When they were barely halfway to the top, the sun slipped suddenly and then was gone. The woods grew dim, dimmer, and the blackness of the trunks merged into total blackness all around.

"Dear God!" Cassandra cried.

As if in answer, a fat complacent moon rose up behind the eastern trees, turning the vanished trunks a milky white, with dense black shadows in between. But now the woods looked different. Cassandra had never been up here at night before and became confused, backtracking twice because the path seemed strange.

A light mist rose up from the earth, glowing in the moonlight, and she looked nervously about, remembering the tale told about this place, that Indians were buried all around and if you came here when the mist was rising and the moon was up, the Indians would snatch away your soul. "Pah! A foolish superstition," she said aloud, comforting herself. Then she remembered how you would not know your soul was gone until you died, and so would not rest easy in your grave, but walk the earth forever. "Pah!" she said again, but she was starting to be frightened. "Come, Independence," she said, speaking to the horse, "you must help me make it to the top."

When at last they broke into a clearing, she gave a little cry of triumph. But Benedict was nowhere to be seen. Tears started in her eyes. She was too late. He had already gone. Her father's words came back to her: "The man has no stability." And something occurred to Cassandra that had not occurred to her before. Anxiously she turned her concentration to her belly. *Oh, God, am I ruined?* A sensation close to anger rose in her. How could Benedict abandon her like this?

But then the whicker of a horse came from farther up the ridge. Yes, there it was again. She felt the blood beating in her neck as she edged her horse on through the trackless woods, pushing aside the branches with her hands, letting them snap back into place behind her, until she broke out into another clearing. And there, against the moon, the dark shape of a tricorn hat, his voice. "Is that you, Cassie?"

She set her hand against her throat. "I thought you would certainly be gone. I thought you had abandoned me."

"Abandoned? Never." He smacked his hand against his thigh. "You'll not get rid of *me* that easily." He edged his horse up close and leaned to kiss her. "Your father has agreed? He has said yes?"

So her imaginings were foolish; she regretted them at once, but the fright she had received stayed with her, and she found herself bursting into tears.

"What is it, sweet? What has upset you?"

"My father says he will not wed his daughter to a pirate."

He looked at her wonderingly. "A pirate? I've never been a pirate."

"He says you are a fop, a Continental charmer, a smooth-skinned fancy fellow of no stability who has spent the best years of his life wandering about in search of wild adventures, and has now decided that he wants to net an heiress . . . Oh, Benedict, forgive me. I have wounded you. It all came bursting out before I thought how it would sound. I didn't meant . . . I was upset . . ." She sniffed. "*I* would like to go adventuring." The thought had not been in her head but as she spoke it she felt emotion take her by the shoulders and shake her angrily.

"Here," said Benedict, and he handed her a cambric handkerchief big enough to wrap her head.

She shook it out. "I hope I have not cried *this* much."

"I have found," he said, "that even strong men weep—adventurers. Sweet Cassie, all my life I have been wanting something just over the horizon. I did not know it at the time, but that was why I did not return to France after the war was done, but quit the army and became a wanderer. I was in search of something, I knew not what. I thought it was some momentous thing, some great enterprise. At first I thought it was America, with its wildness and its freedom, its constant heading out toward new boundaries. And then . . ."

He looked up at the moon and laughed.

"What is it?"

"No, I'm sorry. I didn't laugh at you, but at myself. It just occurred to me . . ."

"That what?"

"That life is very simple after all. Or rather, the things that make us happy are the simple things."

She looked at him.

"Who would have thought that all that time I had been looking for a wife?"

"But what about Papa? He rages at you."

"It's nothing. He speaks out of distress because he is afraid of losing you. Men say awful things when they're upset, and yet they do not mean them. He'll come around, I promise. We must give him time. Meanwhile . . ." He twisted round the buckskin pouch he wore slung across his shoulder and, lifting the flap, withdrew a letter, bent and buckled as though it had been read a dozen times before. This he unfolded, flattening it against his thigh.

"What is it? Some news of your family?"

"Sweet, everything has changed, completely changed. I must leave you. I must go to France."

"You must go *where?*"

"Just for a while. Not long—enough for your papa to cool, perhaps." He held the letter out to her.

"But I cannot see the words."

"Here, like this. Hold it up against the moon. Wait, I'll read it for you."

"No, let me read it for myself."

Paris, July 1790

My dear son Benedict,

It was a grand relief to have word from you at last. I feared my letter to you had been lost or intercepted in some way, the posts are so uncertain. I write to tell you that disaster has befallen us. We cannot turn émigré. Instead, I beg for you to come to France. My son, I did not tell you this before for fear that I would cause you worry, but I must tell you now. Your mother is unwell. Late last year a most uncouth pack of fishwives marched from Paris through a rainstorm and invaded the castle at Versailles, demanding bread and shelter, shouting for the king to sign a "Declaration of the Rights of Man."

Behind them came the mob, armed with guns and pikes and sickles, and after them the National Guardsmen, who are not much good for anything—Lafayette has but weak control of them and they are all antagonistic to the king. Your maman was with the queen, but I was watching with some other nobles from the windows of the Hercules Room and saw everything that passed.

If rain had not discouraged these rioters I think the situation may have turned out worse, and it was bad enough. They lit bonfires in the Place d'Armes, slaughtered a horse and cooked it there, eating and drinking and singing and shouting and cursing the queen, who has come to represent a foreign bogeyman in the eyes of the common populace. The rain came down on all of them all night and we hoped their spirits would be drowned, but no, just before first light they leaped up and started a commotion beneath the king's windows. What we did not see was the crowd that ran up the queen's stairway, shoved their pikes through the Swiss guard who blocked their way, and took to her door with an axe. What we did see was a new commotion in the courtyard and then a head—it was the Swiss guard's head—raised up on a pike and paraded up and down.

We fled for our own safety then. It was impossible to reach the king and queen, and I did not see your poor maman, who, panicked by the attack on the queen's door, ran down an inner stairway and crept out into the Cour de Marbre, intending to hide herself somewhere. But the crowd came rushing, bearing the guard's mutilated head before them. This man had been the dearest of dear friends to your maman and the grisly sight undid her. She took such a turn she slipped on the wet surface and was trampled by the crowd.

Cassandra felt her stomach rise, thinking of the way Baby's little body had rolled underneath her horse's hooves. She turned the paper down.

Benedict held out his hand. "Shall I read the rest?"

"No, I am recovered."

Immediately upon this awful event, we were forced to load her on a wagon and jolt her down the road to Paris—I pitied her more, I confess, than our poor King Louis and the queen in their humiliation on that journey. Since then she has been lodged in the city, cared for by strangers. The physicians say something inside her was injured by the accident, one of her internal organs, but they cannot say which one, and none of their bleeding and poulticing has been worth a fig. In the end, there was nothing for it but to let her rest and recover on her own, which course she had embarked on moderately well, and we felt encouraged enough to make preparations to turn émigré, but then a worse disaster struck.

I do not know how to say this gently, so I will say it outright. Your brother Maximilian and his unfortunate wife have been murdered in their bedchamber by peasants revolting on our property, his wife killed by a gunshot through the breast and Maximilian hung up from the chandelier. We had this from a messenger but since then have had no word at all. All has been in chaos in the area but now seems calmer and I would venture out to see what of our fortunes might be retrieved except I am prevented by my need to be at court—I am reliant on my pension from the king—and also by a sad downturn in the condition of your poor maman, whom I now dread to leave. When she heard the news of Maximilian, she ceased to recover from her injury, instead worsening each day. And her mind has been affected, not all the time, sometimes she is as lucid as I am myself, while at other times . . . it breaks my heart to see her come to this.

Son, she calls for you most piteously, knowing she is à l'agonie. I fear that if you do not come soon you may not set eyes on her again. I know this news will grieve you as it does me, and I am sorry to deliver it, but I must beg you to come home. Since the mails are so uncertain, I have applied to Mr. Gouverneur Morris—the closest we have here to an American minister since Mr. Jefferson's departure—to include this letter in his official pouch. He tells me everyone is asking for such favors and he cannot grant them all, but since you helped his country in its fight for independence from the British, he will make this one exception.

You ask for news of France, and I scarce know what to tell you.

So much goes on here, so many plots and counterplots, some new whisper of disaster every day. The politicians shout and bicker with each other over every word suggested for a constitution. If they do not get it finished and agreed to soon the country will erupt. Huge numbers of the aristocracy have fled, and continue daily, and many are reported to have joined a counterrevolutionary army massing at our borders.

The people grow more unruly every day. They panic over bread, the slightest rumor of a counterrevolution sets the mob aflame. Myself, I barely know what to think about the situation. At first I thought that it would right itself but now I fear it has taken on a momentum of its own and the country heads for a disaster. At the moment, though, things are relatively calm and so I think it safe enough for you to come.

We hear such dreadful things about America, such rumors, that it is so rough and rude, no civilized society to speak of, or none to compare with the delicacy of life with which you have always been surrounded. But enough of that. I long for your arrival, as does your poor maman. Come to the address I have written on a separate sheet of paper.

Your devoted father,

François van Pradelles

By the time Cassandra came to the last line, her hand was shaking so that she could barely see the words. When she tried to speak, a gasping sound somewhere between sob and hiccup came out of her throat. She drew her breath in hard—now was not the time to have hysterics—and spent a long time folding up the letter before she gave it back to Benedict. "I'm sorry for your brother and his wife, and for your poor maman."

He said nothing, looking down at her with a severe expression, but then the tiniest movement of his jaw gave him away. She touched his hand. "I'll come with you, of course."

"No, you will not. It's far too dangerous. You must wait here."

"Your papa says it isn't dangerous."

"Whatever he may say, it is. I must go alone."

"You will forget me."

He set his hand against his breast. "I take your likeness with me everywhere. Each night I open up your locket and set your dear face by my bed to watch me through the night. Each morning I waken to your smile. How could I forget you, sweet?"

Cassandra heard her voice grow stubborn. "It's nothing but a picture in a locket, a sentimental thing, a trinket. One night you'll set it by your bed and dream of someone else. In the morning you will go to meet her, leaving it behind. It will be brushed into the drawer at some inn or at the house of an acquaintance. A maid will find it, slip it in her pocket, sell it for a coin or two. You will forget."

"My, my! What a feverish imagination!" He laughed, but his face was serious. "Cassandra, don't you read the newspapers? They report new violence in Paris every day, and by the time I've made the voyage over the Atlantic, who knows what condition the city will be in?"

"But there's another thing . . ."

"Come, come. No more crying. Give me your hand. What is it? What?"

"Benedict, what if I am enceinte? If you leave me here and my belly starts to swell, who knows what Papa will do? He can be a stubborn angry man, as you have seen. What if he should cut me off, throw me in the street? No, it will not do. You must not go alone. You must take me with you."

An odd expression came upon Benedict's face. "Enceinte? It is not possible."

"That afternoon we spent here in the woods beside the pond . . ."

"Sweet child, do you know nothing of biology?"

Cassandra felt her face go hot. "I was not sure."

"Listen to me, sweet. Your safety is my grave concern. You read my father's letter. France is no place to take a wife."

"I care nothing for all that. I'd rather be with you in danger than in misery without you." She gave a reckless laugh. "We'll be runaways together."

"No, we will not. I cannot steal you from your father. It would be dishonorable."

"Steal me? You do not *steal*. I give myself to you."

"I can't allow it. Your father loves you to distraction."

"And you do not?"

"I do, you know I do. But it's best for you to stay here until I come again. I'll be quick. I'll pack my parents up and leave directly."

"But your papa says your mother cannot travel."

"He's always been too tender with her. He's a contradictory man, my father, with a head hard enough to weather palace intrigue, but a heart that panics at the slightest sign of ill health in his wife. I doubt she's dying. He adores her so much that he coddles her."

"As you are coddling me? Sir, I may be only seventeen, but I am not a child, and I am stronger than you think. I want to come. I can help you with your mother on the voyage home. She'll need a nurse. I offer you myself."

"No. I want your father's blessing. We must outwait him."

"Then I'll tell you straight, Sir, that no matter how quickly you pack your parents up, no matter how the winds blow in your favor on the voyage back, by the time you see me again you'll find yourself too late. My papa intends to marry me this fall to someone else, someone for whom I have not the slightest whim or passion."

"Against your will? It is not true."

"He would keep me from *you* against my will. Why would he not give me, still against my will, to someone else?"

"To whom?"

"Mordecai Worthington—that dullard with his pockmarked face."

"I am aghast."

"It's all arranged. He announced it just this moment. I came directly to you. Benedict, he has quite rejected your proposal. I know him—he will not back down. Unless you take me with you, he'll marry me to Mordecai." She thumped her hand against the pommel of her saddle and her horse twitched back his ears and made a little dancing two-step sideways.

"Whoa, there," said Benedict.

Cassandra pulled back on the reins and looked at him. The moon shone on his face, and on his pearl-gray coat, his white shirt with the ruffle at its bosom. He seemed to glow, and it seemed to her she saw in him her own reflection.

"Benedict, I do not *want* Papa to choose a man for me to love. I don't want Mordecai, or any of these . . . these *boys* about the place. I want a full-grown man, someone who has seen the world, who will not blush and stumble over his own feet. I want a husband who will love me with a *passion*. I want . . . oh, Benedict, I want to have *adventures*."

Benedict turned away with an outflow of his breath and, pulling off his hat, scratched his head ferociously. He set his hat back on and turned back to Cassandra.

"Your father will pursue us."

"We will outride him."

3

*L*ATER THAT NIGHT AT OWINGS HALL, JOHN, red-faced and bulging-eyed with fury, interrogated everyone from Cassandra's quaking sister Charlotte—she of anyone should have shared Cassandra's confidence, did she not lie beside her every night?—to the cripple who had lost his left foot to the British and now hobbled about the place as jack-of-all-trades, by night sleeping in the stable with the horses—how could he not have wakened when Cassandra came to get her horse? Cassandra's maid Susannah, under threat of a flogging with the cowhide, collapsed into a paroxysm of tears, twisting her apron in her hands and swearing ignorance. The other servants, although several obligingly remembered the creak of a door, a muffled footstep in the cobbled yard, the far-off sound of hooves, when they were pressured for a specific time, a detail more, became like damp rags from which all the water has been wrung. No matter how John raged, no one would swear to anything of substance.

At last he spun toward his wife. "Where would she go, woman? Where?"

Colegate quailed before him. "To some neighbor's house, perhaps? The Gists? The Worthingtons? Buchanans?" Although she knew it was not likely to be so.

Thomas was dispatched. Above his head, the moon was round and brilliant in a clear black sky.

The sun was swimming silver in the east when Thomas arrived back at Owings Hall, his horse puffing out her flanks and gasping, sweat flying from the corners of her mouth. In his absence, John had fumed and stamped about the house and yard, once more interrogating every slave and servant, every child and nurse, the children's mild tutor Mr. Meekum, even Colegate who had now barricaded herself into the bedroom, refusing to come out. Over and over again he had demanded every detail of every conversation, details of every move observed.

When there were no more questions to be asked, he sat down on the front step, hunched forward, elbows propped against his knees, calculating how long it would take for Thomas to ride to each of their neighbors, rouse the servants, wait for someone to come yawning down the stairs, to query hopefully, explain, demand, to search the barn perhaps, interrogate the house slaves, persuade someone—who?—to surrender Cassie, and then ride back with her to Owings Hall.

Every sort of scenario played through his mind—Cassandra weeping in a storm of repentance for her foolishness, Cassie petulant and angry, refusing to come home, Cass rebellious, riding off into the night. He strained his ears into the silence, listening for hooves, and tension built along his shoulders. He rolled his head on his neck. *No, man, do not agitate yourself. Sit right here and smoke your pipe. Be calm.*

Stretching out one leg, he tugged a leather pouch from the pocket of his breeches. He folded back the flap and, pinching the rich tidewater tobacco between thumb and forefinger, filled the pipe and lit it. It flared and he sucked at it with his cheeks hollowing and filling, the pipe's bowl hissing and glowing like a small volcano about to erupt.

As he sat there struggling to be calm, it occurred to him that he had been sitting right here on this step, smoking his pipe and telling himself to be exactly that the night Cassandra had come howling into the world, blue-faced and angry, as though she had been interrupted in some other, preferable life. It had been Christmas Eve, seventeen years ago, and what a screamer she had been! Even then the child had been a rebel, tearing at poor Colegate's nipples until they were tender and inflamed, or else rejecting them entirely, storming and screaming into the night, until her mother seemed to go quite mad, claiming that the stoppage of her milk was causing a suffocation of her brain, crying out in strange voices that she would kill herself. Or else she would lie down on her bed and sleep all day, the child beside her, screaming herself stiff while Colegate slept inside the tangle of her hair.

One night, another sleepless night, another nurse gone off that afternoon with shaking head, John's patience had snapped. He had not yet dared to touch the child—it was all sound and fury—but now he felt a growing urge to take it up and shake it into silence. He leaped off the bed and, pouncing to the cradle on its other side, seized Cassandra up so that his face looked directly into hers.

"Enough!" he bellowed. "Enough! Enough!" The last so much louder than the first that Amos came running with his breeches clutched in one hand and the bellows from the fireplace in the other.

John, startled into repentance, clapped the child to his chest and, with wife and manservant agape, commenced to dance about the room with her, singing the first tune in his head: "'If you meet a bonnie lassie, give her a kiss and let her go, but if you meet a dirty hussy, fy, gar rub her o'er with strae,'" beating time with his big red hand against her tiny bottom.

And so the child was tamed. When she screamed at night, John took her up. When she looked near to starving from refusing every breast, he fed her from a spoon, coaxing her with bread softened in cow's milk from which the heavy top layer of cream had been skimmed. And she began to thrive, turning her head toward his voice, gurgling in his arms, falling asleep against his breast.

Colegate began to take an interest in her dress and hair again, to drive out in her carriage, and John, pleased with her improvement, set aside the thought that, while his wife seemed well recovered from her ordeal, she was not entirely the woman he had married anymore. Why would she be? Did not people change as a result of their experiences in life? Her nature, which had been both sweet and fiery, seemed to have undergone a transformation. Now the fire was gone and the sweetness sometimes had a quality like coffee that has been made too strong and filled with sugar to hide its bitter tang. He did still love her, did he not? Of course he did. Had she not given him Cassandra, this tiny, pretty child, with a radiant dark beauty that caused strangers to turn and stare at her, and bouncing black-brown curls he loved to feel beneath his horny farmer's hand? As she grew he would sometimes take her on his knee and rest his cheek against her head and breathe the musky smell of her, and such a yearning would come over him that he would weep into her gleaming curls. "Papa?" the child would say, and turning to him, take his face between her hands and set her soft full lips, her mother's lips, on his.

Between night and dawn there is a time when the entire world seems to enter a period of contemplation, a time when silence hangs suspended in the hills and the sky is neither black nor gray nor light, a time when even the most furious of passions becomes stilled, when the most violent man looks deep inside himself and thinks of life and death and ponders on what matters to him most.

In such a mood now John sat on the step, pulling on his pipe, gazing with unseeing eyes, and thinking of his daughter. She seemed to stand before him, smiling, holding out her arms for his embrace. But then behind her was the Frenchman, with his bold black eyes, his fancy frills and flourishes. She turned away. Oh, God, she turned away. And now a question that he dared not ask himself: was his daughter's virtue tainted? No, he would not think of it. His beloved darling would not serve him in that way. Any moment now Thomas would return with her behind him on the saddle. Then all would be forgiven. She would be his darling once again. It had been his own fault after all. He should have treated her more gently. Was she not still a child? He should have coaxed her, taken her upon his knee and stroked her hair. Yes, he should have coaxed and charmed her. But, in his love for her, his fatherly concern, he had been peremptory, demanding, setting her against him.

But now another thought: what if Cassandra brought the Frenchman with her when she came? He had complained the fellow was too old, too French, that he was a fortune hunter, nothing but a merchant, quite unsuitable. Now he pulled his pipe and thought again. Had he been too hasty in his judgment? This Frenchman worked hard, did he not? He was of good family, dressed well, indeed impeccably. Performed like a gentleman of breeding in society. He charmed the ladies, certainly, but he also charmed the men. He had ambition, plans, might even be an asset to the family. Yes, an asset. His hands were fine and delicate, but surely he could learn to manage land. And as to age, Cassandra was a headstrong girl and needed guidance, a firm hand. Not harsh, but firm and kind, a loving hand, a hand like her papa's. So did this Frenchman truly love her? It appeared he did. Would he spirit her away to France? Why would he return there after all these years? No, the man was just like every other immigrant. He had sniffed opportunity and had pursued it. If opportunity were offered him in Maryland, why would he ever leave? As for Cassie, she had set her heart on him. He knew his daughter. She would not easily be moved.

A cock crowed behind the house, joined at once by the creaking voices of two cockerels. Perhaps he was jealous of the man. Who would not be? A daughter such as Cassandra was a possession to be prized. But marrying a daughter need not mean a father loses his child's affection. He had assumed that because she would love a creature so unlike her own papa and turn in disgust from Mordecai, who was so like him in every way, that it was a rejection of himself. He had been wounded in his vanity. He smiled into his pipe. Yes, he had been too hasty, after all. The Frenchman was a fine match. And he fell to planning which portions of his land he would settle on the newly married pair.

By the time Thomas' horse came clattering up the driveway he had planned it all out in his head, grunting and nodding to himself with satisfaction.

But here was Thomas all alone. John jumped up off the step.

"Why have you not brought your sister home? Where is she?"

"She is not anywhere."

"Not anywhere?" John felt a shaking start inside him. "How so not anywhere?"

"No one has seen her, though I have a theory of my own—no, Father, do not snatch at me like that—I think she has run off with Lieutenant van Pradelles."

"Run off? No, she has not."

"I think it might be so. I saw him loitering about our land this afternoon, watching the house from the shadow of the woods. He seemed expectant . . . no, that is not the word . . . intentional . . . as though someone were at the window looking out at him. Who could it have been but Cassie? And Mistress Buchanan says he was expected at her dinner party this evening but did not arrive. I'm certain he has carried Cassie off."

All John's plans and generous intentions, all his intended forgiveness of his daughter, all his dreams of a rapturous reunion, went flying out of his head. In their place came a hard, furious resolve: he would find this man and kill him, and he would recover his daughter.

A full week of inquiries offered no result. John posted notices in all the newspapers and on the boards of every inn and tavern around the countryside in all directions. Both his sons, every servant he could spare, even poor Mr. Meekum, who was unhandy on a horse, were dispatched to muster every man they could to mount a search. John went himself to pound on the desk of the inn at Towsontowne where the Frenchman stayed when he was in the area. No sign of him. And so on to Baltimore, the owners of inn and hostelry and tavern subjected one after another to his furious inquiry. At one of them he discovered the address of the seducer's lodgings.

It was late at night when this information was discovered, but he rode posthaste to a lodging house close by the harbor at Fells Point, where he beat the big iron knocker against the door until the landlady, fearful that robbers were about to take her, slung up an upstairs window and threatened to empty her chamber pot onto his head. Persuaded of her mistake, she hung her bosom like a pair of cushions out the window and cursed at him. What sort of house did he think she ran? She was an honest woman with an honest house, and honest lodgers, every one of them. Working up a rage to match his own, she accused him of plotting her ruin. "Who will come to me with business if you stand out in the street accusing me of a conspiracy to seize the virtue of your daughter? Sir, you are a scoundrel. Get off with you before I empty every chamber pot in the house upon your head."

But John refused to budge. "Madam, I will stand here shouting in the street until you unbar your door to me. Is this van Pradelles here or not? I must see for myself. I will not leave before I am assured."

And so she came grumbling and groaning down the stairs to slide open the peephole. A pair of eyes slid back and forth. "What so? Are you alone, then?"

"I am alone."

He heard the clack of a bar hauled back and the woman's capped head appeared around the door. "Alone?"

"Alone. Come, Madam, let me in. I'll not harm you."

But the Frenchman's room was empty, save for a few clothes hung on pegs against the wall, a pair of buckled shoes set underneath. John stood staring at the neat cot and the neatly strapped chest set at its end. He bent over it, loosening the straps.

"Fabric samples. Where can the fellow be?"

The woman, realizing she would not be murdered in her house that night, had calmed. "I'm sure I don't know, Sir. The lieutenant is a businessman. He travels all about the place. He comes, he goes. Sometimes he's gone for weeks on end. But I've always found him honest. His rent is always paid, he does not complain about the food, or waste candles, or drink to excess, and always comes alone back to his room. He is a model lodger. Perhaps you judge him falsely, Sir."

"Perhaps I do." And John went off, having extracted from her an oath that she would send him word at once if the Frenchman reappeared. He was calmer now. Perhaps she was right. Perhaps the Frenchman was not involved in this night's excitement after all; he was just off on some business concern. Perhaps Cassandra was right this moment creeping out from her hiding place in the barn or in the stable where she had hidden herself this last week, waited on with food and blankets by her wicked maid Susannah, crying herself to sleep each night, spending her days in contemplation of her duty. Uncomfortable and lonely, she had repented.

Full of hope, and without stopping for rest or food, he rode back home, arriving shortly after dawn to find a messenger from Philadelphia with a letter addressed to him in the elegant swirling hand Mr. Meekum had taught Cassandra.

Seeing it, John gave such a shout that everyone came running—children, house slaves, nurses, old Amos, little Sukie brandishing a flatiron, Eudie panting with her hand against her back, Mr. Meekum limping with a schoolbook in his hand, Colegate with her hand against her breast—and stood staring while he folded back the page and held it to the light of the candle on the table in the entry hall.

> Dearest Papa,
>
> I apologize with all my heart that I have had to take this action. I have but a moment to explain, since we must be on the road again. We are off to France, to rescue Benedict's maman and papa. Be assured we will return, though we could be as much as six weeks on the sea, and six weeks back, and if we are delayed in Paris, perhaps a little longer. A few months—it is nothing! I will be home before you know it.
>
> In the meantime, I beg you, Papa, forgive my offense to your dear affection, but I cannot marry Mordecai. I am in love with Benedict. I know you will be angry for a while, but you have never been offended with me long. Papa, it was always you who made my heart glad when I was distressed, you whose presence I craved whenever you were out of sight, you who took my part against whoever might complain of me. From earliest childhood you have been my greatest comfort. You indulged me, Papa, in everything you overwhelmed me with your kindness. But Papa, you must understand that I am now a woman—I will be eighteen soon.

Already I have left my childhood far behind, but I will never leave behind my love for you, the one who nurtured me. We are partners, you and I. We understand each other's hearts. And so I ask for your forgiveness. Is that so much to ask to make your darling happy? No? I shower kisses on your face in gratitude.

As for Benedict, he is a good man, and honorable. Do not think he does not suffer from the injury he feels he has done to you. He feels that he has stolen me, although there is no truth in it, I gave myself to him, indeed insisted that he take me. He refused at first but relented for fear that you would marry me to Mordecai. So do not blame him, Papa. He is a fine man, and loves me truly. He wishes only for your blessing.

Papa, I love you dearly. Give my love to Mama and Charlotte and all the little ones—oh, and Eudie and Susannah too. Kiss Thomas for me. Tell him he must work hard while I am away if he will have a tale to entertain his sister. And write to me, Papa, write that you forgive me. Send to the address I have written on the back. When I get your letter I will know that you are still my own papa.

Your errant but devoted daughter,
Cassie

As John's eyes climbed down the page and took in the last line—there was no mention of a marriage—his hand shook so violently that the page dipped and the candle flame seized the fragile paper from behind. He jerked his hand away, cursing, and the flaming paper fell onto the fine lace cloth, burning it clear through to the tabletop before he brought the sleeve of his coat down, smothering the fire.

Next morning he set out for Philadelphia with Thomas at his side, but no sooner were they on the road than the sky drew its brows together, frowning down on them. Before they reached Joppa Towne, a storm was raging and they were forced to shelter at the Red Lion Inne, where John heaved a slat-backed chair to the window of the dining room, sat on it with a thump, and set his fists against his knees, watching the lightning crack apart the sky and mumbling to himself. The minute the first bead of blue appeared, he jerked his head at Thomas and the two of them set out again.

Too soon. The storm had only stopped to catch its breath. But when it broke above their heads again, John refused either to turn back or to shelter elsewhere. Blinded with rain, soaked to the skin, and with water filling up their riding boots, man and boy rode on. But at the Susquehanna River they were forced to stop. The river was uncrossable, the ferryman informed them. He sat on a wooden box in a hut beside the ferryboat, puffing out blue smoke. John offered twice the fee, three times.

"Look at she," said the ferryman, jerking his chin toward the open door. "Look at she come down. Not even God could make it to the other side in such a torrent."

So they paid for a room at the inn and sat shivering in a pair of blankets while their clothes steamed beside the fire the innkeeper's wife built for the purpose. Although the rain came down like heaven's judgment, the day was not cold and the banked-up fire heated the room until it was a furnace. In no more than an hour their clothes were dry as bones, hot and crackling as they pulled them on. They went to sit on the verandah where they watched the Susquehanna dance and roar into the night.

By morning the storm was gone, the sky blue, the river, although swollen, flat enough. The ferryman, grumbling about undertows and currents, was persuaded to carry them across. But now the roads were heavy with mud and standing water so that their horses plowed and plodded, up to their hocks, their knees. Twice they had to swim where creeks had burst their banks. Once more they were soaked, their clothes stuck to them like second skins. They made the worst of time.

In Philadelphia at last, they seemed to have a turn of luck. At only the third inn they tried, the innkeeper, in response to a sad tale and a gold coin, confessed to having housed the lovers. But they were gone, he said, staying just one night, heading north next morning. Where to? He did not know. The road led to New York.

4

*A*T THE FRAUNCES TAVERNE INNE ON NEW York's waterfront, Cassandra stood before the dressing table mirror. "We eloped," she said aloud, and saw reflected in the glass a crowd of friends, their faces turned toward her, radiant with the fantasy of a grand romance. She smiled, bowing like a player at a curtain call.

She swung away, edged around the bed toward the window, and peered out through the narrow crack between the drapes. Where was Benedict? She wanted to go out into the street again. She loved the noise and smell of it, the bustle of activity, the shouts and whistles and the clattering of horse's hooves against the cobblestones, the rattling of carts, the ritual of loading and unloading cargoes, barrels rolling off the ships down narrow planks, great bundles swinging through the air, the clattering of furled sails against the lined-up masts. She loved the danger and the wickedness, the vagabonds in rags holding out their hands and caps, pulling at her skirt, wild men in sailors' neckerchiefs grinning with black teeth and eyes that followed her. And then she wanted to come back inside and lie down on the bed with Benedict again. They had made love for half the afternoon and now he had gone off to have a conversation with the captain of the ship on which they hoped to sail. When would he come? She wanted to feel the softness of his hands again—on her legs, her thighs, her belly. Her blood heated at the thought of it.

She went to the door and bent her head to listen for his footstep. Nothing. Only other people's footsteps coming and going in the passageway outside. She went back to the mirror, and her admiring friends seemed very young and innocent. She would never tell them she had tumbled into this adventure quite by accident, that a conventional wedding ceremony had been her desire, with the reading of the banns before, herself and Benedict standing side by side in a garden filled with flowers, family and friends around, Papa sticking out his chest and smiling, Mama weeping on a lace-edged handkerchief, brothers, sisters, Grandpapa Owings, Great-aunt Deye, all her friends and cousins, even Mordecai.

Instead they had fled together like a pair of fugitives. Not daring to attempt a sailing from the port of Baltimore—the infrequency of ships and the closeness of the port to home meant almost certain capture—they had fled north, first to Philadelphia, then, because there was no ship about to sail, on here, to New York.

In Philadelphia, they had hunted for a priest or parson who would marry them, Cassandra insisting over and over that she must be made respectable. An Episcopalian priest had turned them down, and then a Catholic, both saying they must wait six weeks, that was the requirement of the church, to ensure the ceremony was intended seriously, their oaths before God not lightly taken. The Methodist to whom they next applied did not question their intentions but declared he did no marriages on Sunday. It was a day of rest. They must come back tomorrow.

At last, in a poor part of the town along the waterfront, they had beat upon the manse door of the Gloria Dei church belonging to the Lutherans. The reverend had come down, yawning and scratching, in his nightshirt and cap. They introduced themselves and set their plea before him. He replied that his name was Nhils Collins and he would do the deed. His wife appeared, carrying a candle, and led them across a narrow walkway to the side door of the church. They entered a small room and went out the other side, up two narrow marble steps, into the body of the church.

It was black as pitch as they stumbled down the aisle, the pale light of the candle almost swallowed up. But the reverend lit more candles at the altar and they could see each other's face and a pool of light around their feet, the remainder of the church still lost in gloom. They bowed their heads to pray and Cassandra saw, engraved into a marble slab, a grinning cherubim. Words also were engraved: "This marble covers"—*dear Lord, they were standing on a tombstone!*—"the remains of the Rev'rend Andrew Rudman, founder of this church, where he advanced true piety by sound doctrine and good example. Died Sepr 17, 1708, aged 40 yrs." *Poor Rev'rend Rudman! Such goings-on above his sainted head!*

No, she had not meant to do it. When she jumped up to go to Benedict, she meant only to go to him. What she would do after that had not been in her mind. But now everything was turning out to be this wild adventure, like a grand crusade she could not turn away from, a calling she could not resist. She was going to pluck two people out of France—from the middle of a revolution! She was going to save them—rescue them! She felt like Joan of Arc, fancied she could feel the same excitement throbbing in her veins. She would become a heroine—at seventeen years old! They would write about her in the newspapers. People on the street would point her out and ask her to their weddings and their parties. Thomas would envy her. And Papa would forgive her, he would boast of her to all his friends. He would take Benedict by both hands and kiss him like a Frenchman, on both cheeks, apologizing for his opposition to their marriage. Oh, he would be proud!

Outside the window, shouts, a rattling, someone running in the yard. What was going on out there? She was missing everything. She went back to the door, and setting her hand on the big key, turned it in the lock.

And there was Benedict, smiling, kissing her, apologizing for his long delay. In his hand he held the papers for their voyage. They would leave tomorrow with the tide. He had brought her back a gown, a fine new cloak, a pair of shoes, a box of toiletries, a petticoat—she felt herself blushing like a ninny—and here was a gold ring. He slipped it on her finger. "There," he said, "now you are respectable."

In New York, John and Thomas headed for the wharves, making inquiries at every inn and tavern up and down the waterfront. They tracked the runaways to the Fraunces Taverne Inne, a place John was familiar with, for it was there that General Washington had so movingly farewelled his officers when the war for independence had been won. John himself had not been amongst them but the scene was famous and he had visited the place when he had had occasion to be in New York. Once it had been grand enough, but now was fallen into seediness.

Thomas waited with the horses while John picked his way through muck and steaming horse manure to the door. Inside, men went back and forth but no one was behind the desk of whom to make inquiries. A sign said ALEXANDER POWERS, PROPRIETOR. He rattled at the bell but got no response. Went through to the tavern, which was loud with drunken conversation, the floor slick as glass with spat tobacco juice, the smell of bodies and whiskey mixed up together in the air.

A red-faced man with an enormous belly served behind the bar. Not Powers, no. So where was he? A shout. A shouted answer from behind the wall. A man appearing in the door behind the bar. A skinny head, suspicious eye. So what did Mr. Cockey Owings want? A hand held out. A smile. Some coins tucked in a vest. Jerked head.

Back at the front desk, Mr. Powers thumbed the pages of the register. A Monsieur and Madame van Pradelles, a French couple. Were they the ones he sought? Too late, the birds had flown. Flown where? Mr. Powers shrugged. And were they man and wife? He shrugged again: they traveled with no chaperone, they shared a room, he presumed that they were man and wife, and what was more, he did not like John's attitude. "Do I look to you like the keeper of a bawdy house? No, Sir, I am a God-fearing man, an honest businessman. If you cannot control your daughter, am I to be your conscience?"

John had an urge to hit the man, but he was surrounded by others heartier than he and so turned to leave. A boy, a tavern hand, ran behind him to the door, pulling at his cloak. John hesitated, looked down at him inquiringly. A coin placed in another hand. The couple he inquired about were not long gone. A ship was readying right now to leave for France. If the gangplank had not yet been drawn up . . . John leaped outside, bellowing for Thomas.

Now he raged, searching up and down the wharf. And there, out there, on that ship drawing away, was not that tiny figure Cassie—there, standing at the rail? He snatched his hat off, waving it and leaping in the air, bellowing her name, Thomas leaping and shouting at his side: "Cassie! Cassandra! Cass!" And she seemed to turn her face toward him, although she did not wave, just stood staring at him with fixed intensity until she was nothing but a blur and then nothing at all.

That night they ate supper at the Fraunces Taverne Inne, John as morose and foul-tempered as a man could be. Gone off to France! That fool would take his darling girl to France! The whole world knew about the awful happenings there. Just last week the newspapers had carried news of heads set up on pikes around the city. And here was this mad Frenchman dragging his Cassandra full into the midst of it, he an aristocrat himself. What would become of her? In God's name, what would become of her? He punched his fist into his thigh and tossed down another glass of ale.

Thomas, who was enjoying all this hugely, stuck his legs out underneath the table and looked about with interest, listening to the conversations going on around them, the coarse voices and the clank of glasses. Beside him, a man sat reading a newspaper and after a while belched loudly, wiped his mouth with a capacious napkin, and went off, leaving his newspaper untidy on the table. Thomas glanced at it, and a report from Paris caught his eye. He pulled the page across and burst out laughing. "Father, these French are not so dangerous. They cannot so much as get a balloon successfully aloft. Let me read this to you, Sir, for it will cheer you up: 'Since the ceremony of the Confederation, everything here has been revelry and merriment . . .' Yes, yes, and so on . . . 'In the forenoon a review of the national troops . . . ' Ah yes, here it is: ' . . . a balloon was to be sent up after the review. But the balloon-maker, not succeeding in filling his aerostatick machine, disappeared amongst the crowd and the balloon fell upon the heads of the people in the amphitheatre. The country confederates and their spouses, who had heard that balloons are filled with inflammable air, jumped over the seats and balustrade with such precipitation that they risked breaking their necks for fear of an accident. Some young men, with courage quite the reverse, attempted to compleat the filling of the balloon by burning some straw beneath. The consequence was an explosion that scorched five or six of them so miserably that for the rest of their lives they will not be likely to make any more experiments.'"

Thomas grinned across at John, who looked back at him so sourly that he folded up the newspaper and fell once more to gazing round the room.

By morning John's evil humor had grown worse and on the journey home he stewed on the situation, building up his anger against the Frenchman. The man was a libertine, as all these Frenchmen were. With his airs and elegant flourishes, his kissing of the ladies' fingers, his bold black eyes, the way he waved his hands about, he stole away their silly hearts. Colegate had fancied him herself. She hid it well, but he had seen her flirt and flick her fan at him and catch his eye. It was Colegate who had set him on every list of invitations to a dinner, a dancing party, an evening of music in their home. And her friends were just as silly—every evening spent at any of their homes had been an evening spent with Lieutenant van Pradelles.

Not satisfied with that, Colegate had ridden out in her carriage every week to visit one friend or another, taking Cassandra with her, using the excuse that the girl needed new diversions, and like a gaggle of geese, the women had trailed after the Frenchman to fairs and fêtes and plays and race meetings, even cockfights. He, John, had turned a blind eye to their female nonsense: dizzy women with a harmless fancy for a Frenchman. But this Frenchman was not harmless, no. He was slick and subtle as a Satan. While he wooed the dizzy matrons, he wooed Cassandra too. And Colegate, with her head stuffed full of romances, never noticed what catastrophe was brewing. Or did she notice, had she encouraged this? Had she done this to amuse herself, to make a romance of her own?

The closer they got to home the more sullen John became until at last Thomas gave up on conversation and amused himself by whistling through his teeth. By the time they walked their exhausted horses through the dimness of the driveway's overhanging sycamores, John's fury had been transferred from the Frenchman, who was out of reach, to Colegate, who was not. He stormed upstairs with accusation on his face.

Colegate lay sleeping on the bed, a wet rag on her forehead. She did not wake. He stood looking down at her. How could she sleep? How could she rest at all? His eye fell on the row of novels ranged along the shelf beside her bed, titled, every one of them, with women's names: Pamela, Clarissa, Evalina, Trifine, Hélène, Odette, Fantine. Why must their names all be so sentimental? He felt rage building in his throat. As though of its own accord, his arm came up and swept the row of books onto the floor, along with a crystal vase of roses and a miniature portrait of himself, which, landing face upward, smiled smugly at him from its silver frame.

"See what you've done?" he cried. "See what your silly games have brought us to? You've made Cassandra into one more ninny in a novel!"

Colegate jerked upright, holding the rag against her head. She jumped up off the bed and would have fled, but the house slaves had come running, wanting to be in on the commotion, and blocked the doorway, all agog, with brooms and dusters in their hands.

John turned on them. "Your mistress is a silly woman. Do you hear me? Nothing but a silly woman. And you are gaping liars, every one of you. You should be whipped."

And he shoved through them, digging his elbow into Colegate's breast so hard she cried out with the pain, and went outside to rave up and down the yard, cursing his wife, himself, that goddamned Frenchman, God.

After a while he quieted, and Colegate, listening from the open window, heard him weep for the first time in her life. It went on, it seemed, for hours, first a heavy wet spluttering, then a steady wrenching sound, as though he were vomiting up his insides bit by bit, then a quiet rhythmic sobbing, and then silence. He did not come inside that night, and she sat at the window watching his humped body on the grass, blaming herself for her vanity and blindness. How could she have known her whim to make a romance for her daughter would result in this?

All night she sat there dry-eyed, with remorse, like an invasion of her body, swelling up and bloating all her organs until she felt she would explode. Early in the morning, she rose and went to the dressing table, where she took up her little silver-handled mirror and smashed it against the post of the chair. She took the biggest sliver, sat down on the padded seat, and slid the sharp edge into the flesh of her left elbow, drawing it down her forearm in a quick slicing motion. She had meant to do it again, and then again, but when she saw the well of blood against the white flesh of her arm, she leaped up and jerked the bellpull clear off the wall before the room swung on its side and everything turned black.

"She has tried to kill herself," they said, looking at her lying white and bandaged on the bed. "Poor Colegate tried to kill herself." But it was not true. She had meant only to relieve the pressure of her blood. She had meant only to keep her body from exploding.

Now she sank down into what seemed to be a fit of silent madness, refusing to speak to anyone, weeping and tossing her head about. Dr. Bellamy attended her. He bled and dosed and poulticed her. He shook his head.

"Poor Colegate," they said. "She has taken another of her turns."

John sat beside the bed with accusation like a finger pointing at her in his head, trying to forgive her. And he did, he told himself, he did. When she rallied and began to look as though she might recover, he looked into her eyes and said she was forgiven; he would not mention the affair again. But it was not the same with

her now. She had gone against him. She had set herself in opposition to him. She had challenged his authority.

The next morning, when he went downstairs, Eudie came to
him clicking her tongue about the damage caused by Cassandra's
flaming letter. Bad enough that an expensive tablecloth was ruined,
but at least the table could be saved. It must be repaired, she said.
But John refused. Despite its value, despite the fact that it had
been imported from England by Colegate's aunt and given to them
as a wedding gift, he hauled the thing outside and burned it in the
yard. Then, calling for Susannah, he pounded up the stairs and,
flinging open drawers and armoire doors, swept all Cassandra's
clothes into a pile, instructing the trembling girl to burn them,
give them to the poor, he cared not what, just rid the place of
them.

5

*A*LTHOUGH HE NEVER SPOKE OF HER, JOHN waited every day for news of Cassandra: a letter, a message from a friend, from some stranger, a report, God forbid, of her death. Every day, when he came in from the fields or returned from vestry duty, service with the county court, some business at the docks of Baltimore, he hurried through the door and down the hallway to his office, where the mail was set on the rich red leather inlay of his desk. With trembling hands he fumbled through it, and every day called out, "Is this everything? Is there no more?"

Upstairs, Colegate lay on her bed with the curtains drawn and a cool rag on her head.

John's spirits sank lower every day, his temper became more and more morose. His slaves and servants came to fear him, and his children hid in the nursery or schoolroom. When he and Colegate were forced into society by obligation or the insistence of some relative or friend, he sat at dinner with a long face and a sad droop to his whiskers, adding nothing to the conversation. Coerced onto the dance floor, he thumped up and down, clinging so tightly to his partner that he squeezed the breath out of her, or else holding her so lightly that, on a turn or pirouette, she would spin out of his grasp.

He knew he had become the subject of gossip. But something heavy seemed to cling about his head and no matter how he lay in bed at night, resolved to rise at dawn and leave this heaviness behind, he could not shake it off. Sometimes he tossed from dark to dawn in sleeplessness, sometimes strange images roiled in his mind—mocking faces, snatches of Cassandra's face, sensations of wind, of wetness, a whistling and shouting in his ears, a sickening heaving as though his bed tossed in a violent storm, figures rushing and hurtling in a blur he could not get into focus.

And then one night the turbulence inside his head resolved itself into a dream. He saw a ship sailing into a sun that rose on a horizon crimson as a pool of blood. Cassandra stood at the rail, holding tight against the heaving of the deck. She was facing into the sun, and the spray came hissing back along the ship's side, soaking her face and hair so that she seemed to drown in her own tears. Above her head, the sails cracked and billowed, and at the ship's prow, charging with her breasts thrust out across the ocean, was the wooden figure of a woman.

Now a black spot sailed out of the sun, growing bigger, the safe flag of America running down the mast, a pirate's black flag running up. Cassandra's ship leaped in the water, turning. The stranger broadsided and blocked her. The pop of guns was silent as a dream, but he smelled gunpowder. The acrid smoke caught in his throat. He saw Cassandra clutch her heart. She turned to run, skidding on the slippery deck, righted herself with a hand flung out against the rail, then sank down to her knees, hands clasped as though in prayer.

The pirates were upon them now. Grappling hooks sang in the air. Commotion on the deck. Cassandra's face turned up in horror and petition. A cutlass swung. He looked to see who swung it and saw his own arm sweeping down. And then the awful, silent smell of blood.

John woke with a shout, panic pouring from his skin, and did not sleep again all night. The next night he dreamed the dream again, and the next night, and the next, until he feared to go to bed or even to sit down in a chair and doze. Exhausted and light-headed, he went about the business of his day with Cassandra like a mist inside his head, an odor that would not wash off.

One day he saw her. She was standing by the barn, her back toward him. She wore a blue gown with a calico apron tied at the neck and waist, and a puffed white bonnet on her head. She stood quite still, looking into the barn. Then, as though coaxing something to come to her, she bent with her hand held out. It was too far for John to hear, but he *did* hear: Cassandra's voice. "Baby, Baby, come here, girl."

John smiled, watching. In a moment the little dog would come running to jump at Cassandra's skirt, her legs like four springs bouncing her fluffy body up and down. Then Cassandra would bend and sweep her up into her arms and kiss her, and she would turn toward him, her face lighting up. "Papa," she would say. "Papa."

But Baby didn't come. Cassandra dropped her hand and vanished into the barn. John, who had been about to call out, followed her, his heart light and spinning in his chest.

"Cassie?" He blinked into the gloom.

But now it wasn't Cassie, after all. It was Susannah, with a flustered face, straightening Cassandra's dress. And Mr. Meekum, with his rickety bowed legs and a swelling in his crotch.

A few weeks later, John woke late, having fallen into unaccustomed sleep, and lay in bed staring at the blank brightness outside the window. It was an unseasonably warm fall day, all the windows thrown up to catch the breeze. He could hear activity outside: a shout, the sound of horses' hooves on hard-packed dirt, footsteps on cobblestones, the agitated barking of a dog. He must stir himself and be about his business. And yet he could not seem to stir.

At last he forced himself upright on the bed and sat for a moment with his arms around his knees, trying to collect his wits to face the day. There was much work to do. Yes, it must be done. He sighed, climbed down from the bed, took his pants and shirt from where they hung against the wall, and pulled them on. He went across to the brown plush armchair beside which his boots were set and, sitting down, pulled them on, giving each a little jerk to get it past the heel. He rose, stamped against the floor to get his feet set right, then took his hat down from its peg and set it carelessly upon his head.

His breakfast, set out on the table in the center of the room, had long grown cold. He lifted a dish cover, looked with distaste at the ring of grease around the eggs, and set it down. He turned back the linen cover from the biscuits, broke off a crust, and thrust it into his mouth, chewed once, twice, swallowed, choking on the sudden dryness in his throat. Lifted the padded warmer from the coffeepot and felt the metal side. Still warm. Poured a cup, splashing a little into the saucer, then, lifting the cup by its delicate curved handle, went to stand beside the window, scratching his belly with his other hand and looking out at Susannah, who sat at the potter's wheel throwing a new pot. She seemed to sense him watching her and looked up, pushing a strand of hair back from her face. Wet clay clung to her hand and left a streak across her forehead. She wore Cassandra's gown. John felt such an aching in his heart that he could hardly bear it.

That night, lying next to Colegate in the bed, he found Susannah's image rising up before him in the darkness. He heaved himself onto his side. And then the other side. And back again.

"What ails you, John?" came Colegate's voice out of the dark.

He grunted.

"John, are you unwell?"

He did not answer her and she did not ask again. He wanted her to turn to him and let him lift up her chemise. He wanted to be comforted. But Colegate seemed to have entirely ceased to want to comfort him in bed. These days, she laced and hooked and buttoned herself into high-necked, cotton nightgowns and lay beside him unapproachable as stone.

Perhaps the thing to do was take her forcefully. She was his wife. It was his right. But then he thought about the mechanics of such an adventure, the wrestling with all those yards of stiffened cotton, the heavy drawers he had no doubt were underneath, as locked and padlocked as herself. And then, when all the barriers had been torn down, all the defenses ripped away, the wrestling with unwilling, leaden limbs, and her accusing silence. No, he could not do it.

One day he came upon Susannah in the kitchen with her sleeves rolled up, shaking flour to roll some dough, and the exposed skin of her arms made the blood rush in his groin. He turned away, gruff and practical, so as not to catch her eye, and went off to his office, where he stood thinking of the color of her skin—it gleamed like buttered toast. Abruptly, he swung down the pirate cutlass he kept mounted on the wall—it was guaranteed to have belonged to Bluebeard—and brandished it, legs braced against the swaying of the deck, salt wind shrieking in the rigging, while he bore down on some unsuspecting British prize. A voice sounded in the hallway, and he glanced about him like a guilty boy, rehung the cutlass, settled his heavy package in his crotch, and went about his farming duties with a wistful air.

In the days that followed, he took to wandering by Susannah as she worked. Each time he passed she looked up at him and smiled. One day she rose, wiped her hands on her apron and then removed it, and, glancing once at him across her shoulder, walked across the sunlit yard toward the barn. He followed her, and followed her inside. Mr. Meekum was not there that day and neither of them mentioned him.

Gradually, John ceased his constant, silent accusation of his wife and began to treat her kindly once again. Colegate, grateful for what seemed to be forgiveness, responded by rising from her bed and once more taking up the duties of her house.

The weeks went by. Christmas Eve came. The grand party that was to have been held for Cassandra's eighteenth birthday went unmentioned. Christmas was a silent affair, with unspoken sorrows hanging in the atmosphere. New Year came and went. The weather froze. The trees were made of glass. The sky was lead.

As though the sorrow in the house were more than she could bear, Great-aunt Deye declined. Her skin became transparent and her cheeks fell in. She ceased to eat. All day she dozed in her wheeled chair beside the parlor fire, drooling on her neckerchief.

One morning, Colegate heard her calling out and came into the room to find her ashen-faced, half starting from her chair. She ran to her and, taking her by both arms, settled her back down.

"What is it, Aunt Deye? What's the matter?"

The old woman lifted cloudy eyes. "Tommy, is that you?"

Colegate knelt, taking her hands. "It's Colegate, Aunt, John's wife."

The old woman turned her gaze out to the room. "There you are at last."

Colegate turned, thinking someone must have come in behind her, but there was no one. She turned back. Aunt Deye's head was tilted forward. "Oh, Aunt," said Colegate, and kissed the ancient hands. "Oh, Aunt."

In a while she rose and went to John's office. But the room was empty, his leather-bound book of accounts open on the desk. She went to the front door and peered out through the door light, her hand trembling on the glass. She pulled it away and went to the closet in the inner hall, where she drew a cape about her and stepped into a pair of overshoes. She would have sent one of the servants, but she wanted to tell John about Aunt Deye herself, to do it gently, to put her arms around his neck and comfort him. She wanted him to hold her.

Outside, fine new snow lay on the ground and the air was sharp. Colegate made her way across the front yard and around the corner of the house, where she clicked open the kitchen garden gate. Rough flagstones crossed the garden and she went along them with her arms held out for balance, making a little hop from one ice-glazed surface to the next until she reached the gate at the garden's other end. As she reached to push it open, she saw John standing very still beneath the oak tree just beyond. He was smoking his pipe and watching something.

Colegate followed the direction of his gaze and saw Cassandra's girl, Susannah. With one hand she supported something in her apron, corn, and with the other spread it about for a gaggle of chickens who ran splay-toed toward each new handful, gargling in their throats. Behind them, hopping on the edges of the yard, came big black ravens, dropped out of the tree above John's head.

Colegate could have reached out to John and touched him. A whisper would have reached him easily. But something froze her in place and she stood there watching him watch Susannah, pulling at his pipe.

Susannah seemed not to see him either, at least she did not look up from her task, but Colegate sensed she knew that he was there.

John's father, old Joshua Owings, had given Susannah to Cassandra for her tenth birthday. Colegate had never liked her. There was something about her she could not put her finger on. She was too light of skin. She was too tall. She stood too straight, her backside rising up too high and proud. Sometimes something in her expression touched off a sort of recognition inside Colegate's head. It was as though she saw her in a glass that did not give a true reflection, or through a clouded windowpane, or as though she came toward her through a mist that hid but did not quite hide her features. She looked like . . . no, like . . . and Colegate would draw her brows together, struggling to bring her into focus.

Now she shivered, drawing her cape about her, and after a while Susannah finished feeding the chickens, and taking off her apron, set it on the doorsill beneath the jutting porch. Then she wandered off toward the barn, hesitated in the door, half glancing back across her shoulder, and vanished in the gloom.

Colegate's eyes returned to John, who, with a quick decisive movement, pulled the pipe out of his mouth, rapped it against the oak's trunk, shook the ashes down onto the snow, and tucked it in the pocket of his coat.

Colegate did not need to watch to know what he would do now, but she could not tear her eyes away. Down the yard he went, so nonchalant, a hesitation at the barn door as though he called to someone inside, and then he also vanished in the gloom.

Colegate saw her breath freeze on the air. She felt her heart grow cold inside her chest. Turning, she went back across the kitchen garden, through the front yard, and up the steps of the verandah to the house. Inside, she went into the front parlor and pulled the bell for Eudie. Then she knelt before Aunt Deye, set her head down in the frail old lap, and wept.

Weeks went by, months, and not one word further from Cassandra. A dozen times when no one was about, John took up his pen to write to her, to beg for some assurance she was still alive, but before a line was on the page he would make a rumble in his throat and set the pen back down. Where should he send the inquiry? He did not know. Her address had burned up with the letter sent from Philadelphia. Then he would whip himself into a rage again, pacing up and down and swearing. She could go to hell, for all he cared, he told himself, he would never speak to her again.

He became an obsessive reader of the newspapers, searching the fine, slightly blurred print for news of France, something that might provide a clue to her well-being. *The Maryland Journal, The Baltimore Advertiser, The Maryland Gazette*—he combed through them all. It had always been his habit, after dinner in the evening, to read aloud selected portions of the news to his family. Now, though, he never mentioned news of France. Such items he read silently and fearfully, then set the paper down with a sensation in his throat like strangling. Where was Cassie? Why was there no word from her?

For herself, Colegate read no newspaper. Like John, she never spoke about Cassandra, but she was like a shadow moving in the corners of her mind. Imagine it, her Cassie, her own daughter, gone off with a noble Frenchman. What a romance she was living, what elegance of life! She had taken the French court by storm, her lovely daughter. She had become a noblewoman, she had been made lady-in-waiting to Queen Marie Antoinette. And not just *any* lady-in-waiting—the chief amongst them all. The queen was never seen without Cassandra at her side. Cassie advised her on her clothes, her hair, her children, everything. And knowing what power she wielded with the queen, everyone at court fell back for her. They swept their hats off, curtsied, bowed. They came to her with their requests. And in the same way Cassandra had always managed to persuade her father to her wishes, she could persuade the queen to anything. She was a force to be reckoned with in

France, the most powerful woman in the country next to Marie Antoinette. John had always said Cassandra would keep company with persons of distinction. Ah, yes, Cassandra was having the adventures she had always longed for. She lived in Paris a charmed life, rising like a fine confection to the top.

As though Colegate had spoken all these imaginings aloud— surely she had not spoken them aloud?—the rumors spread. The gossips wagged their tongues. They buzzed and hummed. Tales about Cassandra and her nobleman arrived decorated and adorned at every door. Bedecked with gilt-edged inspiration, arrayed in captivating sentences like satin gowns, with coronets set on their heads, rings on their hands, great shining rubies, diamonds, emeralds set at throat and wrist and braided in their hair, they aired themselves about the streets of Baltimore, rode out in carriages, swayed their seductive lines at county balls. And some people believed them, those who wanted to. Others, those who read the newspapers, knew things could not be like that at all.

6

*T*HEY HAD ARRIVED IN PARIS LATE AT NIGHT, nothing to be seen but dark and darker streets, occasionally a sense of people moving, occasionally a lighted doorway with figures going back and forth, occasionally a shout. Aside from that, nothing but the churning of wheels on cobblestones, the rattling of hooves, and then Benedict handed Cassandra down before a town house in a quiet neighborhood, where she stood shivering and yawning in the yellowish light of the street lantern while he attended to the paying of the driver and the unloading of their few possessions.

The house, of a pale-colored brick, had three barred windows looking onto the sidewalk, and above, a pair of wide glass doors with a narrow balcony in front. A wrought-iron balustrade ran across the front edge of the balcony, each upright topped with an iron fleur-de-lys—the king's symbol, Cassandra knew that, very elegant. To the right, a high wrought-iron fence surrounded a small courtyard, the gate attaching to the house wall at one side, at the other to an upright of the fence, also topped by an iron fleur-de-lys.

On one side of the courtyard, a bed of unkempt bushes, roses maybe, with a slightly tilted, tipsy-looking statue of the Virgin. On the other, a wide low flight of steps to the front door of the house.

A ferocious-looking man squatted just inside the gate, a lantern on the ground beside him and a sabre propped between his knees. As they approached, he rose and shone the lantern on their faces, glaring out at them between the bars. Benedict said something to him Cassandra did not catch, but the fellow just stuck his head forward on his neck and jerked his shoulders.

She saw Benedict's hand go to his buckskin pouch. The guard's eyes followed with a narrow glint, his left hand opening, but before anything could be set in it, the door of the house burst open in a flood of pale light and a man came running down the steps. The guard snatched back his hand, hauled up the heavy latch, and, stepping to one side, swung back the gate until it clanged against the house.

Benedict's father, for it was he who was the running man, drew Benedict inside the courtyard and then up the steps and through the door, with exclamations of relief and joy. He paid no attention to Cassandra until Benedict insisted on her introduction.

"Wife?" his father said, turning a startled look on her. "You have brought with you a *wife?*" He looked her up and down. "And so young too."

At once he was all apology, kissing her hand, her cheeks, welcoming her into their most unfortunate family, congratulating Benedict, begging her to call him Papa van Pradelles. "Since it is the only title left to me, all others being done away with." He sniffed. "Even the marquis, your great hero of America, is now only Monsieur Lafayette."

His effusion and obvious goodwill disarmed Cassandra and she found herself warming to this new papa. He was tall and slim, like Benedict, with the same elegant carriage and Benedict's habit of flourishing his hands about as he talked—the habit her own papa had found so irritating. He wore a wig, thick with powder and ornately curled, and his face, which she could see had once been as handsome as his son's, looked worn down, drawn together at the brows and at the chin as though some great matter weighed on him. His sick wife? No, something more. It almost frightened her. He had a peculiar mannerism, a twitch or tic which started at the corner of his left eye and ran down his cheek and upper lip, then traveled down his neck, across one shoulder, and down the left side of his body, as though a tiny frightened animal escaped out of his head from time to time and scurried down him to the floor. He was an effusive and rapid talker, the type of man who lived his life in a state of constant agitation.

He was in the greatest agitation now, drawing Cassandra's arm through his and speaking so fast she missed a deal of what he said as he led them from the candlelit hallway into a dark room, which, when he had succeeded in lighting a lamp, turned out to be a handsome parlor. Here he settled her in an armchair and she watched him chase his shadow from one end of the room to the other, addressing Benedict, who stood in the center of the room, concentration on his face, slipping in a question here and there. With the help of some asides from Benedict, Cassandra managed to piece together the situation.

A year before, when the king and queen had been marched out of their palace at Versailles and brought to Paris under guard, Papa van Pradelles had followed with his wife and the other courtiers. At first they set up in quarters at the Tuileries palace, but his wife, being sickly after her accident, was soon lodged here in this house with a bourgeois couple her husband was convinced would be discreet and loyal, since he had often interceded for them with the king on issues concerned with the manufacture and sale of fabrics to the royal house. Because of this, the pair had grown extremely rich and had bought themselves this house in the Faubourg St. Honoré, and a title to go with it.

"Much good their title did them," said Papa van Pradelles, swinging on his heel and starting once more down the room.

This couple's factory, which was in the Faubourg St. Antoine, had been looted in rioting the year before, along with several others which now stood half-burned and ruined. Fortunately for them, they had not long before moved their household here to St. Honoré, a safer and more fashionable neighborhood, and so they got off with their necks and a good part of their wealth. Being under obligation to Papa van Pradelles, they agreed to take his wife into their home and see that she was cared for. Even when she worsened after Maximilian's death, they did their best for her. Between them and her maid and Papa van Pradelles, who came as often as he could, they kept her hovering on the edge of life. But then, just three days ago, late at night, these benefactors fled the country, taking her maid with them, leaving the sick woman alone in the house with their servants who, so Papa van Pradelles said, were enraged not to have been paid the wages they were owed.

"Now," he said, with a sweeping gesture of his hands, "I am in a situation *formidable*. I can find no other person suitable with whom to lodge your poor maman because everyone of means, everyone of decent family, who has not already fled is planning to, or at least stands ready to, and so is reluctant to take on some obligation that might prevent them when the time comes. I cannot lodge with her myself because I am required at court, and my pension, such as it is since all our pensions have been drastically reduced, depends on my continued service to the king."

"But why has this pair fled?" Cassandra asked. "To leave a helpless woman in that way is wicked."

Papa van Pradelles turned up his hands. "Who knows? Some threat. Some whisper of disaster. Dreadful things happen all the time these days. Everyone with money or position lives in fear. Everybody flees. We planned to go ourselves, but now I fear the trip would finish my poor wife completely."

He and Benedict were discussing the condition of their family lands and property in Flanders, and whether there might be anything to be salvaged from their fortune there, when Papa van Pradelles clapped his hand against his head and cried, "But I must show you through the house," and, seizing up the lamp, set off, talking as he went, so fast that Cassandra lost all track of what he said and contented herself with looking about as best she could, since he flourished the lamp so enthusiastically that the flame dipped and flared and wavered, making things appear, then disappear, then reappear distorted.

It was a grand house, although not large, its fine upholstered settees and armchairs not swathed in the white sheeting normally used to protect furniture during an owner's absence. Everything was left behind, from gilt-framed paintings on the walls to enameled ornaments and vases on the shelves, stacks of dishes and silverware in glass-fronted cupboards, the library shelves well stocked with books. A harpsichord of dark glossy wood stood on delicate legs in the middle of the music room, and a harp off to one side, with several fiddle cases on a bench behind. Running her fingers over the keys of the harpsichord, Cassandra found it still in tune and remarked that it appeared the owners had not left at all but gone off on vacation.

Papa van Pradelles waved a hand. "La!" he said. "They will come back. There are many like them on the borders, and their number grows. Not a day passes but another noble flees to join them. One day they will come back and restore France to order and sobriety." He shrugged. "Do not think I am not for the Revolution. Reforms are needed, certainly. The poor must be fed. The people must be happy. But they cannot rule themselves. *C'est impossible!* Yet these politicians in the National Assembly do nothing but fight and argue amongst themselves. Order must be restored or we will all be lost, the country will go bankrupt. There is nothing for it but to have the nobility take control by force."

As he said this, he pushed back the kitchen door, and a dozen servants, who had been gathered by the fire, rose together, turning on them looks so full of insolence Cassandra did not think it very likely they would stand still for a reinstatement of the old regime.

Papa van Pradelles seemed to think their aggressive attitude was entirely because they had not been paid, wishing aloud that he had sufficient money to do so himself, but his voice wavered as he spoke and Cassandra knew he understood the problem was not pay missed but a deeper grievance, the same that had taken the whole country by its throat.

She was glad to see him shut the door on them, but then such a clamor of voices broke out behind it she wished he had kept it open so they would at least be silent. For his part, he ignored it, as though by so doing it would go away.

Although Papa van Pradelles had been openly concerned that Benedict had brought a young wife with him, it did not take him long to change his mind. As she looked at the two of them together it seemed to Cassandra that the father visibly relaxed into the son's strength. Whereas before he had been too afraid to move his wife for fear that she would die, he now willingly let Benedict persuade him that an ocean voyage would restore her health. And this new wife would serve as nurse. He clapped his hands. The situation could not have been planned better! And he embraced Cassandra even more fervently than before, declaring her to be all sorts of complimentary things she did not understand.

Eventually she grasped that she was to remain here and supervise the care of Madame van Pradelles while Benedict went off to Flanders to see what could be salvaged of the family's fortune there. On his return, they would take the first ship back home to America. Cassandra was dismayed at the prospect of this separation, but it seemed she was a godsend, so she removed her gloves and cape and bonnet and was ready to be transported upstairs to meet the invalid.

At the landing, Papa van Pradelles hesitated. "Something I must warn you of before we enter. Your poor maman has been so sick and frightened that she is, at the moment, not quite herself, although I am confident she will recover before long."

Thus warned, they went on up and entered a well-lit bedchamber at the front of the house. There a strange sight met Cassandra's eyes. She had expected a sickroom, a woman lying in bed with sheets and covers drawn across her, and the paraphernalia of sickness all around. But no, under a bright red floral canopy, Madame van Pradelles sat propped against a mass of pillows that made her sit straight up. She was asleep, her head fallen on her breast, but fully dressed, as though for traveling, in a hooped petticoat and buttoned gloves. Because of the way she sat, the hoops had shot up in the air and her skirts stood up before her like an immense balloon. A wig was on her head, ornately curled and powdered, a grand construction in the old style. Even her shoes were on her feet, tiny, high-heeled silver slippers with flat satin bows. A crimson cloak was folded across the bed's end, as though ready for her to slip on when she rose to leave. On the floor at the foot of the bed, a flowered portmanteau, bulging at the sides. Also a parasol, furled. On a bedside table stood a framed portrait of Queen Marie Antoinette, her coiffure identical to that of Madame van Pradelles.

While Cassandra stood marveling at this apparition, Papa van Pradelles went to his wife and, sitting down beside the bed, took her hand, speaking softly to her until she woke. It was plain there was great tenderness between them.

"Benedict has come," he said, but she turned toward them a face as blank as the white quilt on which she sat, and it was quite some time before, after much cajoling of her memory, she remembered, or half remembered, her own son. Cassandra could see that Benedict was wounded by her forgetfulness, although he hid it from his father, and distressed, which he could not. As for Cassandra, Madame van Pradelles took her for a maid and nothing would move her from this fixed opinion.

7

CASSANDRA KISSED PAPA VAN PRADELLES good night with genuine affection—he had the same warm, accepting nature that had so attracted her to Benedict. She offered to help dress her new charge in a nightgown but he assured her it could not be done, that Maman would not allow it; the most she would accept was a blanket drawn up over her, and he shook one out and did it. Cassandra thought it looked ridiculous draped over the hooped petticoat and gown, like a monstrous toadstool on the bed. Maman, however, did not seem to mind, and immediately fell off to sleep again.

Papa van Pradelles laid a new log on the fire, rattled at the glass doors to the balcony to make sure they were locked, and redrew the heavy drapes. A lamp burned on a little dining table by the window, and he bent with his hand cupped behind the opening of its chimney and blew the flame out with a wet huffing sound. He did the same to the lamp beside the bed and the pair of lamps on each end of the mantelpiece, then kissed his wife by the fire's flickering light and went off to attend the king's folding into bed with protestations of gratitude that his problems with the supervision of his wife's care had been resolved.

Cassandra and Benedict had been assigned an inner chamber off Maman's, a small room originally intended as an infant's room or a private sitting room or library. It was crowded with a bed, a pair of overpadded chairs, a chest of drawers, and a narrow table set against the farther wall. It had no window and promised to be gloomy but Papa van Pradelles had assured them it was safer so, and better for Maman to have them near.

The bed had a thick feather mattress and a feather comforter that smelled of something indefinable and sweet, like newly uncorked wine. Up till now they had not had such a luxury. Their lovemaking had been intense and feverish, emotions and sensations of the flesh magnified by the panic of their flight, the threat of furious pursuit, the suspicious looks of innkeepers, and then, on board the ship, the furtive snatching at each other in a hammock slung in a conspicuous place. Now they slid down into what seemed a heaven of indulgence. Even the knowledge of Benedict's pending departure could not mar the pleasure they found in lying easy with each other, promising in whispers that their separation would not be long, a week or two, no more.

The lack of a window in the room made it completely black. Even the fire in the outer room made but the barest dim red glowing line beneath the door, and that soon faded and was gone. And there was nothing but sensation, Benedict's soft whispering against Cassandra's ear, her heightened breathing on his cheek, and then the knocking of her heart on his, the rise to ecstacy collapsing into laughter as he pressed his mouth on hers to keep her cries from startling his maman, the two of them half suffocating in the dark with mirth.

They slept late, since no light shone in the room, and it was almost noon before Papa van Pradelles appeared and they were forced to tear themselves apart. Before Cassandra knew what had happened, Benedict was gone, dispensed to Flanders to investigate his family's affairs. It left her so dismayed she broke out into tears.

Papa van Pradelles was kind, assuring her that Benedict would be away no time at all, that he would return next week, the week after, as they had planned. "*Ma petite*," he said, patting her arm. "Two weeks—it is nothing."

And so Cassandra set herself to her new duties caring for Benedict's maman with the complacency of one who is aware of doing a good deed. She was doing this for Benedict, and for Papa van Pradelles. As for Maman, she could not think of her as any sort of mother; she was so strange, with her grand coiffure like some dead animal clinging to her head, refusing to be moved. The creature was her primary concern. It must be taken care of, twisted into shape each night, powdered every morning, constantly attended to. No sooner awake than she called out for her mirror, which she held in her left hand, examining herself, and the powder puff, which she flourished in her right. Cassandra's duty was to fetch the box of powder from the top shelf of the writing desk, prize off the lid, and hold it while Maman flapped the enormous puff about her head, filling the room with a cloying scent like moldering leaves. Day or night, she would not take it off.

"It is my best coiffure," she said, "the style Her Majesty prefers on me." She gestured to the portrait of the queen beside her bed. "I must have each hair in place when the carriage comes to take me to the palace. How long will it be now? I must be ready."

And ready she would be, refusing all Cassandra's efforts to have her exchange her gown for a nightgown or chemise, refusing to so much as let her loosen up her stays. All day and night she lay in her traveling clothes and fancy hairdo, her crimson cloak folded across the bed's end, ready to slip into when she left. Not once would she agree to bathe. "No, I have no time to bathe," she said. "What if the carriage should arrive and I am *déshabillée?*" She barely ate or drank, insisted that the room be brightly lit late into the night so she would not waste time fumbling in the dark, and at every sound of carriage wheels out in the street, jerked out of sleep. "*Mes bagages!*" she cried.

Watching her, Cassandra thought of how she would tell this tale to Thomas when she went back home to Maryland. She thought of how his eyes would grow round and his mouth would open and his lips move as though repeating after her. "The Mad Maman," she called this story in her head. She would not put it in a letter though. Papa did not deserve it. He had not written—not one word. It worried her, and yet she told herself that he would write tomorrow, the next day. It might take a little time, but before long he would forgive her and give Benedict his blessing. Yes, of course he would. He could be balky as a loaded mule with those who crossed him, but he never dug his heels in long with her. She could charm him into anything.

Her charms, however, had little effect on the women in the kitchen. She called them "the servants" to Papa van Pradelles but she understood that they were not so much servants as squatters in the lower level of the house. "Why do they stay?" she said to him one evening while they sat together at their meal.

He affected not to understand, as though he wanted to avoid thinking about the women who milled back and forth below his feet, their bold eyes and surly faces watching him through half-open doors or from behind blank windows as he came and went across the courtyard of the house.

Cassandra understood he was afraid of them, not for himself, but because he had to leave her and Maman to their dubious mercies every day. "Why do they stay?" she asked again. "They have not been paid. Why do they not go home, or seek some other work that would put money in their hands?"

Papa van Pradelles gazed at her, chewing thoughtfully. "My dear," he said, "there is no work for them. And I have no doubt that not one of them has any home, or if they do, the kitchen of this house is a grand palace by comparison. No, they are better off to stay here unpaid than to go off looking for a better way to live. I think you do not understand, my dear. France is in a very sorry state."

"Oh, I do understand, or think I understand. You must forgive me, Papa van Pradelles. Since the day we arrived I have seen nothing of the city, so I know no more of what goes on here than I can see from stepping out onto the balcony—and nothing goes on in this street."

"Be thankful for it, child." He tore a hunk of bread from the loaf and crumbled it onto his plate, making little patterns with the piles of crumbs.

He felt her watching him and looked up, smiling, but the little creatures in his head were on the loose again and he struggled to control the left side of his face and body as they made their scurrying escape. Pity welled inside Cassandra, and although she wanted to ask a thousand questions about the state of France, she could see that he was not inclined to conversation on the subject.

"I will find you a new maid," he said. "Then you will be free to spend some time engaged in what amusements come your way."

"Why do we not hire one of the women down below?"

"I do not know them, child. I must find someone we can trust, someone with good references, perhaps a maid who has belonged to some person now gone off to be an émigré." Seizing up his glass of wine, he tossed back a good swig of the dark red liquid. "And before long the ladies of the salons will come rolling in their carriages to leave their cards for you. You will be swept up in society, or what is left of it. The ladies of the court will take you up, you will see. You will be grandly entertained. They will take you to the theatre and the opera, and the palace too. It is very elegant, you know. Everywhere you look it gleams with gold. And the chandeliers, my dear, the silverware, the teacups . . ." He was smiling brightly now, as though he had convinced himself of his own story. "By the time Benedict returns you will be a great sophisticate." He looked her up and down. "But my dear, do you not have a better gown? You cannot be taken visiting in *that*."

"This is all the gown I have. I had another but it was ruined by salt water while we were at sea."

"Two gowns, child? And now only one? What can Benedict be thinking of?"

Cassandra felt her cheekbones blossom into heat. "It's not his fault. We left Maryland in haste. We had no time . . . I mean . . ."

Papa van Pradelles looked quizzically at her. Then he shrugged, his hands turned out, and, going to the wall beside the bed, flung back a pair of doors set flush and papered so cleverly to match the wall that Cassandra had not noticed them before. A giant clothespress was revealed, full of fancy gowns and court gowns in silk and satin, brocade, lace, Lyons-embroidered gowns, linen handkerchiefs and dimity petticoats, stockings, ruffles, headdresses, fichus, lace collars, a stack of bonnets on an upper shelf, a row of dainty shoes below.

Cassandra stared. "These are Maman's?"

"She insisted they be carried to her from Versailles, but she . . ." He stopped, as though a sob caught in his throat. "I think she would not mind."

Cassandra touched his arm. "I would be happy just to have a maid."

"My dear, you shall have one."

A week and more went by. No lady of society appeared or left her card, and still no maid, although each night Cassandra expected to hear the tapping of a second pair of feet come up the stairs behind Papa van Pradelles. Despite his rejection of the notion, she went downstairs one day to inquire of the housekeeper if some girl among the servants might be willing to take the assignment, but when she arrived in the kitchen and stood before the woman, looking up her tall spare frame into an impudently mocking face, she thought better of it, instead requesting as commandingly as she was able that a hot brick be wrapped in a cloth and brought upstairs to warm Madame's cold toes. She did not go downstairs to make requests again that day, but pulled the servant's bell and gave instructions to whomever came.

And so she waited day to day, attending to duties she never had performed for anyone before and never had expected to, and for entertainment contented herself with throwing back the glass doors to the balcony to see what might be happening outside.

But there was nothing to be seen, just blank dark windows looking back at her from blank gray walls, occasionally a beggar, someone rattling by in a delivery cart. If she leaned out across the balustrade and craned her neck, she could see, at the far end of the street, people going back and forth along what seemed to be a boulevard, carriages, from time to time a mass of figures in a crowd. She could *hear* the city, though, a low constant roar rising sometimes almost to a shriek, then falling back again. It made her restless. She wanted to pull on her bonnet and run down to the corner and be part of the activity.

The view from the side window was equally dull—just the blank wall of another house, the ragged flowerbed, the tipsy Virgin, and the ferocious squatting guard.

And then, at last, a new maid was produced. Cassandra looked her up and down impatiently. She was too thin but not unpromising. And now she must be trained. Perhaps a week would be enough to accustom her to Maman's peculiar ways. A week! Benedict could well be back by then. He would take her home to Maryland with nothing to report but the story of "The Mad Maman" and the training of a maid. And yet it must be done, she knew it must be done.

A week turned out to be enough, and Cassandra, confident that she had a steady hand at Maman's side, left the new maid sitting by the bed and went down to the courtyard, intending to investigate the street. As she approached the gate, the guard heaved himself upright, his sabre dangling from his hand. He was of imposing height and quite remarkably ugly, being rawboned and very pale, with a deformed lower eyelid that seemed like a small toad sitting on his face. She could not tell his age.

She made to pass. He blocked her way. She motioned him aside. He folded both arms on his chest, the sabre upright like a warning flag, and blocked her way. She summoned her best French and asked to pass. He did not understand. She explained she would go out, pointed to the street beyond the iron grid work of the gate. He would not understand.

Later, she complained of it to Papa van Pradelles. He looked horrified at her. "The streets are dangerous," he said. "Do not go out alone."

"As if I could with that brute on the gate."

"His name is Pétoin. He will protect you."

"From what? The street is empty."

"Hush, child," he said.

She lay awake that night, sleepless with indignation, and thought of Benedict. Where was he tonight? In Flanders still? Surely he had left by now. He would arrive back any day. Her imprisonment would soon be over. Meanwhile . . . perhaps . . . the brute Pétoin was human and must answer nature's call . . . just a short walk . . . the merest stroll . . . to one end of the street and back, no more.

But then the new maid vanished, and she found herself once more with Maman's care entirely in her hands.

8

ANOTHER MAID ARRIVED. SHE STAYED A DAY, but was arrogant and so unwilling that at the end of it Cassandra told her not to come again. Another came and stayed a day, then two, and then a third, heaving herself about and sighing while she straightened up the bed and tended to Maman and brought the soup. On the fourth day, she stole all the money from Cassandra's purse and vanished, taking her sighs and heaving with her. Yet another, told to roll Maman aside so Cassandra could set a clean sheet under her, jerked so hard and viciously that the poor woman shrieked with pain.

Not one of them seemed able to accomplish the slightest thing. Sent out for a loaf of bread they came back with none, claiming they had been robbed in the street. Set to boil up a pot of broth for soup, they boiled and boiled until whatever meat the housekeeper or Papa van Pradelles had managed to secure was boiled away—or perhaps had not been put into the pot to start with. Each one seemed more truculent and iron-headed than the one before. Training was to no avail, and no amount of threatening on Cassandra's part could make them steady in their service. And all of them refused to call her Madame van Pradelles. They called her "Citoyenne." It was most rude.

One day Cassandra found herself thinking about Mordecai Worthington, with his big feet and clumsy hands, his pocked and pitted face. She thought of how he would arrive for dancing class each week, along with half a dozen other boys and girls, students of the dancing master, Monsieur Louis Pinson. How they would practice minuets and waltzes, cotillions, their dancing slippers hissing on the polished floor. She found herself feeling sentimental toward Mordecai. She had grown up with his hands in her hands, his feet stepping on her dancing slippers. She remembered when he got his pockmarked face. They had been ten years old. Mordecai's mother had sent word he could not come to dancing class that day: he had the smallpox. He was the first in the county to fall foul of the disease and an epidemic followed. Dancing class was canceled weeks on end and Mama lived in terror that her daughters would have their marriageable complexions ruined. At last, when the epidemic passed and dancing class resumed, Mordecai's face had grown so ugly all the girls refused to partner him.

Poor Mordecai; his mother tried to cure his scars by slathering his face night and morning with American Balsamic Ointment, but it did no good. Any beauty that he might have had was ruined by his scars. Still, what if she had obeyed Papa and married him? She would not be a prisoner now, a servant. She would be at home in Maryland, free to do anything that came into her head. She would have her maid Susannah back, and all the willing servants she desired. Perhaps a scar or two might not seem so bad. But then she thought about herself and Benedict together in the bed. She could not imagine *that* with Mordecai.

She thought about her life in Maryland. She had been busy, always busy, always doing something, going somewhere, always finding out new things. And yet she had been restless. It seemed that from as far back as she could remember she had been preparing herself to leap, when the moment offered, out into the world where people had adventures. So was she having an adventure now? She supposed she was, and yet it did not feel like one. She spent her whole time waiting—waiting on Maman, waiting for a letter from Papa, for Papa van Pradelles to come and then to leave, for Benedict to reappear. And for this she had left her friends and family, her comfortable life, estranged herself from her papa, rushing after some mad notion of heroics like a dog after a rabbit.

Maman stirred on the bed, stretching out her hand to some unseen companion. Soon she must be fed and balanced on the chamber pot. The curtains must be drawn, the dazzling array of lamps lit up.

How they glistened in the room. They glistened in the gilt frame of the mirror on the wall. They glistened in the glass. And on Cassandra's face inside the glass, and on her gown. She sighed. If only she could have the pretty gowns and bonnets she had left behind. Perhaps the pale pink satin edged with lace. Or something new and bright and elegant and French. Like one of Maman's gowns here in the press. Yes, this one here, dark purple shot with red.

The mirror smiled at her. Good evening, Madame van Pradelles, you look so grand. Fit to be taken up by high society. Fit for a visit to the queen. She took the portrait of the queen from Maman's bedside table and set it on the mantelshelf and curtsied. A tea party perhaps? With all the ladies of the court. She took her place among them, arranging her skirts with elegance as she sat down, tilting her head graciously. Fine china cups. The tinkling of silver forks and spoons. The snap and rustle of starched damask spread on laps. Hiss of hot liquid through bright scarlet lips.

She was at the palace now, in a room so packed with other women she could barely breathe. Some grand lady in a pale pink satin gown seemed to be in charge of her, but she clearly did not care for the assignment. She stood up very tall and thin and kept her thin high nose turned slightly to one side and up, as though her charge were some offensive thing she had come upon by accident. She spoke, not to Cassandra, but to the air above her head, and when Cassandra begged her pardon because she did not understand, she made her lips into a sour moue.

Some sort of signal must have sounded, because the pack of women moved toward an inner door, a great high thing with fancy loops and gilded curlicues. Cassandra found herself sitting at a round table on a chair with so much padding in the seat that it rose up in the middle like a little mountain and she feared she would lose her balance on the thing.

The grand lady in the pale pink gown had vanished in the jostle through the door and no one spoke to her, or even paid attention. Although women sat at each side of her, she felt totally alone. When the tea was poured there was no cup for her, and when the cakes were passed the platter passed her by. All around she could hear hisses and soft remarks whose meaning she could not grasp, but whose tone she recognized—the tone of women's viciousness and spite. The queen was seated so far off, Cassandra could see nothing but her grand coiffure.

And now she felt around her in the room a gathering malice that made her hands shake and her tongue stick to the roof of her mouth. She looked nervously about, but the ladies were all gone. Maman, wearing the queen's hair, sat propped up on a bed. Cassandra's eyes snapped open. Where was Benedict? When would he come?

When Papa van Pradelles arrived that night she met him at the door. "Are you not yet worried about Benedict?"

"No, child, not yet. These things take time."

9

$\mathcal{M}$AMAN WORSENED. PAPA VAN PRADELLES
sent out for a physician. As soon as he walked into the room
Cassandra knew him for a rogue, but what could she do? No one else
would come. He pronounced Maman's condition to be some affliction called "the king's evil," recommending that they transport her
back to court so the king could lay his hands on her and heal her.

This was a notion Cassandra had not heard about. Although
the old rogue assured her on his soul that all of France had faith
the king's touch would cure the illness, she did not believe it,
either that his touch would cure, or that all of France had faith in
it. She demanded he do something useful for Maman.

So he set about to physic her with an emetic that he said would
flush out her complaint. Flush her it did. She had eaten so little for
so long Cassandra thought she would turn entirely inside out. She
vomited and vomited, whimpering and half fainting, yet the fellow
seemed to think it beneficial.

His ministrations went on for three days, then four, until

Cassandra grew impatient. It was clear no good was being done, harm rather, and she paid him off and showed him the door. It was up to her now. She was no physician but could do no worse.

She found Maman did not resist her now. She managed to remove her gown and petticoats and her enormous powdered wig—poor thing, her hair was almost gone. She lay in her chemise and nightcap, looking more like a dying person than some madwoman about to embark on the journey of her life. Cassandra called for towels and warm water and Maman let her lift her arms and legs and bathe them and set them down again, as though they were no longer part of her. Her skin, which was very soft and papery, smelled overripe, and had taken on a half-transparent quality. Her veins showed through it like a net of red and purple spiderwebs. When Cassandra came with bowl and spoon in hand, she opened up her mouth, obedient as a child, and let her feed soup into it, although it trickled down her chin and from the corners of her mouth. Slowly she slipped down into a half-dead state, as though she realized no journey in a carriage would be made and wanted to leave as soon as possible the only way she could.

And yet, although her fire was gone, Maman did not die, but lay all day with her eyes moving back and forth, watching something close in front of her, as though witnessing some unfolding of events in the transparency of air. From time to time she smiled. Once she wept aloud, calling out for Benedict. What, could she see him? Had she slipped into some world where she was clairvoyant? Cassandra seized her by the arm, insisting that she tell her what she saw, but Maman did not reply, just let Cassandra pull and shake her any way she wished. *I could be cruel—she would allow that too.*

Papa van Pradelles was late today. Where could he have got to? It was his habit to bring whatever was needed early in the evening before the sky turned dark. Now it was completely black. Cassandra came back from the balcony and held her hands out to the fire before she lit the lamp. These days she lit only one. It was enough. Maman no longer called for more.

At last!—a footstep in the hall. Maman turned her head toward the opening door.

"Alex?"

Papa van Pradelles did not hear her. He came smiling into the room with a parcel in his arms, which, when he had kissed Cassandra, he set down on the table and out of which he drew a long baguette. He drew out a bottle of red wine and set it down beside the bread. *"Voilà,"* he said, "I have brought a treat today," and produced from the parcel two red potatoes, a head of cabbage, and a large flat fish. He came over to his wife, and knelt, and took her hand in his and bowed his head.

Cassandra scooped the food up and, summoning a face that said she was in charge, carried it downstairs for the housekeeper to see to. When she came back, Papa van Pradelles had just done with his prayers. He rose as she pulled shut the door behind her.

"Papa van Pradelles," she said, "this Alex—who is he?"

"He is no longer, child. He was murdered in the riot at Versailles."

"The Swiss guard? The one whose head set on a pike so frightened poor Maman?"

"The same."

"She grieves for him, sometimes calling out after him in her sleep. To see his poor head set up on a pike like that was what unhinged her mind, perhaps."

"Perhaps," he replied, giving her such an odd look it occurred to her this Alex might have been Maman's lover.

He seemed to read her thought. "Do not worry your head about it, child."

Cassandra felt herself begin to flush. "Are you still not worried about Benedict? It's been so long now. Surely you are worried?"

Papa van Pradelles, as though grateful for the change in subject, hurried into speech. No, he was not worried. No, of course not. This business of salvaging their fortune had simply taken longer than expected. Records had been lost and must be found, arrangements made, officials persuaded to cooperate, new documents drawn up perhaps, and so on and so forth.

"I think he must be having great success," he said. "Why else would he delay?"

"You think, then, that your fortune will be saved?"

"He works on it. Do not worry, child, he will come back with his pockets bulging with good news."

But his eyes did not look straight at her, and the way the frightened little creatures in his head scuttled down his left side when he spoke disturbed her, as though they were fleeing for their lives.

She told herself it had always been his way. It was not that he was trying to hide from her some awful thing, some disastrous news of Benedict, something frightful skulking in the street outside the house, or in the kitchen where resentful unpaid servants lurked all day. No, it was just his way. He was shy, she told herself, and felt a choky little laugh come up her throat. He was not shy. Then what? Nothing, nothing. It was just his way.

The clock had stopped. It was a wall clock, a grand affair in a gilded wooden case. "*Six heures et demie,*" it said, precisely. Was it six-thirty in the morning? Were cocks crowing in the countryside? Or was it almost night, the farmer's wife in shawl and apron shooing the chickens back into their coop? The sky seemed always to be dim these days, like a thick blank fog forever rolling away but never lifting.

There had been shouting in the street an hour ago, or two, but when Cassandra went to look no one was there. What was happening in France? Papa van Pradelles would not tell her anything. Anytime she asked him what was going on he looked pained and said, "Hush, child, don't worry your head." Or else, "Nothing, nothing, that's the pity of it. Can these politicians not get one small thing accomplished?" When she asked, "What small thing? The making of the constitution?" "Hush, child," he would say.

People were living in the kitchen quarters now, not just the servants but others too. The brute Pétoin was one of them and the rest might have been his family or not. There seemed more of them each time Cassandra ventured down that way. They turned to look at her as though she had no right to be there, and perhaps she did not. This house was not her own. She felt as much of an intruder here as they. How could she order them to leave? She was dependent on them, although they looked so fiercely at her that she sometimes thought they would one day come en masse up the staircase for her head, and the head of Maman too. She might bolt the door against them, but if they wanted they could knock it down.

As the days went by, she felt herself withdrawing from the house around her, not from fear, but from the sort of caution that presages fear. She could hear strange noises down below, directly underneath her feet, a shuffling and from time to time a thud, a muffled shout. The parlor was down there, and beyond it, through a sliding double door, the library. There seemed to be a grand activity. What could be going on? Were strangers coming in to occupy the parlor and the library? How many of them were there? Were they living in the dining and the music rooms as well, sleeping in the study? Would more arrive tomorrow or next week to take over the upper level of the house? Would they crowd themselves into the empty rooms along the passageway and then come beating against Maman's door, demanding she be carted off so they could occupy her bed and set their dirty little ragamuffins down to sleep on the feather mattress in the inner room?

And what if she refused them? What would they do then? She wanted to complain to Papa van Pradelles, but she thought about the frightened creatures in his head and held her tongue. Oh, where was Benedict? When would he come? It had been almost three months since he left and she had suffered halfway through the winter not knowing where he might have got to. She wanted him to hold her in his arms, to stroke her skin, to comfort her.

She began to feel that Benedict did not exist at all, that she had never really known him, that all this was nothing but a dream. If only she could rouse herself. If Charlotte would just turn and jab an elbow in her side the way she used to do in bed. Then she would wake. She would listen to the clattering of hooves below the window of their bedchamber, the slap-slap of Eudie whacking a broom against a rug slung across the clothesline, the sound of Papa's voice calling out to Amos or to little Sukie. If only she could wake. Perhaps Charlotte would pray for her. *Charlotte, please pray for Benedict.*

·   ·   ·

The rooms directly under her were silent now. Whatever had been going on down there was done. Perhaps she had imagined it. She had made up a story in her head to entertain herself. But a story of that sort was no good for an entertainment. It was too grave and frightening. She must make up a different story for herself, a cheerful one, something to make her smile.

But such a story would not come, and so one day she crept downstairs in search of books to read, keeping her eyes about her, her body tingling with the sense of threat that leaked under the kitchen door and through its brass-ringed keyhole. Cautiously, she set her hand upon the parlor doorknob, turned. It was not locked. She pushed it open and slid quietly inside.

The room was naked, ransacked. The silver cupboards gaped and all the fine furniture had vanished. The landscapes had been taken from the walls, and above the fireplace, where once had hung a portrait of the owners with their children, there was nothing but a shape, unfaded on the wallpaper, the smell of dust.

What should she do? Shout burglary? To whom? And what good would it do? The servants still had not been paid. If she raised a hue and cry they might refuse to serve at all, or something worse . . . no, do not think of that. Do not think about their eyes.

She crept across the parlor to the library, where she found the books all in a tumble on the floor, a low door in the wainscoting flung open to a passageway beyond, as though she had interrupted someone in the act of thievery. Not stopping to examine titles, she snatched up a couple of the books and hurried back upstairs.

The books turned out to be a Bible and the works of Horace, both in French. Mr. Meekum had made her translate Horace in his Latin lessons and she had a deal of him by heart, odes and pieces from epistles, so she opened that one first, but could not concentrate to read. She fancied she heard voices on the stairs and in the passageway beyond her door. She checked the door. It was securely locked. She pulled out the heavy key, dropped it in the pocket of her apron, and went to sit beside Maman. She would have liked to hold her hand but could not bring herself to do it.

10

A RAPPING AT THE DOOR, HIS VOICE. AND here he was, completely unannounced. His beard had grown so long and black it made him look wild and handsome, like a buccaneer. Cassandra flung herself on him and he returned her kisses with both arms tight about her, letting her weep and sigh out her exclamations of delight.

"Darling girl, I missed you. Hush, there, hush. It's all right now."

She pulled back, looking up into his face. "But what is it? Why do you flinch away? Have you been injured, Benedict? What happened? And where have you been so long? I was sure you'd been attacked and killed by robbers."

"Sweet, will you let me in? Or must I explain myself standing in the doorway? Here, help me. Let me have your arm."

Cassandra felt her heart sink as he came into the room leaning on her arm, dragging his leg behind him as though it had been turned to wood. She watched as he bent awkwardly to kiss his mother, who seemed to recognize him, or at least to recognize that he was someone kindly. When he lowered himself into an armchair with his leg stuck stiffly out, she seized a footstool and a cushion and helped him lift his leg to make it comfortable, he making little grumbling noises in his throat as though at a dog that would not answer his command.

At last the leg was settled to his satisfaction and he leaned his head against the high back of the chair and shut his eyes. "Attacked I have been, sweet," he said in a weary voice, "and lucky to have got off with my life. Where is Father? Do you expect him shortly?"

"Shortly. He will bring us something for our supper. Tell me everything, at once."

"No, I'll wait for him, or else I'll have to tell the story twice."

"At least tell me this—did you succeed in securing some part of your family's fortune?"

"No success at all. There's nothing for it but to abandon the estate."

"Abandon? Why?"

"Hush, sweet, patience. I'll tell you everything when Father comes. Meanwhile, have you had a letter yet from your papa?"

"Not yet. He sulks in Maryland."

"No, it's the mails. They're all tossed up in confusion."

"Perhaps. But Papa has it in him to be stubborn." She shrugged. "Well, I can be stubborn too. I will not write him another word until he writes to me."

Benedict laughed. "You're a tyrant, Cassie. And no doubt you're right. But now, sweet, I must rest myself."

He fell asleep and slept for more than an hour. When he woke he could barely move, his leg was so stiff and painful. Nothing but a hot bath would do for him.

Since to reach the *salle de bains*, Cassandra had to unbolt the door and go along the passageway, she had not used it recently, nervous that someone might come up and surprise her there. Instead, she had used the water brought up for Maman to wash the two of them. Now her fears seemed foolish, and she set about ordering hot water and a set of warm towels. Some woman she had never seen before hauled up the bathwater, and although she was surly, she brought it hot and saw to everything Benedict needed, even, after much insisting, a small harsh-smelling cake of soap.

The hot water soothed him so that he fell asleep again with his head on the rim of the tub, and Cassandra dismissed the woman, saying she would tend to him herself. She was glad to see her leave—she had not liked her—but when she went to sit beside the tub she half regretted having sent her off. Beneath the water, she could see Benedict's wound, which had healed into an ugly, twisted scar the color of red wine, and all around it black and purple bruising. No wonder he was so tormented by it. The leg below the knee seemed to be attached at a peculiar angle, but perhaps it was a distortion of the water.

A plopping sound, and the soap slipped from the tub's rim down into the water, where it settled on the bottom and, after a while, began dissolving in a misty, shifting cloud. Cassandra smiled, thinking of the time Benedict had told her how he loved the way the ladies of America all smelled of soap, unlike the French, who disguised themselves with scented waters and perfumes. He said this clean, fresh, slightly tart smell had always seemed to him the smell of wild America. It made him want to run, to skip, to leap onto his horse and ride and ride. It was a foolish thing, he told her, laughing at himself, to react so to the smell of something as ordinary as a cake of soap.

She regretted waking him, he slept so soundly, but was afraid he would take cold, as the water cooled rapidly in the cold drafts of the salle de bains. She helped him dry and dress himself in clean clothes, doing the best she could with his unruly hair and beard.

All this took a great deal of time and a great effort on his part, although he swore the heat of the bath had done his stiff knee good. And so it seemed, because he walked unassisted down the hallway to the bedchamber and made several turns around the room before settling once more in the armchair with his leg propped up, where he fell off to sleep again.

While he had been sleeping in the bath, Cassandra had sent a message off to Papa van Pradelles, who came at dusk with a hatful of white rolls, a good-sized wedge of cheese, an entire chicken straight off the spit and dripping with warm grease, and two bottles of fine burgundy, all pilfered from the royal kitchens.

They ate in style that night, even persuading Maman to take a little glass of wine, which revived her enough for her to remember her long-awaited journey and call out for her luggage. A second glass was no sooner down her throat than she gave a great snort and fell asleep.

Benedict ate as though he had not seen food in all the time he was away, and when every crumb had been consumed and the burgundy all drunk—he even ate the morsel of soft inner loaf Maman had let fall on the sheet—Cassandra and his father pressed to hear his story.

He sighed heavily, adjusting his leg on the footstool with both hands as though it were something that belonged to him but was not part of him, and for more than an hour there was no sound in the room except his voice.

11

$\mathcal{B}$ENEDICT'S OUTWARD JOURNEY HAD TAKEN longer than he had expected. The roads far into the countryside were clogged with people whose livelihoods had failed to feed their families and who now, with their possessions loaded onto hand-carts, trudged toward the bread and wine of Paris. They did not give way and he was forced to edge between them carefully, aware of children at his horse's feet, their fathers with hay forks and sickles slung across their carts. The fields were stark, stretched helpless underneath the sky, awaiting the assault of snow.

One evening, as the sun sank, he found himself before a lake. Beyond, a church spire and the walls of a village stood out with startling clarity. It seemed so close, but he knew he must hurry if he would reach it before dark.

A breeze ruffled the surface of the lake and images of light rippled on the trunks of beeches growing at its side. The light reflecting off the water dazzled his horse, who jerked her head aside and stopped, confused. He leaned to stroke her neck and waited, and when the ball of sun fell low enough, set off again.

At the village, he found no life except a skinny yellow dog that slunk out of an alley and followed him along. The cobbled streets rang emptiness beneath his horse's hooves. He called, "Hey! Hey!" but nothing moved except the yellow dog, and nothing made a sound.

He passed that night in a peasant's cottage, sleeping nervously in case its owner should return. At midnight the yellow dog began to howl outside and for the sake of peace he opened up the door, slapping his hand against his thigh to ask it in. It slunk against his leg.

In the morning it followed him, loping at a distance. When he turned, it stopped, looking about with an embarrassed air, but when he turned again it followed still. With this disciple in his wake, he passed through the entrance to his family's property, the high barred gates hanging askew, passed the burned-out chapel on the right, the barn collapsed and burned, the pigpens flattened to the ground, the wheat and barley fields grown up with stiffening weeds. Even the trees had been cut down, the gardens laid to waste, the dovecote nothing but a mess of scattered stones. When he attempted to water his horse, such a rank odor arose from the well he knew it had been poisoned.

The château itself he hardly dared to enter, its condition so cut his heart. One wing had been burned, and great sections of the roof had fallen in. The ornately carved front doors were gone and when he stepped across the marble threshold, he found the rain had come in through the damaged roof, causing the floorboards to buckle up and the grand staircase to half collapse.

He wandered through the rooms with sorrow rising in his chest. The place was ransacked, everything completely vanished—tables, chairs, couches, armchairs, chests, cabinets, and desks, all gone. Everything of value gone, gold and bronze and porcelain and silver, japanned ornaments. Every cup, plate, spoon, and kettle gone, not a painting or a mirror on the walls, not so much as one gilded frame, the tapestries all gone, even the bright-colored Venetian window glass, frames and all. The wine cellar, which had been well stocked, was littered with smashed bottles, the walls and floor stained red.

Worst of all, the burned wing had contained the muniment room, in which had been held all the records of the estate: documents of plat and property, lists of taxes paid and due, records of obligations owed, wills, legal papers. All had been hauled into the center of the room and set afire. Every book and paper, the leather-covered ledgers, burned. Nothing remained but shifting ashes and the ruin of the room.

In the kitchen, before the remnants of what seemed to be a recent fire, he found a mess of straw, as though it had been used to sleep on. From this he concluded that vagabonds had been living in the house, and so crept cautiously upstairs, not just because of the poor condition of the staircase, fearing at every step it might collapse, but also because he expected some enemy might appear above him. But no one, just the empty silence of the house.

He went into the bedchamber where Maximilian had been hung up from the now-vanished chandelier and crossed himself, and stood, head bowed, and thought about his brother.

Being ten years younger, Benedict had not known Maximilian well. He had given up on education early and taken up the hunt. Even as a child, he loved to send a ferret down a rabbit hole, roaring with delight when he saw the frightened creatures scatter out of their back doors. As he grew, his conversation was more and more about the creatures he had shot, or the ones torn up by his dogs, until violent death was all he talked about. His eyes took on the opaque quality of a man whose thoughts and opinions, once arrived at, become fixed inside his head like a wall that cannot be breached, and he grew hard about the mouth.

Was that why his tenants had hung him up—for cruelty? Would it have been different if Maximilian had been a man of tender heart?

Below, the yellow dog yelped in the yard, a man's voice cursed. Benedict swung toward the door. Too late. A clatter on the stairs and the doorway bristled with a dozen brigands armed with staves and muskets. He would have been done for if there had not been such a crowd of them, for they all tried to come into the room at once and got tangled up together. This gave him time enough to leap through a window and tumble down the roof, but he wrenched his ankle as he hit the ground and was slow getting to his horse, giving his pursuers time to get themselves back down the stairs and fire their muskets after him.

They were bad shots, but one did succeed in hitting him from behind, just above the kneecap of the leg he had twisted in the fall, so now his left leg was as good as useless. Somehow he made it to his horse and, with a great hop on his right foot, got himself onto its back and galloped for his life, with rocks and curses and the crack of guns flying through the air behind him. The yellow dog was nowhere to be seen.

Once he was well away, he pulled the horse to a halt and examined his injury. It was bleeding heavily and very painful. There was no question of making the journey back to Paris, so he rode on until he came to a village, where he entered a church, intending to throw himself upon the mercy of whomever he should find.

The church was empty so he sat down to rest and see what he could do about his wound. He leaned down, took the fabric of his breeches in his hands, and the next thing he knew he was lying on a cot in what turned out to be the basement of the church, with a curé bending over him. He wore a loosely hooded robe of coarse brown fabric, belted at the waist with a hank of rope to which was attached the black-beaded rosary he was busy clicking his way around, apparently praying for his mysterious patient's recovery.

Benedict's knee was wrapped in bandages. It throbbed so painfully he could barely put two words together. The curé brought him soup and soothed him and he dozed off, waking and falling back to sleep for he could not tell how long. Day or night, he could not tell the difference, nor did he care enough to ask. When he woke, his knee felt as though it were on fire and he slept to get away from it, but when he slept he dreamed the yellow dog was gnawing on his leg and woke to get away from that.

Once, as though in a dream, he heard the curé say that his leg had taken an infection. Another time he dreamed that some sawbones had come to cut it off, and shrieked under the knife. But when he woke he found the leg still on him, and learned that the curé had been forced to put his healing in the hands of God, as he wanted neither to betray his patient nor himself. Being a refractory priest, one who refused to swear allegiance to the Revolution, he already walked the tightrope of suspicion. And so Benedict lay there in the basement of the church, slipping in and out of consciousness.

. . .

When at last the infection in his wound had eased and Benedict had recovered enough to have his wits about him, he set himself to strengthening his knee by walking up and down with the curé holding his arm and murmuring encouragement. He wrote a letter to his father and the curé sent out for a messenger to carry it to Paris. But the messenger turned out to be a traitor who betrayed them to the same band of vagabonds that had shot Benedict. They arrived with guns cocked, knocked the curé down, and, tying the two men together behind a horse, hauled them away.

Benedict could only hobble, his left leg being useless, and the wretches would have dragged him off his feet if the curé had not half carried him. These fellows hauled them before a tribunal whose plan it was to hang them. Why they did not do it then and there neither of them knew. Perhaps heaven heard the curé's prayers, or perhaps, being country folk, they were too superstitious to hang a man of the cloth, refractory or no.

Benedict, however, his mind once more addled by the torture of his knee, took it in his head that this was their intention and, as they were being hauled outside again, knocked one of his tormenters down. At once a dozen leaped on him. He felt his knee give and the pain screech off into blackness.

He woke somewhere dark and cold, sprawled out on a hard dirt floor. Reaching out he felt a wall, brick, he thought, and also cold. He pushed upright until his back was against it and peered about him into perfect blackness. What, had they blinded him? Or had he fallen into hell? He blinked and peered again. Nothing. Perfect blackness and the cold. A small panic budded in his stomach. He checked himself all over. No pieces missing. That was good. What felt like a bruise right here below his eye, another in his belly. His right fist hurt, as though he had hit someone very hard with it. He flexed the fingers. Nothing broken. Good. His injured knee, though, hurt abominably. He reached to touch it, wincing at the contact, drew his hand away, and, taking hold of his upper thigh, eased the leg until the foot was flat against the ground and the knee bent at an angle that minimized the throbbing. His coat was ripped at the shoulder and his shirtfront hung askew. No hat. Two shoes still on his feet. Good, good. But he was blind. The bud of panic swelled. Cassandra, what about Cassandra? He turned his face up to the dark. Dear God . . .

And then, high up, a lightening in the blackness. A small, pale rectangle. A window, barred. He was not blind. He was in prison, not in hell. The bud of panic blossomed into relief.

A groan. A shuffling. And the curé's voice, "My friend?"

He turned toward the sound. "You are injured, yes?"

No, the curé was not injured. He was bruised and battered but not injured. He could stand. Above, the small pale rectangle cast a pale shaft into the cell. Benedict saw the curé's figure dark against it. He heard the clicking of a rosary, a muttered prayer.

"You had best pray for my knee," he said, "before you pray for liberty."

The throbbing in his knee had eased and now he clutched the bars of the high window. Beneath him, the curé's back was a precarious, slightly moving perch, but even with its elevation he was not high enough to see. He tightened his grasp on the bars and heaved, scrabbling the toe of his right shoe against the wall.

Outside were low, red-brick, white-shuttered buildings set around a brick-paved courtyard. On the far side of the courtyard was an archway, lit up from the other side by what seemed to be the rising sun, judging by the way the bricks of its interior glowed. At its entrance, on the right, a single guard dozed on a low stool, one leg splayed out, the other drawn up to support the musket he held loosely in his lap. Nothing else except a black hen that scuttled through the archway and across the courtyard and vanished out of sight. Benedict looked to see what chased it but nothing followed. Above the thatched roofs of the buildings, the sky was blue with that rare clarity produced by cold.

He eased himself down onto the curé's back, which buckled slightly as it took his weight, then stiffened, bearing it. His left foot struck the ground too forcefully and he winced and grunted. "One guard," he said. "It should be easy. A small bribe . . ."

He reached for his buckskin shoulder pouch and for the first time realized he no longer had it on him. He swung around, searching the cell end to end. Nothing—no. The curé watched him, turning up his hands. No pouch. No bribe. And the cell door made of heavy wood, even the hatch through which their daily bowls of gruel were thrust secured by an iron crosspiece. They had heard it rattle up and clang back down with a harsh metallic sound.

Benedict slid his backside down the wall until it rested on the ground and sat with his left knee drawn up. No doubt his pouch had been stolen while he was unconscious. He felt bereft, not only for the money it contained but for the pouch itself, which he had carried everywhere for years.

He had got it from a settler in Kentucky. The man, Jake Tirrell was his name, had been out clearing traps and, in the delicate act of springing an empty one, had managed to catch himself by the crook of his left elbow. Benedict had come upon him in the act of cutting off the arm below the shoulder. Tirrell had made a circular incision with his hunting knife, packed the site with snow to numb it, and was gathering courage to make the deep slash around and then hack through the bone when Benedict appeared, like an angel out of heaven, as his wife declared afterward when the arm was saved and the wound healed up almost as good as new. Benedict had stayed with Tirrell and his haggard, pregnant wife in their desolate log cabin, hunting food and chopping wood for them until Tirrell had recovered enough to haul his own firewood and go out on the trail again.

When they separated, Tirrell said no word of thanks. Instead, he gave Benedict the only thing he had to give, his buckskin shoulder pouch, thrusting it almost angrily when Benedict demurred, and stood hat in hand watching his horse go slushing down the trail. When Benedict turned to wave at the border of the forest, he saw Tirrell sitting on the front step of the cabin with his knees splayed, still staring after him. He did not lift his hand to wave.

Benedict had kept that pouch about him ever since. It became a sort of talisman. Whatever money it held was all he needed for his life. More than that he did not bother with, and thought of himself as free, unshackled, clean. Now, pondering his situation, he cursed the years that he had wandered footloose in America, his frittering away of opportunity. Now that it was gone, he understood how he had relied on his inheritance. His gallivanting had been excused by it, but it meant that now he had not enough in hand to pay his family's passage back home to America.

Well, all that was done and past, there was no changing it. The pouch was lost—he crossed his wrists and slapped his hands against his upper arms to warm himself—and better that it was. With no fortune of his own and his family's fortune gone—he did not doubt it was completely gone—a young wife to provide for, his mother ill, his father growing old, he needed much more money than would ever fit into that pouch. Everything was up to him. He must come up with an idea, a business opportunity. He sniffed—the cold had made his nose leak. He searched his head for an idea, but there was nothing there.

Later that day he climbed up out of sleep. Cassandra's locket— had they got that too? His hand fumbled at his breast and in a moment drew out from underneath the tattered lace her ivory locket on its crimson riband. This he opened with a tiny click of its gold clasp. At once his grim expression changed. His eyes wrinkled at the corners and his lips seemed to reflect the smile of the young girl framed in gold who smiled back at him. Hair the deep rich color of mahogany. The slightest flush at cheek on pure white skin. A strong, straight nose. He leaned his head against the wall and stared unseeing at the shadowy thatch and rafters up above, thinking of Cassandra.

How would she take his disappearance into air? Would she be strong? Or would she faint or panic? No, he thought, neither. Cassandra was resourceful. She had wanted an adventure and he had got her into one. He clutched his arms across his chest and shivered, smiling ruefully. He should not have brought her here to France. Resourceful she might be, but she must be frightened by this time. When he got out of here—somehow he *would* get out of here—he would make it up to her. He would devote his life to it. He would make a fortune for her, he would build for her a house so grand it would take her breath away.

He tried to conjure up an image of the gracious château of his youth, but all he could find was the devastation that had come to it. Piece by piece it came together in his mind and he examined it. Something in the ruin of it bothered him. Yes, the weathervane was missing, that undaunted one-legged cock who used to point, trembling with anticipation, at the wind. As a child he had imagined that it pointed to America. Once he had climbed up on the roof and, with the ridge between his thighs, inched up on it from behind.

He fell asleep, and was back there on that roof. He felt the roughness of the shingles scraping at his stockinged knees and the scuffling of his shoes. He looked down once—so far to fall—then fixed his eyes securely on the cock. The wind blew in his hair as he hitched his backside down toward it. But it seemed to hear him come and faltered, and when he set his hand against the feathers of its metal tail, it shuddered cravenly.

"*Mon ami,*" said Benedict, "have you ever thought of going to America?"

The curé, who had been keeping warm by striding up and down the cell, spoke across his shoulder. "How could I? I have no passport." He turned at the cell's end and came back. "If I applied for one they would arrest me, and I have no money for a bribe." Turned another time. "Or to pay the high price of a counterfeiter."

Counterfeiter—the word rang in the cell like a sharp blast on a bugle. Benedict said nothing, just sat with his back against the wall and watched the curé pacing up and down, feet a-slap against the hard-packed dirt. But his mind was like a beagle sniffing down a rabbit hole, hindquarters wagging.

And then, one night, some sort of riot in the courtyard. Shrieking and the crack of guns. Feet clattering outside their door, the crosspiece raised, the door flung back, the curé crossing himself and furiously praying. Benedict, unsteady on his feet, prepared to defend himself against the couple of fellows who burst in brandishing a noose.

Although there were only two of these intruders, Benedict's

bad knee and both men's weakened states allowed them to be easily overcome. One pinned Benedict's arms behind his back while
the other slung the noose around the curé's neck and, tossing the
loose end over a beam, hauled him up. Helpless, Benedict prepared
to watch his new friend die, the black beads of his rosary twisted
on his hand.

Just then the commotion in the yard grew worse. Someone blew
a trumpet, very loud, just beyond their wall. Something smashed
against the open door. The assassins took fright and ran, letting
the curé fall onto the ground, gasping and choking, clutching at
his injured throat. And now the flickering of flame, the roar of
thatching set on fire, red light dancing through the window of
their cell, making patterns on the red-brick wall. Both men looked
up at the thatching overhead—not yet afire—and then looked at
the door. It was open still, but the goings-on in the courtyard were
so loud and murderous they dared not venture out. Dark figures
heaved back and forth, lit by the fires rushing skyward from the
thatch like a scene from *The Inferno*.

Benedict and the curé shrank into the shadows, both praying
with all their might that no one else would come for them. No one
did, although a band of fellows chased one another clear in
through the open door and out again. The thatch above their
heads exploded. A flaming rat fell out of it and scuttled, shrieking,
up and down the cell until it found the open door. The heat grew
every second more intense, making them sweat and cough, jerking
tears out of their eyes.

Benedict had readied himself for a run through the seething
mob when, quite suddenly, the clash of battle, like a pump handle
turned down, subsided in a clatter of retreating feet, leaving the
courtyard to the roar of flames and the moaning of the injured.
The curé seized Benedict's left arm and, slinging it across his shoulder, set his own right arm firmly across his back. As the roof began
to fall, they fled, hearing it crash behind them. Neither had any
idea who fought that night, or why.

And so they made their way to Paris, where the curé led Benedict to the home of friends, a pair of Carmelites in hiding, and

they both slept soundly for the first time in what seemed to them eternity. In the morning, the two men embraced, the curé whispered a hoarse prayer—his damaged throat prevented louder intercourse with God—and Benedict went on.

12

"YOUR INJURY," CASSANDRA ASKED WHEN Benedict had finished, "does it improve?" In the same instant Papa van Pradelles asked, "Our properties? Is anything retrievable?" so that the two questions overlaid each other.

"My injury will heal—indeed, it's almost healed already. A little pain, some stiffness." He waved his hand, dismissing it. "As for our properties, there's nothing to be done. Deeds and land records, all the documents, have been destroyed, and since the workers have all vanished—no doubt they are right now begging on the streets of Paris—there are no back rents or taxes to collect. I'm afraid we must conclude our wealth is gone, our lands completely lost."

"Is there no recourse with the law?" Cassandra asked.

Papa van Pradelles sniffed. "Law? There is no law left in this entire land. Cudgel and gun are law, the hangman's noose, the crosspiece of the lantern and a hank of rope."

Benedict ignored him. "I did not come directly here today," he said, "but consulted with a pair of lawyers who have set up as experts on matters of this sort. Their opinion is that unless the army of the émigrés sweeps in to reinstate the old regime, we should regard our lands as lost. Myself, I don't think a reinstatement is a likely thing. I think that when whatever is to come has come, this country will not be the same again. The situation will no doubt be the same as in America when the British were tossed out, claims and counterclaims and legal wrangles over land and property going on for years. Perhaps someday in the future, when this country is at peace again, we might . . . but who knows how long *that* could be?"

Taking Cassandra's hand, he held it to his lips. "It was a waste of time to go at all. I've ruined a good leg and been parted from my wife—and all of it for nothing. I'm sorry, sweet. I'll not abandon you again, I swear."

He struggled to his feet and paced the room with a lopsided, awkward step. "Cassie, we should get you out of France—at once, tonight, tomorrow—back to the safety of your father's house."

"I'm not sure Maman is strong enough to travel, but if you think . . . No, wait! You say get *me* out? Me alone? You say you'll not abandon me and in the next breath—"

"Now, now, don't jump up all excited."

"But why can we not go all together?"

"The truth is we've not only lost our fortune, but I've also lost my pouch, and with it the money for our passage home. And so, although I *want* to send you—*ought*—I cannot, not until I get some more together."

"Then we're penniless?"

"Not penniless," said Papa van Pradelles. "I have my pension from the king."

Cassandra swung toward him. "Is that not enough to get us out of here?"

"Perhaps enough for honest passage, but passage out of France is no longer that. Passports are required, but they are not granted, which inspires every petty official to name his fee. And that is but the start of it. Every hand is out and each one, like a fortune-teller's, must be crossed with coins." Papa van Pradelles shrugged. "No matter. We have waited this long, we can wait. And your maman will be stronger in a while."

Cassandra looked at the way the bedclothes clung against the withered figure in the bed and did not think so. "Then we must find a proper maid at once," she said. "Someone reliable."

Benedict turned from where he had been peering through the curtains to the courtyard down below. "I think it need not be so very long. I did not waste my time in prison, but engaged strenuously in the only exercise available—the exercise of thought. I've come up with a plan."

"So speak," Cassandra said. "What *is* this plan? Will you rob the treasury?"

He laughed. "In a manner of speaking." And dropped his voice. "Father and I are going into business."

"Business? What business can *that* be?"

He came behind and bent to kiss her hair. "It might be better for you not to know."

"But . . ."

"Sweet, come to bed."

Cassandra blushed. She turned to look at Papa van Pradelles, but he was picking up his hat. He smiled at her and then was gone.

She woke next morning with the clear impression of Benedict beside her, but when she reached to touch him, she found an empty bed. What, then, had she dreamed his homecoming? And what about last night? Had she been sleeping with a phantasm? A premonition, maybe? She had drawn him to her, feeling the familiar flaring in her loins, but he had wrapped himself inside her arms and tumbled into sleep like a stone dropped off a cliff. He moaned from time to time, shifting his injured knee, and once cried out, "Cassandra!" but when she tried to comfort him, he flung her off and thrashed until whatever demon harried him grew weary of its game.

Now she heard his voice, low and urgent in the outer chamber, and alternating with it, the voice of Papa van Pradelles. She lay there listening, half stupefied with sleep, but could not make out their words, just a sound like scheming going back and forth. They must be speaking of this business Benedict had mentioned, calculating how to make the money to get them out of France.

Gradually her senses clarified. What could she do to help? Of course—she would write to her papa. Stubborn though he was, when she told him of the straits in which they found themselves, he would soften, he would send the money for their passage home. Yes, first thing this morning she would do it. She would take pen in hand, and a piece of writing paper from the desk, and . . . Like a clear voice in the dimness, she heard her father say, "No good can come of marrying this Frenchman."

And so she could not do it. She could not confess to her papa that she had run off with a man who, as he had predicted, was now penniless. She could not beg.

Later, she stood beside the window and watched Benedict and Papa van Pradelles go across the courtyard. Benedict was limping heavily, leaning on his father's arm. Papa van Pradelles spoke to the brute Pétoin as they went through the gate. Something— money?—passed from hand to hand. What business could Benedict have in mind? She had asked him about it again before he left, and again he had refused to tell her. Why would he not? Was it illegal? Dangerous? She was his wife. He should confide in her.

As the morning went by, she felt increasingly resentful, and it was not until, at noon, another maid appeared saying she had been sent by Citizen van Pradelles that she started to relent. This maid, who called herself Nadine, looked cheerful, and although not stout, well fed enough. She bustled about the room, shaking out pillows and tidying, pulling drawers in and out, putting things away, flinging back the doors of the clothespress built into the wall. She raised her eyebrows at the finery inside, wondering if the gowns should not be hauled out and aired in case of moths. Their value would be lost if they were full of holes, she said.

Cassandra, who had been about to say no, stopped, staring at the stacks of gowns. She went to the press, running her hand across this fabric, then another. She looked down at Maman, who lay with her nightcap slipped across her eyes as though to preserve her from the sight of the plan fermenting in Cassandra's head. Nadine was right. These gowns were valuable. The silks were heavy, the satins crisp, the brocades ornately patterned—and the lace! She fingered a piece designed to fit into the bosom of a gown. It was a lovely thing, and on its own worth a little fortune.

"Haul them out," she told Nadine. "They must be sold at once. Madame has no use for them. But wait, we must be organized. We must label them and make a list. Go down and fetch a thread and needle from the housekeeper."

By the time Nadine came back, Cassandra had notepaper from the desk torn up into pieces to be used as labels and a stack of untorn pieces on which to make a list. Together they set to work, Nadine bustling about at Cassandra's command, laying this gown in this pile of satins, this one with the silks, stitching numbered labels of description onto each one's breast, while Cassandra repeated each description beside the corresponding number on her list, like a bill of lading, as she had seen her father do.

As she worked, she felt her indignation with Benedict transform itself into something more like triumph. So he would not share his plan with her? Then she would show him who was cleverer. Before he knew it, he would have the money for their passage home.

The day had almost passed by the time the sorting and recording were all done. Leaving Nadine to tidy up the room and see to Maman's supper, Cassandra went into the inner chamber to lie down and rest and wait for Benedict and Papa van Pradelles. Tomorrow they would arrange a market for the goods.

She slept soundly. When she woke the room was black, and yet she had not closed the door; she knew she had not. Well, then, she must have slept till night. She rose in a hurry. Benedict and Papa van Pradelles would be here soon. Straightening her clothes, she felt her way across the room to discover that indeed the door was closed. This was strange. She pushed it open.

Maman lay snoring on her bed. The doors of the clothespress were still open, the drawers still hanging out. As for the piles of labeled gowns, every one was gone. The shoes and bonnets had vanished too, not so much left as a feather or the tassel of a belt. Nadine was nowhere to be seen. Cassandra flung out of the room and down the stairs, still in her stocking feet and trembling with rage.

By the time Papa van Pradelles appeared with Benedict—he clean-shaven now and leaning on a stick—she had worn herself out. Even the housekeeper had quailed before her fury. She had stormed into the kitchen full of red-faced indignation, demanding and demanding. No one knew a thing. Nadine had been a stranger, so they said, and the gendarme who arrived to deal with her complaint picked his teeth with a dirty broken fingernail and looked sideways at her with the air of a man whose assistance is for sale— and she with not a sou in purse or pocket she could offer him. She had lost all Maman's gowns as surely as Benedict had lost his buckskin pouch. Now she sat beside the fire, watching him come into the room with Papa van Pradelles. She would confess. She *must* confess. She would say . . . no, she would say . . .

"Where's the new maid?" asked Papa van Pradelles, looking up from his prayers beside Maman. His left eye twitched, and then his jaw. "She did not come?"

Cassandra looked at Benedict.

"Cass?"

"She came and left. She was not suitable."

13

CASSANDRA PUSHED ASIDE THE BEDCLOTHES, shivering, and went into the outer room to stoke the fire. She found a new log roaring, although the room was cold. "Benedict?" But he was gone. He always was these days when she awoke. He seemed to need no sleep.

She went to the window and drew the curtain back. It had snowed again last night, not much, but now the sky was clear. The balcony, which was in shadow, held its snow, but she could hear the tick-tick-tick of water falling and see it running from the roofs of houses up and down the street. A slab of snow on one roof shifted, flashing in the sun, and slid across the edge, spattering the family huddled in the doorway down below.

Papa van Pradelles said the city was entirely full of them, these half-starved people come in from the provinces, but they had not shown up on this street until a week or two ago. Now, with the weather warming, more showed up every day, as though the word was out an empty space was still available.

Sometimes, when she had finished her duties with Maman, Cassandra would wrap a blanket round her shoulders and go out and watch them from the balcony. No matter what the hour, the street below seethed with activity, people going back and forth, their voices whirring like cicadas on a summer afternoon, from time to time exploding into argument, bodies shifting and reshifting in a changing pattern of clumped groups from which—look, it was happening now—a pair of heads would separate, two pairs of arms thrust fiercely at each other, a new clump forming round them, shoving, shouting, waiting for the fall.

Sometimes a head would turn up to the balcony and a face would look up at Cassandra, a hand would point, some words she could not catch would be flung up at her. Then she would jump back and retreat inside the room.

Now she leaned her forehead on the glass door, yawning. She must stir herself and get on with the day. This afternoon, while Maman slept, she would sleep again herself. She needed it, since more and more she spent a great part of the night in the outer chamber, dozing in the chair beside the fire or by Maman. The inner chamber was used for meetings, all at night, most running very late, sometimes until dawn. Benedict had pushed the bedstead up against the wall and pulled the narrow table out, setting the pair of padded chairs on either side. Before each meeting, he carried in the straight-backed chairs from around the little dining table, four of them, and when the meeting ended, hauled them out again and set them back in place. When more than six gentlemen were gathered, Cassandra imagined that they perched themselves along the bed like birds along a fence. These meetings hummed and whispered secrecy, voices but not words. No one invited her to join them, and she did not invite herself because she knew that she would be refused. It irritated and frustrated her.

Her duty was to keep an ear cocked for an eavesdropper or sudden guest. She told herself that one day she would set her ear against the wall and listen in, but never did for fear of what she might discover. Something dangerous buzzed in there. And yet she found it comforting to know these gentlemen with daggers in their belts were gathered in the inner room each night.

Papa van Pradelles seemed more distracted than usual these days, although the creatures in his head were quiet, and Benedict, who once had been a laughing, open man, a raconteur, was now a silent one, his thoughts held tight against his chest. Two other men were often at the house: a Monsieur Tarleton and a Monsieur de la Fitte. Neither were Parisians. Monsieur Tarleton was English, though he was frilled and beauty-spotted like a Frenchman and spoke Parisian French. He bowed elaborately above Cassandra's hand each time he came and went, and yet she did not take to him. Monsieur de la Fitte was his opposite: a big, strong, stubborn-looking man, with an accent to his French she could not place, a sailor's rolling walk, and a way of looking at her with a crooked, half-sardonic smile, while at the same time ignoring her completely. Despite it, she thought that she would like him if she should ever get to know him.

These two, with Benedict and Papa van Pradelles, were regulars, although there was one other who for some weeks had been coming more and more. Cassandra did not know his name or even what he looked like, since he kept his cloak pulled up about his ears and his hat low across his face. He never spoke to her, and she kept her eyes turned down when he appeared, watching his silver-buckled shoes go slipping by her chair. From these, and the delicate way he moved his feet, she knew him for a courtier. Others came and went, but this one came more often all the time, until now he came almost every night.

When the gentlemen were gone, Benedict would lock himself into the inner room. The first time he did this, Cassandra thought that he had gone to bed, but then she found the door was locked, and when she knocked he did not open it. She waited for him, puzzled, and in a short while he unlocked the door and came back out. She questioned him. What had he been doing? Why did he lock the door? But he just set his hand against her neck and stopped her questions with his mouth. Next day, when he went out, she went into the inner room and shut the door and stood there puzzling, as though she would surprise some image left behind. But the air was clear and innocent, the room orderly.

Sometimes Monsieur de la Fitte brought with him his son,

whose name was Jean and who worked for him as messenger. Cassandra found him quite remarkably beautiful, although his voice was still breaking. He was tall for his age, which was about fifteen, and slim. His way of slipping silently into the room made Cassandra think of a cat, or its more dangerous brother the tiger. She had never seen a tiger, although she had once seen a mountain lion and remembered the sinuous movements of its body as it leaped away.

Most of the time Jean huddled with the others in their meetings in the inner chamber, but sometimes he was dismissed to sit with her. At those times she felt both anxious about whatever scheme the others might be hatching—it must be very dangerous if even Jean was not allowed—and grateful for the company. She found it pleasant, a relief, to talk with someone closer to her age.

Jean was shy at first, smiling and murmuring the briefest of answers to her many questions. When he became used to her, he seemed to grow to like her, and soon began to come at unexpected times with little gifts—an orange, or a small round loaf of fresh white bread, which was becoming difficult to find these days. He would also bring a newspaper or broadsheet or the latest cartoon he had picked up about the city. "Here," he would say, "to satisfy your curiosity about what is going on." And he would help her read the words she did not understand, most of which were concentrated on the question of whether France should have a constitution and what it should include.

As a result, she became more fluent in the language, and with fluency came increased confidence. Even when she read predictions that the country slipped and slid toward disaster, reports of murders, someone's head paraded on a pike, she did not feel the hollow panic she had fallen into when she sat alone those first few lonely months when Benedict was lost and Maman strange and frightening.

Papa van Pradelles frowned when he saw the newspapers. "No need to fill the child's head with the nonsense of scribblers." But he did not take them from her.

It had been a week since Jean appeared, or any of the furtive gentlemen. There had been no secret meetings in that time. Papa van

Pradelles had hardly visited at all, and Benedict left early and came late. One night Cassandra fell asleep beside Maman and woke to find the place in darkness, not a candle burning. In the confusion of waking she imagined that Maman had died and she had been abandoned with her corpse. But then she heard low voices in the dark and realized that Benedict and Papa van Pradelles were seated in the armchairs by the fire, across from Maman's bed. The fire had burned down and died and yet they sat on in the dark, their murmured conversation going back and forth.

She was about to speak when Papa van Pradelles said, "It has all been a disaster, then. Thank God the count escaped. He's a good man, but I do not know if he has the strength to keep his mouth shut should they . . ." He sniffed. "They are a bloody lot."

Cassandra must have stirred or made some sound because Benedict's voice broke in. "Hush, she's awake. Don't frighten her."

This sharpened up her senses. "Not frighten her?" she said into the dark. "And why not, pray? Am not I in this adventure too?"

Papa van Pradelles laughed uneasily. "Your wife is becoming quite a little warrior."

"So tell me," she said, "what is this disaster?"

"Dear Lord!" she cried when she was told. "*Dear Lord!* Run off? The king and queen, *run off!* Where would they run off to? To join the émigrés across the border? What recklessness! What *can* they have been thinking?"

Worse, they had been caught. They had been hauled back to Paris. They had been locked up, their little children too. "What will happen now? To the king? The queen? To Paris? To us all?"

"Sweet, don't distress yourself," said Benedict. "Come here. Sit on my knee."

She felt her way across but it could not be done, his knee was still too sensitive. She blundered in the dark, refusing Papa van Pradelles' offer of his chair. "There, child, do not distress yourself," he said, and for a moment she thought it was Benedict who spoke, their voices were so similar. "There, child," he said again.

"I'm not a child," she whispered, but they did not seem to hear her and she made her way back to her chair, where she listened to the two of them, like disembodied voices, speaking together of a suspension of the royal powers, of arguments about a reinstate-ment of the king, of how the queen had suddenly turned gray from this adventure, how she had been accused of sending military secrets to her brother, the Austrian archduke, of plans to avoid a panic of the mob, of a decree being debated forbidding anyone to leave the country, of a choice the king would be obliged to make when the constitution was complete—to agree to it or abdicate.

Abdicate? What then? They talked and talked. Neither of them knew a thing. Or did they know more than they said?

Next morning Jean appeared outside Cassandra's door saying he had been sent by Benedict to sit with her. She drew him in, delighted. How long was he to stay? All day? So long? He carried newspapers and a small box tied up in a yellow riband.

"Tell me about the king and queen, Jean. Tell me what's hap-pening."

He laughed. "I came prepared. The newspapers are full of it. We'll discover what they say together. But first you must open your gift. Yes, I insist. The gift first, and then the newspapers."

Inside the box she found a tiny decorated cake, which Jean insisted that she eat at once, all of it—no, he would have none, just a morsel of the chocolate icing, then, on her fingertip—watching her with luxurious enjoyment, like a cat sitting in the sun. Then he jumped up and insisted that he help her with Maman. "Where's your maid?" he asked. "You still don't have a maid? It's high time your husband got you one."

They set about to read the newspapers. Some artist had made a caricature about the king and queen's foiled escape—Jean said copies had been hung up in shop windows all over the city—which showed them and their two children as pigs being hauled back to Paris in a wagon. Underneath, the caption read, "Bringing the pigs back to the sty." Cassandra thought it very cruel.

She discovered that the entire city had been whispering about just such an escape for months. Monsieur Lafayette and his guards had been alerted to the possibility, had been on watch for it, but they had lost the royal family through a side door of the palace in the night. Nothing could have been more conducive to a panic. The National Assembly, hoping to control it, had put out the story that they had not fled to join the émigrés at all, but had been abducted by them.

The newspapers did not believe a word of *that*, convinced the royal pair had been their own abductors. Did not the king's own brothers lead the army of the émigrés? Did not the queen's brother support them with his Austrian army? No, the royal pair were traitors. They had planned to turn on France with all this force behind them to quash the Revolution and reinstate the old regime.

The papers said Count Axel Fersen had been the organizer and had fled to Brussels. They also said that he was lover to the queen. They argued that he could not have been alone, others had been in on this plot and must be hunted out, some inner circle of confidants who organized the carriage and planned the route and when to go; so many details to attend to—clothes to wear, identities to be assumed, passports with false names to be magicked out of air. It would take a clever man, or men, to make such plans. Who then? they asked themselves. Someone still in Paris? Someone at court? Someone whom the king might turn against because he failed?

Perhaps, Cassandra thought, they were the sort of men who huddled together in windowless rooms, speaking in low voices, passing messages in secret, using boys to carry small wrapped packages.

Jean was just a boy, but he was big enough to be a man, big enough to play the game called treason with the émigrés. And for treason here men hanged, or were stretched until their bones ripped from their sockets, their arms and legs snapped off. The thought of it made her want to run and scream and break out into crazy laughter.

"It's better for you not to know"—is not that what Benedict had said? Better for her why? Because he had set up a conspiracy to smuggle nobles out of France? The king and queen themselves? Was this what all the secret meetings were about?

"Jean," she said, "are we in this affair?"

He looked up at her and winked.

. . .

When Benedict came home that night she asked, "Do you believe that France cannot be brought to rights unless the nobles take it back by force?"

"No. I've lived too long in America. I am a republican."

"But you risk your neck to help aristocrats escape to join the émigrés."

He glanced across his shoulder. "Hush! You must not say such things. The walls have ears."

She dropped her voice. "But you must tell me. Is it true?"

He came up close and put his mouth against her ear. "Cassie, these people are *my* people. I grew up with them. They are my family's friends. I fear that if they stay here, they will come to some catastrophe. I feel it in my bones. Something awful gathers in the air of France. I'd send you with them if you were not so obstinate. No, no"—he set his hands against her cheeks—"we'll not start *that* argument again. You're a stubborn girl and I love you for it. I'll not try to make you go against your will."

He went to the window where he cracked the drapes and looked down into the street. "Besides"—she strained to hear him—"they pay me well."

"They give you *money*, Benedict?"

He came back to her, his face embarrassed. "I'm no philanthropist, Cassandra. I have a wife and"—he gestured toward his mother on the bed—"and my father is no longer young. With our fortune gone, if he should fall from favor with the king . . . Don't look so worried, sweet. I will provide, I *am*. Here, in this circumstance, one must do what comes to hand. And I'm lucky. I can help my friends while at the same time they help me."

"No, no, you misunderstand me. I mean, they actually give you *money*?"

He looked at her inquiringly.

"I mean, where *is* it? Surely you don't put it in a bank? Do you send it to America?"

"It's safe enough, love. Hush."

14

$\mathcal{S}$EPTEMBER, THE YEAR 1791. CASSANDRA WOKE
to the sound of what seemed like a thousand guns. She leaped out
of bed, certain that the archduke, with the army of the émigrés
behind him, had invaded Paris in the night. Benedict had gone off
early as he always did, and Maman still slept soundly with her jaw
hung open, so she was quite alone.

She ran to the glass door of the balcony. Below her, a mass of
people surged all in one direction. Before long, almost no one was
left and she crept out, still in her chemise, and leaned across the
balustrade, listening to the guns, which she now realized were firing in too orderly a fashion for a war—they almost sounded like
the pealing of church bells. What had happened? There seemed to
be a celebration going on.

The sound of artillery and cannon went on intermittently all
morning and on into the afternoon while she went about her
duties tending to Maman. From time to time she went back to the
balcony and craned her neck, but although cheering drifted on the

air, which by now was acrid with the smell of gunpowder, she saw nothing except, once, a huge balloon staggering across the sky.

Late in the afternoon, she went downstairs for some soup to give Maman, but the kitchen was deserted, so she helped herself from the pot hanging in the fireplace, and when she had persuaded Maman to take one mouthful, then another, until she turned away her head, she set the bowl down and went into the inner room and slept.

The smell of fresh bread woke her. Jean stood grinning by the bed, a baguette in one hand and a red straw-skirted bottle in the other. "Wake up," he said. "It's time to celebrate."

She sat up, blinking. "What's happened? Have I slept till night again? What's the commotion for?"

"The king has signed the constitution. Paris celebrates. Come, we'll celebrate as well." And he led her out onto the balcony, where they sat with their legs dangling under the rail, and ate and drank and pointed at the sky, which glowed with a supernatural light Jean said was caused by the illumination of the palace and the Avenue des Champs Elysées. Fireworks began to flash and crackle upward, and for a long time the sky was alight with great colored splashes and fans and cascades ending in sudden bursts.

Cassandra felt carefree for the first time since she had come to France. No one shouted up at her, no threat hung in the air. The people who had not run off toward the celebrations stood gaping at the sky. Cheers accompanied each new burst of light. The noise of Paris, usually an angry-sounding roar, was shrill with the excitement of it all.

Jean and Cassandra cheered as well, like a pair of children on an outing, and not once did Cassandra think of Papa van Pradelles' gloomy face when he told her he had heard the American minister to France say this constitution was as short on ballast as it was full on sail.

When the frenzy had died down, they sat on quietly, even though the air had cooled and rain clouds threatened in the sky, and Cassandra found herself confiding in Jean that she was half-crazy from the loneliness of sitting with Maman. "I want to see the city, Jean. I'm tired of being treated like a child."

He looked insulted. "*I* don't treat you like a child."

"But Papa van Pradelles does. And Benedict."

"I think perhaps they're trying to protect you."

"It isn't fair. You're three years my junior, but I don't see them protecting *you*."

"True. I'm about the city every day." He looked thoughtful. "Perhaps you might adventure out with me."

She clapped her hands. "Oh, Jean! But wait, I have no maid, or none that will stay longer than a minute. And even if I did, that brute Pétoin would not let me through the gate."

Jean laughed. "A handful of sous will make him seem less fierce. As to the maid, I'll see to it myself."

It was the first time anyone had offered sympathy for her situation, and Cassandra felt sobbing start up in her chest. Before she realized what she was doing, she had leaned her head against his bosom and begun to weep.

He did not seem to think it extraordinary that a married woman would break her heart before a boy, but simply let her weep, one arm around her back, the other patting at her shoulder.

"So, are you cheerful now?" he said at last, bending to peer into her face with a look so quizzical and comic that she burst out laughing and declared she loved him, at which she was surprised he did not blush at all. If he had been American he surely would have, but these French seemed comfortable with any sort of womanly emotion.

A day or two later, Jean produced a woman with no teeth to serve as maid. She was deaf as an uppingstone and her speech nothing but grunts and sighs and gibberings, but she managed to communicate by acting out small scenes and gesticulating with her hands, like a mimic in a theater. Her family, she conveyed to them, pointing off into the distance, was from some village in the countryside, but had come to Paris because they were about to starve—here she pointed down her throat and clutched her stomach, looking agonized. Her father, or perhaps her husband, had owned a small farm but his crops had been leveled by hailstorms and his cows carried off by an epidemic of some sort—she represented its effect by clutching at her throat and lolling out her tongue—and then the tax collector—here a scratching at her palm—had become so importunate they were forced to leave their property. Her only child had died of toothache on the road, or so it seemed, although Cassandra had never heard of such a thing before and perhaps misunderstood her.

She certainly looked shabby and disheveled enough to bear out this tale of misfortune, with no stockings and only wooden sabots on her feet. When Cassandra first set eyes on her she thought she must be sixty years old, or even seventy, her face was so furrowed and shriveled, as though she had been left out in the sun to dry. When she indicated with her fingers she was only twenty-eight, Cassandra was astonished.

Her name was Désirée. She seemed intelligent enough and kindly, and turned out to be willing, tending Maman as though she were her own mother. She did not hobnob with the women who inhabited the downstairs of the house—Jean called them *poissardes*, fishwives—but she got on well enough with them, cajoling out of them whatever might be needed. She lacked their meanness of spirit, which delighted Cassandra, and made it very clear she had no intention but to stay as long as she was paid. By the time she had been with them a week, Cassandra wanted to fall on her neck and weep with gratitude. *Désirée*: desired. With her to take the burden off her shoulders, Cassandra found herself increasingly consumed with the notion of going out into the town with Jean.

When she spoke of this to Benedict he was disturbed and, she thought, somewhat smitten in his conscience, since he declared he had been overly absorbed in business—the matter of securing an income weighed heavily on him—and he had quite forgotten she lacked society.

"As soon as possible," he said, and his eyes went to his mother on the bed, "I shall take you back to Maryland where you shall have all the society you want and more, parties every night and new gowns three a week."

"But an outing is all I ask, to see a little of the city, to see with my own eyes. I've tried a time or two to go alone"—he jerked to look at her—"but now I have someone to protect me."

"I hardly think—"

"Just the gardens of the Tuileries, the Palais Royal perhaps, to see the palace. Jean will arrange a carriage."

Still, he hesitated. It seemed that despite all the celebration of the constitution, there had been a riot following the reinstatement of the king. In the course of quelling it, Monsieur Lafayette had come very near to being killed, except the pistol misfired. His guards had been obliged to shoot several people and still went about the streets suppressing violence.

"Well, then," Cassandra said, "I'll have not only Jean to protect me but Monsieur Lafayette and all his guards as well. What more could I want?"

"I'll think on it," he said.

By the time his leg thumped on the stair that evening, she was in a state of nervous agitation. She rushed to meet him and he kissed her solemnly.

"I've consulted with my father, who says he has nothing but confidence in Jean, that he's a fine young man and knows his way about—"

She cut him off. "So you agree?"

He shook his head. "The situation in the city is not . . . Cassie, sweet child, I'd do anything for you, you know it, but in this matter I feel I must accept my father's judgment."

Next morning, she was standing on the balcony looking glumly at the people down below. She had barely slept and her mind roiled with resentment and frustration. These people did not look so dangerous. Poor, certainly, and wretched, certainly, and maybe sometimes violent to each other, but why would they hurt her? She was nobody important. She was not even French. And she was not a child. It was unfair.

Behind her in the room she heard the door click open and click shut, heard Jean greet Désirée.

"A grand day for an outing," said his voice behind her.

She did not turn.

"What's this? The sky is blue, a warm breeze blows, and yet you will not speak to me." He laughed cajolingly. "You do not love me anymore, perhaps?"

She turned. "Benedict will not allow it, Jean. He sides with Papa van Pradelles, who's made a prisoner out of me, and intends I shall remain so the entire time we're here." She stopped, looking him up and down as though she had just that moment seen him. "But Jean, where are your proper clothes? Why are you dressed up like a working man? And what's that package underneath your arm?"

"Come," he said, tilting his head, and she followed him into the inner chamber.

"Close the door behind you."

He set the package on the bed and pulled undone the string that held it, drawing out a gown made of rough cheap fabric, the bodice greenish-brown, the skirt striped brown and white.

"Here, put this on."

Cassandra looked at it with distaste. "But it's the sort of gown a servant wears. Why would I wear a thing like this?"

"It's best to be an ordinary citoyenne."

"You intend for us to walk, then? There's no carriage to be had?"

He looked at her. "You really *do* have no idea of what it's like out there, do you? In spite of all the broadsheets and the pamphlets and the newspapers, you don't seem to understand that in these times to be noble is most *dangereux*. To take a carriage would be foolhardy, like setting ourselves up as targets."

"I'm sorry, Jean. I try to understand, but it all seems like a dream, or like a jigsaw puzzle I cannot piece together. I hear this, I read that, I see the people in the street, the people living downstairs in the kitchen, but I do not understand it. I confess I did not pay close attention to the newspapers in Maryland. It was just some revolution over there in France. I did not think to wonder what it was about. I *do* think, though, it's different from what happened in America because there are no British to be overthrown."

"Well, then," Jean said. "Sit down here on the bed while I attempt an explanation. I think you are entitled. Remember, I'm not a politician, so I do not know . . ." He shrugged. "I *do* know, though, what I have seen. I have seen how hunger turns a man into an animal, how it makes him violent and selfish, even to his family, how the slightest rumor panics him."

"But *why* is everybody hungry? Why is there no food?"

"The crops have been destroyed by hailstorms, and after that by drought, and so the price of grain and flour and bread goes up and up and up. And the treasury is bankrupt, or so close to bankruptcy it hardly matters. Even if he wanted to, the king could not provide for all this multitude of people flocking into Paris."

"Bankrupt? How so?"

"I'm a boy. How can I know anything? I *do* know that the king poured thousands and millions of livres into helping you Americans in your war for independence."

"So it's *our* fault?"

"No, no. There's been so much other spending. It's too disgraceful. Marble gold-leafed public buildings, statues, monuments, grand palaces. To cap it all, the king takes in his head to build a wall around the city. Did you see it when you came? No? It was too dark? It encircles the entire city, and at every gate a grand folly has been built, all this to catch the peasant on his way to sell his wine and cabbages and fowl. No longer can he slip by the tax collector and pocket his own profits. Now he has no option but to pay the entry tax. And he sees this as extortion. He sees the grand gates and the sentry booths, the outstretched grasping hand of government, he sees the king and queen and all the nobles dressing in silk shirts and gowns and playing pinochle and swallowing champagne all day and night, or making love to other people's wives, or hunting game on their estates, while they, the poor, must beg to be allowed to shoot so much as a rabbit to keep their families from starving."

He flung his hands out, dramatic as Papa van Pradelles. "Here he is, then, in his ragged shirt, the soles of his shoes flapping off his feet, his children with their bellies sticking to their spines, watching the local seigneur, with a scented handkerchief against his nose, ride up to his cottage in a fancy carriage, demanding dues and rents. How can this go on? The poor are taxed up one side and down the other, the entire country crissed and crossed with customs barriers, at entrances to towns, at river crossings, boundaries of provinces. For everything there is a tax—the *gabelle*, the *traites*, the *aides*, the *capitation*, the *vingtièmes*, the *taille*, tithes to support some fat aristocratic abbott. On top of that, they have no treatment for their illnesses, their children die like flies, or else they are abandoned while their parents flock to Paris, demanding to be fed. But here, what do they find? They go on starving. And so their temper grows. Every day I feel resentment follow me, as though I'm being stalked by some wild animal. If the people do not get a swift change in their situation, their temper will explode, I have no doubt of it. Then who knows what will happen?"

Through this long speech, Cassandra had sat completely still and silent, looking at Jean's face. Now she drew her breath in hard. "You say you're young and ignorant, but I think that is not true. For one so young, you seem to be extremely wise."

He laughed. "Wise enough to eavesdrop on the conversations of my elders."

"I gather that, like Benedict, you're a republican."

"I suppose so, yes. I had not thought of it."

"You take the people's side against the nobles?"

"How can I? I'm one of them. It's a situation formidable. Myself, I'm for the people governing themselves the way you do it in America, or very like. I'm for the constitution."

"And the king?"

"Who knows if he's serious about it? If he's not . . . if no one takes control . . . But even if he is, perhaps things have already gone so far that no matter *what* he does it will be too late. But enough of talk. It does not bring solution. As for us, we must do what we must do, there's nothing else." He took her hand and drew her to her feet. "You want to see the city? Come, then, I will show you."

He turned his jacket back, revealing a pistol tucked inside his belt, a pair of handles stuck into an inner pocket. One of these handles he withdrew, turning in his hand a short *couteau de chasse*.

"For you," he said. "Stab up, not down, to keep your wrist from being seized before you can complete the motion."

"But Jean—"

"And when you have it in as far as it will go, twist hard."

"But Benedict . . . what would he say?"

"He would say, perhaps, that you protect yourself."

"No, he . . ."

"He what? He would not want you to return?"

"He does not wish for me to go with you *at all*."

He shrugged. "Come. Do not come." And turned toward the door.

"Jean, wait. How can I go without my husband's blessing?"

He looked at her and smiled, and lifted up his eyebrows. "Désirée will not tell."

15

*J*UST ONCE WOULD BE ALL RIGHT, CASSANDRA
told herself, *just once*. And if Benedict found out, she would say . . .
no, she did not need excuses. Was she a child still, to be told do
this, do that, and don't do something else? She was an adult now.
Eighteen! If she had been in Maryland, she would have had a
party. Her mother would have seen to it. Everybody would have
come. But, no, on her birthday she had sat all day alone beside
Maman, and when Papa van Pradelles appeared, she had not the
heart to tell him. What mattered eighteen to him? He had more
urgent matters to attend to. Like Maman. His thoughts were all for
her—*my wife, poor wife, dear wife, my poor dear wife*—he cared for
nothing but his wife. And yet his son's wife he would turn into a
prisoner.

Now the brute Pétoin had turned his head away, now they were
through the gate, now on the street—it seemed that every vagabond
and beggar turned to stare at her. Jean did not turn to the right,
which she knew led to the river and the gardens of the Tuileries,

but at a fast clip headed off the other way, she half running at his side through filth and running refuse, foul odors, bickering din.

Was this the street she lived on? The street she looked down on from her balcony each day? What had happened to it? It seemed to her that up till now she had seen the place as though it were not real, like a play upon a stage, its nastiness painted on a backdrop. When some scene had come before her eyes she could not bear, or someone pointed up and suddenly addressed his lines directly to her in the audience, she had simply gone inside and rung the curtain down. To live like this! To really live like this!

But it got worse—she felt as though Jean tested her. Here six- and seven-story tenements blocked the light from a labyrinth of narrow passageways aswarm with the most miserable of souls, their faces villainous with misery. Beggars with suppurating sores stretched out to clutch her skirt, whole families of beggars, men with twisted grins and violence in their eyes, thin scab-faced girls, women with their hair half fallen out, black-toothed creatures with filthy clothes and filthy faces, their children running naked save for ragged filthy shirts. Here a man pissed unashamed against a wall, here a woman squatted with her skirts up in the shadow of some steps. Here a newborn thrown into the street, and three cats circling. Here a man engaged in such a beating of his wife Cassandra had no doubt that he would kill her. And from it all arose the smell of excrement and rotten meat, and the sharper, strangulating smell of desperation.

So this was Paris. This was France. In America, they had said, "France is in revolution," but it had meant nothing to her. Revolution—what was that? It was only words, stories told at dinner, written in a newspaper. She had not expected this excess, this sensation of roughness in the air, this threat that peered at her from every face.

She had been but a child, an infant, during America's own revolution. Had it been clamorous and loud like this? Had Mama trembled in her house for fear of wild men coming in to murder her? Had she been obliged to hide her little daughter to protect her? Had she fled in panic to the barn or to some neighbor when Papa was off at war? Mama had never spoken of it, but had the revolution come to them? Cassandra felt breathless at the thought of it. She told herself she should go back, go home, should hide, but the fascination of disgust and fear had taken hold of her. She wanted to see every bit of it, the smallest thing. She walked with hand in pocket, closed around the handle of the knife.

But now here came screaming from the street ahead, people running into doorways and side alleys. Jean and Cassandra had only time to flatten themselves against a wall when a bullock came careening with its head half severed from its neck and blood pumping in a fountain. Behind it, shouting and brandishing a cleaver, came a giant of a man, a butcher who had lost control of his victim in the process of a slaughter. As the creature passed, it slipped and fell heavily. In a moment its tormenter was upon it, and with two blows had the head clean off, spattering Cassandra's gown with blood.

That night, when Désirée carried up a boiled beef stew, Cassandra could eat none of it, contenting herself with a little cabbage soup, very watery, and a twist of dark brown bread.

They went again, and then again. Each time she left the house, she told herself this time would be the last. Each time she returned, she looked forward to the time she would go out again. On the days Jean did not come, or when Benedict stayed later in the morning or complained he was fatigued and she feared he might come home to take a nap, or when he promised to be early home, she stewed inside. Whereas once she had longed for him to stay with her, she now encouraged him to stay away. "La!" she would exclaim. "You have more important matters to attend to than a wife." And when he said there was nothing more important than his wife, she said, "Then you must see about your business, since that is what will make her happy."

She found not just the slums but the whole of Paris a sad and shocking place. The Place Vendôme was full of people shouting out for work, the galleries and gardens of the Palais Royal full of vicious characters—pickpockets with shifting eyes, whores with their breasts sagging from their gowns, skirts hitched up to the crotch, calling out obscenities to Jean.

The scenes down by the riverfront were just as pitiful. People

who had drowned themselves, or been flung into the Seine the
night before, were hauled out every morning and hung up along
the bank to dry. The living searched among them, lifting a head
here, a head there, peering into swollen purple faces, weeping to
discover vanished friends and relatives, or glancing slyly sideways
as they rummaged through the corpses' clothes, pocketing whatever valuables they found.

One day they came upon a nun who had been waylaid and all
her clothes pulled off, and two witchlike women in the act of
thrashing her with sticks. She jerked her shaven head about and
wailed, the crowd cheering louder with each new wail. Jean and
Cassandra could not help her, and so they passed quickly on their
way, but Cassandra dreamed of her that night and woke in tears.

Each afternoon when she came home, Cassandra sent Désirée for
water and washed her hands and arms and face, and then her feet.
By the time she was done, both the water and the washing cloth
were black. Sometimes she sent Désirée for a fresh bowl, sometimes a third, and washed again, then bundled her off to launder
out the countrywoman's gown while she pulled on something more
respectable. If Benedict should come and find her with a streaked
face and the stench of the city clinging to her, he would put a stop
to everything. It astonished her each time she got away with it.

Sometimes, while she washed, she would practice the speech
she would make to him when he came home that night. "I am an
adult," she would say, "and not a child. I shall decide for myself
where I may and may not go." But then she would think about how
hard he worked to restore his family's fortune, and the way his eyes
looked when he told her that he loved her, and could not bring
herself to say it.

One day she would, though. When all this was over, she would sit
down on his knee, the way she used to do with her papa, and stroke
his face, and say . . . What would she say? I have deceived you? No,
that would not do. *It is not deceit*, she told herself, *I do not lie. I am
eighteen now, grown-up, and not obliged to tell him anything.*

16

*A*T OWINGS HALL IN MARYLAND, JOHN looked over his reading glasses at his children on their chairs and stools about the parlor. They looked back at him expectantly. He pushed his glasses up his nose, shook the newspaper to straighten it, and cleared his throat.

The king's acceptation of the constitution, and his enlargement thereupon, has diffused a general joy. In the rejoicings on Sunday evening, the greatest decency, politeness, and good humor prevailed, the populace entirely laying aside the ferocity for which they have been lately distinguished. The queen, however, was afraid of exposing herself to the hoots and hisses to which she has been some time accustomed; but M. de la Fayette assured her she would meet with nothing but applause and so it proved when she walked out in the evening with the king in the garden of the palace . . .

He let the paper fall against his knee, folded it, and set it on the table at his side. With his left hand, he took hold of his whiskers just below the chin, sighed out through his nose, and, with a thoughtful air, pulled his glasses off with his right hand, pressing one arm and then the other shut against his vest.

"So you see, my dears," he said, "it's all right now for France. She has become a republic like our own and everyone is safe."

He looked at Colegate from underneath his brows. She slid her needle into a yellow rose she was embroidering onto a small white doily. She did not look up. Since Great-aunt Deye had died, she had taken to sitting in her wheeled chair by the window. John thought it was an affectation, and unhealthy too, another one of her romantic nonsenses. He had said nothing, though. What was the point? She would listen to him, or appear to, and then go right on sitting anywhere she pleased.

He set his glasses on the newspaper and, drawing out a large handkerchief, blew his nose sharply, dabbed the corner of one eye, and, with a heave of buttocks in his leather chair, shoved it back into his pocket.

Through all this, his children said nothing, waiting for him to pick the paper up and go on with his reading. But he grunted, "Bedtime, bedtime. Off with all of you," and sat with his head slumped into his shoulders while they filed one behind the other from the room.

Colegate shook out her embroidery and held it up, inspecting it. John, watching from the safety of his brows, made a rumbling noise, shaking the wattle of his throat. He wanted her to speak, to say Cassandra's name. If she would just say that word, *Cassandra,* this blockage in his heart would go away. Then he could go to her and sink his face into her skirt and weep.

Colegate stuck her needle down into her work and pushed the tip back up. She did not draw it through, but left it fixed there in the rose's yellow heart. She rolled the piece and tucked it in the sewing basket by her chair, and raised her head. John raised his too. Now she would speak. But her gaze, though fixed on him, was blank. She seemed not to notice him at all.

She was watching Cassandra, elegant and proud, walking close behind Queen Marie Antoinette, and all of Paris cheering.

17

ONE DAY, AS THOUGH SHE HAD PASSED HIS test and he would reward her, Jean took Cassandra to visit the grand houses in the Faubourg St. Germain, or at least to visit their back doors and lanes. It was then she came to understand that he intended her for his accomplice, her part being to stand guard while he made some transaction in the shadow of a door, or huddled with his back turned in the dimness of an inner courtyard. If she should see anyone watching him suspiciously, she was to fashion a commotion—throw a faint or a convulsion, cry thief or bloody murder, anything to warn him. And she found she was not frightened. Was she growing hard? But she must grow hard, she must. Else she would spend her life jumping and screaming like a silly girl.

"Jean," she said one day, "what is this business we are in?"

"Benedict has made me swear I will not speak of it to you."

"And why not, pray?"

He shrugged. "He does not want you worried."

"Pah! Not worried? It worries me more *not* to know."

"Perhaps . . . no matter."

"What, Jean? What?"

"Cassandra, Benedict is in a secret business, that's all I can tell you. The fewer who know about it, the safer all of us will be."

"He does not trust me?"

"No, not that."

"Then what?"

"If you should, perhaps, be questioned . . ."

"By whom?"

"The officials of the Commune can be cruel."

"They would not dare."

"Dare or not dare, it is always safer to be innocent, to know only what you *have* to know."

"But I can guess. I can deduce."

"You have that right."

And so Jean's business became Cassandra's business too, and because Jean worked for Benedict, she also worked for Benedict. The thought relieved her. She began to feel quite noble. If Benedict would risk his neck to help aristocrats escape from France, then she would risk her neck to help him. That she did not tell him was just one more secret in a secret business.

This business took Jean and Cassandra into every part of town, from the highest to the lowest faubourg, and there were long periods when they simply walked from one place to another. They talked and talked. He asked about her family. She asked him about his. He said he only had his father and an older brother, Pierre, who was serving in the navy. His father had been a privateer, but when he fell in love he became a businessman in New Orleans, which was where his wife was from. She bore him five children, three of whom were carried off in childhood by the cholera, of which she also died, shortly following Jean's birth. He himself was saved only because a band of escaped slaves had stolen him from his basket where he slept beneath a tree beside the house. They kept him a year and then abandoned him on a plantation up the river, where he was found one morning by a pack of hunting dogs and escaped being torn apart only by the coincidence that their master had just set out on the hunt and had not yet unleashed them.

He said he had no memory of his mother, and little memory of Pierre, who, when his mother died, became so frantic with grief that he ran away and was brought back, this going on repeatedly until one day he was old enough to run away to sea. Jean wanted to follow the example of his brother but his father would not let him. When émigrés from France began to arrive in New Orleans, their hats and boots stuffed full of louis d'or, he sniffed an opportunity and, gathering up Jean, sailed for France, where he offered his services to any who would pay for them.

"What sort of services?" Cassandra asked.

Jean looked sideways at her. "Services to France."

Another time, he told her that his father had been a trader out of Saint Domingue before he fell in love with a New Orleans girl and settled there with her. She was a kind, good woman whose heart encompassed not just her own family but the entire family of man. Every week she went out amongst the poor women living in the swamps, taking with her medicines and clothing cast off by the wealthy people of the town. She had been famous throughout New Orleans as a saint, a ministering angel, and when she succumbed to swamp fever, rich and poor alike crowded to the church to mourn her. Pierre was so distraught he ran off to sea aboard a pirate vessel. Her husband, equally distraught, could no longer bear to live in New Orleans where every scene reminded him of her, and so he came to France, where, in an attempt to make a living, he fell in with this person and that, and now had fallen in with Papa van Pradelles.

Another time, he described his mother in the most minute detail, from the way her hair curled low down on her neck to the tiny mole she had beside her eye. He said she smelled like coffee all the time, and when she died, which was from a seizure of the liver, it overwhelmed the perfume of the flowers piled up on her casket. He said that when she was a girl she had gone privateering with her father and could run up and down a rigging nimbly as any ship's boy. He said she was the daughter of the richest man in Saint Domingue, that she was the daughter of a Kaintock who floated down the Mississippi River to New Orleans and settled there, that she was the daughter of a judge. The only point about his mother he agreed on with himself was that she was now dead.

Still again, he said his father had been a pirate who had spent his entire life at sea. Once, after a battle with a British frigate, he and his fellows had gone ashore near the town of Charleston to make repairs. There they had surprised a party of young women on the beach. All had fled successfully but one, a young woman of remarkable beauty. She was hauled off, struggling, by the pirates, who carried her back to their ship where they proposed to perform unspeakable acts upon her. Jean's father, however, when he first clapped eyes on this young woman, found himself instantly reformed from his wicked life and, in a great feat of daring, rescued her. Her gratitude had been unbounded, as had been that of her father, a wealthy landowner from Charleston. The family had taken him in and civilized him and eventually given him their daughter's hand. The country was in turmoil at the time, being at war with England, and when word reached Charleston that General Rochambeau had brought his troops to help, Jean's father went off to volunteer with them.

When Cassandra heard this, she asked Jean if his father had met Benedict during the adventure, but Jean could say neither yes nor no. She asked him why his speech did not reflect that he been born and raised in Charleston, and he said he had taken on the inflections of his father's speech. She asked what had become of his mother in this version of his life and he said she had taken a bilious fever when he was four years old and had been carried off by it. Cassandra laughed. "I don't believe a word of it." He seemed offended, so she said, in order to distract him, "Of all the places you have been, where would you most prefer to live?" and he said, "New Orleans." "But New Orleans is Spanish, is it not?" she said, and he said, "Spanish! Hah!" She did not challenge him again, since his stories entertained her, and perhaps one of them was true.

On their adventures out into the city, Cassandra discovered not just broadsheets and pamphlets of all sorts, cartoons and caricatures,

handbills, brochures of every shape and size and political sentiment, but also many different newspapers with every sort of name:
*Moniteur, Logographe, Gazette de France, Gazette de Leyden, Gazette
Universelle, Patriote Français, Indicateur, Sentinelle.* There was certainly no shortage of information, and opinions to be found on
every hand, all fighting with each other, many of them obscene,
with indecent pictures ridiculing public figures hung up in windows and at storefronts, crowds of sniggerers shoving at each other
for a peek.

Inside the shops, which were small, the floors and shelves and
counters were so loaded up with papers of one sort or another that
a customer could barely reach the storekeeper to pay for one.

Everything was claimed—that a secret Austrian committee dic-
tated the policies of France, that the king was puppet of his wife,
that he believed in the new constitution no more than he believed
in goblins, that as a young man he used to spit and roast live cats,
that the public hated him, that it loved him, that both the king and
queen hated Monsieur Lafayette, that Monsieur Lafayette was plotting a dictatorship of generals, that all the princes of Europe were
allied to restore the ancient system of French government, that
this notion was ridiculous, that in Avignon there had been mas-
sacres of priests accused of leading citizens astray, that Monsieur
Robespierre, public accuser of the Paris criminal court, had claimed
the most dangerous plotters against France were here at home and
must be rooted out, that the city wall caused ill health, disease,
and feebleness by depriving citizens of light and air, that a new
machine had been invented that would make heads fly off in the
twinkling of an eye, that some man named Clootz had set a scarlet
Phrygian cap upon his head and declared himself Orator of the
Human Race, that the slaves in Saint Domingue had risen up
against their masters and slaughtered them en masse.

This last report seemed to inspire Jean in his storytelling,
because it now turned out his mother died neither of cholera, nor
of seizure of the liver, nor of bilious or swamp fever, but in a slave
uprising on their property in Saint Domingue in which she had her
arms and legs torn off and tossed into the sea.

I declare, Cassandra told herself, *the boy invents himself from day to day!* Still, she thought of him not as a liar, but as a storyteller *magnifique*, her own Mr. Henry Fielding or Daniel Defoe. One day he told her this, the next he told her that. She made big eyes, believing none of it, yet she believed it all. She felt that she had come to know him intimately, and yet she met him for the first time every day.

One evening they were heading home across the Pont Royal. The moon was up, making milky patterns on the surface of the river flowing softly bridge to bridge, shimmering with impressions of tall houses lit up in their gardens and in every window. Although Cassandra knew all this illumination was for safety's sake, to give light to the police if they should need it, she could not help but catch her breath at the beauty of the scene. The air was still, and as she and Jean stood there side by side, the city fell completely silent. The stone wall of the bridge was rough under her hands, and she could hear the river hissing down below. It smelled of waterweed and wetness.

She looked sideways up at Jean, admiring. His lips, to her eye, were his best feature, being full and red, although his hair rivaled them for beauty, being very black and glossy, tumbling in curls. His eyes, by day dark brown, turned black at night, and now reflected back the sparkling of the river.

He felt her watching him and smiled.

She said, "I would be proud to have you as my brother."

He touched her hand. "You are more valuable to me than any sister."

Cassandra felt a warm expansion in her chest. It was the first time he had praised her.

18

ONE DAY COLEGATE NOTICED THAT THE WAY
Susannah walked was different. Whereas before she had glided like
a deer through grass, now she had developed a rolling walk, as
though she carried something heavy in her apron.

Not long after, John was standing at Cassandra's window, as had
become his morning custom, savoring a cup of coffee. Steam hung
above its surface, swirling with a nutty smell each time he sipped.
Then he remembered it was that Frenchman who had brought the
coffee to him as a gift and looked sourly down into the cup. He
would toss the whole lot out, but it had too fine a taste.

He went back to his bedchamber and poured another cup from
the sweating silver coffeepot, set the pot back on the round claw-
footed breakfast table in the center of the room, and, with a little
click, set the cup down on its saucer. He went across and took his
hat down from its wall peg, set it on his head, and with both hands
jerked it into place. Then he took up his coffee and carried it downstairs, planning to take it out to the front verandah where he would

sit and drink and plan his day without interruption. Colegate had become such a scold these days, and so interfering. Why, it was almost as if she wanted to shove her legs into his breeches and button up his shirt across her breast.

She met him in the entrance hall as he came down, an opened letter in her hand. "John, there you are at last. I thought for certain you would stay all day abed."

He grunted at her, "Morning, wife."

"Some visitors for you today," she said, holding out the letter.

He felt irritation rise. First this woman would not talk to him at all, now she talked to him too much, and it was all harassment. Not only did she hound him every minute of the day—do this, do that, get out of bed, get in—but now she had fallen to opening his mail. Why could she not leave him be? She had become an organizing woman of the most annoying kind.

"Since you've already read it, there's no need for me to do so. What does it say of visitors?"

"It's in Christopher Greenup's hand. He wishes an interview this afternoon and proposes to bring with him Walter Beall and Willis Green. They wish to talk with you about a partnership."

"Partnership? What partnership? I've not done business with any one of them."

She turned the letter back toward herself, examining the words. "It says a business in Kentucky. An ironworks."

"An ironworks? In Kentucky? What do I want with an ironworks in Kentucky? If I wanted ironworks I could have one right here in the county. I saw one advertised for sale not two weeks past. I had no interest."

Colegate held the letter out to him again. "You need one, John."

He drew away. "What, woman? Ironworks?"

"No, John, an interest. No, don't turn away. Let me say my piece. Yes, I'll say it even though you glower. Ever since"—she seemed to cast about for words and he waited for the word *Cassandra*—"these days you do naught but mope about the place, avoiding company, frightening your children with your sour face, refusing to take up business opportunities. John, what's to become of us? The farm is slipping down and I've had to take on responsibility for decisions my husband ought to make. Society buzzes over it. Unless you take hold of your life again I must take over all the running of this family's affairs myself."

It was the first time she had spoken so plainly. He looked inside himself and was surprised to find a little part of him that wanted her to take over everything, a part that wanted to curl up and go to sleep forever, the part that dreamed each day of his darling girl, the part that felt every day her hand on his, her cheek against his own. If Colegate would just say her name . . .

"John?"

"Here, give me the letter," he said wearily.

"You will consider this investment?"

"I will consider it."

And consider it he did. For the first time since Cassandra ran away he spent an entire afternoon without her clawing at his mind. The visitors arrived together shortly after lunch and all afternoon the four men sat on the verandah, where they talked and smoked, rustling papers back and forth, totting up amounts of money in their heads. By the time the sun drew down behind the ridge, John was calling for wine and some of that bright yellow cheese with the "very sharpish" taste, and all four were laughing and smacking one another on the arm or shoulder, congratulating one another on their business acumen.

"Well, then, wife," John said, coming back inside when they had left, their horses clanking and clattering down the tree-lined drive, "have Amos pack my bags. I'm going to Kentucky."

19

WHETHER HE INTENDED IT OR NOT, BENEDICT had found a way to stop Cassandra's wanderings with Jean, or shortly would. She had not welcomed it. In fact, she had ignored it, as though by ignoring it she could reverse her condition. She stood before the glass, her gown pulled up, examining her belly. Six months at least. It was astonishing. She barely showed. Perhaps it was the exercise. She remembered how large and cumbersome Mama had been when she carried little Fanny, almost from the first. But Mama had always led a sedentary life, refusing even to go on horseback if a carriage could be had. Yes, certainly it was the exercise, the frequent hours and hours of walking.

Even winter had not stopped her expeditions out with Jean, although it had forced them to complete their tasks posthaste in order to get back before they froze. Now the weather had grown warmer once again, they took their time, inured to their surroundings by each other's company.

She had not yet told Jean of her condition and had kept it from

Benedict so long she hardly knew how to start to tell him. She was sure he had not noticed it—he was too distracted. Soon, though, it would be obvious. It dismayed her. To give birth here in France? To have the double halter of a dying helpless woman and a helpless newborn child? Still, it was done, and could not be undone. She must make the most of the few weeks of freedom she had left.

But now she felt her waistband tighten. Her ankles felt tight too, her back developed a low ache, walking in the city wearied her. With rank odors of every sort—rancid food, animal and human waste—she found it difficult to breathe the air. Indeed, it seemed less air than something viscous through which they had to force their way, as though they waded through a bog.

As though he sensed this, Jean would sometimes take her hand, or draw her arm through his and let her lean on him, or frankly fling an arm about her waist, supporting her. He did not question her, did not inquire about her health, although he sometimes leaned his head to hers as though he would but then decided not to.

The city's mood was changing. Every day fewer carriages clattered on the streets, arrogant young men in cabriolets no longer drove helter-skelter, knocking people down, and the few peaceable citizens who ventured out on foot hurried by with nervous eyes. For the rest, the place was full of ruffians who watched with menace as she and Jean went past, sometimes following behind. Other times they would hoist themselves up from leaning on a wall and walk directly at them, staring at their eyes, avoiding a collision only at the last moment, turning their heads on their necks as they went, their eyes still threateningly fixed.

These, Cassandra understood, were not revolutionary plotters. They were brutal men, wild animals, and women just as vicious, their children sly-faced, with quick, thieving hands. She had no doubt any one of them would have been pleased to slit her throat for a couple of sous or a pearl button. It was only Jean's great height and fearless striding way, the direct domination of his gaze, that protected her.

And she protected him in turn by standing watch while he passed or received small parcels or slips of folded paper, or what she suspected were packets of money, through grilles and windows, through cracked doors or underneath them, to or from some stranger sidling up beside them in the crowd. He did not discuss the nature of these exchanges with her, and she did not ask questions.

A new craze had appeared upon the streets. The *bonnet rouge*, a red wool cap dreamed up by those wishing to advertise themselves as Friends of the Constitution, was now perched antagonistically on half the heads of Paris, giving a bloody appearance to the heaving mess of wearers, who fomented trouble everywhere they went. The National Guard became more and more hard-pressed to keep control. Papa van Pradelles, whose tic had seemed much calmed, began to suffer paroxysms in his face and neck.

One day, Cassandra and Jean returned from their surreptitious tasks about the town to find the brute Pétoin had vanished, leaving the gate open to whomever wanted to go in or out. A commotion came from the lane behind the house, clattering and muffled shouts, but the courtyard was empty, not a soul about, the front hallway too.

Down the hall, the kitchen door was open. No one to be seen there either, the usual clamor of voices replaced by the sound of a neglected pot clapping up and down its boiling lid.

The parlor door stood ajar, which was unusual. It had been locked ever since the day Cassandra ventured after books and found the rooms beyond stripped of all their finery. She seized Jean's hand and, setting the fingers of her other hand against her lips, inched sideways through the door.

The street end of the parlor was stacked from floor to ceiling with metal pikes five or six feet long. More were stacked along the inner wall but not so high. The connecting doors to the music room off to the right had been thrown back and that room completely filled. The library doors had also been flung back, and more pikes stacked.

The commotion they had heard out in the lane they now heard coming through the library, resolved into grunts, the sound of footsteps, low-voiced instructions mingled with a repeated scraping sound and punctuated by the clank of metal against metal, a woman's harsh-voiced curse.

Cassandra's first instinct was to flee but she found herself, with Jean's hand tight in hers, stepping cautiously across the room to peer into the library. At the far end of the room, half a dozen women hauled pikes up one by one and passed them through the window to the lane below. From the pitch and commotion of voices out there, Cassandra judged that the remainder of the women who usually milled about the kitchen quarters were now out in the lane, and there were men as well, she could hear their deeper tones.

And then footsteps coming down the floor toward them. Cassandra swung to Jean, her heart standing in her chest. They stood staring at each other for a moment, then, like a pair of naughty children, scuttled back across the parlor, through the door, and up the stairs, where they bolted themselves in.

Désirée, snoring in her chair beside Maman, was undisturbed by the commotion and they crept past her to the inner chamber, where Jean dropped to the floor, flattening his ear against it.

"What? What do you hear?"

He made a patting motion with his hand against the floor and she eased herself beside him, the two of them lying big-eyed, almost nose to nose, listening to the noises underneath.

Transmitted through the floorboards, the voices seemed louder, and yet less distinct, like a shadow that grows closer but will not resolve itself. And now a clank. Another clank. A thud.

And then a knock. Désirée at the door. They scrambled to their feet, Jean stifling laughter in his hand. Cassandra straightened her skirt and took hold of her dignity. She shook her head and motioned Désirée away. But the incident unnerved her. She felt weak and faint and had to lie down on the bed. Jean sat with her until she fell asleep and then went off. By the time Benedict came home that night, she was so unsettled she was obliged to tell him of her condition, and also what she had seen downstairs.

As she spoke, she realized that had she not been out with Jean, she would have heard activity below. Such a load of pikes could not have been hauled in without considerable noise. These people had taken advantage of her walks, and of Désirée's deafness. She faltered to a halt in her description. Any moment Benedict would think of it, puzzle on it, question her.

He sat down on the bed and took her hand. "You must leave France," he said. "You must not stay another day. You must go back to Maryland for your lying-in. I'd come with you, but Maman cannot travel."

"Benedict, what are they doing with all those pikes? What do they want them for?"

"Don't think about it, sweet. I'll arrange a passport first thing in the morning."

"No, you will not. I'm your *wife*. I'll stay right here with you."

"Cassie, you're very brave, and I am proud of you. But this is not a time for wifely duty. If you care not for your own skin, then think about your child."

"I will not go."

"You must. Please don't make me order you."

"Order anything you like. You cannot make me do it."

He shifted on the bed and flushed. *Oh, dear God, he knows that I go out with Jean.* She watched him, waiting for his accusation, but he rose and went toward the door. *No, he does not know.*

At the door, he turned and drew a hand across his eyes. "From now on you must stay inside the house. Do not go out walking anymore with Jean. These people they call *les bonnets rouges* . . . it is not safe, especially in your condition."

And so he knew. He had known all along. It made her squirm to think of it, and she marveled at his silence. She dared not speak of it to him, either to apologize or to defend herself, and he seemed to have forgotten it, as though it were some little problem that was dealt with and was done. She did not mention it to Jean. Nor did Benedict, she thought, or Jean would certainly have mentioned it to her. She felt embarrassed and ashamed, her skin crawled, her stomach twisted in a small hard unrelenting knot, and she was angry with him for deceiving her. He *had* deceived her, had he not? Had he not smiled and kissed her, murmured to her in the bed, disguising the true feelings in his heart? What had those feelings been? Had he felt angry? Hurt? Betrayed? She racked her memory for some hint, some indication, but all she found was his affection and his gentleness, his love for her, his pride. His pride—yes, he was proud of her. When he had tried to send her home and she refused, she had seen it in his eyes. And he had said it too. "Cassie," he had said, "you're very brave, and I am proud of you."

So, she told herself, he had been proud that she was brave. Yes, yes, of course. It accounted for his silence. He had known about her expeditions all along, but it had not been anger that he felt, or hurt, or any of those other base emotions—it had been pride. He had admired her for it.

So why had he not spoken? For the same reason, she told herself, that Jean did not discuss the business they were in with her. They worked together at it every day and yet did not discuss it. And it was better so. As Benedict had said, the walls have ears, and so he had not spoken either. All of them had been together in the thing. Had not Benedict sent Jean to her at first, had he not encouraged them to friendship? Yes, it had been his doing all along. He had arranged for her to help him. It had not been Jean who tested her, but Benedict. And she had passed the test, and he was proud. He had been proud to have her help him. She understood it now, she told herself, and felt quite cheered. It had been a grand adventure.

As the summer passed, the atmosphere grew hotter every day, and every day more stifling, not just in weather but in some dangerous sensation in the air, as though the rising temperature brought with it a corresponding rise in temper of the citizens. Even though Cassandra sat inside with her growing belly every day, she could feel it out there, pressing in.

She tried to think about her child but could not. She searched inside herself for love, but could not find the place where it might be. When she tried to turn her mind to this new life growing in her belly, she could not separate it from the violence and confusion out there in the city. It, too, was something threatening and dangerous, some small suspicion growing larger as the weeks went by, something to hold her down, engulf her, sweep her off her feet into a violence of its own.

France was now at war, with Austria and with the Prussians, but it was more than that. Troops had come to Paris from Marseilles to protect it from invasion. Protect! The first time she had seen these *fédérés*, it had seemed to her that they were not deliverers but madmen, full of violent intentions. With their clothes all every which way, hairy arms running pus from the blisters of marching in the sun, they tumbled in and out of drinking houses, cursing, fighting, stinking, singing songs of blood and murder, shouting up and down the streets about how they would pull the king down from his throne. And they here to protect him! Jean had said they were a sorry lot, and laughed. But now, the larger and more cumbersome she got, the more inclined she was to worry over him out there amongst the rabble who were rabble and the rabble who were soldiers too. For the first time she began to worry about Benedict and Papa van Pradelles. Why had she not before? She did not know.

The meetings in the inner chamber increased in frequency and length. To take her mind off what was going on in there, she began to read the Bible she had rescued from the library, proceeding quite rapidly because she already knew the sense behind the words. She read about the devils who took possession of a herd of swine, "and, behold, the whole herd ran violently down a steep place into the sea, and perished in the waters. And they that kept them fled." She thought of France. She thought of how her nobles fled.

20

For some time now, the street below the window had been encamped with armies of women and children. With the brute Pétoin no longer on the gate, they swarmed into the courtyard, sleeping on the very doorsill. Jean and Benedict had to fight through them to get in and out of the house. Twice a group had forced its way inside, but the servants, who wanted to keep their territory to themselves, stood together and shoved the intruders out again and barred the door. Cassandra did not know who was the greater threat to their security, these trespassers or the women who hoarded pikes below her feet.

Neither Benedict nor Jean ventured anywhere unarmed, and even Papa van Pradelles had abandoned wig and breeches and went about in trousers like a working man. Cassandra asked him why.

He said, "So I will not stand out on the street."

"Are you in danger, then?"

"Hush, child, hush," he said.

These days it was common for him not to come to the meetings in the inner room at night, but to appear very early in the morning looking haggard and worried, once with a slash in his sleeve, once—God help him!—with a bandaged head. When he came, he paced about the room with the same distracted face she often saw on Benedict, even pacing while he ate. His tic, if anything, had worsened, and sometimes threatened almost to convulse him. He confided to Cassandra that he grew more fearful every day at court, with the mob crowding the windows of the palace, peering in, throwing curses at the queen, or anyone they spied—it was grotesque to treat a sovereign like that. He stooped these days, and the absence of a wig revealed a head of hair completely gray.

He was tender to his wife, though, kissing her, telling her to bear up, all would be well—though she did nothing but stare vacantly in front of her—and constantly warned Cassandra not to set a foot into the street. "Because," he said, "strange things are happening out there." Then he left her to sit all day with her mind running on this mysterious new danger in the streets.

When Jean came she asked him what it was. He told her a new sort of enemy had now been named, the "internal enemies" of France. By this was meant all refractory priests and anyone who in any way assisted or sympathized with the émigrés. This included them. And yet Cassandra did not feel like the enemy of anyone at all, certainly not of France.

Jean came as often as he could to keep her company. If she was in a gloomy mood he stayed until it passed. With him she did not stay gloomy long, even though the news he brought was worse and worse, sentiment against the king and queen more violent every day. If only Maman could be moved. Sometimes she sat beside her saying, *Die*. Then she would press her hand against her mouth and pray for God's forgiveness.

One morning, Maman lay so quietly that Cassandra felt her heart leap in her chest. But no, she half woke, calling out for Alex. Her Swiss guard seemed greatly on her mind these days, as though, while rotting on her bed, she relived their love affair. Perhaps she was closer now to him than to her husband. Perhaps it was Alex snatching at her from the other world. Why could he not secure his hold? It would be better so. *Forgive me, God.*

"Is that you, Benedict?"

  "It is, sweet, yes."

  "This Alex, this Swiss guard, was he your mother's . . . but perhaps I should not speak of it."

  "Why not? I hear her maunderings as well as you."

  "You think he was?"

  "It seems so."

  "But your papa? How could he bear it?"

  "How could he not? He loves her."

The last few days had brought a new note to the roaring of the city. On the balcony, Cassandra clasped her hands around one of the balustrade's iron fleurs-de-lys and tilted back her head, eyes narrowed with listening. What was it? Blood lust? Vengeance? No, more like triumph, or anticipation. Like an explosion on the verge of happening, an eruption roiling toward the surface from inside the earth.

A movement down below distracted her. A young man on a horse had stopped below the balcony, leering up and beckoning, smacking the backside of his horse with a flat palm. He had black teeth, and violent eyes which held Cassandra's for the moment before she backed inside the house. She heard him shout and hid behind the curtain, her body tingling with a dangerous thrill, and when she dared peek out again, she saw his slouched back going down the street above the angled rolling of the horse's rump.

She went to stand before the mirror, examining herself. She thought she looked the same—shabbier, there was no doubt of that, and thinner, although swollen in the belly, with dark rings below her eyes. Still Cassie, though, still Papa's darling, still that young girl who had so impetuously run away with Benedict. No, she deceived herself, she was not Cassie anymore. She was Cassandra now, and had become a player in this play. She wiped the mirror free of dust and saw a new set to her jaw, a new look in her eyes that seemed almost to reflect the fierceness of those squatters in the kitchen and the yard.

The air outside the window shimmered, like a sheet of glass about to shatter.

21

FRANCE WENT MAD SUDDENLY ONE AUGUST
night. The tocsin started ringing not long after midnight, followed
by the sound of drums beating to arms all over town. A low deep
sound came from underneath the balcony, as though the mass of
people on the street had stirred, groaning in its sleep. Cassandra, at
the first stroke of the tocsin, jerked awake and pushed herself up
from her chair, intending to alert the six men congregated in the
inner chamber. She was barely on her feet when the door slapped
back against the wall and they came tumbling out, smacking on
their hats, struggling into capes, faces blank with the listening
expression foxes wear when first they hear the baying of the
hounds. Benedict planted a kiss on Cassandra's cheek and in her
ear an admonition to take care and, wielding his stick as though it
were a shepherd's crook, herded the conspirators off along the passageway. Papa van Pradelles went last. At the stairwell, he looked
back and saw Cassandra watching.

"Bolt the door behind you, ma petite."

Nothing to do but lock and bolt the door, pinch out the candle, jerk the drapes a little more securely closed, and lower her unwieldy body back into her chair, there to listen, sleepless, while the noise went on and on.

Not long after dawn, the sound of marching, like a million feet together, and voices raised in song, that song of blood and triumph the soldiers from Marseilles had brought into the city. Creeping to the window, Cassandra saw wave upon wave of bonnets rouges sweep past, their wool caps glowing red in the rising sun like a river running blood. Men and women both were armed with every sort of weapon—knives and cleavers, muskets, rifles fixed with bayonets, bludgeons, swords, sharpened sticks and crowbars, long pikes like the ones she had seen passed out the window of the library. Some brandished pitchforks. One man flourished a scythe above his head. And all were singing, singing. Behind her, Maman muttered in her sleep.

Within an hour, the street was empty once again, save for a few stragglers hurrying to catch up with their fellows, but by ten o'clock the tocsin sounded still, and now there was a hubbub and the sound of gunfire from the direction of the Tuileries, cannons firing and artillery. The sky filled up with smoke which settled over the city in great black choking clouds. The day itself was sulphurous with heat.

By noon Désirée had not appeared. By two Cassandra gave up expecting her.

Late in the afternoon, Benedict arrived, leaning on his stick and panting, with his hair awry and his shirttails hanging out. "The mob is wild," he said. "The Swiss guard fired directly on them from the palace windows—what a massacre!—and now they've slaughtered all the guards—hacked them to death with butchers' knives and axes, singing at their work, parading off with pieces of their uniforms like pennants flying from their pikes. Now they're stampeding through the streets, tearing down every object hinting of the royal house—statues, murals, decorations—they're even ripping street names off the walls. And woe betide any aristocrat they happen on. I saw one of the courtiers jumped on by a crowd of women till his bowels burst from his sides—they slung them round their necks like jewelry. The poor fellow dragged himself against a wall and died clutching what little they had left him in his hands."

Cassandra clapped her hand against her mouth. "What of the king? The queen?"

"They've hurried them off secretly. I think they're safe, for now."

"And Jean?"

"I have not seen him."

"Papa van Pradelles?"

"Unharmed. I saw him only briefly. He's coming by a different route. He'll arrive at any moment now."

No sooner had he gasped this out than the street was filled with an enormous crowd of people shouting and cursing, waving fists and weapons in the air. Benedict jerked the drapes tightly shut and took Cassandra in his arms. He smelled of sweat and smoke. Something smashed the pane and billowed out the drape so that for a moment she fancied some murderer had climbed up on the balcony to follow it inside. A great crunching came from right outside the window. She squeezed her eyes shut, certain she would never open them again. But the frenzy of activity abated. Whatever had been happening out there was done.

Benedict had drawn his pistol and now signaled her into the inner room, where she half closed the door, peeping at him around it. He went to the window that overlooked the courtyard and, standing sideways to it, moved the drape aside an inch with the end of his pistol. Applied an eye. What, then, were they coming through the gate? The door? She listened for their thunder on the stairs. But nothing came.

When the shouts had faded off along the street, Cassandra went out to Benedict. He pulled back the front drapes to reveal the ruined pane and ruin to the balcony—the iron railing ripped completely off. With his foot, he nudged the broken glass aside and opened up the door, more glass dropping as he moved it, and stepped out, peering over the ragged edge at the pavement down below.

Cassandra snatched his shirt. "Come back! What if you're seen?"

He came back in and shut the door, rattling more glass onto the floor, and secured the drapes in place. "They flung a rope up. The whole crowd must have swung on it."

"But why?"

"It was the fleurs-de-lys. They've ripped down the gate as well."

She cracked the drapes above the courtyard and saw that he was right. The gate had vanished and its supporting iron upright was severely bent, as though the crowd had tried to rip it out but found it too securely anchored. It leaned drunkenly toward the window, its fleur-de-lys snapped off. It looked beheaded. "Fortunate for us they took out their fury on wrought ironwork."

"Not yet. Listen! They return."

A shrill cry from behind them and they swung around. Maman strained forward on the bed, and for a moment Cassandra thought that fright had shaken life back into her. But it was not at Cassandra Maman looked, nor at Benedict. She was gazing with a face of horror at some event unfolding in the air. With one hand she grappled with her breast and with the stiffened fingers of the other seemed to try to tear the scene apart. "Beware!" she cried. "Beware!"

Now the shrieking of the mob was right inside the room, coming directly through the broken pane. There seemed a thousand of them, shouting all at once. The din increased. A cheer went up. "Ça ira!" Maman's face convulsed. Her hands clung to her throat. The crowd swept off, the shouting once more dimmed.

For a moment Benedict and Cassandra stood staring at Maman, who had sunk back onto her pillows, once more lost in vacancy. Then Benedict went back to check the street.

"They've gone? It's all done?"

"The street is empty."

"Heaven be praised. The courtyard too?"

He went to the window above the courtyard and, cracking the drapes, peeked through. He made no sound but it seemed to Cassandra that the room filled with a dreadful wail.

"What? What is it?"

"No!" He reached behind and gave her such a violent shove she stumbled back across the room. The backs of her knees caught the edge of Maman's bed and she found herself sprawled on top of her. She righted herself at once and turned to see if Maman had been injured, and then turned back to Benedict.

In the same instant, he swung away from the window, one side of the heavy drapes still clutched in his hand. With a wrenching sound, the support above gave way and the rod collapsed, tumbling the drapes half off the wall. Benedict stood perfectly still, face white, hands half raised, his chest working like a bellows being pumped to stoke a fire. While Cassandra stood with one hand to her mouth, he was in two strides at his mother's bed, where he sank beside her and, taking her withered hand into his own, bowed his head above it and gasped and gasped as though his breath never would come back.

His mother turned and looked at him as though, after all this time of lying with her ear tuned to another world, she had now come back into the world of mortals. She set her free hand on his head and Cassandra saw in her eyes pity and love and anguish. She looked up at Cassandra and there was recognition and, yes, love on her face. But then she seemed to choke and blood bubbled down her chin onto the front of her chemise.

Benedict fumbled in his pocket for a handkerchief and, supporting her head with one hand, held it underneath her lips. But it was soon full and dripping, so Cassandra fetched a basin. Maman seemed to grasp her intention. She rolled sideways on her elbow and bowed her head above it, spitting and spitting, the blood coming out in thick clots like huge black spiders. It went on for a long time and by the end of it, when her belly stopped its heaving and the flow diminished, she fell back exhausted, confusion taking over her expression once again.

"She will die soon," said Benedict, and his voice was full of sorrow and relief. "I must fetch a priest."

Cassandra rose and went to the window, intending to investigate what had so upset him, but he called, "No, don't. Don't look."

"What is it? Tell me."

"Later. I must fetch a priest. I'll go for my friend the curé."

"But he's refractory. It's dangerous. Is there no one else?"

"No one I can trust. The curé is a good man, and loyal to the king. He'll not betray us."

"It's not his betrayal of us I fear, but his betrayal by another, which would lead to us. Where is he?"

"I dare not whisper it. Suffice to say he lodges in one of the poorer districts. Since the city is in such confusion, perhaps I can persuade him that no one will pay attention to him on the street tonight."

He went to the table where he had set his pistol and tucked it in his waist. Then he went into the inner chamber and appeared again with a blanket and his cloak and hat. He wrapped the cloak about him so that only the tops of his ears could be seen, clapped his hat hard on his head, and rolled the blanket into a bundle which he tucked underneath his arm.

He came to stand beside the bed, looking down at his mother with such a look on his face Cassandra thought he would burst out in tears. "My fear," he whispered, "is that I may not succeed in bringing the curé here in time."

When Cassandra heard his stick thump on the stair, and then the creak of the heavy wooden door below, she crept to the side window, eased herself down onto the floor so as not to be observed, and, separating the curtain at the bottom, looked down into the courtyard. There, on the twisted iron upright of the fence, was a new decoration: the head of Papa van Pradelles. Stuck on it, slanting down across one eye, was the cockade of the Revolution. Around his neck, or where his neck had been, a notice lettered in a large rough hand: COME TO PAPA.

Benedict came into view and she watched as he reached up and removed the sad object, wrapped it in the blanket, bowed his head above it briefly, and passed on through the gate. She felt neither weak nor faint. Instead, she found herself overwhelmed by some powerful emotion she could not name. She went back to the bed and gathered Maman in her arms.

Désirée came. Between the two of them they cleaned the blood from Maman's face and breast as best they could. Désirée signaled to Cassandra that she wanted to remove the soiled chemise for washing, but Cassandra refused. Soon enough to launder it when Maman had breathed her last. Then she could be buried decently.

When Maman had been seen to and a little food brought up, Cassandra dismissed Désirée. She had always proved herself discreet but Cassandra did not want her burdened with the knowledge that Benedict had brought a refractory to say Maman's last rites.

She had been gone but moments when Jean arrived. Cassandra flung herself upon him, demanding to know if he had all his limbs about him. He assured her that he did. "See, here I have an arm, and here another, here a good stout pair of legs."

"And your papa?"

"Four limbs as good as mine, although he was knocked down a time or two. He fled into the passages below the palace, but some-one had the bright idea to flood them, and so he was washed out. He is safe in hiding now, and works to see what can be done about the situation with the king. No, don't fear for him, Cassandra, he's an old bull, with a neck too tough to chop."

His humor, which had been to cheer her up, turned to apology and horror when she drew him into the inner chamber and told him about Papa van Pradelles. They clung together, weeping, com-forting each other, before they went back to take up vigil by Maman.

It seemed an eternity before the door below them creaked again, but this time two pairs of feet sounded on the stair. Sure enough, it was Benedict, and beside him a caped and hooded figure who, fixing his eyes on the still form on the bed, let his hood and cape slip down, revealing priestly robes in an advanced state of dis-repair. Benedict introduced him only as "my friend," and the curé confessed he had no wine or wafer. "In such times, though," he whispered, "the comfort of a prayer, a blessing. Almighty God sees our intentions." And he proceeded with his rites. These seemed to go on a long time and Cassandra grew impatient. This man was a fugitive and she was anxious to get rid of him for fear he lead disas-ter to their door.

Maman's fingertips had taken on a bluish tinge and she had turned blue around the mouth as well. When the curé crossed her forehead with some water he had blessed, she half opened her eyes and mumbled, seeming to address a presence at the foot of her bed. Cassandra tried to imagine how it would be to die like this. Once this old woman had been grand, the gowns stolen from her press the height of fashion. She had attended balls in them. She had attached black beauty spots to her cheeks and painted color on her lips. She had made eyes at swains above her fan. Perhaps Alex was not the only lover she had taken to her bed. Now she lay in this dim room, in the house of strangers, all her grandeur gone, her lover gone, her husband who had loved her gone, the bed, whose drapings once were sumptuous, soiled with her own blood. One corner of the canopy had become detached and sagged above her head like an exclamation of despair.

The curé left the minute his business had been done, and Cassandra heard Benedict outside the door, thanking him and trying to press payment on him for his services, but he refused.

The night went by, the sky above the broken curtain eerie with the flickering of flames, the triumphant sound of singing coming out of everywhere, as though Paris celebrated the awful events of yesterday. And then, like a message out of heaven, daylight made a banner high up in the room. Maman's eyes snapped open. She turned her face toward it. She sat straight up, clawing at her breast. Her throat worked with a rattling sound.

Cassandra leaped to support her with an arm across her back. Jean called out to Benedict, who had fallen asleep in his chair. Benedict did not respond. Jean stepped across the room and shook him by the shoulder. "*Vite! Vite! C'est Madame! Elle est à l'agonie.*"

Too late. Maman gasped and gobbled at the air, and then Cassandra felt a breeze rise past her cheek. She looked toward the ceiling and the golden air up there seemed full of something tragic.

"Poor soul," she whispered. "Poor dear soul."

Gradually the presence faded. The band of golden air tilted down the room and dimmed. Maman's body slumped and, with Jean's help, Cassandra lowered her against the pillows. She stood looking down at her. The blue around her mouth was gone. She was all gray: gray face, gray open eyes, a dark gray tongue inside the sagging mouth. She had pitied this old woman, but she had never loved her. Now, as she bowed and set her lips against the dead gray cheek, she felt a cold hard lump of grief come out of her.

· · ·

That afternoon Cassandra's pains began. Jean sent word for Désirée. He wanted to send word to Benedict, but she said no, he was occupied enough. They had by now discussed his father—Cassandra had insisted—and he had gone off to see about a burial. She was as close to panic, though, as she had been during her entire stay in Paris. Such a time to be seeing to the dead! And yet, she felt a sort of reassurance on account of it. That Benedict loved his parents so much he would risk his life to see them to a decent grave was indication of a dedicated nature. If he would be so faithful in his duty to his parents, then she could trust him to stand by her whatever horror threatened. All the niggling criticisms that had arisen in her mind from time to time these last few months—his inattention to her while he went about his moneymaking business, his new self-conscious awkwardness in bed, his foolhardiness in aiding and abetting people with whose politics he so violently disagreed—all vanished as she lay there in that room.

She brought herself to think of Papa van Pradelles. Before she met him, she had thought that she would be in awe of him, a confidant of royalty, but this unassuming man, with his gentleness to her and his unquestioning devotion to his wife, had inspired in her not awe, but pity and affection. She thought of how she had looked forward to his company each night when Benedict was lost, how each day she had turned over in her mind their conversation of the night before, his tales of people she could barely imagine, courtiers and conspirators and politicians. She thought, too, how, like a sackcloth lining to a velvet cloak, fear had always scurried in his head, as though he could see from the corner of his eye something standing in the periphery of the room that she could not, and she regretted blaming him for keeping her a prisoner.

Désirée came again. Cassandra could see that Jean, despite his show of confidence, was much relieved. Désirée bustled, readying the bed, seeing to hot water, rubbing Cassandra's belly with each pain. It was a treatment Cassandra had never heard about before and she found relief in it. Désirée clearly had experience with childbirth and seemed entirely unperturbed and competent. Jean trotted about the place obeying her signals as though he had been born to serve her.

As her pains went on, Cassandra found her mind fixing on Maman's bloodied chemise, worrying about it, accusing herself for failing her at the end by not sending her decent to her burial. It was a foolish thing, she knew, but by attaching to this detail she saved herself from panic. What she dared not think about was Benedict out there surrounded by the murderous violence of the city. As she went into her final pains, she clung hard to Jean's hands, sank her fingernails into his palms and squeezed until he winced and ground his teeth. "Whoa!" he said, and "Whoa!" as though she were a bolting horse.

The child came suddenly, slipping like a rabbit from its skin, and lay there quietly between her legs. Cassandra saw Désirée seize it up. Saw the miniature arms and legs, the tiny bloodied head, and something came together low down in her stomach, like a gathering of forces, a knotting and a churning and a rising. *This is love,* she told herself, *this is how it happens—it comes up.* But now she saw the limpness and the pallor, and she heard no cry. She saw Désirée's eyes meet Jean's. She thought that she would shriek, she would cry out to God, would beg him, curse him, demand his explanation: *Sir, speak up, how do you account for this poor rag of death that you have given me? Is this some lesson I must learn? Sir, you are cruel, cruel.*

She could say none of it. Her head was heavy and her eyes clung to the inside of her skull. Jean was shaking her, she felt the motion of the bed. From deep inside herself she looked at him. He seemed so strange. His face swelled large and shrank away and swelled. His mouth opened and closed, a hole that sound came out of, a whooping swollen sound that faded to an echo in her head and swelled again. Her head was swelling too. It hurt. It filled up with a rushing sound. She felt bones crack and shift. Her skull had gone away and there was nothing left to hold her in. She swelled and swelled and the rushing was like water, someone weeping in the water, then only weeping, and a going out, and weeping.

It was the jerking in her chest that brought her back. She was attached to it somehow, and each jerk shortened the connection.

She was a bucket on a rope being drawn up from inside a well, her chest was winding up the rope, the windlass in her chest, with a hard convulsive sound like sobbing. Now she understood that she was crying in her sleep. Something had happened, something dreadful, in her sleep, and she was crying. She could feel wetness on her face and her lungs spasming, releasing, spasming. She was almost at the top of the well. It was getting lighter and the clanking of the winch was getting louder. The clanking was her own breath in her throat. Papa van Pradelles was dead. Maman was dead. Her child was dead. It was a punishment. She had sat at Maman's bedside saying, *Die*. She had wished for death to come, and it had come. It had taken Maman. It had taken Papa van Pradelles. It had gone inside her belly and had killed her child. Now it would kill Benedict and Jean. A wailing came up the well shaft after her. The clanking stopped and the wailing went out into the light.

Benedict was looking down at her. She must stop this wailing. He would be upset. She set her hand against her mouth but the wailing wouldn't stop. It was very thin and high and Benedict held it cupped between his hands.

"Your baby wants her maman," he said, and smiled down at the tiny howling creature. It thrust out stiff blue trembling arms and legs and wailed the louder. "Here," he said, "let me put her in your arm." He moved Cassandra's elbow and set the baby into it. It gave a great hiccup and lay there blinking. "See, she quiets for her maman."

"So much black hair, all standing up on end." Cassandra's voice came out weak and tremulous and she cleared her throat, controlling it. "We must give her a name."

"Her name is Anne. It was my mother's name. What, you do not like it? Come, sweet, do not upset yourself."

"I did not know. In all this time I did not know her name."

22

$\mathcal{S}$USANNAH'S CHILD WAS BORN. WHEN COLE-
gate heard of it, she demanded that the thing be brought for her
inspection. Eudie brought it wrapped up in a piece of blanket, with
little Sukie trotting at her side. They came into the parlor where
Colegate stood, back rigid, in the center of the room.

"What is it?"

"A boy, Miss Colegate," Eudie said.

"Don't stand there gawping in the door. Bring it here."

Eudie stepped into the room, holding out the child. Sukie,
reaching to clutch the trailing corner of the blanket, came behind.
The child was very pale, paler even than Susannah. Colegate
looked into its face.

"Take it away."

Now she knew what it was about Susannah that bothered her so
much. That expression she sometimes wore: John wore it sometimes
too. So did his father, Joshua Owings. As the implications of this
traveled to her conscious mind, Colegate felt herself grow nauseous.

For a long time she stood completely still, then she went out walking in the garden.

On her return she was no less agitated, and she rang for Eudie, commanding her to bring Susannah.

"Tell me, girl, what is your mother's name?"

Susannah swayed before her, barely recovered from the birth. She named a slave on Joshua's plantation.

"And your father's name?"

The girl shrugged. "Why, Miss Colegate, everyone know that. Old Master Joshua hisself."

23

$\mathscr{A}$LTHOUGH CASSANDRA'S STRENGTH CAME back rapidly, her milk would not come down. At first she thought nothing of it. *Tomorrow it will come*, she told herself. But tomorrow did not bring it, nor the day after that. At first Anne took her breast, seizing it eagerly, but finding nothing there broke off, red-faced and howling. Cassandra tried to calm her, and herself, by singing to her, assuring her that if she would just suck a while the milk would come. But the child refused to coax and wheedle at ungenerous breasts. Instead she raged, arching her back and flinging her head about.

Désirée went in search of cow or goat milk. Nothing could be had. She soaked a handkerchief in broth and trickled it into Anne's throat. The baby choked on it and screamed. Désirée tried again. The same result. Cassandra took the handkerchief from her and tried herself, one drop at a time, but Anne clamped her mouth tightly shut and when Cassandra tried to force it open with a fingertip, she turned red-faced and raging once again.

When at last she became desperate enough to swallow, sucking furiously at the handkerchief, the broth disturbed her stomach so that when she fell asleep she woke almost at once, tight-bellied, bellowing in pain. Once the wind was pressed and patted out of her she wanted feeding once again, and with the same result. In despair, Cassandra sent Désirée in search of a wet nurse. No wet nurse could be found. The housekeeper was applied to with the same result.

"At least she stays alive," said Benedict, pulling on his stockings by the bed. He had come home early in the afternoon exhausted—Cassandra knew it from the way his injured leg dragged on the floor—and lay down to take a nap. He had got no sleep the night before for the howling of his daughter, and could get none now and so gave up the attempt. Yet he was philosophic. "Be patient, sweet, and rest," he said. "Your milk will come. Meanwhile, I will go myself and see about a wet nurse." And he took the baby from her and went into the outer room, where Cassandra heard him speak to Désirée, heard the door open, close, his stick clatter on the stair.

Cassandra pitied him. He had said nothing of his parents' deaths since Anne was born, and if he had wept, had not done so before her. She knew that he was worried over their delay in getting out of France. The meetings in the inner room had stopped. Their names were on the civil list, he had it on authority, and it was only a matter of time before some *fédéré* came rapping at their door with papers in his hand for their arrest. As each day passed, Cassandra became more agitated instead of more relaxed, and yet Benedict still refused to leave, arguing that a dangerous journey—and it would be that—would serve only to delay her flow for longer. "Rest, sweet, rest," he said ten times a day. "When your milk comes it will be time to leave. Not one moment sooner. I do not want to risk our daughter's life to save our own."

Now, though, in speaking of a wet nurse, it was as though he spoke in code—he had told her that he thought their situation was becoming desperate. Still, he had gone off businesslike and cheerful. He had always managed to produce whatever goods were needed for whoever wanted them, why should he not produce a wet nurse? But what if he could not? Or what if he produced one and she refused to flee with them from France? How would they feed Anne for all those weeks at sea?

Benedict returned. He had consulted with some ladies of society and all reports came back the same. A wet nurse? It was not the thing in France these days, on account of Monsieur Rousseau. Monsieur Rousseau? What madness was this? His writings, it seemed, had persuaded the entire womankind of France that the only proper way to feed a child was from its mother's breasts. He had persuaded them that all society's depravities resulted from the mother who did not suckle her own child. It had become not just a fashion but a tenet of the Revolution. By inquiring for a wet nurse they made themselves conspicuous.

"Worse," said Benedict, "they are selling off the houses of the émigrés; it has begun. Eventually they will get to this house. Then we will not even have a roof above our heads. Anne can do no worse if we leave. Nothing can be done but flee and pray that the relief of our escape will bring your milk. Once we find passage on a ship, at least she will have its surgeon to attend her."

And so it was arranged. Cassandra asked after Monsieur Tarleton, who had come to all the secret meetings, but Benedict said that he was British, he could take care of himself, and went off to notify Monsieur de la Fitte.

Dismissing Désirée, Cassandra readied herself for departure, expecting at any moment to see Benedict come back with Jean and Monsieur de la Fitte. Anne lay quiet even though awake. Her face was pinched and thin, her eyes sunk in deep shadows. Cassandra picked her up. "Come, my darling, try," she begged. "Please don't give up." Opening her gown, she pressed the baby's lips against her breast, but Anne puckered up her mouth and turned her head away. *Sweet God, please don't let her die.*

But what was this commotion on the stair? The door burst inward and she braced to defend herself against whatever new horror had arrived. It was Benedict, dragging Jean, who appeared to be half-crazed with grief, or fear. Lord, how he shrieked and wailed, jerking his body back and forth. Cassandra did not know how Benedict managed it alone, with Jean's full strength against him, but he dragged him through the door and forced him down onto a chair, holding him there in an effort to control him while he settled down.

But Jean would not be settled, struggling the worse and screaming out horrendous oaths at—who? At Monsieur Robespierre? She had heard he was a fierce and righteous man, but the public accuser had never done Jean any wrong. What could have happened to so destroy his natural composure?

He raved on and on. Must he be held down all night? Poor Benedict would soon become exhausted. A look between them, a tip of Benedict's head toward the inner chamber, and with Anne's head bobbing up against her shoulder, she ran to swing wide the door. In less than a minute Benedict had wrestled Jean into the inner chamber and locked the door on him.

"It's for his own good, sweet," he said, gasping from the pain the encounter had caused to his knee. "To keep him from rushing out and doing something foolish."

"What? What's happened?"

"A horrible event. Monsieur de la Fitte has been accosted on the street and dragged off to the Abbaye prison, accused of conspiring with the émigrés. Someone has denounced him."

"Dear God, what will happen?"

"If they find him guilty he could be hauled off to this new beheading machine they have set up in the Place du Carrousel."

Cassandra saw again the bullock that had been slaughtered right in front of her, the way the creature's head had swung half off its neck as it came careening down the street, the way the legs buckled as though the body suddenly had grown too ponderous, the skidding, jarring fall, and then the upswing and the powerful downthrust of the butcher's cleaver, the way the head fell heavily. She felt herself grow faint, a clamoring began inside her head, but she was brought back to her senses when Benedict cried, "I must go and see what I can do to save the man." And he lurched off, clattering his stick, disheveled and distraught.

The incident had frightened Anne, who now wailed miserably. The sound of Jean's furious howling in the inner chamber, the stamping of his feet, did nothing to help. And now Cassandra heard what sounded like a head dashed against a wall.

"He must be calmed," she said aloud, "before he does himself an injury." She thrust Anne into the folds of Maman's bed linen, bracing herself for the scream of protest, but none came, as though the baby had been flabbergasted into silence. Going to the inner door, she turned the key and softly turned the handle. She slipped inside. Jean did not hear her come. He stood with his back to her, fists clenched, head bowed between them, rocking back and forth, moaning and calling down perdition on his father's enemies.

"Jean, my poor dear friend."

He started and swung around, his face distorted so that he seemed to be some other, violent, person.

"Jean, it's me, your friend Cassandra."

He came to her in one long stride and, flinging himself onto his knees, buried his face in her skirts and wept with an abandon she had never seen, even in a child. His breath came in great wrenching gasps, and he wailed and cried with such force that she thought he would surely tear his lungs out of his body. There was nothing she could do but stand with his head between her hands and let him saturate her skirt with tears.

On and on it went for what seemed hours. Then she sensed a softening, a hesitation, hiccuping. Soon he would exhaust himself.

"Come, dear, lie down with me."

He let her guide him to the bed where he stretched his length, still heaving out great rasping breaths. She climbed up beside him and he clasped his arms about her. Without thought of propriety, she drew back her gown and, setting a hand behind his head, guided his mouth against her breast.

As his lips closed on her, Cassandra felt her entire body surge with a delirium of milk. Before long it was a river, running down his throat and spilling from the corners of his mouth. He sucked so long she thought that he had surely emptied her and, pulling gently back, gave him the other breast. But her body, which she had almost given up on, gave and gave, and as he drank from her his agitation faded and a soothing calm took hold.

Cassandra did not know how long she slept with Jean's head between her breasts, but when she woke her gown and his shirt and the bedding under them were soaked with milk. She must go to

Anne. She had left her for too long. She kissed Jean twice and slid down off the bed.

It was silent in the outer chamber. A faint light came from above the damaged drape, so she knew it must be almost dawn. Anne was wide awake—had she not slept at all? Cassandra took her in her arms and the child looked up into her face, then turned her head against her mother's naked breast. By the time Benedict returned the only sound against the silence was the sweet gurgle of her nursing.

24

SEVERAL DAYS WENT BY IN WHICH BENEDICT
and Jean came and went with preoccupied expressions, Jean sleeping by night in the bed Maman had occupied. He had come back
to his senses and he and Benedict were now absorbed in the business of procuring the release of Monsieur de la Fitte. Cassandra
was left alone with Désirée, who constantly pressed food on her, at
the same time puffing out her breasts and patting them, from
which Cassandra gathered Désirée was telling her she must eat
well if she would keep on feeding Anne, who now seemed always
to be against her breast, feeding in a bubbly, milky frenzy, only
pausing when lack of breath threatened to choke her.

Outside, the city bustled with a new sort of activity. Whereas
the atmosphere before had been explosive, now Cassandra felt
something steadily relentless in the air. And she was right. Benedict
and Jean brought daily news that the Commune was going door to
door, arresting anyone they could accuse of taking the king's side
in the Tuileries affair, and refractory priests were being rounded up

as well. Cassandra thought about the curé who had risked his neck to say the last rites for Maman. Was he now in prison? And they, themselves? With Monsieur de la Fitte arrested, would they not soon be too? Herself as well, with Anne? Her baby flung in jail? What if she were condemned along with Benedict and Jean? What would the verdict be on Anne?

And so she passed the days and nights in expectation of a heavy rapping at the door, a circle of accusing faces, rough hands taking her, yet on the other hand she felt a sort of recklessness growing inside her, as though she were becoming capable of anything. Now she had a child to protect she felt both weaker and more powerful. She felt her eyes hard in her head, a sternness in her heart, a cold resolve, as though all her female sensibilities had turned to stone. She no longer had a dagger in her pocket, but she felt as though her entire being had become a weapon. When they came they would not find her unresistant.

August became September. Saturday became Sunday. Morning became afternoon. Somewhere a cannon fired the three blasts of its alarm. Drums beat the *générale*. Once more the tocsin rang in every quarter of the city. Cassandra could smell violence in the air.

Toward evening Benedict came home. "We leave tonight. Jean will be here shortly."

"What is it, Benedict? You look distraught. What's this commotion that's been going on all afternoon?"

"I hardly dare . . ."

"Speak. You must."

"Dear God, they're slaughtering the prisoners. They've set up a tribunal at the Abbaye, but denunciation, condemnation, and execution come one after the other in breathtaking succession, as though the law's cool head of reason has been severed from its body. What results is nothing but a massacre. They're hauling them out of the prisons by the hundreds, those unfortunates, and a mob of butchers is busy hacking them to bits. And the poor Princesse de Lamballe! The queen's best friend! They have chopped off her head. They have tossed her body to the fishwives. Those harridans have torn her entrails out and made of them a 'royal belt' for her to wear while they drag her naked body through the streets. Others ran off to the palace with her head stuck on a pike, presenting it at the queen's window like a voyeur from the grave. Sweet, I'm sorry. I shouldn't speak of it, but I saw the creatures at their horrid games myself. It shook me to my soul. That France should come to this!"

"What of Jean's papa?"

"Still safe, please God. He'll not go to the tribunal. His jailor has been bribed to 'lose' him through a side door of the prison. He'll come to us and we'll slip away together."

"What if he's seen entering the house? There are people all around. They watch us day and night."

"He'll come disguised. Anybody watching will take him for just another of our visitors come here for a meeting. They'll not think a thing about it. We'll wait here together until the coast is clear, and then slip away. You've gathered up your things, yes? Bring what you *must* have, nothing else. Hush, what was that? Someone at the door?"

"It must be Jean."

But it was only Désirée, a tray of supper in her hands, some gruel, a hank of black bread hard as rock, a jug of rough red wine. Benedict took it and sent her off. When he had eaten and Cassandra had swallowed all she could, he set the rest aside for Jean and, glancing once at her, went into the inner room. She followed him, but he pulled the door to close it. She pulled it from the other side. He hesitated and then shrugged.

"Come, then."

Going to the bed, he pulled off the sheet and ripped it into long strips, which he spread side by side on the floor, then flipped the mattress to reveal a mutilated underside.

When she saw this, Cassandra understood the mystery of his secret visits to the inner room. "Here, let me help," she said, and together they laid the strips of sheet end to end with gold coins, which they dug out of the stuffing of the mattress. Benedict folded the strips lengthwise, right to left and left to right across the coins, thereby encasing them in a long thin sheath. He tore a narrow strip of sheet, hacked it into sections with his knife, and with these tied the sheeting in between each coin, securing it in place. Then, having removed his coat and shirt and undershirt, he showed Cassandra how to bind this treasure to his chest and back and waist like an enormous, priceless bandage.

"There," he said when it was done, "you have a good fat husband now." He laughed and took her in his arms, but she could feel him trembling.

Jean came. Since recovering from the shock of his papa's arrest, he had been remote and businesslike, but now that an escape had been assured for him, he was half-delirious with a tension that seemed almost like happiness. Closing the door behind him, he came across and kissed Cassandra on both cheeks. Then he kissed Anne. Then Benedict.

"They say the Prussians are upon us," he said. "They say they're almost at the city."

"It can't be true," said Benedict. "No army moves that fast."

"True or not, we have no time to lose. I've heard a rumor that the Commune is planning to secure the city gates. If we don't make it out of here before they do, we'll all be trapped."

They waited. Where was Jean's papa?

"It's nothing," Benedict assured them, "a delay somewhere, a crowd in the street."

They sat in darkness, cloaked and shod, their few possessions tucked about them. Jean had brought a bonnet rouge for each of them, and they set them on their heads, he thrusting the one for his papa into his shirt. Cassandra had found Benedict's ivory locket dangling by its riband on the bedpost and slipped it in her pocket, along with an ebony comb that had been Maman's. Beneath her cloak, Anne slept at her breast, bound to her body with the remainder of the bedsheet.

Still Jean's papa did not arrive. Cassandra felt fear and tension growing in the room and was glad she had fed Anne earlier when they were hopeful. She at least was calm, although if they delayed too long they would have a hungry screaming child to carry through the streets.

He did not come.

At dawn, just as the sky began to lighten, there was a commotion underneath the window. Benedict sprang to see. At the same moment came a rapping at the door. Jean leaped for it. Benedict cried, "No!" and he halted, one hand on the latch. "Who is it? Name yourself." And then a shuffling of paper underneath the door, the sound of footsteps hurrying away.

Cassandra had risen and all three stood staring at the paper underneath the door. At last Jean bent and picked it up and folded down the note. With a ghastly face he handed it to Benedict.

"My father has been taken down to the tribunal. We have been betrayed."

"By whom?"

Something turned inside Cassandra's head. She saw Désirée outside the door, the supper tray held in her hands, and a look on her face that was not vacant with deafness.

"Désirée. She was outside the door last night. She overheard our plan."

"No, she's deaf."

She looked at him.

"Not deaf, then?"

"I fear not."

Benedict turned on Jean. "You brought her here. Where did you find her? Did she come recommended?"

"I found her through the citizen who used to guard the gate. He said she was his niece."

"The brute Pétoin?" Cassandra said. "I never trusted him."

"I trusted him, God help me," said Benedict. "I fear the man has set a spy amongst us."

"It's my fault, then? I've killed my father?" Jean was becoming wild-eyed once again. "Lord help me, did I kill your father too?"

Cassandra interrupted him. "The fault is mine. If I'd been more perceptive I'd have noticed, I'd have found her out."

"No, Cassie, it's not your fault," said Benedict. "Nor Jean's. If fault is to be found it is my own. I was so concerned with a thousand other things I let everything settle on a wife who is young and inexperienced. It's I who should have inquired into the woman's background. But we mustn't stand arguing amongst ourselves. We must get out of here. We daren't stay even one more moment."

Jean seized him by the arm. "But we can't abandon my father. We must go quick to the Abbaye. We must beseech the tribunal commissioners. We must persuade them he is innocent. Somehow we must rescue him."

Whether Benedict agreed with this or not, he did not say. He simply took Cassandra's hand and turned. Afterward, she would barely remember getting out of there. They dared not attempt escape by the front door, but lowered themselves from a back window down into the lane. She felt Jean's strong arms about her waist and Benedict's upon her legs, guiding her feet to where they ought to go. Then they were on the street, surrounded by confusion. In their bonnets rouges, they merged into the crowd.

Benedict went first. Cassandra clung hard to him with one hand, and with the other held Jean's with such a grip her arm would be sore for days. She was grateful she had Anne tied to her body since she had not a hand to spare. They were pushed and jostled by what seemed thousands of people shouting and raging, calling for the blood of this one or that—of the king, the queen, Monsieur Lafayette, the entire court, the priesthood. Drums beat somewhere close at hand, the tocsin jangled in the air, the ground trembled with the stamping of feet.

They set out walking as quickly as the tumult would allow, intending to cross the river at the Pont Royal, but their way was blocked by a carriage a group of soldiers was busy commandeering. They had hauled out the occupants, a lady and gentleman, and now shoved them in their backs, ordering them to walk wherever they were headed. The crowd got into the adventure, rocking the carriage, which tilted over. The driver sprang to the ground and made to flee. A soldier smacked him sharply on the head with the butt end of his rifle, and he ran half a dozen steps with his brains bursting from his skull before he fell.

The horse was in a panic, caught between the traces, thrashing his head and struggling to get up. With a great effort he heaved upright, or almost upright, since the position of the carriage prevented him from standing up entirely, but a heap of people fell on him and he collapsed again. Cassandra did not see anyone deal a death blow but he gave a great shriek and died, perhaps of fright.

They passed on quickly, heading for the Pont Neuf, and had almost reached the middle of the river when a cart came rattling toward them, the driver shouting to the crowd to let him by. He drew up his horse and two others jumped down from the back of the cart and set about unloading a stack of bodies, which they laid along the edges of the bridge. The crowd fell silent, and Cassandra could feel Jean's attention fixing on each body as it came. While this was going on, the driver stood up in the cart and shouted, "Claim your own! Everybody claim your own!" like a man selling newspapers on the street. Then he flicked his horse's reins, rattled on across the bridge, turned his cart around, and rattled back across, leaving the other two men to guard the bodies from being robbed.

"Come," said Jean. "He's heading for the Abbaye."

At once they were swept up in a sea of people intent on following the cart. The best they could do was stay upright and together, and soon they reached the Abbaye prison, a great gray building, square, with a pointed roof and a turret at each corner. The crowd did not stop there, but went on after the cart, which rattled on down the narrow street and turned into the garden court of the Abbaye monastery.

Here an execution was taking place. Three men with sabres were the executioners, their victims pushed one by one out through the Abbaye doors. Some struggled as they came, some screeched and howled, and some—these terrified Cassandra most—came proudly and silently, their eyes fixed on the sky as though they had already entered heaven. The men with sabres seized them on the steps and knocked them on the head, the sound of the sabre on the skull making a loud ringing sound. Most fell down at this first blow but some staggered or tried to run away. None of them escaped, though; all were hacked to death.

As each prisoner appeared, a profound and gloomy silence took the scene so that every blow could be distinctly heard. As they were finished off, a cry of "*Vive la Nation!*" started and before long was a din of whooping and applause which went on until the next unfortunate appeared. The courtyard was littered with their bodies and more joined them as fast as their owners could be dragged out. Blood washed across the rough stones of the courtyard and ran in rivulets into the gutters, its hot, metallic smell rising up like a con-tagion. From time to time the executioners refreshed themselves by swigging from flagons of red wine, and the wine ran down from the corners of their mouths and mingled with the blood in which their clothes were soaked. Meanwhile, half a dozen men and boys were dragging the fallen bodies by the hair or heels to where they could be loaded on the cart.

Cassandra stood stunned, clinging to Jean and Benedict. She felt nothing, neither horror nor pity, as though all her emotions had been frozen. She felt Jean release her hand, saw him leap into the courtyard, where he succeeded in reaching the steps before one of the executioners turned and set his sabre flat against the boy's chest. As the man did so, he turned his head and Cassandra saw the deformed lower eyelid like a small toad sitting on his face. She jerked Benedict's arm. "It's the brute Pétoin!"

"I've come for my father, Monsieur de la Fitte," Jean said boldly. "I've come to plead with the tribunal."

The crowd made not a sound. Cassandra saw the brute Pétoin smile close up in Jean's face. The wine had stained his teeth dark red, as though he had been drinking blood. She saw him lower his sabre. She saw him take Jean's arm as though he were a friend and lead him down the steps. He led him across the courtyard, where he turned a body with his foot, and then another. Six times he did this, each time advancing his bloody smile into Jean's face when the body turned out to be a stranger's. He stopped before a seventh and turned it with his foot. Jean dropped to his knees, but the brute Pétoin jerked him up again.

"Have you no heart?" Jean cried.

"Is it a heart you want? I wager you've never seen the heart of an aristocrat. I'm going to show you one." Letting go Jean's arm, he took his sabre in both hands, slashed open the body on the ground, and bent over it. He rose, his forearm dripping. "Come, *mon enfant,* kiss papa!" And he thrust it at Jean's face.

As Jean's lips touched his father's heart, it seemed to Cassandra that something passed out of it and into him. A great tremor went through his body and he closed his eyes and balled his fists and seemed to concentrate on something going on inside himself. When it was done and he looked up at the brute Pétoin, something new looked out of him, something hard.

Cassandra heard herself cry out into the silence. The brute Pétoin turned and leered into her face. Recognition flickered in his eyes. He stepped across and grabbed her by the arm. At the same moment she heard Benedict shout beside her, *"Down with the counterrevolutionaries! Kill them! Kill them all!"* She swung to look at him. His face was savage and contorted and he thrust his fist into the air as though he had been suddenly transformed. Around him, others took up the cry: *"Kill them! Vive la Nation!"* And within a moment the air was filled with it. The crowd surged forward, Cassandra felt the brute Pétoin's grip break, and she was lifted from behind and hauled backward out of there, through arms and legs and elbows and the stench of blood.

And then Jean was with them and they were on the Rue Sainte Marguerite, where they continued on amongst an amazing noise and confusion of people shrieking and shoving, and soldiers shoving back at them. Cassandra saw a child ridden down by a fellow on a horse who did not so much as look back to see what he had done. She saw the flailing of the arms and legs and then the stillness. She dared not stop. By now Anne was wailing and she herself half-collapsing with exhaustion. When she staggered and began to fall, Benedict and Jean each seized an elbow, hustling her on. "Don't let her stumble," Benedict shouted out to Jean. "A twisted ankle could be fatal to us all." It was threatening rain and the weather was chilly for the date, which was the third day of September, the year 1792.

25

AT LAST THEY CAME TO A SECTION OF THE city where only a few miserable souls wandered up and down or crouched in doorways. Here they stopped to rest on the stone wall of a well, where Cassandra drew her gown back and gave her breast to Anne, and Jean hauled up the bucket. The water was cool and although it had a strange metallic taste, it was refreshing. But when Cassandra tried to stand again her knees buckled underneath her.

"Could we find a horse? I think I can't go on."

"There is not a horse or carriage to be had, sweet, not anywhere. All have been impounded by the military."

"Refuge then, we must find refuge for the night. I'll have more strength tomorrow."

"Refuge? No. We must go on."

"But how?" Jean said. "She can barely stand upon her feet."

"We must walk. We *must*. It's the only way. We must walk until we reach some country inn or village where transport can be had."

"Then I'll carry her."

"No, it would attract attention. Here, give Anne to me. Help me, Jean. Bind her to me."

"No, your leg is weak. Give her to me, Cassandra . . . There, she will not easily be snatched out of *that* firm knot."

Benedict, who had started to protest, nodded. "Pull your coat about her. Close, like that. Cassie, hold tight to my hand. Jean, hold her other. Cassie, think of nothing but to put one foot before the other. Don't look any stranger in the eye, and pray, my darling, pray with all your might."

They pulled her to her feet but though she willed her legs to walk, she dragged against their hands. Benedict looked down at her despairingly. "Try, sweet, try. You must, before the gates are barricaded shut against us. God knows, it may already be too late."

"What then? How will we escape?"

"Don't panic. Walk. We're heading for one of the lesser gates, la barrière des Ministres, where perhaps security will be more lax. Time enough to panic if we find we cannot pass."

As they struggled on, the number of people on the street increased and shouting came from the direction they were headed. A couple of horses, of the sort used by the king's boundary patrol, came high-stepping through the crowd, riderless and disconcerted, their nostrils flared and snorting, ears swiveling on their heads.

The road widened into a square, not large, and at its side, a small customs house with guard quarters behind and a sentry box in front. The city wall loomed dense and threatening on each side of the road. The way through, though, was clear—no blockades yet, although a pair of fédérés in bonnets rouges stood guard, leaning on their muskets and watching a small tumult going on at one side of the square. Benedict drew Jean and Cassandra into the shadow of a doorway. It had begun to rain, not hard, but bleakly drizzling, and a storm rumbled overhead.

Shortly it became apparent that the crowd—some fédérés, others ordinary citoyens—had a couple of fellows on the ground, perhaps the two boundary patrolmen whose horses had just bolted down the road, and were giving them a thorough beating. From what she had already witnessed that day, Cassandra felt sure they had no hope of coming out of it alive, but then, as though heaven had cast its vote against another death today, the sky lit up and crashed and a torrent fell down out of it. The crowd scuttled for cover. Benedict shouted something, but the thunder drowned his voice. Cassandra felt Jean's hand slip out of hers and snatched for it, but he was gone, vanished in the rain.

Hardly time to panic and he reappeared, sliding his dagger back into his belt, the bundle that was Anne running bloody water at his breast. He seized the hand Cassandra still held out for his. "Now, for God's sake! Run!"

Then they were beating through the rain toward the gate, although it seemed to Cassandra that she did not run at all, but floated, as though she had somehow become disconnected from her body and now observed the situation from the safety of another world. Here was the heavy sentry box, here the two sprawled bodies of the fédérés, here the looming presence of the wall, the city's wide encircling boulevard, and beyond that, three hundred feet or so of open ground, and then the mess of peasant huts, the woods beyond.

It was not until Benedict and Jean, moving as one, yanked her sideways into the protection of the woods that she came back to herself, her head buzzing and strange shrieking noises coming from her mouth. Benedict tried to wrap her in his arms but she jerked away, snatching at Anne.

"Jean, is she dead?"

"Dead? Of course not."

"Accomplice to a murder, then?"

He seized her by the shoulders. "Stop it, Cassandra! Stop! Do not become hysterical. Not now. No, don't collapse. We have no time to rest. We must get out of here in case we're followed."

That prospect put more life into Cassandra than any resting could have done. She found herself absolutely running, her feet guiding themselves. And all the time conjuring up thoughts of what would happen to them when the dead fédérés were discovered. There would be a shout and they would stop, confused about which course to take, but before they could decide, their pursuers would be upon them, tearing them limb from limb, her baby's head ripped off her little neck and set up on one of their foul pikes. That image in her head, her feet grew wings and she ran hard, tears streaming down her face, breath coming in great heaving gasps.

The rain had eased somewhat but still came down steadily, the ground getting soggier by the minute so that eventually they were forced to come back onto the road to take their luck there. Several times they heard a rider or a wagon, but each time had warning enough to jump back into hiding. Once a sound of marching came toward them and they flattened themselves against the backs of trees while some sort of army passed. After that the rain intensified again and before long they were plodding through a downpour. They met no more traffic, perhaps because of it.

By nightfall it was raining still and had grown considerably more cold. Anne wailed to be fed again and they stopped briefly while Cassandra gave her breast without unbinding her from Jean. By the time she was done, she was shivering all over and walked fast to warm herself, while Jean wrapped his arms tight around Anne and held her close against his chest, attempting to pass his warmth to her. Benedict had lost his stick in the mêlée at the Abbaye and, although he made no complaint, he stumbled constantly so that Cassandra found she was now supporting him. Disheartenment crept up to become their fourth companion.

But now here were lights, a village, thin suspicious people who, at a ruinous price, provided food and allowed them to dry themselves before the fire and tend to Anne. At a price even more ruinous, they managed to secure from them a cart with not so much as a driver's bench to sit on, but at least with a canopy to keep off the rain, which still came down hard and steady. One horse only was available, an old swaybacked nag no good for war.

And so they set out, with Jean crouching at the front, thrashing the reins against the creature's back, Benedict and Cassandra jerking and jolting black and blue behind, stiffening with fatigue and cold.

At first the cart rattled along at a great clip, or at least it seemed that way, but after a while it slowed and no amount of coaxing or thrashing could persuade the nag to do more than loll along. Then, as though hit with sudden inspiration, it picked up its feet again and bolted down the road, the whole contraption swaying crazily. And so it went on, first a mad dash, then a lurching amble, then a mad dash again. But after an hour or so the animal grew tired, the mad dashes became halfhearted and then ceased. Before long, the lurching amble ceased as well and Jean was forced to climb down from the cart and lead the stumbling creature through the rain.

Cassandra had no idea in which direction they were traveling, the night was so completely black. The rain continued to fall and Jean's figure up ahead was lost inside it, Benedict awash at the cart's front edge, calling out to him about their route, Jean's ghostly answers floating back like debris washed up by a flood.

Cassandra sat clutching Anne with one hand and the cart's side with the other, pitching back and forth, listening fearfully for shots, the rattle of a blockade, shouts commanding them to stop. But nothing. Just the grinding of the wheels, the clattering of hooves, and from time to time a whistle of encouragement to the horse from Jean.

On that journey she gave thanks to God for the condition of the roads. If they had been traveling through the countryside of Maryland the cart would surely have bogged down, but no, it rattled on, with the rain roaring and beating on the canvas canopy. Once there was a smashing sound as though the horse had broken through some barrier. She waited for shouts above the downpour. Nothing still, just the snapping of the canvas overhead and from time to time the crack of lightning and the heavy roll of thunder.

The ocean stretched before them, ships clanking and groaning at the wharf. The sky was clear, although the wharf was puddled, people slapping back and forth above their own reflections. A light wind blew, carrying the smell of salt and rot and seaweed.

An inspector looked at them suspiciously and conferred with two or three others. Their papers were coughed over and frowned above. Money passed from hand to hand, and then some more. Then turned-up hands, and shrugging of the shoulders and apologies. Questions hovered in the air.

Cassandra kept her eyes turned from Benedict's bulging midriff.

Suddenly it seemed conspicuous—such a thin man with a belly of that grand dimension. If these fellows should suspect . . . On an inspiration, she drew off her wedding ring and held it out. "Here, take it—it's all the gold we have left to our name." Benedict would swear afterward it was her voice saved them in the end, having the accent of America, but Cassandra knew, by the way he did not mention it, that he was distressed she should have given up her ring.

Within moments they were through the barricade, into the midst of a confusion of others seeking quick passage out of France, and in not much longer had discovered the brig *Nancy*, which by a miracle was to sail that very day for Philadelphia. Benedict went aboard to make arrangements with the captain, leaving Cassandra with Jean, but he, without warning, dashed off somewhere, she did not know where. She tightened her arms around Anne, bracing herself against the jostling of the others on the wharf, and a great sigh came out of her, and then another, as though she would turn inside out with tension and relief.

When Jean reappeared and seized her in his arms and kissed her soundly on the mouth, she demanded, startled, if he had gone mad. But no, it was a farewell kiss. He had discovered a ship about to sail for Saint Domingue and was set on making the voyage in search of his brother Pierre. When he pointed out the ship, Cassandra was aghast.

"Jean, what are you thinking? You'll be lost. That sorry tub looks half wrecked already. It'll not last a night at sea."

But he was determined, and in a hurry, since the seamen were already hauling in the mooring ropes. He flung his arms about her once again. "I love you," he said, suddenly in tears. "Here, let me kiss you one last time." And did it whether she would say yes or no.

She was breathless now, her mind in disarray. "Remember me," she said, and slipping her hand into her pocket for some keepsake, came up with Benedict's ivory locket, which she slung around his neck.

"I'll wear it always," he said, kissing her a third time. And he turned and ran, leaping aboard his tipsy vessel with not a second left to spare.

She ran to the wharf's edge, shouting up at him. "But Jean, what will become of you? Will I never hear from you? Will we never meet again?"

The ship jerked and he grabbed the rail. "We'll meet again, Cassandra, I promise on my soul." He leaned toward her, straining to touch her hand across the murky, jigging water, but by now the distance was too far. "When next you hear of me, Cassandra," he shouted, laughing now, "I shall be *famous*. No, more than that, I shall be—" The ship's whistle blasted and his voice was lost.

Benedict came urgently behind her. "Cassie, where is Jean? Where is the boy? We must go aboard at once."

"Gone. Gone off to Saint Domingue." She pointed to Jean's vessel, which by now was well pulled out, although not so far they could not easily perceive him at the rail shouting something they could not hear and brandishing his bonnet rouge, which, with a grand gesture, he flung into the sea.

"Damn the boy for a fool!" exploded Benedict, waving furiously back. "He'll go off and get himself drowned in a storm, or set upon by pirates in the southern sea, or slaughtered when he gets to Saint Domingue in some uprising of the Negroes." And so he went on, furious with what seemed rage but what Cassandra knew was loss because he loved Jean like a son.

At last he calmed and, since there was nothing to be done for it, led her aboard the *Nancy* where he introduced her to the captain, an Irishman named Mr. Hathaway, who himself conducted them below to where a tiny cabin had been assigned to them. It had a single hanging cot and a narrow wooden bench.

"There," said Benedict, when Mr. Hathaway had gone, "have I not found us accommodations of the most luxurious sort?"

He took Cassandra in his arms and, kissing her, wept, apologizing for having, in the first place, taken her into such danger, and in the second, for having treated her so roughly during their escape.

Cassandra felt sighing take her over once again and could say only, "Don't say that, don't think it."

And they clung together until the ship jerked under them and they heard the shout of seamen hauling in the ropes. Then they climbed into the hanging cot and, with Anne between them,

wrapped their arms about each other and surrendered to its swaying. They slept all day and all night too, Cassandra barely waking
when Anne nuzzled up against her breast to nurse.

At last the crash of buckets and the squeal of pumps, the rasp of
holystones against the deck above their heads awakened her. She
lay listening to the shouts and cursing of the sailors as they
scrubbed the ship, and thought she had not heard a sound as sweet
in all her life.

26

*T*HEY WERE WELL AT SEA NOW. BENEDICT spent most of his time below, resting his damaged knee, which all the activity of the flight had made inflamed and swollen. At first it was so sensitive he could barely put foot to floor, but the ship's surgeon had made a project of it, dosing him with laudanum and attaching leeches, trying every sort of compress to relieve the pain, and Benedict assured Cassandra he was having some success. She offered to sit with him but he said he needed time alone to think about their situation and what business he should enter when they got back home to Maryland.

And so Cassandra gave herself up to motherhood. They had been at sea barely two days when Mr. Hathaway produced a woman willing to serve as nursemaid, but Cassandra would not have her. She wanted to do everything herself. Later, when she looked back on those weeks of voyaging, she would think of them as the most profoundly peaceful of her life. It was the first time since her baby had been born that she could be quiet with her, and she found she could not bear to let her from her arms. She wanted every moment to feel the sensation of Anne's head against her arm or shoulder, the pushing of her tiny legs against her hand—such tiny feet, and such a tiny child—the way her fingers curled around her own, the miracle of her pink ear. She looked into her face and saw, on one day, Benedict, on another day, herself, her little sister Fanny, her papa, Thomas, Charlotte, no it was Mama, it was Charcilla, Mary. Once she even imagined that she saw Jean in the little face.

Sometimes Benedict thrashed in his sleep and woke up sweating in a panic. When Cassandra asked him what it was, he told her he had seen his father's head stuck up on the fence again, or had dreamed that he was trying to remove it and it would not come. Then she would hold his hand until he slept. Sometimes she wondered why she did not have bad dreams herself but thought it was because of Anne. As long as she could hold to her she could sleep easily.

She thought about her love for Benedict. It seemed stronger than it had been when they ran away, and yet his injury had changed their lovemaking. Once they had come together almost violently, with no regard for anything but the sensation of body against body, the hot fusing of flesh as though a fire burned below their skins, and then the urgent thrusting and their two breaths rising, hesitating, rising, savoring the journey to the top—oh, he was a master at the art of love!—and then, suddenly, the point of no return, the great erupting gale of—what? Of ecstasy? Desire? She could not find a word that captured first the brilliant tingling like a coin inside her belly, then the outward spread through chest and head, the spiraling through arms and legs, the sparking out through toes and fingertips, a sensation so powerful that sometimes she would turn and look, half-expecting to see singeing on the sheets.

Since Benedict's injury, however, everything had changed. The hot flaring in her loins was as it always had been when he touched her, but the violence of their coming together had been muted to protect his knee. Sometimes he could not perform the final act at all, there being no position which would allow it without agony. Once she had gently pushed him on his back and taken her own pleasure from him, but although he allowed it, she had felt embarrassment rise off him like a cloud, and so did not repeat the experiment.

These days, when he could not do his normal duty as a husband, she would lie quietly and he would touch her with his fingertips up and down her body, soft as feathers on her skin, until, thrusting her breasts up to his lips, she would seize his hand and force it down between her legs and hold it there while her body arched and bucked. Yes, she had learned another way to make love too. She had no doubt that she and Benedict were as close as any two could be.

The wind was sharp behind them, driving them along as though in sympathy with their impatience to arrive, and not another ship hove into sight, either friend or brigand. Cassandra prayed Jean's journey would be likewise uneventful. She thought about his father. She had not known him well—he had not allowed it. He had been dark like Jean and handsome like him too, but with a reckless, knowing air. She thought she could have loved him if he had let her, but he had not let her. He had loved his son, though, it was evident from the way Jean spoke of him, and Jean loved him, no doubt of that. Did he also wake sweating and crying in the night, and no one on that tipsy tub to offer comfort? She wished he had not gone off to Saint Domingue, although she sympathized. He wanted family, as she wanted her own.

She thought about her father. Captain Hathaway had assured her that the posts were going through. And so she had been right. He had not answered her. He had not written. And yet, looking down at Anne, she did not believe he would withhold his love forever. How could he stop loving his own child? It was impossible. When he saw her once again, when she set her head against his heart, when she held him in her arms, everything would be all right.

The low hissing of the bow through water, the tapping of the salt wind at her cheeks, the knowledge that Benedict was always to be found not far away, gave her a feeling of security she had not had since she left Maryland. She was surprised to find that she was happy, not in the way she used to be when—so long ago—she was a child, but in a calmer, contemplative way.

She looked back at France in numbed astonishment at all that had happened there, and all that was still happening. She said a prayer for Papa van Pradelles and Maman and for Monsieur de la Fitte. She thought of Désirée, and then prayed for herself because she could not forgive her for betraying them.

Night fell. She stood beside the railing with the deep blackness of eternity above her and let her eyes run star to star until they dazzled her. Her nipples stood up underneath her gown, her breasts sang with her milk. She thought of Jean. Sometimes, when she suckled Anne, he would come and sit with her. She would feel his eyes upon her breasts and fancy that he watched her hungrily. It was an unsettling thought, and she put it from her.

A word from Horace came into her mind: "When we cross the sea we change the sky above us; we do not change our souls." She thought, though, that she had changed her soul, for good or ill she did not know. Soon she would go down to Benedict.

27

*J*OHN CAME BACK FROM KENTUCKY. HE inquired of Amos why Susannah was nowhere to be found.

Amos shook his head. "She run off, master."

"Run off? Why?"

"Miss Colegate done set about to sell her. When Susannah hear of it she run."

"Sell her? Where did she go?"

"Dunno, master. Somewheres north. The little baby too."

Sell her? Sell Susannah and her child? It could not be true. But yes, it was. Amos did not lie. He knew the man. He did not lie. Perhaps he was mistaken, then, confused. It was a rumor only, gossip, some sort of cruel joke. But Amos did not joke. He was a solemn man. Well, then, perhaps it was the truth. Why else would Susannah run? She had a good home here. She was well treated, even loved. Why would she run? Because Colegate had arranged to sell her. But Susannah was no field Negro to be bought and sold. How could Colegate think of such a thing? She might want to do it but she would not dare. She would not dare. Susannah was not her property to sell. Why else, though, would the girl run off? And she was gone, there was no doubt of that.

He had questioned Eudie now, and the overseer, and Sukie too, and gone door to door amongst the slave huts, and ridden out into the fields, interrogating everyone—Jason, Cyrus, Lucy, Beck, Carmia, Ruth, Bess, Bob, Ajax, all of them, their children too, calling them to him by name to stand beneath a tree or in the shadow of a slanting porch. Some seemed to pity him, some looked narrow-eyed, triumphant, but all their stories were the same. His overseer said he ought to whip the truth from them, but John did not have it in his heart. He knew the truth. Colegate had set about to sell Susannah, and she ran. That was the truth.

Perhaps, though, she had not gone north, not yet. Perhaps she was still in hiding somewhere close at hand, waiting for an opportunity. Addie Kemp would know. She would tell him where Susannah was and he would go to her and ask her to come home.

At the Quaker meetinghouse, Addie Kemp came down the path and met him at the gate. He had been about to tie his horse up to the hitching post but when he saw her coming, he stopped, and stood before her with the reins held in one hand.

He took his hat off with his other hand. "Good morning, Addie."

She inclined her head. "Good morning, John." She did not smile.

Another woman came out of the meetinghouse and, after her, another. John knew them both, but slightly. They came to stand at each side of Addie just inside the gate. They did not smile.

He said, "Good morning, ladies."

"Good morning, Sir," they said.

Susannah was behind them in the meetinghouse. He could feel her. He looked up at the window. Nothing there. No face. And yet her presence pressed against the glass. If he could speak to her, if he could . . . no, she did not want to come back home. She did not want to come to him. And if he forced her? If he pushed his way past Addie Kemp and her lieutenants? He had a right. Susannah was his property. What, though, if he took her home and she ran off again? What would he do then? Would he go after her with dogs? His mind recoiled.

"Good morning, John," said Addie Kemp again, and this time it was not a greeting, it was a farewell.

He set his hat back on his head. "Good morning to you, too, Addie."

He wanted to shout at Colegate, to argue, punish her. No, he would speak reasonably. "What's this I hear about Susannah?" he would say. "What have you done?"

He went to her. She sat stiff-backed in Great-aunt Deye's wheeled chair beside the parlor window. She did not look at him. Her hands were folded in her lap. Above her head, Great-aunt Deye gazed down at him, an expression of what seemed to be amusement on her face. "So, John, what will you do now?" she seemed to say. "How will you deal with this?"

He stepped warily across the room and stood before his wife, feeling not like a husband come to punish and upbraid, but like a supplicant. He cleared his throat.

She turned her head and looked at him. "John. You have come back."

He eased his neck inside the collar of his shirt.

"You have some information to communicate? Some news of Kentucky?"

Formality took him by the scruff. "Be so good, Madam, as to have Thomas called out of the schoolroom."

"You seem not to realize, Sir, that time has passed. Thomas is not a schoolboy anymore. He is gone sixteen years."

"I am aware of my son's age. Where is he?"

"Somewhere along the bottom run, supervising the construction of a fence."

"Have him sent for. I will take him with me to Kentucky."

"When will you return?"

"I cannot say. Do not expect me soon."

"And Thomas? When will he return?"

"He will not. I'm putting him in charge of my new iron-smelting works. It's time the boy took responsibility for a business of some sort."

"You do not call our property a business?"

"You have a second son. Set John to work on it."

"But John has signed up for the navy. He has no inclination for farmwork."

"I have been," said John, his own voice ringing in his head, "I have been in communication with my agent, Mr. Price. He compliments your management of my affairs. I have no doubt you will continue to do so."

He stopped, waiting for her to speak, to remonstrate, to make some sound of loss or disappointment, but she kept her eyes fixed on his face, expressionless.

28

_I_T WAS MID-OCTOBER, ON A WEDNESDAY AFTER suppertime, when they arrived in Baltimore. They went directly to an inn, where, when they asked after a room, the innkeeper looked them over skeptically. Cassandra had insisted they leave Philadelphia the moment they arrived, and since they had nothing but the peasant clothes in which they had fled France, the innkeeper could be forgiven for taking them for a pair of wandering derelicts. At last they managed to convince him they were not and were assigned a room and had their supper carried up. When they had eaten, Benedict lay down on the bed with his hands beneath his head and his leg up on a pillow, watching Cassandra nursing Anne.

She looked up at him. "What is it?"

"Nothing, it's nothing."

But she insisted, "What?"

"I pray that your papa will treat you kindly, that is all." And he levered himself up off the bed and went in search of a bath.

Cassandra felt a sensation climbing in her throat like exhaustion, or tears that would not come. When Anne was done, she made a nest of cushions for her in a corner of the room and settled her down into it. Then she stretched out on the bed to wait for Benedict. She felt herself begin to drift, and yet she did not seem to sleep. She was back home at Owings Hall, standing before the front door, knocking and knocking and pulling at the bell and calling out, "Papa, Papa." Footsteps came behind the door, and voices in the hall, but the door stayed locked against her. At last she went back down the steps and turned to leave, then turned and looked up at the house. There, in the sidelight by the door, was her father, watching with a cold hard stare. She saw his mouth move and, even though the sidelight was tight shut, she heard him curse her.

She woke, leaping in the bed, and he was cursing still below the window. Benedict stood before it, the drapes crushed between his hands, peering at the curser. "An inn is no place for a gentlewoman," he said across his shoulder. "Why, sweet, what's the matter?"

Even after she had swallowed down a dose of calming gin, and listened to Benedict's soothing voice telling her it was nothing but a dream and all her fears were foolish—she was her papa's darling girl, he would welcome her back home, would not reject her—she lay awake clinging to his arm, his hand, his wrist, the image of her father's face leering at her from the corners of the room.

Early in the morning, Benedict sat up with his hair disheveled to find Cassandra, surrounded by a mess of balled-up papers, crying at the writing desk. "Come, come," he said in an astonished voice. "What's the matter here?"

"The words will not go right. Every time I start to write a sentence I hear Papa's angry answer to it in my head."

"Why do you write? There is no need. We'll go to him."

"I dare not face him suddenly. What if he is still put out with me? What if he should reject me after all?"

It was still dark outside and she had a candle by her. As Benedict picked his way across the littered floor, the light glinted on his hair and a giant shadow loomed behind him on the wall. He knelt beside her, favoring his injured knee as he went down. "Love, you'll frustrate yourself trying to get the words right. If you're nervous, let me go alone and plead your case with your papa."

"No, that won't do. You'll likely get nothing but a load of buckshot in your backside for your pains."

He laughed. "I can be persuasive, I assure you."

"I think Papa may resent that character in you. If he blames me for running off, how much more will he blame the man who persuaded me to it? No, I must send a letter to prepare him." She frowned, clicking her tongue. "But I cannot get the words right on the page."

"Here, let me write it for you." He gripped the edge of the desk with one hand and the arm of the chair with the other and pulled himself to his feet. "Come, sweet, let me. I'll make a fine job of it, I promise."

"Then do it. I suppose you'll make no worse a job of it than I." And she drew a clean piece of paper from the drawer and rose and began to pace the room.

When he was done, Cassandra agreed he had made a fine job of it, humble and yet confident, pleading yet insistent, contrite yet expressive of the deepest affection and willingness to be accommodating. He said he would hire a horse and carry it to Owings Hall himself, but when he stood up, wincing painfully, she forbade it.

"You don't need that long ride. Your knee is barely half-recovered. And besides, you can't appear before Papa in those old rags. We must order some new clothes. I'll do it right away. For the moment, you must sit down in that armchair, and set your foot up on that stool, and let me find a messenger."

"You'll send a stranger?"

"I'll pay him well."

She became brisk and busy, bustling about the room picking up the abandoned letters and placing them in the wastebasket by the desk, dressing hastily. "I'll see to it this minute, and while we wait for a reply I'll see to our new clothes." She took the letter and went out of the room.

Anne whimpered in her nest of cushions. Benedict went to her and lifted her onto his shoulder, crooning a French lullaby. She craned to look about the room, her head bobbing unsteadily, but as his voice went on she set her head against his neck and her eyelids came down heavily across her eyes, lifted once, came down.

Downstairs, Cassandra sent out for a messenger. An honest-looking fellow with a stutter came within the hour. She gave him his instructions, paid him half his fee, promising the other half when he came back with a reply, and followed him outside, where she stood watching him grow small and smaller on his horse. Then she turned and walked rapidly off down the street.

It was a brisk day, although not cold, and her steps sounded sharply on the paving stones. She felt hopeful now, her night fears seemed foolish. She could feel the color coming to her cheeks and looked eagerly about, drawing in the sights and sounds and smells of home. She had heard people who had come back from a journey say that the time they were away seemed like a dream, that no time at all had passed and everything was exactly as it had been before. But it was not like that for her. Although it had been only a little more than two years since she left Maryland, the city looked and smelled both foreign and familiar. Although she turned each corner with confidence, stepping briskly down the sidewalk toward the next turn in the road, she found herself looking about as though at a place she had never seen before. Every building seemed suddenly sprung up, the early street vendors calling out their wares in a language that seemed barely comprehensible. Their faces were like faces from a fairy tale, the smell of ocean on the air exotic and ambiguous, the dip and screech of gulls like visitations from another world.

She fell to thinking about the expeditions that she took with Jean through the tumultuous streets of Paris, and a sigh escaped her, of relief because she was no longer in that city, and of wistfulness because her friend was no longer at her side. She imagined him en route to Saint Domingue, standing with his hands upon the railing of the ship, his black hair whipped about his shoulders by the wind, and he laughing into it, cheeks flushed with the delight of travel. Did he think about her too? Tears sprang to her eyes and she hurried up her step, brushing them away with the back of her hand. Once more she heard his voice: "We'll meet again, Cassandra, I promise on my soul." Once more she saw the tears sparkle in his eyes, once more felt his lips pressing against hers with such urgency that had he not been a mere boy—no, it was wrong to think of him that way.

On the voyage home Benedict had asked about his locket. He had left it slung across the bedpost. Had she noticed it? Had she brought it with her? Surely he had not lost it, his most prized possession? Cassandra had felt heat rush up her neck. "Oh, Benedict," she said. "I'm sorry." But she did not tell him she had given it to Jean.

Now she had arrived outside a window holding a display of fabrics and a sign that read, MONSIEUR HENRI, COUTURIER. She had never heard of him but since he advertised himself in French she thought she could trust him to produce some clothes fit for their visit to Papa. *Dear Lord, please let him answer soon. Please let him want to see me.*

Anne had cried all night and Cassandra could not tell why. Perhaps the change in diet had made her milk too rich. Or perhaps the baby tasted tension. Now it was almost noon and Anne, at last, was sleeping. Cassandra had finished nursing her a little while ago and still sat with her in her arms, afraid that she would wake and cry again if she set her down. She had not yet bathed today, nor even combed her hair, but sat in a half-daze, exhausted from lack of sleep and a thousand imagined rejections from her father.

Across from her, Benedict was stretched out on the bed, a compress on his knee. Before they left the *Nancy*, the surgeon had shown him how to prepare his own concoction and had given him instructions on how long to soak the compress, how often to apply it to the knee, and for how long. Since Benedict was anxious to pursue some business venture as soon as he had clothes in which he could appear, he had been assiduous in following the remedy. Twenty minutes, yes, it was enough. Now he must exercise the knee for a like time. He rose, folding the compress into a metal dish beside the bed. "Rest, sweet. I'll be back soon." And he took his stick and made it out the door without a limp.

Cassandra rose and settled Anne into her nest of cushions in the corner of the room. She must wash. She must do something with her hair. She would feel so much better when she did not have to wear this dreadful gown.

Monsieur Henri and his Negro boy had come yesterday, late in the afternoon, the boy hauling an enormous pouch of fabric samples and sketches of designs, Monsieur Henri with a tape measure, and a leather-bound notebook in which he jotted notes and measurements for garments he would make. He had assured them they would have one complete outfit each by tomorrow, and the rest in one more day, or maybe two. Cassandra was doubtful about the quality of work he could produce in that short time, but he assured her he had half a dozen good French seamstresses and as many tailors, all of whom could wield a pair of scissors and a needle faster than a flash. If he was right, they could set out for Owings Hall tomorrow. Cassandra prayed that they would have good news by then. She prayed that she would get some sleep tonight.

But now a knocking at the door, the houseboy's voice. At last— a message from Papa! Cassandra called for him to enter. The door swung open and the messenger came into the room. And now it was as she had feared. He still had her letter in his hand.

"No one would take it, Ma'am."

"A message then? A note?"

He handed it across to her. She turned the paper down: "Mr. John Cockey Owings knows no one by this name."

When Benedict came back, Cassandra was raging in a fury up and down the room.

"The news from your papa is bad? He will not see you?"

"Not only will he not see me, but he will not even tell me so himself." She snatched the note and letter from the desk. "Look, look at this. My letter comes back to me unopened, and . . . here, read this note. It is Mama's handwriting. Papa has had her do his dirty work for him."

Benedict's neck grew red. He punched his hand into his fist, then drew out his handkerchief and blew his nose with a trumpeting sound. "The man's forgotten all civility. It's up to me to teach him some. I'll leave for Owings Hall at once."

"Benedict, no. What if he should kill you?"

"I'm as good a man as he. Let him come at me."

"You'd leave me a widow, then? Your child an orphan?"

"How can I stand by and let him treat you in this way? How *can* I?"

"How he treats me, Benedict, is none of your concern. It's between him and me alone. If there's a lesson to be taught to my papa, then it's I who will teach it, no one else."

The cold determination of her tone caught Benedict up short. She had risen from the couch and stood between him and the window. The brightness of the outside sky flared around her so that all he could see was her dark form in silhouette. He could not see her face. She had the letter and the note from her papa held in her hand.

"I mean it, Benedict. It's up to me alone."

"What will you do?"

She went to the window, raised the sash, tore the note and letter into shreds, and tossed them out.

"Cassandra, sweet . . ."

She turned to him. "If my papa will turn his back on me, then I will turn my back on him. If he will cut me off from family, then I'll make a family of my own of which he is not part." He saw her shadowed arm go to her belly, as though she felt a crowd of unborn children moving there. "We will leave here," she said, and there was no waver in her voice. "We will leave here bag and baggage, never to return."

"Where will we go? To Kentucky?"

"Not Kentucky. I have no fancy to be slaughtered by some Indian."

"But the whole world goes to Kentucky. By now it is quite civilized."

"No, we'll go to New Orleans, where your countrymen will welcome us."

"New Orleans? But it's governed by the Spanish."

But all Cassandra said was, "Spanish! Hah!" And he did not challenge her again, since she was clearly set on it and he had no desire on earth except to please her. "I'll go at once," he said, "and make arrangements for a passage."

When the door had closed behind him, Cassandra turned and gazed out of the window, her thoughts on her papa. All her life he had cosseted and spoiled her, granted everything she asked. But she had asked too much: forgiveness for rebellion. She saw now that his love was not without condition. Obedience was demanded in exchange. As long as she made his demands her own, he had given her his heart to hold inside her hands, but when she went against him, he withdrew it. Still, she would not buckle under it, she would not take the blame. She was his daughter, hardheaded as himself, and she had made her choice.

The smell of ocean carried on the breeze, the slap and clank of ships at dock. Below her, someone shouted. A horse and carriage clattered by. A woman in a large hat passed on the street. She leaned on her companion's arm and looked up, laughing at him, so that Cassandra saw her face. She did not know her.

29

$\mathcal{I}$T WAS DECEMBER 20, THE YEAR 1803, AND Mr. Jefferson had just bought Louisiana. Benedict stood on the town square, leaning on his cane, his free hand resting on the curly dark head of his son and namesake, five years old, who clung against his leg. Colegate and Juliana, ten and nine, stood in front of him, three-year-old Charcilla perched on Colegate's hip. Cassandra, holding baby Mary in her arms, stood on his right, while Anne, now eleven years, fidgeted between her parents, one hand holding on to her baby sister's woolen-bootied foot.

It was a damp day, and chilly. A low mist hung above the river, and the sky, which was entirely covered up with clouds, cast down an eerie brightness on the scene. The crowd was not so large and there was small enthusiasm in the spirits of the people as the red-striped, star-struck banner clambered up the pole, snagged once, resumed its journey up.

Benedict reached to touch the blue-black ringlets falling down Anne's back. She felt her father's touch and sidled into him, rubbing her cheek against his sleeve like a cat responding to a stroking hand. There had been a time when he would not have allowed her outside in weather such as this. These days she was rosy-cheeked and healthy, a laughing, tenderhearted child, but in her early years she had been sickly, with a sunken-eyed wan look, prey to every chill and cough and inflammation of the lungs that came along.

Sometimes, after supper, when Benedict sat with his injured leg up on a stool, he used to watch her in her mother's arms and feel his heart contract. No matter that Cassandra wrapped her baby up in love, flinging herself into motherhood as though she had invented it, no matter that she insisted on nursing Anne herself, even though a dozen wet nurses were easily available, no matter how she cajoled her into swallowing this tonic or that potion, the child refused to fatten. As each new life came into his family, it had seemed to Benedict a little more went out of Anne. At five years old, she was no bigger than her little sister Colegate, her hair very black against porcelain-white skin, and her delicate bone structure made him think of her as breakable.

Because of it, he could not help but love her best of all his children, as did Cassandra, who used to take her everywhere she went, as though she feared that if she left her for one minute fate would scoop her up. When Benedict was home, he would indulge her shamelessly, and when he was away, would hurry back as soon as business would allow, and she would run to him and clutch him round the knees so hard he could not take a step until he swung her up into his arms. Then he would sit down on his chair and take her on his knee, and she would lean her head against his chest and he would sing to her in French. Even now, sometimes, she would come to him and sit down on his knee and stroke his face, and they would sing some song together. She had survived. His heart was grateful.

Grateful, too, for this occasion. He had always hankered for America, ever since he was a child. Smiling to himself, he thought about the day his grandfather had taken him on a business journey to the port at Brest. The ships jostling at the wharf excited him, but the ocean had amazed him, the vast expanse of it, going on and on, dark blue fading into green, and full of depths. What had entranced him more was the horizon, the way it cut the sea with such finality. He had seen horizons on the landscape but had never been affected in this way. It was the straightness of it, the precision, like the downthrust of a butcher's cleaver.

"What keeps the water in?" he asked his grandfather.

"Why, the shore, of course," his grandfather replied.

"But what keeps it in out there?" Pointing out to sea.

His grandfather had not laughed, although he had seemed enchanted by the question. Looking about, he spied a vendor selling fruit and, taking his little grandson by the hand, led him to the cart, where he selected an orange that was perfect in its roundness. Then he led him to where they could see out between two ships and, crouching at his side, explained how the earth was like an orange, round, and he made a line on it with his thumbnail to show where the French shore met the ocean, and another mark for the horizon, and a third mark for the shore that held the ocean on the other side.

"It's called America," he said. "It's a brand-new country in the world. It is still wild."

"Can you take me there this afternoon?"

"No, not this afternoon."

"Then when?"

"Maybe you will take yourself there when you are a man."

It had been like a promise, a secret held between the two of them. They never spoke of it again, but the notion of a brand-new country called America had taken root in Benedict's imagination, and as he grew, it floated out there past the sharp horizon of his thoughts. When Cassandra had insisted that they come to Spanish New Orleans, he had been disappointed, and all the time they had been here he had hankered for Kentucky, the way he used to hanker for America when he was a child.

Now Mr. Jefferson had made his dream come true. He had not magically transported him to Kentucky, but he had restored to him America. Perhaps—he hoped it, he *did* hope it—perhaps his luck in New Orleans would turn at last.

When first they had arrived here, he had rented one of the little houses in the French section of the town, a crude affair, as they all were, wooden, with a roof that sprang a new leak after every patching. It was decent, though, with a palmetto-thatched hut at the bottom of the dooryard in which he installed a big, bright-turbaned housekeeper named Mattie with her two young sons, Seth and Syphorian.

When that house burned—half the town vanished in a leap of flame—Benedict drew in his breath, let it out again, and taking the last of the louis d'or he had brought from France, used it to buy the still-smoking devastated lot, where he built a new house of his own. It was small but a step up from the house that burned, of brick, not wood, a tiled roof instead of shingles, and extra cisterns, very large, at the back corners of the house so they would catch rainwater for daily use and enough spare to fight a fire if there should be another. It had a rental property below it, a bakery, the income from which, he hoped, would recoup his investment.

On the day they took possession, their downstairs tenants came tapping at the door, a hearty woman with enormous breasts whose name was Emmeline Tournelles, and her husband, a weed of a fellow with smiling yellow horse's teeth and a persistent cough. A little black boy with a tray of fancy breads and cakes came on behind.

Within the week, Emmeline, whose nature was amiability itself, had become Cassandra's friend. Despite her husband's feeble lungs, which often left him breathless, he was a fine baker and as fine a pastry cook, and Benedict and Cassandra woke each morning with the odor of his early morning diligence fresh in their noses.

Benedict assured Cassandra that this was just a start; there would be a large grand house before too long, and nursemaids and a hostler and a handyman, a butler if she wanted one, and all the lovely clothes and furniture her heart desired. And yet he could not make it happen.

At that time, New Orleans was a tiny, backward place, full of vagabonds sprung out of every nation, many of them coarse Americans, wanted men, who had fled there to avoid being taken by the law. The police, in their frock coats and blue breeches, cocked hats on their heads, went determinedly, and somewhat hopelessly, about the town all day with muskets in their hands, attempting to suppress robbery and violence. The night patrol, by the light of oil lamps slung on chains across the intersections of the streets, addressed themselves to the nefarious activities of unruly blacks, or the vagabonds who took up nightly residence in the doorways of official buildings, or the burglars breaking into homes and stores and warehouses, paddling boats about in floods and scrambling onto the galleries of houses, where they came in through the upper windows after silverware, fine linens, money, whatever they could find. Slaves brought in from Saint Domingue incited ferment amongst local slaves, who, up till then, had been contented or resigned, and the town was wracked by constant agitation over rumors of attack by the wild men of Kentucky, who, resentful of how the Spanish played fast and loose with their rights to use the docks, were threatening to gather arms and descend the Mississippi River, thousands of them on their flatboats, to conquer New Orleans.

As if all this were not bad enough, the place was beset by hurricanes which knocked down the levee every fall, freeing the river to rush upon the town, lifting coffins from the ground, and sweeping every enterprise away. Plants were washed out of the soil, warehouses ripped off their foundations, construction projects ruined.

Emmeline and her wheezing husband would stack sandbags up against their doors, their goods and furniture on tabletops and counters, and haul their sacks of flour and sugar upstairs, where they would stack them along the four walls of Cassandra's tiny parlor. Then they would haul up their mattress, and their little songbird in its cage, and camp there while the house groaned on its foundations in the rushing waters. The first time this happened, Benedict went out onto the gallery that overlooked the street and saw a mule come sweeping past, floating on its back with its four legs stiffly in the air, and two dogs swimming like a pair of wild-eyed demons after it. Just beyond the house, the mule snagged in a tangle of wedged branches and swung there in the waters like a floating feast while the dogs climbed upon its body, ripping at the flesh. It made his heart sink, because it seemed to him some sort of omen.

And so it seemed to be. He had arrived in this unruly place with no idea of how to make a living and, having struggled mightily for more than ten years now, could see no prospect but to struggle still. Every sort of venture was available, and yet every venture fell away from him, like a rotting board laid over a morass. He would step out onto it, whistling and lighthearted, and suddenly be mired in debt again. He could not understand it.

He did not speak about his worries to Cassandra. She had no idea how close to bankruptcy they lived. He gave her lovely clothes and dressed his babies in the best, and hired a man to mend the roof when it was torn away, and ground his teeth above the bills, and worked and worked, but his dream of building a grand house for his wife remained a dream, as did his dream of building back the fortune he had lost.

But now a murmur in the crowd. The flag had reached the top, where it unfurled, wrapped itself around the pole, and clung there, as though gathering courage to embrace this new resentful populace, until the breeze reached out and jerked it to its duty. There was some shooting off of guns and someone—some roistering American—let out a cheer that fell into the gloomy silence like a stone dropped down a well.

Benedict felt a cheer rise from his belly in response, but he suppressed it, glancing at Cassandra. Her face was pale and her expression solemn. He wondered what she thought, she who had rejected everything American and made herself into a New Orleans Frenchwoman.

He had been astonished at the way she turned her back so steadfastly on her papa, though it meant the loss of her entire family. Though he should be the best of husbands to her, though he should one day make her wealthy, a grand lady about town, though he should love her till his soul ached and his every thought be to increase her happiness, he could not deserve such sacrifice. Several times he had tried to persuade her to write another letter to her papa, at least to send him her address, but she refused. "Papa has made me choose between himself and you," she said, "and I have chosen you." But still guilt nagged at him, and he longed to make a fortune he could carry home to her, as though by this means he could make up for her loss.

Cassandra felt him look at her. She glanced at him and smiled. The years had rounded her. Where once she had been slightly sharp of chin, slightly angular of shoulder, she now seemed somehow smoother in appearance, somehow more mellow. She had been accepted from the first as a Parisian émigrée, and it had seemed politic to let that impression stand, since neither the French nor the Spanish of New Orleans had any great affection for America. Now she had been French so long that when she saw the flag of the United States snap open on the square of the Cabildo, she felt a small jolt of surprise.

She looked up at the familiar flag against the bright white sky and seemed to see, behind it, like an old painting that has been covered by a new, a big stone house with a shady low verandah at the front, and Papa smoking his pipe in that slatted rocking chair he had bought from a tradesman down from Pennsylvania. She saw Mama come out the door and bend to speak to him. It was a moment only, two strangers in a dream, and Cassandra's heart had not yet started to constrict, tears had not yet started in her eyes, before she pushed the scene away and became once more resolutely French, as resentful as the rest at this betrayal of Napoleon's, selling them off like a pack of used-up slaves to the despised Americans.

Now some fellow, William Claiborne, climbed up on the gallery of the Cabildo, where he made a speech saying that America thought of them as brothers, but nobody took account of it since he spoke in English, which added insult to injury.

It turned out that this William Claiborne was their new governor. He was a tall man, of imposing stature, with heavy dark brows above intelligent brown eyes. His hair was also brown, almost a chestnut color. It was thinning on the top and he brushed it forward to disguise his pate. His nose was strong and his lips unbalanced, the top one being thin, while the bottom one was full. He stood very straight and, when he spoke, had an unnerving way of looking directly into his listeners' eyes, as though he read their thoughts inside their heads. This habit of his did nothing to endear him to the French of New Orleans, who always danced up to a matter sideways. The Americans built him a grand house by the levee, at the corner of the Rue Toulouse, and he was much resented.

Yet while the old residents of New Orleans schemed to place every obstacle in the path of their new governor, they were adept at the old game of holding in a tight embrace the one they schemed against, and so were politic enough to socialize with him. From the smiling faces lined along his dinner table every week, and the gracious bowing in his ballroom, no one would have thought he had an enemy in all the world. Sometimes Benedict thought he was the only one in New Orleans delighted to be made American.

Cassandra, for some mysteriously instinctive reason of her own, took against William Claiborne from the start and refused to have anything to do with him. When Benedict came to her with some invitation in his hand that would rub them up against him, she would flare her nostrils and declare they had better things to do. And so, while every two-faced Frenchman seemed able to turn his new nationality to a profit, being made American did nothing to advance Benedict's fortune. He was like the frogs his children caught and lined up in glass jars along the kitchen windowsill: he could see where he wanted to get to, but something invisible and hard prevented him.

So after all, he asked himself, as he had asked himself a hundred times before, had he made a mistake coming here to New Orleans? Should he have allowed Cassandra to persuade him? Perhaps he should have insisted they go to Kentucky. She had thrived here in this rude, unruly place. Why should she not in Kentucky? Then he would once more fall to calculating how to pay his debts off so he could start again.

And then William Claiborne's wife and little girl died of the yellow fever. Disaster that this was, Mrs. Claiborne's death turned fortune's smiling face on Benedict, since the woman who replaced her was Cassandra's dearest friend, Clarice Duralde.

Cassandra was now obliged to temper her aversion to the governor with a pinch of tolerance. Since Clarice had stood up for her at the baptism of her children, and her own, into the Catholic faith, there was nothing for it but that she stand up for Clarice at her wedding and be civil to her husband.

Clarice was a good wife for a governor—charming, gracious, beautiful, with periwinkle eyes, a fair complexion, and hair the soft gold color of sand upon a beach. With a portion of her papa's great wealth settled on her, she could entertain as lavishly as she had a fancy to without ever asking for a penny from her husband. Cassandra's intimacy with her made it natural that Benedict and Mr. Claiborne should be often thrown into each other's company.

Before long the two men were friends and, as though the universe had shifted on its axis, Benedict found himself sought after in the town. Would he condescend to dine, to drink a glass of gin, of port, a cup of coffee, to introduce, to offer an opinion on, to give a small word of advice? When he appeared at café, or at courthouse, or in the hallway of some other public building, younger men buzzed at his back, jostling for advice on this business opportunity or that, or perhaps they wanted him to underwrite some business venture for them, while others, more mature men with experience and money, came hail-fellow to slap him on the back and broach the prospect of a partnership in some new enterprise. Before long, he became the sort of man who sat with other men who looked like him, deliberating around tables in important rooms, the sort of man whose opinion was respected.

Kentucky flew out of his mind. He bought land, expanded to construction, loaned his profits at a good return, and began to think about himself as wealthy. He did not say the word, though, for fear that saying it aloud would bring all his enterprises tumbling down around his ears, but he ceased to lie awake at night watching the mosquitoes massing, like an army planning an invasion, on the outside of the muslin net above the bed, worrying his head about bills and debts and payments to be made. He forgot financial worries altogether and was prolific in his generosity. He produced a brand-new wedding ring to replace the humble one Cassandra once wore, a wide gold band with a glittering diamond set flush into the gold. "For you," he said, and slipped it on her finger. "Swear that you will never take it off, not even if it means my death." And she swore easily, laughing at his melodrama, and kissed him on the mouth. The world sang all about him. He beamed upon his family.

Even his knee ceased to bother him every minute of the day. He bought himself a new cane, a handsome thing of polished ebony with a silver tip and ornate silver head. He swaggered on it, brandished it, used it to point at maps and charts, and, as time went by, found that sometimes he forgot to lean on it, but simply tapped it along the ground as though it were nothing but an affectation. Those who did not know the truth assumed he had sustained an injury in battle. Since he said nothing to relieve them of this belief, he came to be regarded as a hero of the American war for independence. Sometimes, alone with Cassandra, he laughed and said he was no more a charlatan than Monsieur Lafayette, whom he considered to have been a grand rogue.

He became less self-conscious about making love, sometimes in the heat of it forgetting he ever had an injury, forgot, too, how he used to imagine that Cassandra gazed across his shoulder in the act as though she looked for someone else. He even found that he could dance again, awkwardly, but still, he danced.

One day he came home to Cassandra and led her to the parlor, where he invited her to sit, and sat down across from her, keeping his face solemn.

"Cassie, I have something important to discuss with you."

She did not answer, just sat looking at him, an intense expression on her face.

"If you could have anything your heart desires, what would it be?"

A distressed look came into her eyes, as though he had told her he suddenly had fallen into bankruptcy, but then she jumped up from her chair and flung herself onto his lap, scolding him and laughing.

"So," he said, "tell me what you want. Anything at all."

She looked about her. "I would like a grand house at last, with a wing for the children and a courtyard with a fountain and a little private gallery above it, and a wide gallery above the street with a fancy iron balustrade and potted trees and . . . oh, I do not know what else."

"Then let me tell you this. The house next door is going up for sale—"

"Oh, but it's too small."

"Wait, hear me out. If I should buy it, we could tear both houses down and build ourselves a grand one."

"Tear down? But what about the Tournelles' bakery? I could not throw Emmeline out on the street."

"Then we'll build around it."

"Where would we live while this grand house was being built?"

He laughed. "So many questions, but I've thought about that too. You and the children will go upriver to stay with friends and I will stay in a boardinghouse and supervise."

Cassandra scrambled to her feet. "But I must find some paper. We must make a drawing."

And so the planning was begun, and then the building, Benedict going every day to suggest an improvement here, an added something there, a better grade of wood for this, a more expensive marble tile for that, and before long he found himself wandering through the completed rooms of an even finer house than he had dreamed about. As soon as the last tile was set, the last paint dried, he moved his family into it, with the Tournelles undisturbed in the bakery below.

One day, smoking an after-supper pipe with William Claiborne, Benedict found himself offering the governor advice on how to straighten out the vagaries and perplexities of land ownership and transfer. Who owned what was a matter of considerable confusion at the time. Many papers had gone missing with the Spanish, never to be found again, and there were claims to be considered, and counterclaims, surveys to be done, land grants and concessions to be investigated, abstracts and titles to be prepared. Mr. Claiborne fretted over it. He needed someone he could trust, he said, someone willing to apply his mind to straightening the whole mess out. Benedict advanced a name, and then another, but no, neither would do. Then how about . . . ? Or how about . . . ? The two men spent the evening weighing the pros and cons of each suggestion, but by the time Benedict rose to leave, Mr. Claiborne had not settled on a candidate. He set his pipe down and rose to see his friend out, still worrying his head as the two of them walked down the passageway. When they were almost at the door, he made a sound of exclamation, and reaching out his hand, set it on Benedict's

shoulder—the very man! Would he consider a position as commissioner of lands? He would write a letter recommending him to
Washington that very day.

Benedict did not hesitate. What was to be lost? And he discovered that he had a head for matters of this sort. In politics and government he was a great success.

Next year, he was appointed notary public and justice of the
peace. And his ambition rose—he had his eye on registrar of
lands—and with it rose responsibility. These days he worried about
his duties day and night, was overburdened with much paperwork,
and frequently called away to settle cases in distant parishes, where
he would be delayed by disputatious people, dubious claims, elusive
records, uncooperative weather.

Sometimes Cassandra worried about highwaymen and river
pirates, but then she would shake her head and reprimand herself
and think of pleasant things: her comfortable life, the way the
money flowed as though conjured from the air, how her allowance
grew larger all the time so that now she could buy anything
she liked—the best musicians for the party she would give next
week, the silver soup tureen and ladle, the new green velvet cape
with the embroidered peacock on the train, books with color
plates to entertain the children.

Sometimes when Benedict was out of town, early in the morning before the children were awake, she would go out to the gallery
above the street and sit there with a cup of coffee in her hand, and
rock. She did not think or plan or dream or wonder or imagine, just
sat there with the gentle motion of the chair beneath her and the
warm sensation of the cup between her hands, noises of the waking
street below—voices, footsteps, rattling of carts and buggies, clatter and thud of footsteps, a laugh, a small child's wail, a dog's bark,
the sweet damp smell of mold.

From the bakery below, she would hear Emmeline calling to her
husband about some task—the heating or cooling of the ovens, a
delivery to be made—and smell the yeasty smell of pastry, the
sweetness of damp icing sugar, rising on the air. Then she would
look up at the sky, half-silver with a petticoat of salmon, and
thank God for her luxurious life, and for her healthy family.

30

*A*ND THEN, AS THOUGH HER GRATITUDE had made him notice her, God decided that she had too much. It happened in the summer, the time of year when New Orleans was beset by armies of insects—gnats, tiny biting things, dancing in clouds above every patch of damp across the city, sluggish, heavy-bellied blowflies, little darting stinging flies, beetles with wing casings so hard they could be cracked only with a stone or flatiron, insects with splayed legs and sticky feet, a sort of jumping black cricket, enormous moths and tiny moths and every size of moth between, palmetto bugs the size of mice.

In the evenings, clouds of furious mosquitoes came howling up out of the cypress swamps like bands of vengeful Indians, and although Mattie draped muslin across all the windows, and slung muslin tents above the beds, they could not be kept out. They crept under doors or bombarded the muslin at the windows, breaking in around the edges to fling themselves into the candles or the lard oil lamps. Mattie's boys, Seth and Syphorian, waged a constant war against invasion by these creatures, but every morning the spent lamps were set about with tiny bodies, burned or stuck onto the melted wax, some still half-alive, waving their tiny wicked legs.

As the heat and dampness of the air intensified, robbing man and beast of energy, the entire city fell asleep just after noon and slept till almost four. Even the sounds of birds and insects ceased at this time of the day, and dogs flopped down on their backs in whatever shade they could discover, sleeping with their legs splayed and their pale hairless bellies exposed to catch what breeze might be around. The stench of human waste and rotting vegetation filled the air.

It had become Cassandra's custom to take her children off to the country during these dreadfully hot months, by this means avoiding not only the sickly season but hurricanes as well, but this year she had stayed in town because the house was being redecorated and she wanted to be there to supervise. Benedict was once more out of town and she planned to have all the wallpaper torn down and replaced, the draperies as well, so she could surprise him.

She was so taken up by this project that at first she barely paid attention to what was going on around her and it was not until the first cemetery carts began to rattle in the streets that she started from her trance and swept her children up and made departure for the country.

By then tar fires had been lit at every corner and the city choked with smoke and thundered with cannon being fired across the swamps in an effort to dispel the deadly vapors. White flags fluttered on the doors where death had struck and the roads were clogged with people fleeing out of town, taking with them carts and carriages and wagons loaded up with household goods. Long lines stood at the city's exits, where inspectors searched for mattresses and pillows, hauling off any they found to be burned or tipped into the river, because they might be carrying the miasma of the yellow fever in the air between their feathers.

Cassandra and her children traveled lightly—they had been through this before—but at every turn they were held up by less experienced travelers. By the time they reached the clean air of the countryside, it was too late. Anne was already sick. At first

Cassandra thought she would recover, since she went on for a week with only a mild fever and a slight headache but no vomiting. She sent off for a doctor but he came too late. She sent a messenger for Benedict, who came at once, arriving late one afternoon. He rushed into the house, but no sooner was he at Anne's bedside than she worsened suddenly. Her forehead burned, and she began to toss about the bed and scream.

By midnight she was sunk down senseless and in that state lasted until morning, when her spirit left her body with such gentleness that although Cassandra had her in her arms she did not realize it until she started to go cold.

Benedict, who had been standing at the window, looking at the moonlight on the sugarcane, heard Cassandra gasp. He came back to the bed and knelt as he had knelt beside his mother all those years ago in France. He kissed Anne's lips and reached to take Cassandra's hand, but she clung fiercely to her daughter.

They stayed like that, with Anne's body in between them. Benedict fell asleep with his face against the bedding, but Cassandra did not sleep. All night she lay with her daughter in her arms and struggled with her soul. So this was love, she thought, a man and woman together in a room watching over their dead daughter, and bitterness rose up to choke her.

Toward morning, it came into her head that she would bury Anne beneath a tree, the way Mama had buried her dead infants beneath a giant oak. She had no oak, but she had a piece of land where she could make a garden at the edge of town. Benedict had secured it some years ago as part of an effort to beautify the flood-prone area abutting the city's fortifications. He had given Cassandra the duty of developing the place, but she had not been delighted with the project and did no more than hire a colored man, the half-Spanish son of a local voodoo healer, to be the gardener, directing him to tidy up the lot and build a levee round the edge, and put in some trees, whatever he thought suitable.

A month later, this gardener, Fernando, appeared at the doorway of the kitchen, cap in hand, looking up at her and smiling, inquiring after wages, and so Cassandra settled on him a monthly wage and an allowance for the garden's cultivation and let the matter slip out of her mind. She had not been near the place since then, but now she felt the notion of making a memorial for her dead daughter take hold of her imagination.

Benedict had feared Cassandra would go mad with grief—he felt half-mad himself—but she did not. She had Anne's body carried back to New Orleans, where she ordered a white tomb carved with flowers on the top and angels on each end, spreading out protective wings along the sides. Then she set out to survey her land.

The city's old fortifications were now in ruins, but a number of gardens flourished in the area, most of them miniature market gardens lined with rows of vegetables and herbs. She went on past them and before long came to a lot where someone had taken the notion to make a decorative park.

Along the sides grew high bamboos with moonvine and morning glory and honeysuckle growing in a riot over them. Crepe myrtles and azaleas and hibiscus and mimosa flourished at the front, and wisteria on a latticed arch grew above a small white picket gate. Beyond the gate, a path surfaced with ground-up oyster shells wound off into the tumultuous scent of flowers.

Cassandra stood before it, tears starting in her eyes—this was what she wanted, exactly this, for Anne. She set her hand against the gate and pushed it open—no one was about—and started down the path.

And then a voice behind her and she turned. A colored man stood there, cap in hand. "Madame," he said.

It was Fernando. He seemed quite unsurprised, smiling up at her as though he had been expecting her that day.

"I will show Madame around?"

He led her along curving paths through banks of pink and white camellias, clumps of giant purple violets, columbines and callas, lady's slippers, feathery parkinsonia, and other flowers she had never seen before. Scarlet and purple and yellow trumpet vines trailed over trellises, and pink and yellow water lilies floated on a pond, where bright red-orange carp swam back and forth.

At the center of the garden Fernando had set a weeping willow.

"A tree that loves the wet, Madame," he said, but it seemed to Cassandra that, somehow, he had known, somehow he had looked ahead and seen the day when she would need a garden with a willow tree to weep above her daughter. Did this man have second sight?

She had a pretty sign made, ANNE'S GARDEN, which she hung above the gate, and had Anne's tomb installed beneath the willow, and beside it, a matching white stone bench with flowers around the edges of the seat and around the curving claw-foot legs. When Benedict saw the single bench, he understood the way Cassandra's grief would go. Anne was to be her private sorrow, this garden her place of private mourning. She had no wish for company, not even his. It grieved him, but there was nothing he could do but give comfort to his other children, distract himself with people's squabbles over property, and wait for her to work her sorrow through.

While Cassandra had been busy with the planning and construction of her child's memorial, loss did not overwhelm her, but when it was done, the stone bench set in place beside it, and she sat beside her daughter in the comfort and the dreadfulness of solitude, she found she could not mourn, she could not pray, could not offer God a word of thanks for the five children she had left, could not even pity Benedict.

Something had gone wrong with her heart. Something had gone wrong with it. It had become a void, a deep, dark, sucking emptiness through which she tumbled headlong every day. If she reached the bottom she would vanish, she knew that she would vanish.

She could not speak of this to Benedict. She could not find the words to make him understand. And when she spoke of emptiness to her confessor he said that God would fill it, but He did not.

Day after day she sat beside Anne's tomb, eyes dry, hands folded in her lap, and fell and fell. Night after night she fell into the dark. She could not eat, or sleep, or understand the words her children spoke to her, or bear for Benedict to touch her, as though Anne's death had killed the part of her that had desired him. She grew gaunt and thin and her eyes took on a hollow, staring look. Doctor Masderall was called. He shook his head. He said think about your children. Think about your husband. He prescribed a physic. Suggested that she take a little brandy with her tea. Spoke sternly. Reprimanded. Recommended that she have another child.

As time went by, the falling stopped, and now Cassandra felt as though she were suspended. Winter came. The weather took on a damp chill. She wrapped herself in a hooded woolen cape and came every day to sit beside Anne's tomb. It seemed to her that she was waiting; for what, she did not know. She felt as though her life till now in New Orleans had been a dream that one day she would wake from.

Spring came, and with it came the rains. The streets turned into quagmires and the city was beset with frogs which came up out of the waters like one of Moses' plagues, hopping into every open doorway. Cassandra pulled on high boots, unfurled a giant black umbrella, and went to sit beside Anne's tomb. Soon daffodils and tulips sprang up along the paths, blossoms hung on every tree and bush, the air was once more full of sweetness and so thick with pollen that the whole place had a yellow glow. When it rained, pollen washed up against the tomb's white pedestal like golden spume left behind by waves receding from a beach.

One day, above Cassandra on a branch, a bird began to scold. She looked up and a nest was there, the mother bird perched beside it on a twig, looking down at her and making her remarks. For a while she bounced her little reddish body on the twig and threatened, and then she flew away.

A strange emotion took Cassandra, a restlessness, a yearning, an excitement, the sensation of something momentous about to happen. She jumped up and looked about, but no one was there. She went out to the street. No one there either. But there was something, someone, somewhere. She straightened up her skirts and set off into the city.

As she had craved solitude, Cassandra now craved company. She threw herself into activities, appearing at friends' houses unannounced, demanding tea and conversation, demanding that they come to supper tomorrow or next week, arranging dinner parties, dances, concerts, taking her children on expeditions to the circus, Benedict to the opera or the theater, where he sat smiling, nodding to acquaintances, hoping that Cassandra would soon let him make love to her again.

But although Cassandra's surface sparkled, underneath it was a feverish restlessness that drove her out into the city every day. Whereas before she had reeled from one day to the next, consumed with grief, now she walked and walked about the streets in agitation, looking for she knew not what.

She adventured everywhere, into the poor areas and the free colored areas, out beyond the ruined city wall into the marshy countryside, where water birds flapped up in a panic and flew off at her approach. If she stood very still, they would come back, one after the other skidding onto the surface of the water like skaters dropped out of the sky. They would tuck their legs up and their heads into the water, or stand on long thin legs, poking in the weeds and mud with long thin beaks. She envied them. To fly like that!

Then she would turn and go back through the city's center, past the rows of galleries above, the businesses below, where bootsellers and booksellers and sellers of madras and silks and laces pulled at her sleeve to tempt her to a purchase, on into the rowdy areas of town, the barbershops and cockpits, shooting galleries and gin houses, where cutthroat characters and soldiers drank and caroused, where foreign sailors tumbled in and out, singing in the streets and calling after her, men of every color and complexion, Americans as well, Kaintocks, Tennesseans, men from Mississippi and Ohio, every sort of northern trader come down the river on their barges and their flatboats to wrangle over sales of furs and logs and cotton and tobacco. They were a rough lot, big unkempt men with bold eyes and loud voices, who spat tobacco juice as though their insides were made of the stuff. They hung about the gaming halls and saloons and drank hard and brawled and whored and roared about the streets and beat each other up and raised unshirted hell all over town, and later bellowed in the calaboose when they were slung there for a cooling off. Yet Cassandra never came to any misadventure. No one ever threatened her. Perhaps it was because the intense concentration of her gaze gave her an air of self-containment.

On toward the wharves, past the slave markets, with their pervading smell of human waste and lye, where Negroes decked out in blue suits and flowered dresses paraded up and down before the pens, looking boldly at her, assessing her among themselves as a potential buyer, laughing at some underhand remark, and, when a trader came with whip in hand, dropping their heads to stand like sycophants, their eyes swinging with the swinging of her skirts.

The wharves she loved, where New Orleans shouted and bustled with activity. She loved the smell of it, the sound of ropes spun, the rattling of rigging against mast, the shouting and cursing of the flatboatmen, the hypnotic, dirge-like singing of slaves unloading bales of cotton. People of every race crowding up against one another, from Englishmen in silk top hats to half-naked Indians with tribal markings on their faces. And in the evening the wind came rolling up the river and the sun flamed low down in the sky.

31

$\mathcal{T}$HROUGHOUT HER LONG DEPRESSION, Cassandra's friends had done their best to comfort her, to interest her in the world again. Clarice tried constantly to trap her into company, a tea party, a shopping expedition, a visit to a friend. Emmeline took on the supervision of her family's meals, arriving at the door each morning with her Negro boy, Methuselah, bearing bread and cakes, poking about in Mattie's pots of stew, sprinkling rosemary onto her roasts, advising her on dishes that might tempt Cassandra's palate.

She insisted Benedict eat eggs each morning to fortify his constitution, would not allow him port, and sent him off to the Land Office with a pocketful of nuts or raisins or some hard sweetmeat wrapped in paper slicked with butter. She cosseted and nagged him, listened to his worries at the office, made sure Mattie darned the socks he took on expeditions out of town, and reassured him he must go, it was all right, he must see about his business.

One morning Cassandra was sitting with Clarice in her little parlor at the Government House, helping plan an entertainment. Between them they were drawing up an invitation list and menu while they criticized the local poets and musicians. It was a fine day and the window was thrown up, letting in the rattling of cart wheels, rumbling of rolled barrels, the hiss of furling and unfurling sails, the slightly rotten smell.

Mr. Claiborne joined them. He greeted Cassandra and kissed Clarice, who was far along with her first child. Then, with a black frown on his face, he went over to the window, where he stood with his hands beneath his coattails, looking out across the harbor.

"What ails you, William?" said Clarice.

He grunted. "Nothing, damn his eyes!" he said, leaning out the window to get a better view of whatever he was looking at.

"Damn *whose* eyes?"

"That blackguard Pierre Lafitte."

Cassandra, busy with her list, had been paying no attention to their conversation, but now her head jerked up. "Lafitte? You can't mean Pierre de la Fitte?"

"I know him only as Lafitte."

"He has a brother Jean?"

William turned toward her with an odd look on his face. "What are these men to you, Cassandra?"

Something in his eyes made Cassandra wary. "It's nothing. I knew a Jean de la Fitte in France. He said he had a brother Pierre."

"If these are the same fellows, I advise you to forget your old acquaintance."

"Forget? Why, pray?" She felt herself begin to flush with irritation and turned her head down, pretending to be busy with her list.

William ranged himself in front of her. She could see his shoes and the way his stockings sagged a little at the ankle.

"Now, William, there's no need," Clarice said in a placating voice.

"These banditti that infest our coasts—"

Cassandra's breath came sharp. She wrote *Jean* on her list, and crossed it out.

"Now, William," said Clarice.

He left then, and Clarice made a little moue and laughed. "You've managed to rile William up again. You have a talent for it."

. . .

Cassandra left Clarice's house that day feeling dizzy and electric. So this was it. This was what she had been searching for. She seemed to float along the street, as though her senses all pulsed out, away from her, ranging out across the city. Jean was here, in New Orleans, yes, he was out there somewhere.

She wanted to climb up on a roof and shout, "Jean! Where are you, Jean?" She must be mad. She had an inflammation of the brain. It had been fifteen years since she had seen him. He could be anywhere, or dead. Pierre Lafitte was just some other person not his relative. And yet some instinct told her he was close. To react so to the mention of his name!

She told herself she must calm down, she must go home; no, she would go and sit with Anne and let the garden soothe her. But when she got there she could not sit still. As though some sealed container in her mind had cracked, Jean's presence poured into her consciousness. Once more she walked the streets of Paris at his side. Once more she sat and waited for him in that miserable, dying room. Once more she flung her arms around his neck. She thought about the day Maman had died, the day that Anne was born. She felt again the panic that had risen when her milk refused to come, felt Anne's lips against her breast, the tingling sensation as the milk came down.

But then the memory of that awful night when Jean had grieved for his papa came flooding back, and she realized it was not Anne's lips she felt, but Jean's. She blushed and looked around, as though she would find him watching her. If he could just be here. If she could talk with him. They used to talk of anything at all, had always understood each other. They had been dear and intimate, like a brother and a sister. If she could just set her head upon his breast and weep and talk to him again, the way she had when she had been so lonely there in France, this desolation in her soul would go away.

So was she mad? Was this what grief had done—conjured up a ghost to mock at her? No, this was no sudden thing. She realized now what she had not before: this was why she had persuaded Benedict to come to New Orleans. She had not known it then, and since had been so preoccupied with life it had not risen to her consciousness. Now, though, she understood that ever since that day he kissed her on the dock in France and swore that they would meet again, Jean had been anchored just outside her mind.

He was in her head now all the time, and on her tongue. She wanted to say his name aloud, to ask after him about the town, among her friends, ask Benedict if he had heard some news of him, and yet she never said his name. Walking in the streets, or going about her duties in the house, or visiting a friend, or at the theater or an entertainment, she felt his presence every day. When the doorbell rang, or when she came into a room, she expected him. Every time she turned her head she felt he would be there. It was not that she said to herself, "Today I shall see him," or "I must wear my best gown today so I shall look my best for him." It was more an awareness, like a dream, the way a bereaved mother listens all the time for her lost child, hearing her return in every clatter on the stair, in every child's laugh on the street, catching her breath at half-seen strangers, hurrying after them, only to be disappointed.

It thrilled her, this sensation of being linked to someone outside her family and the circle of her friends, as though a line had been tossed between herself and Jean, like a grappling hook tossed aboard its quarry by a pirate ship. Every day she could feel him coming closer, hauling in the line. One day, she knew, he would fetch up beside her.

It had been a clear, warm day, one of those magic days New Orleans sometimes offers up. The air shimmered with a crystal clarity, birds sang in the courtyard. The bustle of the city—horses' hooves on stones, the rattling of cart wheels, fragments of foreign conversation floating from the street, a laugh, a shout—all sounded like a distant happiness.

Since early morning, Cassandra had been busy planning a new gown for Colegate's birthday, looking through designs and drawings, consulting with the seamstress over strips of fabric and samples of fine lace. Colegate's friend Michèle Donaldson had spent the day with them. Her mother had died in last year's yellow fever epidemic and Cassandra had agreed to see to gowns for both the girls. Juliana and Charcilla danced excitedly about the place, teasing Colegate about Harold, Michèle's older brother, who was to lead her in for supper at the party. They said he had an eye for her, and Cassandra did not doubt Colegate returned his affections since she blushed so hard. Benedict had spoken approvingly of such a match and when Cassandra protested that Colegate was too young too marry, he had laughed at her, saying she was a fine one to complain.

When at last they had settled on design and fabric, Michèle bore Colegate off, with Charcilla and Juliana trailing on behind. They were to dine together at the Donaldsons' and attend the theater with a group of friends. It was a great treat for the little girls. Mary's nurse brought in her charge to kiss Mama good night before she bore her off to bed. Young Benedict was off at school, since the brothers required their pupils to live like monks all week so they could exert a stronger influence on their morals.

Benedict had gone off to Attacapas County to see about Judge Nichols, who was rumored to have been practicing extortion. No straight answers were forthcoming from the man by mail and so Benedict had set out prepared to threaten him with the same law he was appointed to uphold. Before he left, he had sent a letter to Mr. Albert Gallatin, who was secretary of state in Washington, applying for the position of Louisiana's registrar of lands. It would be a grand promotion and Cassandra waited every day for news.

Left alone, she sat running the fine stuffs through her fingers, thinking of her wedding day. She had never told Colegate about that impetuous ride to Philadelphia, or about the late-night search for a priest willing to marry a pair of rain-bedraggled strangers. As far as Colegate was concerned, her mother had always been what she was now, a model of domestic respectability. Cassandra felt a tiny sadness touch her heart. How little her children knew of her.

A breeze stirred the curtains. She set aside the samples of finery and, slipping on some sturdy shoes, went downstairs to walk. She went toward the docks, planning to climb up on the levee and watch the sun go down. Already she could smell the putrefying mud and river water, the fish fried up in batter, the sweet sharp scent of pipe tobacco.

She found the place in an uproar. A cargo of hogs had been unloaded and the stevedores, in herding them along the levee, had lost one of the beasts, which had run into a stack of sugar barrels and brought them tumbling down. Then it had bolted off into an open-fronted store and wedged itself under the table where the trader's wares were piled—a load of fancy belt buckles and buttons— and now did not seem to know which foot to put in front, agitating back and forth, trying to throw this strange obstruction off its back. Each time the hog moved, the whole load shifted with it, threatening to tumble everything onto the ground. The trader, a German in a pair of tight short leather pants, jumped about excit- edly, cursing and whacking the creature on its broad pink rump so that it squealed and struggled all the more. A crowd had gathered and there was much laughter and shouting of advice.

Cassandra stopped to watch, and when the owners of the hog had managed to retrieve it by roping it about the hind legs so that it collapsed and was hauled out without one buckle upset or any of the jars of buttons overturned, the crowd let out a cheer and every- body turned to go about their business.

She had been so distracted by the affair that when someone fell in step beside her, she barely noticed it. It was not until she came out of the crowd that she realized she had a companion. Still, she did not so much as turn to look at him, it seemed such a natural occurrence.

For a time they walked together silently, then, "You have found Pierre?" she asked.

"I have," he said, and paused. "I have your locket still."

She stopped and looked up into his face. He was the same, a little older, with side whiskers, but the same, and smiling down at her with the same comfortable familiarity.

"My locket?"

"Your locket, yes." And folding down the collar of his shirt, he drew out Benedict's ivory locket on its crimson riband and clicked it open, holding Cassandra's portrait up beside her face. "You look the same as you did fourteen years, eleven months, and fifteen days ago."

She wanted to take him in her arms and kiss him but they had a hundred and more people on the wharf for audience.

32

*A*S EASILY AS THOUGH THEY HAD NEVER been apart, Jean slipped back into Cassandra's life. They saw each other every day. It was a simple matter for him to slip in unremarked through the side gate after the children were in bed, their nursemaids with them, and Mattie and her boys gone off to their little house beyond the far wall of the courtyard.

She delighted in having him completely to herself, like a secret she could savor before she had to share it. When Benedict returned, she intended to produce him with a flourish, imagining the great smile that would break open on his face, the hand held out, the warm embrace, their old friend once more drawn into the family.

Several times she told Jean of some plan she had, a little celebration. She would prepare a special dinner. Benedict would sit down and inquire about the extra place set at the table. Cassandra would smile mysteriously. When everyone was settled and the napkins set in laps, the wine poured into glasses, she would nod to Mattie to fill the glass before the empty seat. Benedict would look up with inquiring eyes and Cassandra would nod again to Mattie, who would vanish from the room. A murmur, and the sound of footsteps in the passageway, and then . . .

Jean laughed easily at her but, "No," he said, "let me do it my way. Let me bide my time. Let us enjoy each other for a while and then, when the time is ripe, you will perform your little trick of magic."

She wondered at this hesitancy. Jean was not a man anybody would have called retiring. If anything, he had grown up flamboyant, with a hold step and a bold eye, though a gracious and disarming manner. Sometimes, when he did not observe her, Cassandra would admire him. How sleek and beautiful he had become. How arrow-straight and slim of hip, with broad strong shoulders and the lean hard body of a man accustomed to hard work and temperance. Unlike his brother Pierre, who, he told her, had a penchant for hard drinking and luxurious dining, he drank no rum or whiskey and ate sparingly. Pierre, he said, had what he called "a very handsome lady" by the name of Adelaide, a Spanish woman born in Saint Domingue, and a little son, also named Pierre. Jean had no wife and when Cassandra suggested that perhaps he had "a very handsome lady" too, he denied it. She believed him, though she did not know why. The women of the world must all have lost their minds to let someone such as he slip through their fingers.

One thing marred her easiness with Jean—that he did not ask her about Anne. Cassandra did not mention her, waiting for his question, but it did not come. And so one evening she asked if he would like to walk, and led him to Anne's garden, through the gate and down the winding path.

Fernando was kneeling by Anne's tomb, pulling out some weeds. He rose, smacking his cap across his knees. "Madame," he said. "Monsieur Lafitte." And vanished off toward the gate.

"You know Fernando, Jean?"

He bowed his head before the tomb and crossed himself, and then reached out and with his fingertip traced the carved letters of Anne's name.

"You have been here before? How did you know?"

He turned and took her hands, folding them between his own. "I feel that I have lost a daughter too, Cassandra."

That evening they did not talk at all, but sat together silently, and Cassandra felt between them that intimate communication which marks the relationship of old and trusted friends. She thought about that dreadful night in Paris when she had soothed his grief, and it seemed to her that it had bound the two of them together in a way unlike that in which she and Benedict were bound. Jean was a part of her, not like a husband, to whom she must, albeit lovingly, defer, but like an extension of herself, an equal.

Benedict had been in Attacapas County almost four weeks now. It was late one night and the children all asleep, the servants gone off to their beds. Jean and Cassandra were sitting together in the dim lamplight of the parlor, entertaining each other with small gossip of what had happened in their lives that day. He was telling her a story about a delivery of goods he had received from Barataria. He did not mention smugglers—it was assumed. The whole town did slippery business with the gentlemen of Barataria. That Jean also had connections of this sort was, to Cassandra, unremarkable.

They were laughing over some aspect of the tale when a knock sounded at the door. Still laughing, Cassandra went out to answer it and found, standing with a letter in his hand, Mr. Brown, the district attorney.

"Come in," she said. "I have a friend with me. Here, let me introduce you."

They had come in through the parlor door, Cassandra with one hand out to make the introduction, when Mr. Brown froze in his tracks.

"Lafitte?" he said.

"You know each other, then?"

Jean had risen on their entrance and Cassandra noticed he had taken up a shepherdess figurine, holding it as though he had just been examining the thing. "Why, Sir, delighted," he said to Mr. Brown and, freeing his right hand by transferring the figurine into his left, held out a hand in greeting.

Mr. Brown did not respond. Jean's hand hovered in the air and then, smooth as milk, settled underneath his left, as though to protect the shepherdess from falling. He set the little lady on the table.

"I am delighted, Madame van Pradelles," he said, "that you are happy with your purchase. As soon as I lay my hand on the other of the pair I will have it brought to you." And with that he swept his hat up, bowed, first to Cassandra and then more formally to Mr. Brown, and he was gone.

Cassandra was confused, and yet something told her she must cooperate in Jean's charade. "Ah, yes," she said to Mr. Brown. "A lovely trinket. Monsieur Lafitte has a magic touch with finding objets d'art."

Mr. Brown had drawn his brows together and seemed about to make some inquiry. Whatever it was, Cassandra knew she wanted neither to hear it or to answer it.

"But, Sir," she said, "I keep you from the purpose of your visit."

He shook his head and blinked, as though he had just awakened from a dream, or had seen a vision which had now evaporated. "Madame," he said, holding out the letter, "I have this for your husband, from Mr. Albert Gallatin in Washington."

It was the announcement of Benedict's promotion to registrar of lands. Cassandra clapped her hands and thanked Mr. Brown for his thoughtfulness in coming to notify her so promptly.

"Not only that, Madame, but I have news of your husband, who has sent word he has departed Attacapas County and will arrive home shortly."

Cassandra retired to bed that night so delighted with both pieces of news that Mr. Brown's peculiar behavior, and Jean's as well, went clear out of her head. The following morning she received a note from William Claiborne asking her to come at once. Its tone was urgent, in fact it seemed more summons than request. It worried her, since Clarice was not yet ready to deliver. Surely she had not miscarried? She applied a shawl and bonnet and was at the Government House within minutes.

"Is it Clarice?" she demanded of the Negro houseboy who opened up the door.

He did not answer, which made Cassandra's heart sink with

foreboding, but showed her directly into William's private office, and closed the door behind her.

William half rose from behind the desk and, without so much as a greeting or an offer of refreshment, waved her to a chair and took his seat again. He said nothing, just looked at her across the papers piled along the front edge of the desk, his pen still in his hand and a severe expression on his face.

All this increased Cassandra's agitation. She stared at him, expecting some awful announcement. Clarice dead? Dear God, surely not!

"I've had disturbing news," he said, "from Mr. Brown."

Not Clarice then. It was Benedict. A river pirate? Some marauding highwayman? Murdered in a slave uprising? This was why Mr. Brown had been so uncomfortable and odd in his behavior. He had known of this disaster but was afraid to speak. She sat waiting for William to continue, her bottom lip caught in her teeth.

"Mr. Brown tells me . . ." He coughed.

"It's all right, William, go on. I know how to be brave."

He gave her an odd look. "I think bravery is not the issue here, Madame, but rather decency."

"Decency? I do not understand. I thought you had some distressing news of Benedict."

"*Of* Benedict, or *for* him?"

"You speak in riddles, Sir. I do not understand."

"Then I'll be plain. Mr. Brown informs me that you entertained last night."

"And so he did not feel it delicate to speak?"

"On the contrary, he felt it not his place. It is for a husband to correct his wife, but since your husband is not here—"

She cut him off. "Correct? What is this *correct*? You say you will be plain, yet every word becomes more mystifying."

"Madame, if you'll kindly let me speak."

"Sir, I—"

"Be silent." He looked so fiercely at her that she shut her mouth. "I've been informed that Monsieur Jean Lafitte was a visitor at your house last night. And that you were alone. That it was late."

He stopped, looking meaningfully at her. She frowned and leaned forward in her chair. He jerked his hand. "We are not children here."

"Sir," Cassandra said, "I do most earnestly resent your tone, not only that, your accusation, and on top of that, your presumption in calling me here today to reprimand me for some imagined impropriety. Let me make it very clear, Sir, that I am no responsibility of yours."

She rose, straightening her skirt, and fixed him with a haughty look, although she would have preferred to have reached out and wrung his irritating neck. "I did not understand, Sir, that you were such a stiff-necked, straitlaced, moralistic, self-righteous, judgmental, interfering . . . Sir, you are—you are . . . I am affronted, insulted, injured, offended. Why, if I were a man I would—"

"Cassandra, sit. Sit down. I don't mean to accuse you or insult you. Come, calm yourself." He rose and came out from behind the desk, looking about distractedly. "Will you have some tea? A little whiskey, then? A cordial?" He took her by the elbow. "Please, sit down again."

She shook him off and stood stiffly, glaring at him.

"There, there, come, come," he said. "Let me explain."

"I think you owe it to me."

He went to the window and stood with his back to her and his shoulders set in a concentrating attitude, as though he were gathering his sentences. When he turned back, his color, which had fled, had resumed its normal shade, and his breathing, which had heightened, was now imperceptible.

"Cassandra, as you well know, the marshes about New Orleans, especially the area of Barataria, crawl with low humanity. I don't mean the fishermen, or the boatbuilders and farmers, the Acadians, but those persons who involve themselves with smuggling and piracy and that lowest of activities, the importation of raw Negro slaves, an activity to which I mean to put an end. This company of men grows larger and more violent, more brazen every day. Pirates menace the seas around our shores and seize not only Spanish ships but ships of every nation, American as well. They slaughter passengers and sailors and seize their cargoes, which they haul to Barataria, from there to sell them to the citizens of New Orleans, and others up and down the river. You know of this, Cassandra. All New Orleans knows it. Good men close their eyes to the wickedness of it every day in order to bring home some piece of trumpery, or to secure some strong new back for cutting sugarcane. The laws are mocked at. I am mocked at too, which I can bear, but not the mockery of law, which is more important. If the law is not followed we'll soon be living in a state of mayhem. We'll be taken over by some pirate king and all of us forced to go about the place in a gold earring and a striped head rag, settling our differences with daggers.

"And now, you, *you*, Cassandra, entertain one of these men in your own home. How could you? How *could* you? Did I not warn you when this fellow's name first came up between us? Did I not tell you that you must forget this old association with Lafitte? How can you shame your husband so? Because in shaming him you shame your government. Cassandra, do you not understand that Benedict is rising in importance in this government? And he'll rise further. He's a good and honest man, reliable and diligent. Of all the men who serve under me he is one of the very few who can be trusted not to take a gratuity passed underneath the table or to do a favor for a twisting of the law. Do you not understand I cannot tolerate that a man of position in my administration should enter-tain at home one of the very rogues that I am set against?"

Cassandra watched him with dismay. He had got himself all worked up into a state. How was she to explain his great mistake? At last, when he had sputtered to a stop, she said, as gently as she could, "William, you wrong Monsieur Lafitte. Perhaps he trades a little with the Baratarians. You say yourself that all New Orleans does so. Perhaps he doesn't understand the nature of the goods he barters for, or doesn't want to know. Is he any worse in that than a thousand other reputable citizens? Perhaps a meeting should be held. Perhaps the situation should be explained as you have just so lucidly explained it to me. But it's unjust to condemn one man for what a thousand do."

"You don't understand. This fellow is a ringleader. Cassandra, he's a smuggler."

"Smuggler, juggler. He's a blacksmith."

William sighed. "No, no, it's a front. The man's a rogue. His brother is a pirate. I suspect that he is too."

"Have you met him? Do you know him?"

He shook his head.

"How then can you judge him?"

"The Bible tells us that a man is known by his works. I know his works."

"I know the man. He is a gentleman."

William laughed. "Many a gentleman has been disreputable."

"You slander him."

"You are a woman with a woman's sensibilities. You do not understand the world."

She could see there was no point in further arguing with him. She would have to wait for Benedict to come home. She would put the matter to him and he would clear the whole confusion up.

"William," she said, "I'll not argue with you longer. You may take the matter up with Benedict. But let me tell you this: Jean is our friend. We love him. We will have him to our house."

Although shaken by this incident, Cassandra soon recovered, and by the time she arrived home was quite cheerful, shaking her head over this new piece of William's earnest nonsense. Since Benedict might be home at any moment, she busied herself with making the house spic-and-span, seeing to new flowers in the vases, ordering the makings for a special supper.

He appeared next day, early in the morning. Cassandra had just finished dressing and come down to supervise the getting of the breakfast and the seeing of the children off to school. She rushed to give him the news of his appointment, but he had already heard.

Since his journey had wearied him, she suggested he go and lie down on the bed. She intended, as soon as she was free, to send a note to Jean inviting him to join them that evening. She could hardly wait to spring her surprise and had readied herself to present her fantastic conversation with William, which the two of them would laugh about, and later put their heads together to decide how best to rectify the matter.

But Benedict had ideas other than bed. He dismissed the children, who had been bombarding him with questions, and drew Cassandra off into the morning room. He shut the door. A peculiar sensation stole over her. Had she not seen another man behave like this but yesterday?

"Sweet," he said, "I hear you've had a visitor, your old friend Jean Lafitte."

"Ah, I'm disappointed. I wanted to surprise you."

"I didn't know you were aware he was in town."

"I came upon him accidentally, out walking."

He looked alarmed. "You've not been out in public with the man?"

"What's this, Benedict? You turn on an old friend?"

"Cassie, you don't understand. He's become—how shall I say?—not quite respectable. His brother too, Pierre."

"I'm offended. How can you say our friend is not respectable? Are you not happy for him that he found his brother?"

"Yes, sweet, I'm happy for him. But the Lafitte brothers aren't accepted in polite society."

"Not accepted? They've barely arrived."

"They've been here quite some time."

"You knew it and you didn't tell me?"

"I thought it better for you not to know."

"Why, pray?"

"Cassie, you don't understand. Jean's become a smuggler."

"William says that he's become a pirate, as though his blacksmith shop has magically sprouted sails."

"He takes orders in his shop for goods from Barataria."

"And this is criminal? The whole town buys from Barataria."

"He deals with pirates."

"That doesn't make him one."

"It's a fine line, Cassie. William thinks he's stepped across it."

"But he's our friend. William can say he's a smuggler or a pirate or the devil himself, he's still our friend."

"Cassie, don't take that tone with me. Think of my position."

"Is it because of your position Jean is not welcome in our house?"

"It isn't wise."

"You're afraid for your reputation?"

"I am afraid for yours."

"He's my friend. I love him. I'll have him to my house."

"Cassie, don't stare at me so fiercely. In France the circumstance was different. It was a wild time, and all decorum was turned upside down. But here, for a married woman to announce she loves a man who is not her husband is reproachable. Here Jean is an adventurer, someone to do a little business with from time to time, perhaps, but not the sort of man to bring into the family."

Cassandra felt rage flame on her neck. "You were reputed to be something of an adventurer when we ran off together."

He flipped his hand impatiently. "That was years ago. I was a young man then, and reckless in my ways."

"Reckless enough to steal a good man's daughter?"

She had not meant to say it. Such a thought had not been in her mind. But when Benedict flinched behind his eyes she knew that something serious had happened, as though a wild dog had come barking to stand on four stiff legs between them.

"You hold me culpable for that?"

"I was a child. I did not understand the consequences."

"You've always held me culpable?"

She made no answer. It was only to control herself, to keep from saying more she would regret, but he took it as assent. She looked at him standing in the thin light of the early morning, his face crumpled up with pain, and for the first time since they had been together she saw him as another, as someone separate from her, someone on whom she could pass judgment. She stepped toward him, reaching out her hand, but he brushed her off and turned away and went out of the room. She heard the front door open, close.

Cassandra struggled to persuade herself that Benedict was right. She told herself it was not wicked that he should turn away from Jean. If advancing his position meant cutting off old friendships, so be it; she understood why he would do so. It was not for himself he sought advancement. His father's family had lost everything, and so he must bring his own family to the top. He was fully taken over by this responsibility. Commissioner, registrar—these positions were nothing, just the low steps of the ladder he had set against the high wall of success. He had never mentioned it, but she could see inside his heart the title *Senator*. And all this for her and for her children.

And so, she told herself, she understood her husband's very good intentions. And yet she was at loggerheads with those intentions. She loved her husband and her family, and yet she loved Jean too. He was her friend. She did not have it in her heart to cut him off.

33

$\mathcal{S}$HE WENT TO HIM. SHE HAD NEVER BEEN SO indiscreet before, but had always sent a note with Syphorian or Seth. Today she almost ran, her shoes clattering through the half-awakened streets, brushing past slaves and servants clutching long thin loaves of bread to take home for their masters' breakfasts, tradesmen rattling in their carts, vendors setting up their stalls, night-soil workers hauling off their stinking loads. Horses clacked and jingled, strutting in the briskness of the early morning air.

She knew that people stared at her, a hatless lady rushing past as though she had heard alarum of a fire and was bent on helping with the brigade of buckets. Jean had told her the location of the black-smith shop behind which he and Pierre lived, and she had secretly passed the place a dozen times before. Now she went directly and beat against the courtyard door. A woman opened it, looking out at her inquiringly, and Cassandra knew at once that this was Pierre's "very handsome lady." She was dark-skinned and a little fleshy, with black eyes, a full red mouth, and long black silky-looking hair that fell around her face. She wore a brightly colored gown with a bright shawl drawn around the skirt and looped up at the side. Cassandra was too intent on her purpose to notice whether her gown was red or green, or her shawl blue or yellow, just that she seemed very highly colored and exotic, like a cluster of hibiscus.

"Adelaide?"

The woman did not seem surprised that a total stranger knew her name, as though such things happened to her every day. "Wait here," she said, and closed the door. No more than a moment after, the door reopened and Jean slipped out.

"Jean—"

"Not here, Cassandra."

He turned and strode away, with Cassandra half running behind him, until they reached a seedy, crowded part of town, as though he would hide their association amongst the jostle of people going back and forth. Here he slowed, allowing her to catch up and take his arm, and she told him everything, from William's summons and his accusation, to her argument with Benedict. "Jean, you must meet with them. You must explain yourself. You must persuade them you're not the man they think you are."

He soothed her, but she felt something stirring in him. Anger? Fear? She thought not. Defiance, then? A sort of schoolboy naughtiness? Whatever it was, he did not seem the least enthused by the notion of explaining himself to either one of them.

"Jean, you must. They say you're a smuggler. William says you're a pirate. Jean, are you a pirate?"

He did not answer her at once, but stopped and stood looking at a parrot swinging in a cage outside a store. When she thought he would not answer her at all, he said, "An adventurer, maybe."

That word again. It stirred Cassandra's memory to the night her father had so violently argued against Benedict: "The man is an adventurer." And it occurred to her that what had made her fall in love with Benedict was that he had been cut from the same cloth as Jean. She had smelled on him the scent of somewhere else, of action and excitement, the seductive scent of danger.

But youth and exigency make men into adventurers; the demands of family and position make them steady and reliable.

And now Benedict was steady and reliable. He was a man to lean on, a man to be there when the need arose. No matter what catastrophe befell, as long as she could be with him her world was safe and actual. She loved him totally, she did not question it. And yet with Jean she felt as though a part of her that had been lost had been restored.

As though he read her thoughts, he looked down at her with a subtle wickedness behind his smile. "I swear to you, Cassandra, I shall see to it that we are never parted."

He left her then. She knew that he would keep his word, although she knew not how and did not feel consoled. On an impulse, she went to the cathedral and burned a candle for the soul of Papa van Pradelles, and then another for the soul of Jean's papa, which she imagined as a sort of pirate spirit loose upon the ocean of the sky.

By midday Cassandra had become exhausted with emotion. Her anger with Benedict and that meddling Mr. Brown and that self-righteous William Claiborne was all mixed up with disappointment and something she was sure was heartbreak. She went into her bedchamber, and calling out for Mattie, had her remove her gown and bring a basin of cool water with a towel. Then she dismissed her.

Drawing her chemise above her head, she dropped it on the floor and loosened her undergarments, intending to bathe her arms and neck to cool herself. But the strength of her emotions had made her very hot so bit by bit she cooled a little more here, a little there, until finally she cast all her clothes aside, and lifting the basin down onto the floor, stood in it and squeezed water down her back and breasts and thighs and down the insides of her arms.

Careless of spilled water, she went to stand before the open glass doors to the courtyard gallery. The breeze, which had been crisp that morning, had dropped, and the city stultified under a midday haze. Everything was still, the children all at school, the servants no doubt snoring on their beds, nothing but the distant mournful lowing of a dove. Naked, she stepped out onto the gallery and stood dripping water down onto the marble tiles. Nothing stirred. A shiver of daring went through her, as though she expected something wild to happen, for the heavens to make some declaration, for a million voices to shout—what? In all her life she had never stood naked outside a bathroom or a bedchamber. She felt as though the whole world stared at her, though there was not a soul about, and the sensation of it made her shake with an unusual excitement.

She looked down at her body. She could almost see the water drying on it. It made her skin feel crisp and cold and so sensitive that if anything had touched her then, the merest feather stroke, she thought she would have shattered like a crystal glass.

And then she looked up and saw a spider watching her. She could have sworn the creature watched her. She had made herself a web across the angle where the upright joined the eaves, and hung head downward just above its center, her tiny fangs erupting from her face between two angled front legs, fine as hairs, which stretched toward Cassandra, slightly spread, as though in welcome. Two shorter legs clung upward, as though she were suspended not from her web but from the sky, and two pairs of even shorter legs balanced her at either side. Her web was littered all across with carcasses: flies, moths, beetles, tiny shapeless creatures bound up into neat, wrapped packages. She did not move, just hung there watching, and Cassandra fancied that she smiled.

She shivered, and with one hand hid her breasts. With the other hand she crossed herself. Then she went back inside and lay down on her bed. Any other day she would have shouted out for Mattie, who would have come running with a broom and knocked the creature from its lair, but today, for what reason she did not think to ask herself, she left it there.

She pulled the sheet up to her neck and tried to sleep, but no sooner did she start to doze than she dreamed about the little bodyeater hanging in her web, and started back awake. She turned and turned, but sleep eluded her. The sheet suffocated her and at last she pushed it off, and spreading out her legs and stretching up her arms above her head, she imagined that she was a spider, hanging upside down, completely still, with violent death wrapped up in parcels all around.

She must have fallen off to sleep because suddenly she was alert. For one incoherent moment she thought a moth had fluttered down into her web, and tensed herself to spring. But then she opened her eyes and Jean stood in the room. She did not move, just lay there looking up into his face for what seemed like eternity. She saw him look down at her feet, and at her thighs. His eyes went dark and hot. She did not move. She felt his eyes upon her breasts. Her nipples burned.

And then it was as though a madness took her in its arms. She could not think of anything but him. She heard the side gate click and the voices of her children laughing in the courtyard. She felt life leap inside her.

When Jean had gone, slipping through the window to the gallery as silently as he had come, she lay in a stupor and was still lying there when Benedict came home. He came so quietly she barely had time to draw the sheet around her. Dear Lord, what would he think of her lying here in bed completely naked? And the bowl of water uncollected from the floor, her clothes all in a jumble, the smell of wantonness still heavy on the air? She closed her eyes, pretending sleep. She felt him lean above her. Felt the pulses in her neck and head begin to drum. Waited for his accusation. But he said not a word, just kissed her on the forehead.

For a moment she thought he would turn and creep out of the room, but then she heard a rustling and a snapping sound. Whereas before her pulses had been racing, now they seemed to stop entirely. Because the sound she had just heard was her husband taking off his belt. And now she heard the rustle of a shirt, the sound of shoes kicked off, of breeches dropping to the floor. His hand drew back the sheet.

It was the first time he had made love to her since Anne died. He did not ask her, and she did not refuse, in fact, she wanted him, wanted him to touch her everywhere, as though by doing so he would remind her body of its duty and this mad desire for Jean would go away.

When he had done, he did not roll away, but kept his arms

about her and his face against her neck. "Cass, I'm sorry for our argument. Will you forgive me?"

She felt shame take her, mixed up with love, and pity for him too, yet underneath was triumph. She had wronged this man in his own bed, yet it was he who begged for her forgiveness. In that moment, Cassandra felt herself become another woman, a stranger both to Benedict and to herself. She heard this woman saying brazenly, "I will forgive you if you tell me Jean is not to be a stranger in our house."

"Cassie, the governor requires it."

"And you? What do *you* say?"

"I must forbid the friendship."

He said it in a whisper, and clung hard to her, as though he expected her to leap up and harangue him, and would hold her down. But she did nothing of the sort. She thought about that awful Paris night when she had given Jean her breast. She thought of how his lips had burned, as though the boy had branded her as lover for the man. And she realized that, as she had disobeyed her father, she would now disobey her husband.

"There will be no friendship then," she said.

She felt his breath go out—she had not realized he was holding it—and his grip, which had been tight and hard, turned into an embrace.

34

*H*OW THEY KEPT IT SECRET SHE WOULD NEVER know. Gossip in New Orleans leaped roof to roof like fire. But the danger of her conduct did not so much as flit across Cassandra's mind. Love deranged her senses, chasing prudence out the door like a wet frog hopping on a broom. Every morning when she woke, her heart woke first and shouted out her love the way the birds outside her window shouted at the dawn. When she rose, she rose as a young girl. Her legs were supple and her arms were strong and full of energy. When she looked into the mirror she saw she was still beautiful. Her skin glowed and her hair was dark and lustrous at her neck. Her lips shone and her eyes shone and her breasts stood up like two proud figureheads. From morning until night she was a spring doe, leaping and skipping across the mountains of desire. She was greedy for Jean's love.

It was Anne's garden where they kept their rendezvous. It was well grown up and private there; the elegant long branches of the willow tree came down around them like a curtain drawn around a bed. And all around, the riot of the garden, its pinks and reds and yellows shifting with the subtle shifting of the breeze, spicing it with perfumes. No one disturbed them there, or heard their cries. Even Fernando had turned invisible.

One day Jean said, "Why did you come to New Orleans?" and Cassandra said, "Because I knew that I would find you here." It seemed so simple and so clear. He accepted it without a word.

He was not the same person she had known in France. And yet he was the same. As then, he told a dozen stories all at once, all conflicting with each other. He had the same easiness with her, the same unquestioning assurance that she delighted in his company. And yet there was a difference underneath, the difference of fifteen years of—what? When she questioned him about his life since France, he told her tales of uprisings on Saint Domingue, dramatic deaths and rescues, combat at sea, tales of men lost in swamps, taken by alligators, by violent fevers, tales of pirates who had pursued him and Pierre, tales of foreign lands whose names rang strangely in her ear. Every story ended with a laugh, a kiss, a tumbling to make love again. Every day he left her with a buzzing swarm of entertainment in her head, impressions of a swashbuckler, a grand adventurer, a hero dashing for his life, a man of enterprise, roguish good humor. But she had no direct account of him, no plain recounting of his doings in the years since France. He was a shifting set of images, kaleidoscopic, smiling, charming, sweeping off his hat, her off her feet, like a river with a glinting surface, but underneath, a deadly spinning current. He was entirely wicked, she knew that.

There was about him something so like and yet so unlike Benedict, as though God had repeated him, but made him not quite wholly accurate. When she tried to work out what it was, she could not make a sentence in her mind that held the thought. It would come toward her like an animal creeping through a mist, but when it was within her reach and she tried to throw a net around it, it would struggle for a moment and be gone, a white roiling vanishing back where it had come from, leaving her with nothing but the sensation of slick pelt against her hand, the drumming of a heart, the wild smell of its breath. Yes, it was wild, she knew that it was wild.

They never made arrangement, never said goodbye, or greeted one another when they met. It was as though they lived through one long day, and because of this they never had to ask or answer, "When?" If she was there, he came. If he had come and she was still not there, she would feel him reach for her and draw her through the streets. Sometimes he brought a picnic with him: apples, pastries, cold meats, a fresh baguette, a bottle of red wine. Sometimes they loved and ate and lay disheveled in each other's arms all morning and on into the afternoon. Other times they hurried through the streets and fell upon each other and hurried off again.

Benedict was off at work all day, and often out of town, and her children spent a good part of the day at school. Because of this, her absences went unremarked. Even Clarice did not question her less frequent visits to the Government House, since she was taken up with her new baby son. But Mattie knew, Cassandra felt it, although she never said a word. The first time she came home with pollen in her hair and mud-bespattered gown and said that she had fallen in the garden, Mattie took the gown away to wash with no more than a murmur of concern. The second time, she held it up, examining the grass stains and the soil, and shook her head. The third time, she muttered in her throat.

After that she kept her face a mask and her lips tight shut, and carried off the soiled gown the minute she could get it off Cassandra's back, as if she understood that she was now accomplice and must keep the evidence from all eyes but Cassandra's and her own. Once Cassandra surprised her in the kitchen on her knees, hands clasped at her breast, weeping at her prayers, and knew she prayed for her. There were those who said that Negroes had no souls, but she could not think that Mattie's prayers did not go up to God. In a strange way it was comforting.

Sometimes she felt that this woman into whose skin she had slipped was beyond the reach of prayers, beyond reach of all redemption. Sometimes, lying next to Benedict in bed at night, she tried to think dispassionately about her situation, but no matter what her head told her, her heart would not, or could not, comprehend its wisdom or rebuke. When she was not with Jean, he was with her. Everywhere she went, he was a voice inside her head, a hand upon her waist, a pair of soft lips on the flesh between her shoulder blades. When she sat at someone else's house, she felt his questing hand between her legs. At the opera, it was his voice that echoed and re-echoed off the ceiling and the walls. When she climbed a stair, she saw him at her feet in the shadows of the treads. When she ate, she tasted him upon her tongue, and when she drank a glass of wine, she drank the fluid of his love. He came to her in dreams—his slim hard hips, the firm flesh of his belly, the soft fur of his chest—and she would wrestle under him and moan. Sometimes she would wake to find Benedict leaning on his elbow, looking down into her face. "Love, you are not sick?"

Behold, thou art fair, my love; thou hast dove's eyes. Oh, she was sick with love.

And yet she did not turn her back on Benedict. She pitied him and because of it she loved him even more. With him she was quite different from what she was with Jean. Benedict was a tender lover. When he took her in his arms she felt a warm expansion in her breast. His hands moving on her skin made her think of butterflies—so delicate, so sensitive, so almost feminine. He murmured as he worked, or hummed, a low sound like an echo or a whisper. Everywhere he touched she tingled, nerves rising up to meet the brushing of his fingers, and she would lie in his embrace half swooning, somehow purified, forgiven.

With Jean she was aggressive. She flung herself on him and made her own love to him like a man. And he would treat her roughly, although he never hurt her. The two of them together were a pair of yearling tigers wrestling, the constant threat of slashing teeth and bared, extended claws an added stimulant.

With Benedict she lay stretched out, completely naked. With Jean she was in disarray. And she loved both ways of making love. She loved both men, she had no doubt of it, and needed both. Jean was her darling rogue, and Benedict her darling. And yet she understood that this was not a normal thing. Had God, for reasons of his own, given her more ability to love than he granted other women? Or had he intended her to be two women, but in some moment of thoughtlessness had made two women one?

One day, sitting with Clarice, she said, "Do you think it possible to love two men at once?"

Clarice, who had been stitching a silk gown for baby William, looked up with bemusement in her soft blue eyes. "Of course it is impossible. And wicked too."

"How can it be wicked if it is impossible?"

"What do you mean? I do not understand."

"I mean that if something can be judged wicked, then it must be possible, otherwise it could not be judged at all, either wicked or not wicked."

Clarice laughed and resumed her stitching. "Ah, I see now. You're playing a word game with me. Your question wasn't serious." The needle hovered in the air. "It wasn't, Cassie, was it?"

Cassandra heard the echo of Clarice's laughter spring out of her throat. "Why, no, of course not, silly." And she turned the conversation to another topic.

It puzzled her, the way she loved both Jean and Benedict, how she desired them both. Her head told her Clarice was right, that she, like Jean, was wicked now, but she did not feel wicked. She searched inside herself for this thing, wickedness, imagining it sometimes as a sort of darkness, a pooling ink inside her soul, at other times as some horrid creature lurking there, and yet no matter how she held her heart up to the light, no matter how she traveled through its mazes with a candle in her hand, she could find nothing bad—no spreading stain, no crouched beast. All she ever found was an expanding whiteness through which she traveled lightly, joyously, her feet not touching earth.

Late one afternoon, Benedict went downstairs to the bakery, intending to find some sort of treat for supper. The bakery, he knew, was closed by now, but he had often gone down after hours before and so thought nothing of entering the side door without a knock. Hearing voices, he went along the narrow passage to the kitchen, and turned into the open doorway. There, spread out on the pastry table, was Emmeline, with not a stitch of clothing and her fleshy legs wound around her husband's skinny back, while he stood at the table's end, pumping at her with all his might, kneading her enormous breasts and, through his yellow horse's teeth, making remarks the vulgarity of which Benedict had heard before only in a bawdy house.

The vision hit him as hard as if the door had been fast closed and he had walked right into it. He stood there riveted, unable to back off, unable even to turn his head away. The pastry table clapped and shifted on its legs as Emmeline, working her knees hard, drew her husband tight and tighter up against her. The heaving of it, the slapping of their flesh, the smell of their arousal. He felt his member rise. And now Emmeline moaned and keened, sweat rolled down her reddened breasts, and then her body stiffened and she seemed to take a fit, head tossing side to side, hands beating a tattoo against the pastry table. Her husband's thrusting reached a fever pitch. He threw his head back, eyes screwed tight and nostrils flared, and roared. And then they both collapsed, Monsieur Tournelles wheezing in his chest. Benedict stepped back into the shadows and slipped quietly away.

In bed that night, when he rolled toward Cassandra and took her in his arms, he found that he was watching himself with her the way he had watched the Tournelles. How different they were in love, how sensitive, refined, and delicate, how gentle. Had they always been this way? Had Cassandra always lain so quiet under him? His mind went back to those first weeks of their lovemaking, when they were on the run. Had he been more like Monsieur Tournelles then? Had Cassandra been more like Emmeline?

No, Cassandra was no Emmeline, no brute woman with her legs flung up, stout heels beating at his back, thrusting out her pelvis like a wanton. She was a queen. A man did not approach a queen as Tournelles approached Emmeline. And yet he wondered what it would be like to have Cassandra gasping naked on that pastry table.

Next morning, as he set off into the town, he went into the bakery to buy a roll to eat along the way. He had never done such a thing before, had always eaten breakfast with Cassandra. But today he had excused himself, he must be off, was late for an appointment, and had pushed away his plate.

Emmeline was bending above a tray of little cakes, icing funnel in her hands, and he found his eyes fixed on the shadow inside the neckline of her gown. He felt a tingling in his groin, an urge to thrust his hand down there and grab at those big breasts. For a moment he fancied himself humping her like a stray dog off the street, and quickly turned away and hurried off. He must see about that contract . . . that land abstract . . . that contested title . . . and then there was the issue with Judge Nichols out in Attacapas County that was still not settled . . . Should he go back out there and confront him? . . . Oh, and then there was that matter of . . . and then . . . A thousand things to see about today.

That evening, dressing for a dinner party, Benedict pulled on the new brocade waistcoat Cassandra had made for the occasion. As he did, he glanced toward her at the dressing table and saw her reflected in the glass. She wore a pure white gown, cut low, and was pinning a red rose into its ruffled neckline. It put him in mind of the gown she had been wearing in her portrait in the locket he had left behind in France. She looked so lovely that he felt an aching start up in his heart. He came behind her at the mirror.

"Are you happy with me, Cass?"

She eyed his image up and down and smiled. "It's the best-cut waistcoat I ever saw."

"I didn't mean the waistcoat."

"What then?"

He touched her shoulder. "Nothing, sweet."

35

*S*HE WAS ENCEINTE. SHE WAS CERTAIN OF IT now. When she told Benedict, he was writing a letter reporting his activities to Mr. Albert Gallatin in Washington and did not respond.

"Love, I am enceinte," she said again.

Once more, no response. Instead, he turned toward her with an expression of concentration on his face and asked her to aid his memory on some dates when he had been away from New Orleans. Cassandra felt her heart stop. She stuttered out a date. She watched him write it down. Watched him list his absences and his returns. Pinch the chalk between his fingertips and sprinkle it to blot the ink. Fold and seal the letter.

He set it on one side and, pushing back his chair, regarded her. "Sweet," he said, "I swear that pregnancy agrees with you. You look more lovely than you ever did. Come here and let me kiss you."

So it had been nothing but her own inflamed awareness. He did not suspect. He did not know.

. . .

Cassandra hid her pregnancy from Jean. She did not want him suddenly becoming gentle. She wanted their affair to go furiously on and on. She wanted him to knock her to the ground and tangle up his legs in hers, to spread his weight on her and struggle with her body. She wanted it to last forever.

But the day came when her condition was impossible to hide. She had thought he would turn gentle, but she never saw a man turn more contentious. This was his child, he said. She was his wife. She must leave Benedict and come to him. The thought that Benedict might be the father apparently had not occurred to him and she did not propose it, since it had not occurred to him, apparently, that she might still make love with Benedict. Like the flutter of a tiny predatory bird inside her chest came the start of realization that the bliss of loving two men at once might not be seen as bliss by either man. She heard her voice turn edgy.

"Nonsense, Jean," she said. "This may be your child but I am not your wife. I'm married still to Benedict."

"Then you must leave him and divorce him. You must marry me at once."

"Don't be foolish. Catholics don't divorce."

"Let him give you a divorce or let him not, you're still my wife."

"Jean, I'm not some quadroon to be set up in a *mariage de la main gauche*. The world would call me whore."

"Let the world say what it will, you are my wife. I love you and it's me you love. You give me evidence of it every day. You cannot give my child to Benedict."

"Jean, he's an excellent papa."

"He's not my child's papa. I am, and I will be. I'll have my own child in my house, and I will raise him, not another man."

And so they went on half the afternoon, Jean alternately raging at her obstinance and falling on his knees to plead his case, like a dramatic actor on a stage.

"I'll carry you off," he said. "I'll carry off the child. We'll go away from here, to Cartagena, or to Texas, somewhere no one will know us or pass judgment."

"And what about my other children? I've lost one family. I will not lose another."

That brought him up short. "I hadn't thought of it. Oh, Cassandra, what confusion, what confusion."

He sat thinking for a while. "I'll challenge Benedict. I'll make a widow of you."

She leaped up off the ground. "You will not, Jean, you will not. I'll not hear a word of it. Love, don't look so agonized. You'll watch him growing up and you can love him. While he is a child, I'll bring him to you from time to time, and when he's grown, who knows? Perhaps the two of you will become friends."

"I can't wait until he's grown. I want him now."

"No, I'm firm. Not now."

"When he's six, then? Fourteen? Yes, give him to me when he's fourteen. I'll take him on as my apprentice."

For the first time that day Cassandra laughed. "So I'll set my son to be apprentice to a pirate?"

"Don't call me that. I am a businessman."

"Mr. William Claiborne calls you that."

"I care not for the opinions of Mr. William Claiborne. Let him call me anything he wants."

As fate would have it, Benedict and Cassandra went next day for dinner at the Government House. Cassandra had avoided seeing William since their argument and did not look forward to the opportunity of seeing him again. Still, there was a certain perverse pleasure to it. She sat there at his table watching him be powerful and gracious and, after all this time, starting to be respected too, slipping so smoothly from English into French and back again that either might have been his native tongue—his marriage to Clarice had benefited him in many ways. Watching him, Cassandra heard a voice inside her head: "Powerful as you may be, my friend, I have outwitted you."

It would have remained at that, a little private gloating, but William, as he had done ever since she first clapped eyes on him, provoked her. She could have sworn he loved to do it, like a brother who takes a child's perverse delight in tormenting a sister. A conversation had been going on about William's continuing efforts to control the flow of slaves entering Louisiana by way of Barataria. Inevitably there arose his obsessive notion that Jean had ambitions to become a sort of pirate king.

Now he looked along the right side of the table, caught Cassandra's eye, then looked along the left, so that when he spoke it was not apparent to anyone but her to whom his remark was addressed. "They say," he said, "our pirate has a mistress, although her identity he manages to keep a mystery. No doubt she's as slippery a character as he, since a man is like a river in his love affairs—he finds his level in the women that he beds."

She knew from the way he said it that it was not an accusation—perhaps he could not conceive of the notion that she would so dangerously disobey him—but an effort to discomfort her, while there she sat, a guest bound by a guest's civility, unable to protest. And she did not protest, but let her eyes drop to her plate of soup, studying the clever way the carrots floated while the beans did not.

William would not leave well enough alone. "Oh, by the way, Madame van Pradelles," he said, and looked directly at her, "how is our charming rogue? I understand he is a friend of yours."

She could not help herself. She took his bait. "Sir," she said, "as you are well aware, I knew your so-called pirate as a child. He gave no indication then of any slipperiness of character. I'm sure his mistress thinks herself a lucky woman to have found a gentleman so discreet that even the rankest gossip of the town has not unearthed her name."

William's face grew cold—he was a freezing, not a boiling, man—and turning to Clarice, he said, with a chilly little laugh, "My dear, perhaps you should not associate with Madame van Pradelles, since *her* associates are dubious."

The entire table fell silent, all heads turning to Cassandra.

She did not blush. "Hardly, Sir," she said. "I've not set eyes on Monsieur Jean Lafitte for years. You can hardly call him my associate."

She waited for him to challenge her, but he did not, perhaps, she thought, because he took her remark as an apology of sorts, as though by denying the association she had declared to him that she was sorry to have caused him worry over it.

He inclined his head. "Well, then," he said, "if you've not seen him since he was a child then you know nothing of him, do you, Madame van Pradelles? Lafitte is now a man, an unscrupulous man. And you are just a woman and know nothing of these matters." And he turned away and took up conversation with the lady on his left, Madame Labiche.

Across the table, Cassandra saw Benedict shift uneasily and look toward her with a warning glance, but she pretended not to notice. She was inflamed with William once again and would have spoken further if Clarice had not fixed her with her eye. That silenced her. She would not have mortified Clarice for all the world.

A dinner party loves the spark of gossip and the conversation turned to speculating on the identity of this mysterious mistress. The ladies especially took delight in chewing on the topic and from the way they spoke—Monsieur Lafitte was this, Monsieur Lafitte was that, so sleek, so suave, so elegant, and so on and so forth— Cassandra had no doubt that more than one of them indulged in private fantasies of this forbidden rascal who each day became more visible about the town. With each of them so anxious to insert her own opinion, no one thought to ask for Cassandra's notions on the matter. Listening to them, she thought about how, long ago in Maryland, the gossip used to circle around Benedict in just this way, and she smiled smugly to herself—of all the women who had wanted him, it had been her he chose; and now it was the same— these women lusted after Jean, but he was hers.

Her smugness was cut short when Madame Labiche looked up into William's face and, simpering, said, "They say our pirate's mistress is a married woman of the town. They say he keeps her portrait in a locket on a crimson riband round his neck."

William's nostrils flared. "Do they indeed, Madame?" he said, and from his tone Cassandra could tell he thought she was a stupid woman and had made the story up to get attention.

But across the table, Benedict had flinched. "A crimson riband, do you say? What color is the locket?"

Someone said that it was ivory, but no one knew for sure, and at once a dozen voices went baying after this new topic like an unruly pack of hounds. Benedict looked across the table at Cassandra, framed between a vase of pure white lilies and an enormous haunch of pork. Candlelight flickered on his face, making him look beautiful and deathly. "It is too much," he said, "too much," his voice so low she understood his words only because she saw the movement of his lips. She had the sudden feeling that William watched them, but when she turned her head he was looking somewhere else.

On the ride home, the only sound between them was the tapping of Benedict's cane against the carriage floor. Inside the house, he left Cassandra standing at the door. His cane clacked in the passageway. He came back with her jewel box in his hands and set it on the table in the entryway. "The locket you gave me isn't here."

"I know it, Benedict. You know it too. But it's been years. You've not mentioned it for years. Why are you searching for it now? Do you think I hide it from you in my jewel box?"

He looked up at her with dazed confusion on his face. "You told me it was lost."

"I thought it best."

"Then it's true? Jean wears my locket round his neck? You gave it to him?"

"It was all I had about me. It was years ago, when he left us on the wharf in France. I thought I'd not set eyes on him again. I wanted to give him some keepsake so he would remember me. It was all I had about me."

"And now all New Orleans knows he wears the thing around his neck."

"Benedict, no. No one knows whose image he hides there. It's a secret."

"A secret for how long? Tonight a dozen people gossiped of a locket. Tomorrow every parlor in New Orleans will tattle with the news. Tonight you sat at dinner at the governor's table and defended Jean. Tomorrow the whole town will make anything it will of your defense. You have been indiscreet, Cassie, indiscreet. No matter how he keeps that locket closed against his breast, your image will leak out of it. They'll say you are his mistress. Then they'll sharpen up their tongues. They'll say this child that you are carrying . . ."

He came to her and held her in his arms. "Oh, Cassie, sweet, I cannot bear to think of it."

36

$\mathcal{T}$HE INCIDENT SHOCKED CASSANDRA. SHE DID not go to be with Jean again. She did not dare. If they should be discovered, prim propriety would reach out its mud-bespattered hand and soil their love. Whereas before she had ignored that danger, and perhaps had been protected by her brazenness, now she recoiled in horror at the thought. Every gossip in the town would be aflame with it. She would be cut off from society.

Why this had not occurred to her before she did not know. She had been so taken over by her passion she had not seen what might lie on the road ahead. She felt a tension in her stomach and a rising, a pounding heaviness high up inside her chest, like fear—no, more like anger mixed with fear, a furious resentment, a strangling weariness, as though she were a tiger locked inside a tiny cage, pacing, pacing, and yet paralyzed.

She sent a message off with Seth telling Jean there had been gossip, forbidding him to see her, that she was too far gone in pregnancy to be walking in the streets, that she planned to rest until her lying-in. Aside from that she had no plan. She went from day to day wrapped in confused anxiety, wanting to see Jean, not wanting it, wanting to make things right with Benedict the way that they had been before, wanting to thump her fists against his chest and rail.

He said not another word about the locket, but pampered and indulged her, came twenty times a day to kiss her and hold her in his arms, clung to her at night. As the weeks of pregnancy went by, Cassandra found the lethargy of her condition took her over and she relaxed into his love until she found that sometimes she could put Jean from her mind for half an hour, an hour, a day. The child was Benedict's, she told herself. Yes, it was Benedict's.

The child was born October 29, 1808, an easy birth. As the midwife set him in Cassandra's arms, a tiny apprehension took her, but he looked no more like Jean than like Benedict—a black-haired, black-eyed, energetic child—as though he had been sired by both. She loved him instantly and her milk came in as though she had been designed to feed him. Sometimes, when she put him to her breast, his nursing made her thrill and tremble until she arched into a spasm.

Two weeks went by and she was feeling quite recovered. It was approaching noon. The rain that fell all morning had passed over, the day was warm and still and lazy, and she had propped herself against the pillows of her bed to nurse. When it was done, she set the sleeping baby on the bed beside her and lay half dreaming. The buzz of insects drifted through the open doorway to the gallery. Water tinkled down into the cistern at the corner of the house. Some small creature rustled in the fig tree by the rail.

Mattie roused her. "Madame, your friend is at the door."

Cassandra blinked up at her, pushing back her hair. "Friend, Mattie? It's early yet for callers. I'm still déshabillée."

"Madame, he insists."

She knew then who it was. "Send him away."

But he was in the passageway at Mattie's back, then in the room. He came directly to the bed and kissed her. She pushed him from her. "Jean, you mustn't. Mattie, show Monsieur Lafitte the door."

But Mattie had already gone and Jean ignored her protest. "Cassandra, these past months I've been living on Grande Terre. I've not come to town in all that time because I knew I couldn't keep away from you. But now . . ."

He took the child up off the bed and stood looking down at him, his face alight with—what? With love? No, with something more akin to pride of ownership. He bent and set his lips against the little forehead, then looked up at her.

"His name is Jean?"

"His name is Albert Gallatin."

"Albert Gallatin? What sort of name is that?"

"Mr. Gallatin is secretary of the treasury. It was he who saw to Benedict's appointment as commissioner and as registrar of lands. My husband is most grateful. This is how he shows his gratitude."

"Your husband? But the child is mine."

She felt her womb contract, and then contract again.

"Cassandra, come to me. Leave Benedict and come to me."

"You're a fool, Jean. Here, give Albert back to me."

"His name is Jean. It must be Jean."

"Hush! Not so loud. Will you make trouble in my house?"

"I love you, Cassandra. I've always loved you. You must be my wife. You must let me have my son."

And then Mattie was coughing at the door. The clatter of a cane along the passageway and Benedict was in the room, Mattie agitating at his side.

Jean had reached the doorway to the gallery and Cassandra realized he still had Albert in his arms.

"Jean, no!"

He stopped. He turned. Held out his hand to Benedict.

She watched their two hands moving toward each other through the air. She could not bear for them to meet. And when they did, it was as though they had agreed on her adultery.

"A fine son we have here, my friend."

Ah, cruel Jean!

Benedict looked him in the eye. "Six tomorrow morning. At the big oak. We'll not need seconds."

Jean turned to Cassandra. "I hope you'll not think me not a gentleman, but I cannot accept this challenge. I have no taste for murdering your husband." And he set the baby into Mattie's arms and turned, and, stepping through the door onto the gallery, vanished out of sight.

Benedict stood staring after him. "He has come to you this way before. In our own bed."

Mattie scuttled from the room, the baby clutched against her breast.

"Once only. Once."

He did not look at her. The light outside the window dimmed, the cicadas ceased their buzzing. And now, as though it were a trick, she saw Benedict grow old. His shoulders stooped. Lines grew on his face. Black hair turned gray. He leaned against his cane.

"I loved him like a son. I did not want to ban him from my house."

Tears rushed behind her eyes. Dear Lord, what had she done? Suddenly her love affair with Jean took on a different character. While it had been going on, she had thought of it as magical, the passion of two people destined by fate to be eternal lovers, like a grand opera played upon a stage. When it was done—*It's done. It is done. Yes*—she had stored it in the secret chambers of her memory, told herself she had forgotten it. Now it was as though the whole thing had taken place in darkness, and the darkness had hidden its true nature. Like a torch raised in a tomb, discovery revealed it was corrupt, some sort of rogue adventure. Why had she done it? What had she been thinking? How she had hurt poor Benedict, who had never done a thing to her but hold her in complete devotion.

She wanted to leap up off the bed and go to him and fall down on her knees and beg for his forgiveness, but she could not move. She lay completely still, feeling inside her a peculiar pain, as though she had been split apart and half of her had somehow and mysteriously vanished. She closed her eyes, and when she opened them again, Benedict was gone. Had he so soon abandoned her? Panic gave her strength. She dressed in haste and, despite all Mattie's protestations, went out in search of him.

. . .

At the cathedral in the square, Benedict knelt painfully before the altar. He had a pistol in his belt. His sword was in its leather scabbard at his side. He clasped his hands and gazed up at the figure of the Virgin. She gazed back down at him, smiling enigmatically. Her face was purest white, her limbs smooth and round and lucent. She clutched her gown across her breast, and yet to Benedict it seemed this modesty was feigned. Her radiance seemed carnal, wanton. It was as though she sided with Cassandra, mocking him.

There came into his mind the memory of the Swiss guard who had been his mother's lover. He remembered how Cassandra asked him, speaking of his father, "How could he bear it?" and how he had said, "How could he not? He loves her."

Now he had become his father. From that moment back in Maryland when Cassandra had said, "I do not *want* Papa to choose a man for me to love. I want to choose my own," he had had no wish except to please her. He had taken her to France when his own desire had been to leave her safe in Maryland. And there she had met Jean. He had taken her to New Orleans because she preferred it to Kentucky. And there she had once more found Jean. He had led her to the arms of her seducer. He had loved her too much, demanded too little, and, in the end, had lost her to a man who demanded of her everything. The Virgin smiled at him complacently.

He heard a step behind him in the aisle and Cassandra knelt silently beside him. He did not look up, but reached and took her hand and pressed it to his cheek. "My love, my only love." She leaned into his neck and wept.

Benedict did not come home that night. Cassandra lay for hours staring at the dark, straining her ears for some movement from the courtyard down below. But there was none. In the small hours of the morning a storm came howling up out of the gulf. The wind bawled and the rain came down in torrents, thundering against the roof. She must have slept because when she woke everything was calm again and it was almost dawn. She heard a ship's horn blare. Below her, in the courtyard pond, a bullfrog lifted its lugubrious voice. A bird spoke in a tree, another, and another. Soft wind stirred the curtains. It would be another lovely day.

She rose, her head heavy with weariness and anguish, and went into the kitchen. Mattie had laid breakfast in the courtyard, but Cassandra could not eat. Upstairs, she heard her children calling to their maids, the sound of water poured into a basin. Someone laughed. The baby made soft mewlings in his wooden cradle at her side. She picked him up and opened up her bodice. A cat appeared from nowhere and wound itself around her ankles. She reached one hand down to stroke its back, listening to it hum its low, contented song. She smelled disaster in the air.

All day she waited but Benedict did not return. By evening she was half-crazed with fear. She sent the children early to their beds and sent the servants off as well, and sat alone and watched the sky grow dark, and waited. All that night she sat up in her chair. It stormed again. At dawn she started out of sleep, listening to the silence. He did not come.

The third night she sat up again, giddy with exhaustion. From time to time she fell into a nightmare of black rushing shapes, then jerked awake, her heart loud in the silence of the house. And then, outside, very early in the morning, she heard whispering, the sound of Mattie's voice. The servants' door groaned on its hinge. The muffled sound of feet, a shuffling in the kitchen.

She was down there in an instant. The house was black but a candle flickered in the room. A band of men was in there, crowded all together, rough men, evil-looking men in head rags and gold earrings, bending over something on the table. It was Benedict, she knew it. They had him laid out there and were stripping off his clothes. What, was he dead? She stood frozen in the dark.

And then a figure, silhouetted in the kitchen doorway. "Cassandra?"

"Is he dead then, Jean? Have you killed him?"

"Hush, hush. He's not dead, not dead. We found him in the swamp. In God's name, what was he doing out there all alone and in the middle of a storm?"

"He was coming after you."

"He planned to kill me?"

"I suppose he did. He had a pistol and a sword."

"He planned to storm Grande Terre alone? Take on a hundred men? Had he gone mad? Did he not realize he would be peppered full of lead before he made three paces up the beach?"

"I suppose he didn't think . . . he didn't care . . . Jean, have I killed him?"

"I think he'll live."

"Let me through. I must go to him."

"No, not yet. I have my surgeon treating him. Let him do his work. Then we'll carry him to bed."

"Surgeon? Work? Whatever is the matter? What's going on in there? Jean, let me through."

He swung his arm up to prevent her but she slipped beneath it, through the door, pushed between the men, and reached the table. And fainted dead away.

Later, Jean told her they had caught the alligator that took Benedict's leg, but she did not believe him. He had made the story up to comfort her. "At least be glad," he said, "it was the crippled leg it took and not the other." But she found no consolation in the thought.

The surgeon was a giant hairy man with stiff hairs sprouting from his nose and ears and an unwashed smell about him. He had a kind heart, though, and seemed to know his business. He assured Cassandra that the leg had come off cleanly, there was no infection, it would heal neatly in a shiny stub that could be fitted with a wooden leg.

"So you see," said Jean, "Benedict is better off. He'll no longer be tormented by his injury. He'll stamp about New Orleans like a brand-new man. Come, Cassandra, let me cheer you up."

But her spirits were in no mood for cheering, and for good reason. Although Benedict's leg behaved exactly as the surgeon said it should, he himself did not recover. For a week he lay in bed and barely moved. He spoke only in a whisper, smiling a half-apologetic smile as he told her how he had got himself into this pass.

He had left the cathedral and taken a pirogue, heading for Grande Terre, but there had been no moon that night and he lost himself in the maze of bayous. In attempting to reverse his course, he ran up against what he took in the dark to be a mud bank. He hefted up his paddle and pushed against it, meaning to swivel the pirogue around. The mud bank hoisted itself up in turn and the next thing Benedict knew he was thrashing for his life beneath the water.

Why the alligator did not eat him totally he did not know. Perhaps it had already eaten, perhaps something startled it away. He remembered nothing after that until he woke with a sharp pain in his leg and a big ugly hairy face looking down at him. It was Jean's surgeon, Monsieur Dessalines.

Jean hung about the house, alternately worrying about Benedict and begging Cassandra to run away with him. She forgave him for the latter since he was distraught. She would not allow him to come into the sickroom, though, for fear it would upset Benedict, and after a few days sent him away, telling him to go back to Grande Terre. He did not go. He and his surgeon took accommodations with Pierre and every time Cassandra sent out for Monsieur Dessalines she knew that Jean came with him. She could feel him outside in the courtyard. It touched her, but it worried her. She sent her children off to stay with friends upriver, the baby too, although it meant that he was so abruptly weaned her breasts swelled up and hurt.

Monsieur Dessalines seemed to enjoy the change from Barataria to New Orleans. He spent his time playing cards and billiards at the Absinthe Bar. He did not drink, though. Cassandra never smelled it on his breath. Perhaps he was afraid that Jean would have his eyes gouged out or some such awful punishment if he should arrive drunk to care for Benedict.

As for Cassandra, all her agonies of soul-searching were swallowed up by her concern for Benedict. Every moment, every thought, she dedicated to his recovery. And at first she thought he *would* recover. He took water and a little food, although from time to time he rubbed his hand against his head, complaining of a headache, and was very irritated by mosquito bites, which rose in livid swellings on his face and arms. In his haste to do Jean in, he had forgotten to take vinegar to rub into his skin to keep them off.

On the third day of the second week, he complained that he was cold, and though Cassandra wrapped him well and had Mattie set a hot brick in the bed, he shivered. Monsieur Dessalines examined him and declared it was nothing but the shock of surgery, it would take a little time.

On the fourth day of the second week, Monsieur Dessalines decided that he needed to be bled. He bled him all that morning, Seth and Syphorian moaning back and forth with bowls of blood to pour into the drain along the street. At noon he purged his bowels with ten grains of calomel and fifteen grains of jalap. At six he gave the dose again but did not give another, saying his patient was too weak for such a violent cure. He said to keep him hot even if he complained of it, that sweating would rid the body of its harmful humors.

By the sixth morning of the second week, Benedict refused to eat a single bite and could not drink. Cassandra tried to force a little water on him but he gagged, complaining that his stomach hurt. She felt a shadow settle on her heart.

By midday he complained his muscles hurt. By night she did not need to set her hand against his head to know that he was burning up. His pulse raced and his skin had broken out in bright red blotches. She sent out for Monsieur Dessalines, who came at once.

"What is it, ma petite? He has grown worse?"

She described Benedict's new symptoms and Monsieur Dessalines said nothing. They went into the bedchamber, where Benedict lay with his eyes closed and two bright spots burning in his cheeks. Dark bile trickled from the corner of his mouth.

Monsieur Dessalines crossed himself. "It is the black vomit."

Dear God, the yellow fever, the same as took her darling Anne.

It was that silent time between night and dawn when Benedict left her, before the birds had started on their morning hubbub. Even the insects, which shout and rattle all night long, fall silent at that time. It is the hour of death, when nature bows its head before ascending souls.

She had dismissed Monsieur Dessalines and sat alone beside the bed. Gray light crept into the room and woke her from a doze. She rose and stood looking down at her poor wreck of a husband. He seemed to be dreaming, his eyes moving behind his eyelids as though following some scene.

A smile flickered on his mouth, and suddenly Cassandra saw him as she had seen him so many years ago, when she knew him only as a stranger in a crowd. She saw again the way he moved and walked and gazed into a woman's eyes when he conversed with her, the way he concentrated on her when they danced. She saw his smooth, slim body moving in his clothes, his elegance of manner, the dark beauty of his face, extraordinary in a man and yet entirely masculine. When she grew to like him, then to love him, the distance from which she viewed him had closed so that she never again saw him as completely separate from herself, until her infidelity split them apart.

He stirred, his eyelids lifted, and Cassandra saw proof of the disaster that had befallen him. His eyes, normally a pair of deep brown circles floating in the purest white, were a peculiar faded dun, and around them, yellow, shot with a fine red web of veins.

She seized his hand. "Love, you swore you'd never leave me. Please don't leave me."

He looked up at her and seemed to smile. "After it's over, you will go to him."

Guilt rose up in her like sickness, but she ignored his meaning. "It was the miasma of the swamps, love. You've caught the yellow fever. You must rest."

He closed his eyes and coughed.

37

SHE BURIED HIM AT ST. LOUIS CEMETERY, AT dawn, too early to expect a crowd of mourners, which was her intention. Perhaps it was the hour, or perhaps fear of breathing in the pestilence, but only she and William Claiborne came, besides the priest and undertaker. It pained Cassandra that her children could not come to see their father laid to rest, but she dared not expose them to infection.

Clarice had carried off baby William to the country. Indeed, the minute word got out of Benedict's affliction, the carts and carriages had begun to rattle out of town. Everyone who had a place to flee to fled, and those who were left waited with their breaths held, thinking fearfully of the stagnant waters of the swamp surrounding them, its gasses drifting toward the city like a cloud of death.

But that year not another person died of yellow fever. Not a single white flag flickered outside any other door. It was a miracle, or else a punishment, as though God's fist had reached out and shaken over Benedict alone. Cassandra had his tomb made out of brick, raised high off the ground, with a flat stone for the roof. She had it plastered thick and whitewashed and his name carved on the top. At first she had thought that she would go to the Cabildo and beg the mayor to let her bury him with Anne. There was now a requirement that victims of the yellow fever must be buried at St. Louis cemetery, and she thought she would try to make him set the law aside. But then she thought it would be cruel to Benedict to let him lie forever where he had been betrayed. She did not know it then, but she would never go to visit him. This place held too much sorrow, both hers and other people's. To think of him she would go and sit with Anne.

The priest made short work of the ceremony, as though he did not trust God to protect him from infection. William, though, surprised Cassandra with his tenderness. He stood by her and held her hand, and when the last word of the prayer was said, he squeezed it hard, until she thought that all the bones would break, and held his other hand against his eyes.

He said that he would see her home—he had a carriage—but Cassandra said that she would walk, the exercise would calm her. He kissed her before he left, as kindly as a brother. "I'm sorry that you hate me, Cassie."

Cassandra was so surprised at this remark she told herself she had not heard it. He had whispered something else, some condolence, and in her confused state she had misheard him. She knelt beside the tomb and prayed for Benedict, and for herself and William and her children. And then she prayed for Jean.

She rose and lifted back her veil. And there was Benedict, watching from behind a tomb. She felt the hairs rise on her neck. But then she saw that it was Jean.

"I've lost him, Jean. Dear God, I've lost him."

He came to her. She would not let him touch her.

"Cassandra, marry me. Let me have my son."

She turned her back on him and walked away. Behind her came his voice, so low she did not catch the words. She did not stop.

.   .   .

After the funeral, Cassandra fell into a pit. No sooner had she come back home than the world beneath her yawned and swallowed her. All day she wandered through the house and wept, and all night lay stiff and sleepless on her bed. By day she refused to open up the drapes, by night refused a lamp, not so much as a candle to carry room to room, but felt her way around the house as though she had gone blind. Her breasts ran milk still, and hurt so much she could hardly stand the fabric of her clothes to touch them, yet she could not bear to bring her baby back so soon. It seemed to her he was, and always would be, the physical reminder of the disaster she had brought down on Benedict. Whereas before she had convinced herself that he was Benedict's, now she was convinced that he was Jean's. Why else would God have punished her so cruelly? After Anne's death, she had blamed God; now God blamed her. And in a strange way it was easier. When Anne died there was nothing she could do, no one she could punish. But she could join with God and blame herself for this, and punish herself too.

She could not bring herself to see Clarice or any of her friends, or Dr. Masderall, or anyone at all. She barely ate and the flesh dropped off her bones, while Mattie spent long hours in the kitchen concocting dishes that would tempt, only to throw them out next day or give them to the poor.

The days went by so slowly, and yet they rolled into each other as though each day was not separate from the one before or after, but all were one long day, the nights unnoticed in the dimness of the house. She felt unwell and she was weak and trembling in the knees from time to time. Sometimes she fancied that she sat once more by Maman's bed in that dim room in Paris, willing her to die. *Dear God, forgive. Dear God, take me as well.*

Other times she fancied it was Benedict who lay there in the bed. He had loved her all these eighteen years and never once looked slyly at another from the corner of his eye, but the instant another man had looked at her, she had let fly from her head the long consistency of his devotion. She had let fly faithfulness, forgotten that most precious virtue—how to be a wife. And she had killed him.

Why had she fallen into love with Jean? Was it because he wanted her and she had been so flattered she could not resist? Had his desire inspired her own? Or hers inspired his? Was it because Benedict had become domesticated, staid, responsible, and Jean still had about him adventure's heady scent? But she had loved them both and could not separate them out, as though they had been not two men but one, almost as though—no, it was foolish— as though Benedict were the idea of which Jean was the realization. Or was it the other way around?

She thought about the time she had told Jean how, after all these years, Benedict still saw in dreams his father's head skewered to the upright of the gate, how he would twitch and cry out in the night. She had asked Jean if he had nightmares too, but he had not replied. Instead, his face went hard and blank. It frightened her because she understood she did not know him anymore.

Benedict she had grown to know so well she could predict his every mood, almost his every thought. There had been at his core a steadfast gentleness. Jean's soul was opaque. Sometimes she had fancied that she saw down into it, but what was there seemed shifting, centerless, as though the core of him had somehow been misplaced. He was not as pure a soul as Benedict.

She could not make confession to a priest—her sin had been too monstrous—and so confessed it to herself. Day after day, from morning until night, she sat with her eyes fixed unseeingly, or paced about the echoing rooms, confessing and confessing, until Mattie became frantic with concern.

One day Jean appeared outside her door. She had him turned away. He came again. She had him turned away again. He came along the gallery and rattled at the locked door of her bedchamber. He sent a letter to the house. She tore it up unread. He sent her flowers. She had Mattie throw them out.

At last he sent his surgeon, Monsieur Dessalines, to plead with her. When Mattie spoke his name, Cassandra found herself once more in tears. This huge rough man had been so kind to her, and so gentle with Benedict. "Let him come in," she said. And so he came. They sat together in the parlor while he called her "ma petite" and offered her Jean's heart.

Although Monsieur Dessalines was clearly embarrassed by his mission, he was so tender in presenting it that Cassandra wanted him to sit forever in her parlor and rumble fondly at her in his big deep voice, and gaze at her with fatherly concern. She wanted to climb onto his lap and let him comfort her. She found herself coherent in his company.

"Monsieur Lafitte must trust you very much," she said, "if he will trust you with his heart. Tell your master I have cut him out of mine. We have sinned together, he and I, and we must bear the consequences. His punishment will be that he will have a child he cannot call his own. Mine will be that I have a father to my child that I cannot acknowledge."

She did not call Mattie to show him to the door, but got up from her chair, intending to do so herself. But she was weak from lack of food and sleep and staggered. Monsieur Dessalines leaped to catch her and, with all the gentleness of a big man, lowered her back into her chair. "Oh, ma petite," he said. "Oh, ma petite." And went off to the kitchen where he secured hot broth and a spoon from Mattie and came back to crouch in front of her and spoon the broth into her mouth, insisting she take every drop, making her promise him that she would take three meals a day. "If you should die," he said, "Monsieur Lafitte would have my head." It made her laugh and with laughter came the start of her release.

Next day she kept her promise and ate three small meals, and again the next day, and the next, until her appetite was up, her strength increasingly returned, her spirits making their long climb out of the pit. On the day she gave instructions for her children to be brought back home, Mattie went down on her knees before the kitchen fire and prayed so hard and long the pie she had just made for dinner burned.

Shortly afterward, Cassandra heard that Jean had built himself a mansion on Grande Terre, and an auction warehouse between Grande Terre and New Orleans which he called, mockingly, "the Temple." Now he rarely came to town. Instead the whole town went to him. Within months he was notorious. Gossip about him whistled and murmured on street corners and in drawing rooms, but he cut such a dashing figure and was so sought after for the provision of untaxed exotic goods that no venom attached to it. It was as though he had sent a message to the governor: "You call me pirate? Then a pirate I shall be." William fumed and fretted over it and all the town supported Jean and thumbed their noses at him.

His knife-sharp elegance of form, his sleek black charm, his ability to conjure anything a body needed out of clear blue air was so like Benedict back in the days when he was courting her that when Cassandra thought of it she caught her breath. Jean could well have been his son. And Benedict had said he loved him like a son. And was betrayed. It tore her heart.

The weeks went by, the months. Cassandra lived her life devoted to her family. Her four daughters were as dark-eyed and dark-haired as she was herself, and as lovely as she could have wished them. Benedict, a solemn boy, looked like her brother John. Albert was her favorite, she could not help it, though she told herself it was not because of his paternity. If Jean's name sometimes floated in the air she never spoke it. Gradually, like a vapor, his image grew thin and then invisible. When she went to sit with Anne she no longer thought she heard his step come crunching up the path. She ceased imagining she heard his voice. She told herself that he was nothing but a memory. And yet, when she looked into her baby's face, she saw him there. Albert was Jean's son; she knew he was Jean's son.

When her mind was torn and her heart twisted in her breast, she would go to the cathedral and kneel down at the altar and attempt to pray. At first she felt that God's harsh gaze would never soften, but over time He seemed to bend to her and listen. Gradually, she became contented with her widowed life, although to stay so she kept busy. If she did not, if she had an afternoon without a visitor and no project to absorb her, she sometimes felt a sensation in her head like falling. Then she would hurry to invent something to do or some purchase to be made. She dreaded solitude and inactivity. She never heard Jean's name connected to another lady.

On Albert's first birthday, a gift arrived, a miniature silver drinking cup. With it came a note: "From your papa." Cassandra locked it in a little secret cupboard in the morning room. She did not write a note of thanks. Besides herself and Jean, Monsieur

Dessalines was still the only one who knew that Jean claimed Albert as his son. She intended it to stay that way.

William, who had become kinder to her, still teased her about Jean, but now his teasing lacked its old sharp edge. Sometimes, at a social gathering, he would approach her with an eyebrow raised. "How fares our charming pirate?" he would say, or, "My dear, how goes the world of plunder?" And she would laugh—what else to do?—but she worried that one day he would look at Albert and see Jean.

On Albert's second birthday, another gift arrived, a tiny silver candlestick: "From your papa." She locked it in the secret cupboard with the first.

And then the yellow fever came again and took Clarice. It struck Cassandra unawares, and William too. One day Clarice was well and readying her house to have a ball. The next, she lay against her pillows with her eyes gone yellow and blood leaking from her nose and mouth, as though her internal organs seeped.

Cassandra sat with her all day. William wanted her to leave in case she took infection, but she would not. They sat together all that night, and in the morning, Clarice took a fit and thrashed about the bed and shrieked. Blood sprayed from her mouth and nose across the bed, and then she died.

Cassandra never saw a man more broken down than William. She thought that he would die of grief. He leaned against her breast and wept for hours. She could not make him stop. When at last he lifted up his head, his face was terrible. She took him in her arms again. He wept again. She coaxed him to an armchair and he clung to her and wept.

He went back to his duties but he could not make himself recover. He wept before the city council and the legislature. He wept before his servants and the public. He sent a message to Cassandra every evening, begging her to come and sit with him. And he would take Clarice's little boy onto his lap and weep. He hardly dared let the child out of his sight for fear that he would lose him too. He worried over every cough and sneeze, and if the child was not hungry for his dinner, sent out for Dr. Masderall to examine him. He drove the child's nurse half-crazy with his fuss.

William got it in his head that the filthy levee at the waterfront outside the Government House was responsible for Clarice's death.

"I'll write to Mr. Madison," he said, "and beg to have the residence removed. I'll describe to him the rank stench of foulness I suffer every day, how this entire city slops its waste, like a calculated insult, right outside my window—old vegetables and fish entrails, rotting pigs' heads, bones with matter clinging to them, the soil of chamber pots and privies, dead cats and birds and dogs and slaughtered rats, old used-up mules—once I even saw a new-born Negro child—and not even the care taken to tip this refuse fully in the river, but they let it spit and spatter all along the levee where the sun boils it up and stews it into noxious vapors, poisoning the air. Two wives I have lost to the rank atmosphere of this fetid, wretched city, and a little daughter too, a kind and decent secretary, and more friends than I can count. A man trembles to hold out his hand in friendship in this place lest he make a friend today and have him flung down on his back to die in blood tomorrow."

And he jumped up to find pen and paper to write this awful record down and send it to the president.

"Wait, wait," Cassandra said. "I don't think you should complain to Mr. Madison. Instead, you should apply to him for leave of absence. You should take a holiday."

And so he did. He wrote to Mr. Madison and then set off for Washington. He would ascend the river and then travel overland. Cassandra was glad to see him go for she was growing weary of his grief. She went with him to the wharf and waved her handkerchief, and then she turned and walked.

Arriving at a church in the American sector of the town, she went in and knelt in a back pew. The church was Protestant and a service was in progress, a requiem for some dead child. She found herself weeping for this unknown child, and, at last, for poor Clarice.

38

$\mathcal{W}$ILLIAM CAME BACK FROM HIS VACATION
well recovered. He had dined with Mr. Madison in Washington,
and with Mr. Winder, the governor of Maryland, in Baltimore,
and with important men in Philadelphia, New York, and Boston
too. When Cassandra heard that he had dined in Baltimore with
Levin Winder, she was overcome with curiosity. She had known
Levin as a child. He had come to dancing lessons at Owings Hall.
She longed to beg for news, but William had always thought she
was Parisian, and would most certainly have questioned her about
her interest. Even though her relations with him had grown
warmer since Clarice died, she had no fancy to confide in him her
intimate emotions.

That winter, Monsieur Tournelles coughed himself to death,
leaving Emmeline a widow. Her sister, Madame Trepagnier, whose
husband owned a sugar plantation, died shortly after, of the bloody
flux, so grieving widow married grieving widower and Emmeline
sold off her furniture and sacks of flour and sugar, and went off to

live the country life. She had always been an enterprising woman with a sharp eye for a profit and she had got herself a fortune now, and a vast estate.

Cassandra missed her. It had been comforting to know that Monsieur Tournelles was down below her making bread, or Emmeline squeezing intricate icing decorations onto petits fours. But Emmeline had never had a child, and now she took her sister's clutch and brooded over them. She grew stout, and her breasts, which had been copious, grew vast. She was as contented as a woman ever was and Monsieur Trepagnier was well satisfied with her. Although she missed her, Cassandra could not begrudge Emmeline her new happiness.

After the Tournelles' departure, a young lawyer by the name of Mr. Grymes came to Cassandra with a proposal to turn the bakery into a suite of offices. He was American and new in town, but had decided it was better to live in the French Quarter, which was central, than in the newer area where other Americans were building houses. He was a quiet man, canny and industrious, and often, when she came home late from some event, Cassandra would see him through the window, his oil lamp burning and his head bent over legal books and papers. Before long, clients were rapping and tapping at his door all day, or swinging their heels in his waiting room, clutching wills or deeds or summonses or bills of sale or statements of investment or account.

Sometimes, when Cassandra was sitting in her courtyard, he would appear, coughing politely, asking some question about French customs in this place, and she would ask him to join her for a cup of coffee. It turned out he was in love, but at a loss how to proceed, and although Cassandra saw it as an irony, she gave him what advice she could, which seemed to help, because before long he was betrothed to a young girl by the name of Suzette Bosque. In return, he helped her with business matters and investments. He did not become what she would call a friend, but they were very civil to each other.

Shortly after that there was a slave revolt. It broke out in the Parish of St. John the Baptist on the west side of the river above New Orleans, and before anybody knew it, five hundred and more Negroes made themselves into an army, with flags and officers for each division, and came marching down the river to the beat of drums, setting on fire plantation houses as they came. Five burned to the ground, the owners and their families having fled.

Emmeline's new husband, Monsieur Trepagnier, became a hero. He was a gentle man, most civilized, who loved to play the fiddle and was as lenient as any of the planters toward his slaves. Emmeline had complained from time to time that he was over-lenient, that his Negroes sang too much about their work, and that he would improve their output greatly if he would only get himself a cowhide.

"Wife," he would say, laughing, "I would as soon listen to them sing as listen to them howl." And calling for his fiddle and his children, he would go out to the high circular gallery around his house and make his children jig.

He was no Nero, though. When his slaves rose with the others, he sent his family away and turned himself into a one-man army. He loaded half a dozen fowling pieces with buckshot and set them in a row along the balustrade, where they could be taken up one after the other. Then he took his fiddle and played himself a tune, watching for a tumult to come bursting through his gates. When it did, he set his fiddle down, picked up the first piece in his arsenal, and emptied it above the heads of the approaching foe.

The entire mob stopped in its tracks, milled about in panic, and backed off through the gates, leaving no more damage to his property than the echo of their shrieked-out oaths to return and slice his throat.

Not far down the river, the rebels were trapped between militia coming down from Baton Rouge and up from New Orleans. With a great wailing cry of rage and disappointment, the entire company fled into the swamps. Sixty-six were shot as they ran off, and a good number taken and hanged on the spot. The rest died in the swamps, save for sixteen, who were caught and hauled to New Orleans for trial. The whole thing was reported in the papers.

When it was discovered that all the ringleaders were slaves sold out of Jean's Temple warehouse, William flew into a rage. He would have liked to get his hands on Jean and hang him for it, but instead he had the Negroes' heads cut off and stuck on pikes along the riverfront. Half the town went out to see the spectacle, but Cassandra had no stomach for it.

Albert turned three years. Another gift, a silver napkin holder with his initials carved: "From your papa." Cassandra locked it in the cupboard with the others.

Next year, Louisiana was admitted to the Union as the eighteenth state, and New Orleans had its first election. William stood for governor and won. He was most gratified. After all the years of struggling against him, the citizens had finally decided he was a worthwhile man. He developed a small strut in his walk and Cassandra thought his face would fairly crack apart the way he smiled so much. He became avuncular and gracious, although she never saw him condescending.

He invited her to be his hostess at a celebration ball and they got through it nicely, without a single argument. It was a grand affair, with fireworks, and everybody who was anybody came. The Government House glittered with a thousand candles and the streets around it glittered with more fancy carriages than anyone could count. People came from miles around. Every inn was full, people sleeping cheek to jowl on every bed and cot and couch, jammed end to end on rugs and quilts spread out on floors. The grand supper was set as a buffet, and the ballroom floor had been polished to a glistening sheen. Frivolity jostled with frivolity in all the public rooms, and Cassandra was sure Jean had made a fancy profit decking everybody out in finery. Curls. Feathers. Flashing rings and bracelets. Lace at wrist and throat. Candles gleamed on white breasts. Cream was licked from dainty fingertips, eyelids lowered, raised. A hand kissed here, a bow. Madame, you look entirely captivating. So charmed that you could come. Romantic competition filled the air like the heady scent of roses and was sharpened by the wit of malice. Whispers floated. Heads tilted, nodded, turned away. Eye met eye over feathered clicking fan. Messages were passed. Conversation rustled, murmured, punctuated by a laugh or girlish squeal, the deep hum of a comment from the corner of a

mouth. And through it all, Cassandra rustled in a pure white ruffled gown, tapping with closed fan an elbow here, a shirtfront
there, drawing this one to talk with that, lubricating tensions with
an offered glass, triumphant in her own success.

When it was all done, William led her to his private sitting
room. It was a fine room, with paneled wainscoting and the best
of furniture. A wine-colored leather armchair, high backed, well
cushioned, and with thick rolled arms, stood on the right side of
the hearth, and a matching lady's armchair on the left. There was
no fire, since the weather was extremely warm, and the fireplace
was hidden by a screen in the shape of a brass peacock with its tail
spread out, most fancy.

Beside William's armchair was a small round table, highly polished, with a pure white doily, round. On it was a silver candlestick
with a tall white candle, lit, a crystal decanter of whiskey, a squat
pair of crystal glasses, a large meerschaum, and a fat tobacco
pouch. Cassandra thought William would smoke, or take a glass of
whiskey, but he did neither. He showed her to the lady's chair and,
when she had made herself comfortable, went to stand before his
own with his coattails in his hands as though he would sit down
but could not make up his mind to it.

"Cassandra, there's something I must say to you."

"Not bad news, I hope? Sit down, William, you're making me
uneasy."

"No, good news, I hope." He sat down and then stood again,
then sat and, setting his hands against his knees, leaned toward
her, speaking earnestly.

"Cassandra, since Clarice died you've been a great help and
comfort to me."

"Thank you, William. You're very kind."

"No, that's not it."

"Not a help and comfort after all?"

"You tease me. I'm being clumsy." He coughed. "Cassandra,
Benedict was most fortunate to have you as his wife. You are a perfect hostess and intelligent in conversation too, the sort of wife a
man needs for his success. I've no doubt that with such a lady at his
side he would have achieved high office. No doubt we would have

sent him off to Washington as senator if he hadn't taken it into his head to go to heaven before we had the opportunity. But I distress you. I didn't bring you here to tell you that." He stopped and gazed about the room, as though he had forgotten what he had intended and would read it in the pattern of the wallpaper.

It was late and Cassandra was thinking about bed and so she prompted him. "Say on, William. I'm discreet. You can tell me anything."

He shifted his neck inside his collar and, with no further preamble, turned to her and said in a stern voice as though it were a reprimand, "I have it in my head to marry you." And got up from his chair and came to kneel in front of her.

All the air went out of her. "Marry me, William? And what other extraordinary notions have you in your head? Get up, get up. You mustn't kneel to me. It is undignified. You're the governor. It is *I* who should kneel to *you*."

"You think you'll have me, then?"

"I think you have gone daft. A prize cat and dog together *we* would make. Since Clarice died we have gone a long way to repair our differences, but *marry* you? Why, I'd as soon marry—"

She was casting in her head for some incongruous example when she saw his face darken. He leaped to his feet.

"I'll hang the man!"

She looked at him astonished. "Then he's lucky I couldn't put a name to him."

But now he was off on one of his tirades, pacing up and down the room, and she realized he was talking about Jean. How this man could rile her!

"Be silent, William. You let obsession carry you away. You didn't hear me mention Jean Lafitte."

He turned on her. "How *can* you, Cassandra! How *can* you, as the widow of an upright and estimable man? This rascal you hanker after is a rankling sore to this administration, flaunting his illegal wares, seducing even our most honorable citizens to fly in the face of law and order, laughing at me up his sleeve."

"I know nothing of his sleeve, but you'll not hang him for some imagined hankering of *mine*."

"I'll hang him anyway. If you don't wish to witness it, you may pack your bags and pack your children up and go on back to Maryland where you belong. No, don't try to contradict me. You're no more Parisian than I am myself. You're Cassandra Deye Cockey Owings of Owings Hall in the County Baltimore. You gape, Madame, and well you should. Did you take your cousin for a fool?"

"My cousin? What's this?" Cassandra burst into tears and it seemed to bring him to his senses. He stood glaring for a moment and then his face softened. Once more he came to kneel before her. He took her hand and would not let her pull it back.

"Cassandra, I'm sorry. We are cousins. Can we not be friends?"

"William, you've always had a talent to upset me. Now you would astonish me. When did you discover this?"

"I knew it from the first."

"And did not reveal yourself to me?"

"How could I? You hated me."

"I didn't hate you, William. You would needle me and needle me until I flew into a rage."

"I've always had a fondness for you."

"A fine way you had of showing it. Please, will you get up?"

He got up, and pulling up a footstool, sat on that instead, looking at her in a mournful fashion, like a hound who has been punished by his master.

"Did I torment you? I'm sorry for it, Cassie. May I call you Cassie now that we are cousins?"

"You may call me anything you want. Call me Cassie, call me cousin, but do not call me wife."

"But I am a grand catch now that I'm elected. Indeed, I am a prize. *Anyone* would marry me."

She laughed. "Then marry anyone."

He did. Within the month he married Suzette Bosque, a child as dark as Clarice had been fair. Or stole her, rather, out from underneath Cassandra's nose. She had been sweetheart to the lawyer Mr. Grymes for twelve months now, and when she abandoned him to become the governor's wife, Cassandra was glad he did not understand she was the cause. William had probably been right when he said he could have any woman in the town, but Cassandra thought he wanted to make her understand the good prize she had lost, and so, to rub her nose in it, he stole the sweetheart of her neighbor.

As though in punishment for William's perversity, Mr. Madison, on June eighteenth of 1812, proclaimed the country was at war with Britain and called all New Orleans' troops away to fight. At once William became embroiled in figuring a way to protect the city from invasion, since he had it on intelligence that the British planned to take it. It would be a prize for them. From New Orleans they could go up the Mississippi and attack the country from behind while their sloops of war attacked it from the sea. And so William spent his time running from here to there, writing letters, sending memos, drumming up volunteers for a militia.

Suzette, who had no mother and had been spoiled by her father, found herself neglected. She became petulant and demanding, and it was not long before William came to Cassandra, calling her cousin, wanting to make up their quarrel, begging her to "take the child in hand." But Cassandra said that he had made his bed and now should lie on it.

39

*A*LBERT TURNED FOUR YEARS. AS USUAL, A gift arrived, this time a tiny silver scabbard with a tiny silver sword: "From your papa." Cassandra locked it with the others. Colegate married Harold Donaldson and went to live in Natchez. Cassandra did not like Harold much. She thought he had grown into a priggish sort of man. Juliana took vows and locked herself up in the convent of the Ursulines, intent on charity. Young Benedict went out for the militia, at barely fourteen years, and Cassandra went to the cathedral every noon to pray for him. Mr. Brown resigned from his position as district attorney and horrified William by buying a plantation and a mess of slaves from Jean. Mr. Grymes became district attorney in his place. Mattie's boy, Syphorian, died of an aggravated spleen, or so the doctor said, although Mattie swore that it was voodoo brought in from Saint Domingue.

Cassandra repented of her attitude to Suzette Bosque and was gratified to find Suzette welcomed her advances. She began to go to dinner at the Government House again, and to advise Suzette on matters of entertainment, invitation lists and seating, and other diplomatic matters. William beamed on her and Cassandra told herself that their antagonistic days were over.

But then Mr. Madison put out a call for privateers. William scrutinized New Orleans' applicants and gave out three letters of marque on Mr. Madison's behalf, and then another one. Not long after, Jean sailed up the river in a brig, *Goellette la Diligente*, bristling with cannon, and tied up at the quay in front of William's house. It was a long, dark vessel, low in the water, with very tall masts, and gleaming pure white sails. Port authorities approved it for registration but William grumbled when he heard of it. "A letter of marque is what the man is really after. For that he may go hopping."

And he put a proclamation out against him, commanding him to cease all his unlawful activities, adjuring every official of the state to watch out for him and try to catch him in the act so they could arrest him, prohibiting the people of the state from holding any kind of intercourse with him. In all this he did not name Jean exactly, referring only to "the pirates and banditti of Lake Barataria," calling them dishonorable and a foul reproach and subversive to all laws, human and divine, threatening the severest punishment. But the whole town knew against whom this proclamation was directed and Cassandra puzzled over why, since William was so set against Jean, he did not put out an explicit warrant for his arrest. She thought him something of a coward that he would not go head-to-head with Jean.

As she passed his office one day, she saw him at his desk, bent above some piece of paper. She stopped, and coming back to the doorway, said, "An arrest warrant for Monsieur Lafitte, perhaps? You told me once that he's a slippery character. Do you think you'll catch him?"

He set his pen down and removed his spectacles. "I'll put money on his head and he'll be led to me."

"So you can throw him in the calaboose? There's not a soul in town ready to betray him. Where else are they to get their fancy goods, with your government so set on keeping trade under control? Everybody says your taxes and the customs that you levy are prohibitive."

"The war goes badly. We need the public money to defend the city."

"The people want free trade. If you'll not give it to them, Monsieur Lafitte will."

He rose, ponderous and statesmanlike, his face gone all white. "Let me give you some advice, Cassandra . . ."

But Cassandra wanted none and quickly made it out of there. She did not know it then, but this speech of hers would change her life entirely.

The day was hot and stifling. The doors and windows all stood open, the paintings were wrapped up in gauze, like old men groaning with the toothache, to protect them from the gnats and moths and flies. Cassandra had gone into the morning room and was sitting quietly, sipping a cup of tea, when Mattie came to say she had a visitor, and in a moment there was William, with a letter in his hand.

He came into the room and set it on her lap. "From Maryland," he said, then, as though he would wait upon her for an answer, he went to stand beside the window with his hands clasped beneath his coattails.

Cassandra turned the letter over. It was written on fine parchment paper and addressed in the hand of a stranger, full of loops and swirls and elegant slanted crossings of the effs and tees, which showed it had been written by a woman. Mattie brought her spectacles and the bone letter opener, which Cassandra slipped beneath the flap. She did not fold the pages down at once but sat looking at the letter with a cautious feeling in her chest. Since she came to New Orleans she had not received one word from anyone in Maryland.

With a quick movement she smoothed it open, and turning to the last page, read the signature: "Your sister, Fanny."

Tears started in Cassandra's eyes. Fanny, that child, that little baby. A great heaving of the chest seized her and she sat with the unread letter in her hand, weeping helplessly. William did not move.

Mattie ran in. "Madame?"

"It's all right, Mattie. Close the door." And sat there weeping and shaking for she did not know how long. By then the ink was smudged with tears and she blotted it with the corner of her handkerchief so as not to miss a word. Then she wiped her face and blew her nose and tucked the handkerchief into her breast. Still William did not move.

My dear Cassandra,

Several years ago, I learned I have an oldest sister I have never met, one who ran away with a Frenchman before ever I knew what was going on in the world, never even knew I had any sister older than Penelope, Charcilla, Mary, and Charlotte. Since then I have been searching for you, and have now discovered you and yearn to meet you, especially as Papa has spoken so lovingly and sadly of you. Cassandra, what have you been thinking all these years to treat him so?

A panicked feeling rose inside Cassandra's chest. What was this? Papa had spoken lovingly of her? But then joy came to take the place of panic. He had forgiven her! A delighted laugh broke out of her. She leaped up from her chair and walked excitedly about the room. She would go to him at once. She set her hand on the bellpull and was about to ring for Mattie to come quick and pack her clothes, but the letter was in her hand and she had not even finished reading it. Settling herself once more in her chair, she read again. And now it was bad news.

Several months ago Papa had a falling out with our brother Thomas over a business venture they have together in Kentucky. It upset him so that he suffered an attack of the heart and since then has taken to his bed. The doctor says he could recover if he made his mind up to it but instead he has made up his mind to die and lies day after day working at it. I have always been his favorite, even above Charcilla, and he will let none but me sit beside his bed. He tells me all about his life, all the things that have happened in it. He does a deal of talking, I can tell you, hardly sleeping at all, just talking and talking, and all the time he keeps calling me Cass, or Cassie, or Cassandra.

At first it puzzled me and I pressed him on it but he only closed his eyes. I tried to ask Mama, but she is so muddled in the head these days that I could ask away forever. And so I asked Charlotte, and then Charcilla, and my other sisters. Gradually a story of you came together, although it came reluctantly, since it turned out Papa had forbidden them to speak of you, and they had not done so for years.

I suppose you wonder why I did not ask our brother John. I could not, since he is not here. John is in the navy, fighting with the British. We beseech God for his safety every night, and since we have heard nothing for some weeks, presume that he is safe. But I must go on with my story. After I had got all the information that I could out of my sisters, I resolved to go one neighbor to another until I got the full truth of the matter, and if that brought no success I would take out advertisements in the newspapers. (Many people do it, looking for lost slaves or wives.) But although many still remembered you, no one knew your whereabouts, and only people seeking money answered my advertisements.

Then I had occasion to go to dinner at the home of Mary Winder. Her husband is now governor but they spend more time in Baltimore than in Annapolis. Mr. Winder was entertaining our cousin William Claiborne who was visiting from New Orleans where he is the governor. But of course I need not tell you that.

I was seated next to William, but instead of drawing him out to speak about himself, I was so consumed with the idea of finding my lost sister that I could speak of nothing else. Afterwards I thought he must have found me very dull, because he sat all night very quiet, with a look of bemusement on his face, and now here comes a letter from him telling me you live under his very nose in New Orleans and have ever since he came there. I do not understand why he did not reveal this to me earlier and am considerably put out with him. Still, I suppose he has his reasons.

He tells me you are a widow now, that your husband was a good man and much relied on in the town, and that you have six children of your own—six! He commented you have an inclination to keep company with pirates, following the remark with exclamation points, as though he were laughing as he wrote it, so I suppose it is some private joke between the two of you.

Cassandra dear, I do not know your reasons for remaining hidden from your family all these years, but Papa's health declines each day. It would give him great comfort if you would visit him before he finally succumbs.

I do not know if this will reach you, since the posts are all awry these days. The British sit outside the harbor in their sloops-of-war, preventing mail by sea, and all the useful men have been called into the army, leaving the decrepit and young boys to act as post riders. Of the two courses, I plan to entrust this to a blockade runner by the name of Mr. Hicks, who is a canny sailor.

I embrace you tenderly.

Your sister, Fanny

Cassandra set the letter down and sat staring straight in front of her, her mind back in that afternoon so long ago in Baltimore when her letter to Papa had been brought back to her unread. She had blamed him for it, assuming that his pique with her had been so great he could not even bring himself to write a note rejecting her. And so, she had thought, he had Mama write it instead. But if he grieved for her, if he had longed for her return, then what venom had guided Mama's hand? Her own?

Cassandra's heart continued on a steady beat, like a clock ticking, clinging to regularity as if even a small disturbance would send it off into such a wild clanging and jangling that it would fly apart. After a while she rose and passed the letter silently to William and watched him as he read, but she could not divine his emotions from his face.

When he had finished, he looked up and saw her watching. He came to her and took her hand and stood there patting it. It was the first time Cassandra had ever seen him at a loss for words.

At last he said, "I'm sorry, cousin."

Cassandra felt sorrow rising like a poisonous cloud, making her eyes water and her breath catch in her throat. All these years, these years. Why would Mama have done it? How could she use her so? She felt herself begin to shake. She felt rage rise.

And then a voice inside her head: *She used you no worse than you used Benedict.* And suddenly the rage and grief were gone. William came behind her. She turned and set her head against his shoulder, and he held her.

That night another great storm swept up from the south. The crops all up and down the river were flattened or dragged out by their roots, houses lost their roofs, some were completely blown away, others sank at their foundations, and ships at anchor in the harbor were tossed up in the air to come down higgledy-piggledy on each other.

Cassandra could not sleep. She got up and went to the front gallery, where she watched the street roar and rush with clotted leaves and vegetable matter snatched from someone's garden or washed across the levee, here a cypress branch trailing a rippling train of moss, drowned rats, the ripped-off timbers of a house. She listened to the thrash and batter on the roof, like some swamp creature that would break in and drown her in the tumult of her whirling thoughts.

In her life she had been through many things. She had witnessed poverty and horror and revolution. She had seen blood running in the streets, men's heads torn from their bodies and paraded. She had seen her house explode in fire and everything she owned devoured by flame. She had seen floods laden with the plunder of despair, and lived in damp, and constant heat, waiting for the sickly season when deadly gasses rose out of the swamps, creeping into the city like the angel of death, first one and then another dropping in its path, bodies piling up in pyramids inside the cemetery walls, each breath of wind across the city laden with the breath of their corruption. Sweet Anne, dead; Benedict, dead horribly because of her; Clarice, her best friend, dead; a hundred others vanished in one hot, dank October month. And she had suffered guilt and anguish and the joy and pain of passion that took her in its jaws and would not let her go.

In the small hours of the morning, all this fell away as though none of it had happened. She wanted to be young again, to start anew. She wanted to stand on the steps of Papa's house in Maryland and watch a purple storm come sweeping down from Pennsylvania and smell the purity it left behind. She thought about the little red-barked maple Papa planted in the yard the day she had turned six, saw in her mind its thin red limbs outlined against the snow. She imagined she was going to a Christmas party, at the Gists' or Worthingtons', felt once more the sensation of the sleigh slicing its way across the snow with its bells jingling and the horses' hooves crunching, the shouts of laughter and her fur-edged hood tickling at her neck. Now she was skating on the pond behind Grandpapa Owings' house, her ankles chilling with the swish of frozen air. She felt the blood rise in her cheeks, heard the splash as some unfortunate fell through the thin ice at the end, and then the shouts and scurrying to rescue him.

As abruptly as it had attacked, the storm gave up. It sobbed a little rolling off toward the north, and hiccoughed once, then everything was still, just the tick-tick-tick of water falling from the eaves, the rustle of water in the drains along the street. Cassandra clasped her hands together on the balustrade and gazed up at the moon, a round hole in a pure black sky through which she could see Maryland.

As soon as it was decent, Cassandra hurried through the streets until she came to the Government House, where she found William eating a solitary breakfast in his courtyard. He embraced her kindly, remarking that she was more cheerful than he had expected, and they sat down together over a pot of coffee to discuss her situation.

"What will you do?" he asked. "Surely you'll not go to Maryland?"

"I must. Of course, I must."

"But we're at war. The seas are full of British gunships. The ports are all blockaded from New England to the Mississippi mouth. Only pirates in sharp vessels dare to sail the coast."

"Then I'll go with one of those."

He gave her a dry look. "I don't doubt you could arrange it, but your shipmates would be more danger to you than the British navy."

"Then I'll go overland. I'll go up the river to Natchez and overland from there. How long will it take?"

"I couldn't say, but I had it in a letter from a friend that the Virginia roads are bad this year. The British blockade has forced merchants to transport their goods by wagon or by cart. Their wheels tear up the surfaces and the weather does the rest. He says he took thirty-eight hours to get from Fredericksburg to Alexandria, the distance fifty miles."

When Cassandra heard this lamentable statistic she jumped up from her chair. "How can I go by road? Papa will be dead and buried, rotted in his grave, before I ever get to Maryland. No, I must go by ship. Don't expostulate about it, William. You'll not persuade me from it. I'll go with this blockade runner, Mr. Hicks. Fanny says he is a canny sailor."

"Canny enough to carry cargo. I'll not have him carry my own cousin into danger."

"But surely you thought of the British blockade before you sent your letter off to Fanny telling her that I was here? What did you think I'd do? Stay here and let Papa die without a reconciliation? And William, why did you not reveal me to my family earlier? Why did you say nothing at your dinner with the Winders—when was it?—almost three years ago? Why did you let me go on suffering from this separation? Have you no heart?"

He looked alarmed. "It was because I have a heart that I did *not* reveal you. Cassie, I've never asked you why you hid from them. I thought it not my place to question you."

"So why *now*, when there's a war on?"

He looked sheepish and set his coffee down. "I confess I wrote the letter in a fit of pique that day you taunted me about my ability to catch Lafitte. I regretted it when I had sent it, but struck it from my mind, certain it would go astray. The post riders these days . . ." He trailed off, staring down into his coffee cup. "And then this Mr. Hicks came thumping at my door. I'm sorry, Cassie."

"What did you hope to gain?"

"I don't know." He shifted in his chair. "I suppose I thought that if I could reconnect you to your family you would, you would . . . Will you return to New Orleans?"

Something in his tone made Cassandra suddenly suspicious. "Return? What do you mean?"

"Do you have reason to return?"

"Reason? What other reason than my children?"

"You'll not take them?"

"I must go quick, before Papa dies."

"But you could send for them. I could keep them at my house and you could send for them."

"So, cousin, would you have me out of here for good?"

He made a noise in his throat. "I think of your own interests. And, now you are my cousin, the interests of our family."

"And what interests might those be?"

"You know to whom I'm referring."

"William, why must we go round and round with that old story? Why don't you *take* the man if he upsets you so? You say you have good cause. Then haul him into court and hang him. Or are you afraid of him? William, are you afraid of him?"

When she saw his hand begin to shake, she knew that she had happened onto something serious. She watched him push his chair back and press his palms against the table. Watched him rise. He walked off down the courtyard, where he stopped before a flowering gardenia and broke a blossom off and raised it to his nose. Watched him turn with it in his hand, and come back down the courtyard and set the wax-white flower before her on the table. Its sweet, heavy scent rose up. He sat down, leaning on his forearms, looking at it while he spoke.

"Cassandra, cousin, it's because of you I have not hanged him long ago. But I must hang him now. His crimes are too egregious. Cassie, you've lost Benedict. I do not want to further break your heart. I do not want you here to witness it."

She looked at his bowed head, the way he would not meet her eye. Surely he did not know? How could he know? No, he did not know. It was nothing but his same old meddling. And then he lifted up his head and looked at her. He knew.

40

*I*T WAS ARRANGED. SHE WAS TO GO WITH
Mr. Hicks on the *Corinthin*, a little craft but very pretty, slim and
low-slung in the water. Cassandra knew the type. They were not
comfortable and prone to be unstable in the hands of amateurs, but
none was faster on the sea. Mr. Hicks boasted she could outfly any
sloop-of-war or cruiser, and Cassandra had no doubt it was true.
The schooners out of Baltimore were famous for agility and speed.

Mr. Hicks had turned out to be a genial rogue, with a quick eye
and a ready bellowing laugh. He was not a privateer, he told her,
and had no intention to get into a fight. Since the port of Baltimore was bottled up, his plan was to go ashore at a secret place he
knew and haul his cargo overland. He told her he had made this
run a score of times before and would be a rich man when he had
made that many more. He would lie back then, and smoke good
cigars beneath a tree.

The journey downstream to the Mississippi mouth was a hundred twenty miles, he told her, but it was silted up and treacherous

from the recent floods, making navigation tricky. He also told her, laughing wickedly, that these floodings had left an enormous mass of decaying vegetable matter built up along the riverbanks, which, having been cooked and steamed up by the sun, now stank almost past enduring. But, he said, she must endure it like a man. She must think of it as an adventure. Adventure, did he say? With the entire British navy waiting in the Gulf of Mexico to catch them? And she would entrust her life to such a daredevil? But if she did not go fast she would not reach Papa before he died, so she must hand herself to Mr. Hicks as though she were a cotton bale or sack of sugar.

This arrangement made, she set about to make preparations. Since Mr. Hicks had neither room nor inclination for the carrying of children, she accepted William's plan that he guard Albert and the two girls till it was safe to send them on. And since Mr. Hicks would allow no luggage but her pocketbook and one small trunk, she must ready everything for auction, with the exception of some things both sentimental and of value—her jewelry, Benedict's cane and silver inkstand, some framed portraits—these would follow with the children. All the rest would go for sale.

The house and Anne's garden were to be sold to Mr. Grymes, who had agreed to buy a portion of the furniture as well—the main bed with the matching dressing table, the stuffed armchairs from the parlor, the crimson velvet couch with the turned legs, the inlaid secretary, and some other of the finer pieces.

He made a generous offer on Seth and Mattie but Cassandra said no, she would free them, and she had him draw the papers up. Seth was to stay one month to help Mr. Grymes resettle and reorganize his household and then he would go off to pursue what opportunity he found. He was a good boy and Cassandra wished him fortune. Mattie would stay on. She said she was too old to make another life, and while she was glad to no longer be a slave, she had no objection to being a hired servant. These two were Cassandra's only slaves. The remainder of her servants had been alerted to find themselves some new employment and several stayed with Mr. Grymes, including Fernando, who was charged with the care of Anne's garden and her tomb.

All the packing and the stacking had been done before she remembered the little secret cupboard in the morning room. She unlocked it and opened the door and there they were, Jean's gifts to his son, four of them set neat and blackly tarnished side by side, each with its label: "From your papa."

She took them down and, tearing off the labels, set them with the other silverware for auction. But as she went about her tasks, her eye kept catching them, until at last she set them in the trunk of precious things to follow with the children.

Later, she lay in bed and listened to a million insects shouting their complaints out to the night. Since William had revealed he knew the truth of Albert's paternity, she had found Jean coming more and more to mind. Now a notion came into her head, a fantasy. She put it out, but it occurred and reoccurred: *What if?*

What if? Ah, what foolishness and power in those two words. Jean was wicked, she had always known it, but what if she should reform him? He had said when they were lovers that he was her slave, her captive, that his heart was hers forever. Were those just fancy words or were they true? Were they true still? And if they were, was not his heart connected to his body? If she ran off with his heart, must not his body follow? Would he follow her to Maryland? She had left her life behind and followed Benedict because he had her heart. Would not Jean follow her? William adored her. He would pardon Jean and they would marry at St. Thomas church in Maryland. When she was dead, they would carve upon her grave "Here lies Cassandra, who took a pirate's heart and made an upright man of him." She would go down in history, like Bluebeard, only virtuous.

She fell asleep with her head full of this nonsense. She must have dreamed it too, because when she woke she was still caught up in it. As though she could reform a pirate king! His ship was reputed to be faster in the water than that of any other pirate, and more deadly too. Customers came streaming to the Temple every day to buy his goods, and planters from Natchez, three hundred miles upriver, and even farther, came to buy his slaves. He sold them cheap, one hundred seventy dollars for a good strong back, and grew richer every day.

But how rich was rich enough? And had he not flung himself back into this desperado's life because she had rejected him? If she could loose a pirate on the world then surely she could tame him?

Bah! Falderal and poppycock!

She rose and dressed and flung herself into the business of the day, but late that afternoon she wrote a letter to him. She did not request a meeting, merely told him she was auctioning her goods and making ready to depart. She told herself it was nothing but civility.

On the morning of the auction, she left proceedings under the fastidious eye of Mr. Grymes and took the children to the Government House and William. Seth had gone earlier with a cart, taking their belongings and the trunk of precious things, as well as Cassandra's small trunk to go to Mr. Hicks, and so they walked alone and unencumbered. She was sad to leave her children, since she did not know how long it would be until they came to join her, and she cried a little, quietly. Charcilla, who was thirteen now, and Mary, who was ten, were both sweet children, timid in their natures. Although Cassandra loved them dearly, she had never doted on them as she did on Albert, who by this time was almost five years old. He was her darling boy, her favorite child. Now, as she watched him trotting on before her with his sisters, she felt a constriction in her throat and stopped to let it pass before she followed them to William's door.

Albert seemed to sense his mother's agitation, because he did not follow his sisters inside, but turned and came trotting back to her with his face raised for a kiss. She hugged him close and whispered to him that he must always live with her, that when he married he was to bring his wife to live with her and they would be a family together. He listened solemnly and answered solemnly, "Of course, Mama, I will always live with you." And yet Cassandra knew how men travel for adventure, how they vanish and come back and vanish once again, how they cannot be held in place.

William appeared in the doorway with William Junior at his heel. He came down the steps, and taking Albert by the hand, connected it to his little son's. "Cassie, this is difficult for you," he said. "Go, just go. Say no farewells." And when he saw her hesitate,

"Cousin, they're my family too. I'll guard them with my life. As soon as this fracas with the British has been settled, I'll send them on to you. No, I'll carry them myself. I'll not trust them to another."

By now Albert and William Junior had scrambled up the steps together and vanished in the house, but still Cassandra hesitated. William set a hand upon her arm, and with the other lifted up her chin and kissed her on the forehead. "Cassie," he said, "you may not love me, but you *can* rely on me." And so she left them there.

When Cassandra got back home the auctioneer's voice was loud and sonorous inside. All sorts of people, purchasers and agents and those who had come to gossip and to gawk, hustled back and forth. For a moment she felt panic start to rise.

Mattie met her on the stair. She rolled big eyes. "Your friend is bidding up a storm. He has already bought your best set of silver tableware, the best linens, all the serving dishes and the fine china dinner set, the heavy silver candlesticks, the porcelain lanterns—"

Cassandra left her in the middle of this recitation and hurried off in search of him. She found him in the street, securing a load of boxes on a cart.

"What's *this?*"

He gave the rope a tug. "I'm rescuing your things," he said across his shoulder.

"Rescuing from what?"

He finished lashing the crate, flipped the rope's end up on top, and turned to look at her.

Cassandra had come away from Benedict's funeral firm in her step and resolute in her determination: she would not speak to Jean ever in her life again. But the body whispers secrets of its own. And resolution fades. Looking at him now, she realized none was left. She wanted him again. But with desire came guilt, and with guilt, disgust for her own weakness, antipathy for Jean.

She swung away, but he had seen her eyes. He caught her arm and made as though to kiss her. She pushed him off. "Not on the public street."

"May I come to you tonight?"

"You may not."

"When? It has been long enough."

"Have you no respect for Benedict?"

"Cassandra, Benedict is dead. I'm sorry for it. I did not intend it. Indeed, I did my utmost to prevent it. But it's done. His bones lie in the tomb . . . Come now, don't turn away. I'll not press you. I'll wait till you are ready."

He waved at the stack of boxes on his cart. "But this is nonsense, this selling off your valuables. There's no need to sell. I've space enough for everything, and if not, I'll build a bigger house."

"Are you speaking of Grande Terre? Jean, I'm going home to Maryland."

"To Maryland? You wrote a letter and said you were to come to me."

"I did not. I merely said that I was leaving. The rest you made up in your head."

"Cassandra, but I love you. I've been waiting five years for this day."

And here it came, bursting out of her mouth, like any silly schoolgirl. "Then give up pirating and come to Maryland with me." Embarrassment swarmed on her skin.

He did not laugh, and she felt grateful to him for it. "I think not Maryland," he said. "We'll go to Cartagena, since I sail under her flag."

"So now you will confess you are a pirate?"

He looked pained. "I'm not a pirate. I'm a privateer. It's a legal occupation. I can show you the letter of marque to prove it's true."

"William Claiborne says he'll hang you."

"I'd like to see him catch me."

"He says he'll put money on your head."

He flicked his hand across his face as though he flicked a fly. "Pah! I'll double it on his, or triple it."

"Will you give up this so-called privateering? For me?"

He closed one eye. "I'll give up Barataria for you. If you don't fancy Cartagena, we'll go to Texas."

"But my papa . . ." And she told him about Fanny's letter and how Papa was ill and dying on his bed. "You see," she said, "it's imperative I go to Maryland."

His face, which had been crumpled in a frown, relaxed. He smacked his hands together. "So it's settled, then. We'll marry. You'll go to Maryland and see to your papa, and I'll guard the children while you are away. No, no, don't protest. I'll take everyone. I'll be father to your children, all of them. I'll be grandfather to your grandchildren, and great-grandfather too. As soon as you return, we'll all sail off together. I'll take good care of them while you are gone."

"Nonsense. They're to stay at William Claiborne's house."

"You give our children to my dearest enemy?"

"I trust him."

"Trust! I've trusted no one since the brute Pétoin."

Cassandra blinked. The brute Pétoin—she had not thought of him in years. Standing there with the bustle of the auction all around her, she felt herself transported back to France. Once more she was standing between Benedict and Jean in the courtyard of the Abbaye. The crowd was hushed and the coppery smell of blood hung on the air. Once more she felt Jean's hand slip out of hers as he leaped toward the steps, felt the thud of recognition as the brute Pétoin stopped him with his sabre flat against his chest, saw the grisly searching through the bodies scattered on the ground. She saw the downthrust of the sabre and the ripping fist. Saw Jean's lips touch his father's heart. The tremor of his body, the way he closed his eyes and concentrated deep inside himself, and how, when he opened up his eyes again, something new and hard looked out of him.

"Cassandra?"

Looking up into his face now on this street in New Orleans, Cassandra recognized the hardness that had risen from inside him on that day in France. It was the same that backed his eyes today. So this was what his wickedness was all about, his defiance of authority, his recklessness, the way he gambled with his life, as though he taunted death each day and cared not if it came.

"Cassandra? What is it?"

She felt pity surge inside her. She wanted to take him in her

arms and comfort him, while at the same time understanding that
once a man has hardened in his soul, not even love will soften him.
She touched his arm. "Jean, I know you must still grieve for your
papa, but that was long ago. The world has changed. William is no
brute. He's your enemy only because you contravene the law. And
it's turned out he is my cousin. He's agreed to bring the children on
to me when the war is over and it's safe." She hesitated. "If you
must be their papa, you'll have to follow them to Maryland."

A subtle change came over Jean's expression. "Well, then," he
said, "since you're determined, we will go to Maryland. But the
children must not be left with William Claiborne. He has a war to
think about. It's only fitting that they stay with me. I'll wrap up my
affairs in Barataria and bring them on to you myself. They'll have
safe passage with their new papa."

This had been her fantasy, and yet Cassandra felt quicksand
tremble underneath her feet.

"You frighten me."

"I love you." His voice was soft, and yet there was that hardness
under it.

"I think I do not know you anymore."

"I swear I love you."

"It is your son you love. You want your property."

She saw his jaw go tight, his pupils darken and expand. He
turned back to the cart, and with one hand tested the tightness of
the rope.

"Jean?"

He swung himself up on the cart and nodded to the carter, who
made a clicking in his throat and flicked the reins.

William found Cassandra weeping underneath the stair. "William,"
she said, "what made you think that hanging Jean Lafitte would
break my heart?"

"I'm not a fool, cousin, nor a stranger to the passions of the
human heart. I know it from the way you turn away from him, and
from the way you never fail to spring to his defense. Is it not true?
Look me in the eye and tell me that it's not."

"I cannot look at you. I am ashamed."

"Cassie, it's the past. You must think about the future. If you wish it, go to him. It's been five years since Benedict departed. Five years is long enough to mourn. And long enough for penance."

"You would send me to your enemy?"

"An enemy you love. Listen, Cassandra, Lafitte may be a rogue, but when I consider the great sorrow Clarice's death brought down on me, and from which I suffer still, and when I think about the darling child she left behind, and what solace he brings, I cannot but think that every man should have his son, his wife, and any other family he can gather about him. Our time here on this earth is short, our grasp on life so dreadfully precarious. Each day we wake could be our last. Each night we lie to sleep we might well never wake again. You've seen death, Cassie, you've seen the fragility of the human body, how it will succumb at the slightest whim of fate. Because of Albert, Lafitte is now my family too. I judge him for his public deeds, but I pity him in private. You may think me mad, or you may think me wicked, but a man should have his family. You have given him a son. Let him have his son."

She laughed, still crying. "Lafitte, your family? Here's a turn-around of fate. Yesterday you planned to hang him. Today you'd marry your cousin off to him. I wager the bishop would take a dim view of your advice."

"Here, dry your eyes."

He produced a pocket handkerchief and she snuffled into it. "I had a foolish notion in my head I could reform him."

"Lafitte will not reform. You must take him as he is."

"Ah," she said, "by pleading his defense you have convinced me that I have a choice: I must throw in my lot with him and become a pirate's wife, or I must rid myself of him entirely."

"And your decision?"

"I know that as a general thing a man has a right to raise his son, but our case is different. Jean may be Albert's father, but Benedict was his papa. He wouldn't want his son raised on Grande Terre, apprenticed to a pirate, doomed, in the end, to be shot on some deserted beach, or slashed apart in an encounter on the sea, or—William, in the end *you* would do this to him—strung up on the looped end of a rope, an example to society. No, Albert belongs to Benedict. Albert believes that too. How can I tell him he's a bastard, that his father is a wanted man, a criminal. How can I say to him, 'Here is your true papa. Kiss him well today, because tomorrow he will hang.' It would be too cruel."

"And so you choose against him?"

"I do. But I know this will not be the last of it. Jean gets what he wants, no doubt of that. I fear that if I leave Albert here with you, one day you'll turn around and find him vanished."

"Lafitte has threatened you?"

There was a coughing at their backs: Mr. Grymes, begging the governor's pardon and desiring Cassandra to sign the bills of sale and settle with the auctioneer. She wiped her eyes again and sniffed, and straightened up her hair, all of which Mr. Grymes affected not to notice.

By the time she had finished with the tasks he laid on her, she was sure that William would have gone off, but no, he was waiting in the courtyard, full of an idea. "We'll trick Lafitte," he said, "by playing his own game. I'll make it known about the town that the children are my guests"—he looked about him as if he thought Jean might be listening at the gate—"but I'll keep only the girls. Albert will be smuggled out to you a moment before Mr. Hicks casts off. That way, the girls will be safe with me, since Lafitte has no interest in them, and Albert will be safe with his mama. If Lafitte will run his smuggled goods past me then I'll run mine underneath his nose." And he beamed on Cassandra as if it were the best plan in the world.

"But Mr. Hicks told me categorically he will not carry children."

William rubbed his hands together like a schoolboy in a play. "Can *you* deny him docking rights? I think, after the briefest word with me, Mr. Hicks will find he has a very strong desire to carry Albert."

"Jean will discover it, as he discovers everything. I don't know what he might take it in his head to do. William, I may be fool enough to love him, but I'm wise enough to fear him."

"Don't concern yourself about it, Cassie. I'll keep my nieces closeted inside the house and go about the city bragging loudly of them and my handsome nephew. By the time Lafitte discovers I have only nieces with me, it'll be too late. You'll be well away to sea." He grew serious again. "Cousin, you understand he has a well-armed brig, *Goelette la Diligente*. As long as he is free, he can go anywhere he wants. This time you might trick him, but no matter where you are or where you hide, as long as Lafitte lives, your son will be in danger. How will you protect him?"

"You must catch him, William. Catch him and sling him in the calaboose."

He became completely still, his eyes fixed on her face. "And then?"

She took a breath. "If hanging him is what it takes, then hang him."

After William left, Cassandra found herself trembling with fatigue. The coming separation from her daughters made her hate herself because she had not loved them as well as she loved Albert, and now she would abandon them for who could know how long? The dangerous plan to smuggle Albert made the blood pound in her head. The perverseness of her desire for Jean tormented her, and she felt half in love with William for his kindness.

Mattie made her sit down on the one chair remaining in the morning room, while she brought a stool for her to put her feet up and a cup of hot sweet tea to calm her nerves. After a while she rallied, and resolved that she would go and bid farewell to Anne. Tomorrow she would leave this town forever. It would be the last time she would set her lips against that dear white tomb. Thinking of it brought the tears again. Mattie clucked and patted her as though she were a child, and Cassandra leaned her head against her breast and gave up to her solicitude.

When there were no more tears to cry, she kissed Mattie's hands and thanked her, and then a carter was rapping at the door and Mattie went off to see about him, leaving Cassandra feeling much recovered.

She went looking for her boots and found them in a pile with Benedict's. She smiled, stamping down on one heel then the other, thinking about those first days in New Orleans when they had marched together to some entertainment, their boots half-vanished in the muck, her skirts hiked up above her knees, Benedict leading with a huge umbrella, one of Mattie's boys holding up another one for her, the other slopping on behind, a pouch slung from his shoulder with their dancing pumps or buckled shoes.

She would need the boots now, no doubt of that. It would be the first time she had been to Anne's garden since the recent storm, when the levee at Kenner's plantation up the river broke and an inundation swept across a portion of the city. The low-lying gardens had taken the runoff and still sat awash. And so, clad in her boots and with her skirts pinned up at the sides, she set out to say her farewells to her daughter.

As she went, she found her mind on Benedict. She rarely dared to think of him. Benedict—how he had loved her. She would not go to his tomb, had never been. She had never felt that he was there at all, not dead and buried, rotting flesh and bones, but living somewhere still, somewhere where his injury no longer pained him, and where the people whom he loved did not betray.

The garden was watery still and very soft and giving underfoot. The shallow-rooted plants had floated off and lay cast up against the trees and bushes with a firmer foothold in the ground. The willow standing guard above the tomb had flourished, though, and looked more lush and green than it had been before—it must have grown a foot since last she saw it.

The stones around the edges of the pond could not be seen—they were entirely underwater—and the carp had either washed or swum away. The whole place stank of rot, and mildew, and the evil smell of festering mud. The stone bench had not washed away, although its neat curved feet were lost in slush, and rotting vegetation clung about its legs and seat, caught there when the flood came rushing through. Anne's tomb seemed like Moses' basket floating on the waters, and the willow spread its leafy branches out across the blank brown surface like a bridal train of green.

The mud was thick and sticky near the willow tree and very deep, and it took all Cassandra's exertion to make her way. When she came close enough to part the willow branches, meaning to set her lips against the tomb, she sank so low she could not draw her boots out of the mud, and stood there struggling and half crying, because by now the night was coming down and she could neither go to Anne nor leave. The more she struggled the more firmly stuck she became, and the more she stood unmoving the more she sank down in the mud.

Then the sun was gone and suddenly the place was black, nothing but the sucking mud beneath her, and its thick smell rising up. Cassandra crossed herself and cried out, "Save me! Save me!" although no one was about.

But then a movement back behind her in the darkness and the sound of water swishing, strong arms about her, and Jean's voice reprimanding and consoling. He lifted her clear out of her boots and carried her back home. All the way he uttered not another word, just held her tight against him, and—God help me, oh, God help me—she forgot her fright, forgot everything and clung to him, her lips against his neck.

All night she struggled with him, five years of separation exploding from her body like breakers crashing on a beach. Five years had altered nothing of the way his flesh melted into hers as though they were not two, but one, his breath her breath, the beating of his heart the beating of her own. She had always been a wanton in his arms, and for these five years she had been starving for him. Each time she cried out she knew for sure that she could bear no more of it, that her heart would burst inside her chest. But each time she fell away from him, he set his hand between her legs and his mouth against her breast, and once more she was aflame.

And yet with all this, deep inside her a cold hard eye was watching him. She could not see his face. It was too dark. But she could see his soul, and she could see clear through his soul to his intentions. It was his son he wanted.

At last he gave a groan and rolled onto his back, falling into sleep as suddenly as if he had tumbled down the sheer drop of a cliff. Cassandra did not sleep but lay beside him in that state of physical suspension that follows the satisfaction of desire, like a drunkard fallen smiling in the street.

She did not know how long she lay there in that state, or whether she slept and only thought she waked, but she was brought back to her senses by the mist-muffled blare of a ship's horn from the direction of the docks. In one movement she slid out of bed and swept her clothes up off the floor. With them bundled in her arms she stood looking down at Jean. He slept easy as a child, one arm flung above his head, lips slightly parted—so beautiful, like a vision of an angel. And she would hang this man for loving his own son? Then she should hang herself, for she was just as guilty of that crime.

She bent to kiss him one last time, softly, so as not to wake him, and found her eyes fixed on the crimson riband round his neck, the bow that held it resting on the sheet. She felt her breath stop, and freeing one hand from the bundle of her clothes, reached out toward it. She gently pulled. It gently slipped. He moved. He muttered in his sleep. And now her heart was thrashing and she had the locket in her hand.

She flung her clothes on in the passageway, then crept into the morning room to fetch her pocketbook, which was on her writing desk. She picked it up. And set it down. Drew out a sheet of notepaper and leaned above the desk and dipped her pen: "William, I have changed my mind. I cannot let you hang him."

With it in her hand, she turned, and it was as though a phantom stood before her—Jean, appearing from behind a tomb the way he had the day she buried Benedict. Once more she felt the hairs rise on her neck. He came to her, his hands stretched out. She put her own behind her back. "Marry me, Cassandra. Let me have my son." This time she did not walk away, but shook her head and waited for the words she had not caught five years before. She saw his face go hard. "He is my son, Cassandra. I will have him." Then it was he who turned and walked away from her.

The moment was so real she followed him, but there was no one in the passageway and Jean still lay sprawled out, sleeping on the bed. For a moment she stood watching him, and it was as though a doorway opened in her mind. Through it she could see a lake, and long-necked birds rising from its surface, up into the sky. And it came to her that she had nothing more to say to Jean. It was all gone—that madness, that benighted love, that awful, awful pain.

She crumpled up the note, and going back into the morning

room, drew out another piece of paper: "You will find him in my bed if you are quick." The next moment she was in the courtyard whispering to Seth. "Run quick, quick as you can, to Mr. Claiborne's house and put this in his hand. Be sure you give it to no other."

Now she hurried through the streets toward the docks. That she had murdered Jean she had no doubt. And yet her step was resolute. It was the only way that Albert could be safe, the only way her heart could finally be free.

41

*A*T OWINGS HALL IN MARYLAND, JOHN
Cockey Owings cried out in his sleep. He had seen Cassandra with
a small child at her skirts, a boy. The image was so real it wrenched
him half awake and he lay, confused, against the stacked-up pillows
at his back, his belly jerking with the effort to draw breath. Something came rattling up his throat, like a stone that had been lodged
there. He coughed, tears sprang from his eyes, and with his hands
before his face, he wept, snorting and gasping at it like a child.

Feet rushed into the room. "What is it, John?" More feet. And
now an agitated chattering. Someone other than himself began to
weep.

"John, what is it? Dear God, what ails you, man?"

Now a bright white light was in his belly, climbing toward his
chest, expanding and expanding. He swung upright on the bed,
clutching at it to contain it, but it leaked out through his fingers. It
was filling up the room, and Cassandra was inside it with her child.

At first he could not distinguish where they were because their image rocked up and down in a peculiar way that made him nauseous. Then he saw that they were on a ship and in his dream he knew this ship was to bring them home to Maryland. It was very early in the morning. Cassandra had risen because her little boy had been made fractious by the creaks and moans of wood on wood, the shouts of seamen, and the shrilling of the bosun's whistle calling the sailors to this task or that, the smell of salt and pitch and hemp. Now she stood beside the rail, the child's dark head pressed against her side, crooning to him and marveling at the brilliance of the rising sun. She was thinking about him, her own papa, smiling at the thought of taking him inside her arms and feeling his about her once again.

How did John know it was because of this she smiled? Because he had entered on a miracle. In it he knew everything. He knew the tight-wrapped bud of emptiness that for all these years had been at the center of Cassandra's heart. Despite a husband's adoration, the sweet caresses of her children, the passion of a lover, and the tenderness of friends, still she had longed for her papa.

John moaned, reaching out one hand into the light, with the other clutching at his breast to keep its source from tearing him apart. He could hear voices calling him as though from the far end of a tunnel. A bustle in the room, the peculiar smell of Dr. Bellamy's gray hair, a cold ear on his breast, a voice cajoling. "John, are you still with us? John?" Someone—was it Colegate?—weeping by the bed. He dropped away from them, back inside his miracle.

Now the sun had struggled up out of the sea and hung, pale and trembling, just above the line of the horizon. Now it gathered strength, spinning out its glistening tentacles. And now it was so bright Cassandra could not look directly at it. She raised a hand to shade her eyes but it was not until the sun had risen high enough for her to see beneath it that she saw the other ship, tiny and black against the brilliant sky. A shout came from the rigging overhead and feet ran down the deck behind her. Spyglasses were raised. Sailors turned, head close to head, as though in conference. The ship's bell rang. John felt a thrill of fear. But no, it was all right. The flag the ship flew was American.

Another shout. The ship, still hurtling toward them, had run its flag down and another flag was being raised: white hourglass against black background, white time running into dark. Whose time was it? Whose time was running out?

A hand against his arm, the vicar's voice intoning a farewell. A hand against Cassandra's arm, the captain's voice commanding her to go below. She seized her child up in her arms and turned, but as she did the pirate ship swung broadside. John saw the row of gun heads down her side, saw the sailcloth slung to hide her name. Saw Cassandra's foot slip as she scrambled down the narrow ladder, saw her child's mouth open in a shaft of fright, saw them tumble down on top of one another. Then she was up, her face gone all awry, dragging the child behind her to the locker where the extra sails were stored, while up above, ship answered ship with eardrum-bursting volleys.

Then all was confusion. Curses, shrieking, clash of steel, the sound of thumping feet, the locker door flung back, Cassandra and the boy discovered where they crouched inside, three men with cutlasses and evil faces pulling at her, dragging her back up the ladder to the deck, the child clutching at her arm, her skirt, her leg.

For a moment John was blinded by the light, but then the nightmare scene was back. Cassandra's child was torn howling from her arms and swung across the rail, suspended by his wrists. A shout from down below and he vanished out of sight. She shrieked, lunging after him. The ship heaved under her. She slipped in someone's blood and fell, hitting her head against the deck. A voice—his own?—screamed, "Do not hurt her! No!"

Smashed heads, mutilated limbs, steel clash, gun bark, ship heave and moan, tossing of the whole mess back and forth. And now harsh hands were on his ankle and he felt himself hauled across the deck, skirts dragging up across his face. Then he was flying through the air, blind with fear, and falling, falling.

Afterword

WHAT HAPPENED TO CASSANDRA IS A mystery. The ship on which she sailed entirely vanished. Some say it was taken by the pirate Jean Lafitte, some say by another pirate. Or it could have been the British, or a storm at sea. Her crested silverware and linens were recovered in a raid on Jean's hideout on Grande Terre.

Her youngest daughter, Mary, married Dr. John Rochester Moore of Kentucky, a religious man who used to visit the prisons of New Orleans of a Sunday afternoon. One day, "an awful old pirate" told him of a murderous shipboard raid in which he stole some jewelry from "a pretty little matron from Maryland" who begged for mercy on account of her six children. When Dr. Moore asked who the captain of his ship had been, he set one finger up against his nose and refused to say. The recovered jewelry was identified as Cassandra's. It is not known if her locket was among the items.

The portrait of Cassandra on the cover of this novel comes from a miniature on loan to Dickinson College in Carlisle, Pennsylvania.

It is the property of Cassandra Lee Keer, a descendant of our Cassandra's sister Mary, who married Alexander Nisbet, son of Charles Nisbet, the first president of the college.

William Claiborne never did succeed in hanging Jean Lafitte. Instead, Jean became a hero of the Battle for New Orleans, supplying General Jackson with men and the gunpowder he lacked, and so William was obliged to secure a pardon for him from the president, James Madison. After the war, Jean vanished out to sea and reappeared on Galveston Island, where he named his settlement Campèche. From there he organized a new base for his marauding operations. He is reputed never to have married, although he maintained mistresses, and is reported to have had a child living with him. He abandoned operations there in 1821 and vanished out to sea. New Orleans folklore hails him as its most notorious pirate.

William Claiborne served Louisiana, first as its appointed, then as its elected governor, for thirteen years in all. In 1816, he became constitutionally ineligible for reelection and was sent to Washington as senator in January of the next year. He was fated not to serve his term. In November of that year, he died in New Orleans after a long and painful illness. The city grieved. His widow, Suzette Bosque Claiborne, married Mr. Grymes.

In 1857, Albert Gallatin van Pradelles entered history as the first postmaster of Wallisville in Chambers County, Texas. He married Mary Louisa Thomas and died in 1884, at the age of seventy-six, and was buried there.

Cassandra's eldest daughter, Colegate, who had married Harold Donaldson of New Orleans, was a widow before March 1814. Juliana became a nun at the Ursuline Convent in New Orleans. It is not known when she died. Benedict Junior died of unknown causes in 1819, at the age of twenty-one. Charcilla married William Moore in 1835, in the Baltimore Cathedral in Maryland, and went with him to Texas, where she died in 1838, at the age of thirty-eight. Her older sister, Colegate, took Charcilla's widower, William Moore, as her second husband, and lived to fifty-three. Both Colegate and Charcilla were buried at Moore's Bluff, Liberty County, Texas. Extensive files on the family's descendants are held at the Wallisville Heritage Park in Chambers County, Texas.

John Cockey Owings did not acknowledge Cassandra in his will. Thomas, whom he cut off with a dollar, became a wealthy man and was elected to the Kentucky legislature. Owingsville, in Bath County, Kentucky, is named for him. He died in Brenham, Texas, bankrupt.

Fanny married John Taylor and went to live in Alabama, where she fought for the cause of higher education. After the Civil War, she returned to Baltimore a widow and died there three years later, in 1870. In her will, she bequeathed to the Sherwood Episcopal Church on York Road in Cockeysville "one acre of land to be used as a graveyard." She also provided for an obelisk to be erected in memory of her sister Cassandra. The inscription on its western side reads: "Cassandra D. van Pradelles. Lost at Sea, 1815. Aged 40 years." Cassandra actually met her fate in 1813, but the family did not discover it for two more years. Fanny lies beside Cassandra's obelisk, their sister Charcilla close by. The names of their parents, John and Colegate, and brother John, are engraved on the obelisk's north, south, and east sides. I could not discover where their bodies lie.

Cassandra's bones lie somewhere at the bottom of the ocean. You can come any day to the Sherwood Church in Cockeysville, just north of Baltimore in Maryland, and see her empty grave.